Exotic Desires Box Set

By M.S. Parker

Table of Contents

Exotic Desires Vol. I

Chapter 1

Reed

Paris, France.

I'd arrived three days ago, coming by way of London, Glasgow, Vienna, and Rome, as well as Moscow and Berlin. None of these places were like home and I was grateful for that.

Home.

I ran my hand through my hair, ignoring the appreciative looks from the women in the café. I knew I was good-looking. I wasn't conceited, just honest. That was one of the vows I'd made to myself when I left Philadelphia a couple months ago. No more lies. Lies were the reason I'd been traveling around Europe, wearing out my welcome with various college friends. If

I'd just been honest back then, with *her*, things might've turned out different.

I shook my head and drained the last of my drink. I didn't want to think about Piper Black. After all, the entire point of coming to Europe was to get away from her. I managed a wry smile. Another lie. It wasn't just Piper I was running from, the same way it wasn't her who'd made me turn my entire life upside-down. She'd just been the catalyst who had started the whole damn thing.

I looked across the street to where the Eiffel Tower stood and took a moment to enjoy the regal landmark. I tossed a few bills onto the table and stood up. I hadn't been over to see it yet. I'd been a little more interested in the Paris nightlife than the city's history. After all, I was twenty-seven, far from an old man, and I'd spent the last five years of my life concerned more about work, about doing what my family expected of me. My little tour of Europe was my time to have fun.

I looked up at the tower and then around. After dismissing a few possibilities, I found exactly who I was looking for. Putting on my most charming smile, I approached her.

"*Bonjour. Voulez-vous me prendre en photo?*" I held up my phone.

"American?"

Her accent was thick, but I was more interested in how her long brown hair would look spread across my hotel bedspread or the way her curves would feel under my hands.

"Yes." I pulled my thoughts to the present. "I'm Reed."

"Monique." She flashed teeth too straight to have been completely natural. The nose was a little too perfect too. My eyes flicked down to her ample breasts. Probably fake as well.

"Would you take my picture, Monique?"

2

"Of course." She took my phone, letting her fingers brush, then linger against mine.

I smiled at her as she snapped a shot of me with the tower in the background. When she handed me back the phone, I winked at her and, on a whim, sent the picture to Piper. I'd been keeping her updated on my trip. Well, more or less. Things hadn't exactly ended badly in the angry sense, just me being hurt. I wanted to let her know that I was okay. And I *was* okay...sort of.

"You are here alone?" Monique asked, her voice as erotic and soft as the finger she ran up my arm.

I was about to be very okay.

***

Monique's big brown eyes widened when she saw the hotel where I was staying, but she didn't seem overwhelmed. I'd definitely chosen well. I had no problem with Europeans who were enamored with Americans. What I didn't need was someone looking for money and a green card. Monique might not be Stirling rich, but she dressed well enough to let me know she wouldn't be coming after me for some big payday. There were too many women who thought they'd fuck me and I'd take care of them for life. Or the ones who tried to do things like get pregnant or some shit like that. Finding a random hook-up was getting to be as complicated as having a relationship.

Not that I'd really know. Pretty much all of my relationships had been shit.

"Reed?"

"Come on, *ma chérie*." I slid my arm around her waist and pulled her towards the elevator. "You're going to love the view."

As soon as the elevator doors closed, she was on me. Her mouth was firm, no hint of hesitation. Definitely something I liked about European women, especially the French. If they wanted someone, they went for it. I wrapped my arms around her waist and pulled her even more tightly against me. She moaned and nipped at my bottom lip. I dropped my hand lower and squeezed her ass. If she was half as good in bed as she was at kissing, this was going to be fun. And probably just what I needed.

The door to my room had barely shut behind us and she was already unzipping her dress. I lost my shoes and started unbuttoning my shirt while I watched her slowly shimmy out of the confining material. I let out a low whistle. She looked even better out of the dress than she had in it.

"In case you are wondering." She ran her hands over her flat stomach and up to cup the crimson silk holding her breasts. "They are real."

Had I misjudged her? Could she really be this perfect?

She reached behind her and unhooked her bra, releasing a pair of the most magnificent breasts I'd ever seen. Easily a D-cup. She smiled at me as she hooked her thumbs in the waistband of her matching silk panties. She slowly lowered them, revealing something I'd come to learn about French women. They were as diverse as Americans when it came to their grooming habits.

"You like what you see?" she asked, running her fingers over her bare pussy.

I closed the distance between us in two quick steps and covered her mouth. My tongue pushed at her lips and they parted. I ran my hands over her back and down to that firm ass as I explored every crevice of her mouth. She tasted like coffee and expensive chocolate.

Her hands found their way under my shirt, palms burning against my skin. When her nails scraped over my nipples, I moaned and felt her smile. She broke the kiss and pushed my shirt from my shoulders.

"*Magnifique.*" She lowered her head and flicked her tongue against my nipple. She looked up at me through those thick eyelashes, gave me one of the most wicked grins I'd seen in a long time, and bit down.

"Shit!" I buried my hand in her hair as she worked her mouth across my chest, biting and licking until my cock was pressed painfully against my zipper. I'd barely spent a night alone since coming to Europe, but the last couple ones had been rather passive and I was starting to get bored. I'd definitely picked a good one today.

"Let us see what you have to offer." She went to her knees in front of me, her hands at my waist, making short work of my pants. Her dark eyes brightened as she lowered my pants and saw the bulge at the front of my underwear. "*Très bon.*"

"Like what you see?" I grinned down at her.

"Very much." She curled her fingers under the waistband of boxer-briefs and yanked them down.

My cock jutted out in front of me, thick and hard, eager for attention. Monique reached around and grabbed my ass, nails digging into the muscle as she wrapped her lips around the head of my cock. I groaned as she circled the tip with her tongue, then took me deeper. Her mouth was wet and hot as she took me all the way to the root, her lips stretched wide around me.

"Fuck!" My hands curled into fists. Damn, she knew what she was doing.

One hand released my ass and came around to cup my balls. She rolled them as she bobbed her head, taking my cock all the way into her mouth and down her throat each time. A lot of women gave head because they thought it was expected or that it was the best way to get a man going. Then there were women like Monique, ones that obviously enjoyed it. Or were at least enthusiastic about it.

"Ma chérie." My voice was strained. "That's enough."

The hand on my ass flexed, nails digging in, giving me a bite of pain to go with the pleasure. Then I was sliding from her mouth, my cock swollen and glistening. I held out my hand to her and she took it, letting me help her to her feet. It was then that I noticed she was still wearing her heels. Heels and nothing else. Fuck, that was hot.

She released my hand and gave me that naughty smile again. She licked her bottom lip, then bit her lip with those perfect teeth. She winked at me and sauntered over to the French doors. I kicked off my pants and underwear as I followed her, stopping only to grab a condom from my pants pocket. She pushed the curtains aside and put her hands on the glass. Feet apart, ass out. There was no doubt what she wanted.

I stood behind her, taking in the line of her body, the smooth skin of her back, the curve of her ass. She was gorgeous. Just like every other woman I'd fucked since coming to Europe. Sometimes I felt like that was the only thing I'd been doing. Party, drink, fuck. Repeat as needed. Hope that I'd somehow figure out what I was going to do. Where my life was supposed to go next. So far, it wasn't working.

Still, it didn't mean I would stop trying, especially with a woman who looked like this.

I ran my finger down her spine and she arched her back. I palmed her ass. Damn that was firm. My cock throbbed in anticipation, eager to finish what her mouth had started. It would have to wait though.

I leaned against her, pressing my cock against her leg. My hand dropped down between her legs.

"Already wet?" I dipped a finger inside her and she made a mewling sound. "Do you really like sucking dick that much?"

"Very much." She pushed back against my hand, but

I didn't give her what she wanted.

"And what do you think I should do to you now?" I removed my hand and lightly smacked her ass. Based on what I'd seen, I thought she might like it and I wasn't proven wrong.

"Harder, *se il vous plaît,*" she begged.

I brought my hand down a little more firmly and she let out a gasp that was pure pleasure. I alternated cheeks, each smack making her cry out. I didn't stop until my hand began to sting and her ass was a brilliant shade of red. I shook my hand as I bent down to pick up the condom I'd dropped. I tore it open and rolled the latex over my erection. The immediate need to come had eased a bit, but I was still ready to go.

I leaned my body over hers, intentionally rubbing against her sensitive ass as I did so. "I'm going to fuck you now." I cupped her breasts, squeezing them until she writhed against me. "Take you hard and fast right here against this window." I pinched her nipples and she made a sound half-way between a yelp and a moan. "Is that what you want?"

"*Oui, se il vous plaît.*"

I didn't need to know French to understand that as a definite affirmative.

I kept one hand on a breast, pinching her nipple, as the other hand slid down her stomach and between her legs. She gasped as I found her clit and rubbed the tip of my finger across it. Just when I felt her body start to quiver, I stopped.

She let out a stream of French expletives that made me chuckle. I straightened and put one hand on her hip. I teased around her entrance with the tip of my cock until she shot a glare over her shoulder. With a snap of my hips, I drove myself into her and her glare turned into a beautiful portrait of overwhelming sensation. Her entire body jerked and she swore again. I stayed still, giving her a moment. There was a fine line between painful pleasure and straight pain. I liked the first, but never wanted to cause the latter.

I rolled my hips and she cried out. *"Prêt?"* I made sure to ask it in French so there'd be no misunderstanding. She seemed to like it rough, but I didn't want to start moving until I was sure she was ready.

She nodded her head and I pulled back until just the head was still inside her. When I thrust into her this time, she wailed loud enough for me to hope that no one was in the room next to mine...and that the glass door she leaned on would prevent the people outside from hearing her. Then again, if anyone looked up, there'd be no doubt as to what was happening.

She kept one hand on the glass and used the other to play with her nipples, pulling and twisting until they'd turned from pale pink to almost red. She pushed back against me with every stroke, forcing me deeper even as she squeezed my cock with her pussy.

"Fuck," I swore through gritted teeth. I didn't know where this girl had come from, but someone had definitely taught her how to fuck.

I moved my hand around to her front, once again finding her clit. She moaned as I rubbed the little bundle of nerves. The pressure inside me was building, but I was going to get her there first. I might not have always been the gentlest of lovers, but I liked to think of myself as considerate. I always did my best to make sure my partner came first.

"Spank me," she said, her voice as strained as I felt.

I smacked her ass twice and apparently that was all she needed. She came with a high-pitched squeal that would've made me wince if she hadn't clamped down on my cock at the same time and triggered my own orgasm. I closed my eyes as I came, focusing on the pleasure coursing through me, the way her muscles flexed around my cock, prolonging the pleasure until it almost hurt.

It was only during these moments that I felt at peace,

that I forgot about all the shit I had waiting for me back in the States and the vast, empty future stretching out before me. A few precious moments where it was pure bliss and all was right in my world.

Then it was over.

Chapter 2

Reed

I'd always thought I had stamina, but Monique definitely put that to the test. By the time she left around midnight, I barely had enough energy to dry off from our joint shower and make it into bed before I fell asleep. The best part about being that exhausted was that I didn't dream.

I couldn't exactly say I'd been having nightmares before, because they weren't disturbing or anything like that. No, it was more like my brain had decided to deal with my issues when I was asleep since I refused do it when I was awake. Sometimes it was my parents asking me why I'd left and begging me to come home. The guilt trips my imaginary parents gave were almost as convincing as the real thing.

Then there were the ones with Piper.

Most of the time, my mind replayed every moment we'd spent together, trying to figure out where things had gone wrong. What would've happened if I would've done things differently? Like if I'd told her the truth that day I'd run into her at my sister's high school reunion. Would we still have ended up in bed together or would she have turned me down when I'd kissed her that first time? What if I'd called my engagement to Britni off sooner? Would I still have ended up in Vegas, seeing Piper work, or would I have stayed in Philadelphia to look for her? What if I'd changed things later so that we'd still had the same meeting, but instead of being an ass and essentially asking her to be a bought-and-paid-for mistress, I'd broken up with Britni to be with Piper?

In some of the dreams, Piper and I ended up together in some sort of weird alternate universe where my family accepted her and my sister apologized for being a bitch for so many years. I always woke from those with my hand stretched out to the other side of the bed, thinking she would be there. Then I'd remember. Worse were the ones where, no matter what I did, she still ended up with *him*. In the dreams, I could feel how futile my attempts were, but couldn't stop myself from trying to make a difference. Either way, I'd wake up knowing that I'd lost her.

When she'd told me she didn't want us to be together, it cut me to the quick. She'd said that what we'd had hadn't been real. Maybe not for her, but I'd thought for sure it had been for me. Only over the past couple weeks did I start to wonder. I'd met her when I'd been very close to marrying a woman I didn't love, a woman my parents had decided was a good fit for me.

As much as it pained me, I couldn't help but wonder if I'd fallen for Piper because of timing and circumstances. I'd feelings for her, that much was true, and I'd wanted her – a man would have to be either gay or stupid not to want her – but was what I felt for her more than that?

I lay in bed, staring up at the ceiling. There was gratitude, I thought, for giving me a reason to divorce Britni. Or, more accurately, showing me the reasons to divorce my wife. That had started the chain reaction that had led me here. Part of my rationale for doing the things I'd done had been for Piper, but they'd also been for me.

I'd spent so much of my life giving up things I wanted just to make my parents happy, to make my family proud, that I'd never considered what I wanted out of life. Until now.

I frowned. I'd spent the last couple months considering and wasn't any closer to an answer than I had been when I'd left Philadelphia.

My phone rang and I sighed, rolling over to grab it.

"Hello?"

"Good morning, Reed."

"Mom?" I blinked at the clock. She had to be up early to be calling me here. Then I registered the time. Almost noon. Which meant it was nearly seven o'clock back home.

"Are you just waking up?"

I flopped back on my pillows and closed my eyes. I was an adult, thousands of miles away, and she could still sound like I was some lazy kid sleeping in late.

"Yes, Mom, I am." There wasn't much point in lying to her.

"Your father's on the line too," she said.

Fuck. My parents had to be two of the few people who still had landlines and liked to use them for conference calls. I had a feeling if they'd been in charge of the technical advancements, our companies would still be using computers that took up a whole room.

"Morning, Dad," I said. I silently wondered what the hotel would think if I threw my cell phone off the balcony and into the pool below.

"We need you to come home, Reed." At least Dad didn't try to make small talk. "You know I can't run the businesses by myself, not with my health."

Dad had been playing the health card since he'd been rushed to the ER three years ago with chest pains. The doctors had said it was a panic attack, but he'd refused to believe them, instead insisting that he'd had a heart attack and the hospital was conspiring against him. Conspiring

13

with who and why, he never said. Only that there were people who wanted to make sure he was ruined. I was just grateful he kept his theories to himself. The last thing we needed was our stockholders thinking the old man was nuts.

"You have Rebecca to help you," I reminded him.

My little sister was in her early twenties and had been after my dad for the past couple years to let her run one of the companies. He'd always refused and I knew she thought it was because she was a girl. While that was part of it, I happened to know that my father also believed that Rebecca didn't have the temperament to be a good CEO. I didn't disagree.

"Rebecca doesn't know what she's doing," he said bluntly.

"Your father and I tried to get her to see that," Mom cut in. "We even had things worked out with the Westmores to have Rebecca marry Blayne."

"Isn't he the screw-up?" I asked. From what I remembered, he was a couple years older than me, but was still acting like he was in high school. Maybe college if he was in a frat.

"His father had been eager to get his son married and settled. We thought he and Rebecca would be a perfect match."

Apparently, my parents hadn't learned from my disaster of a marriage that, in this day and age, in our culture, arranged marriages didn't work. Telling them that wouldn't do any good though so I kept my mouth shut and waited for finish with their little pitch.

"Then he went out and married some immigrant or something."

I could almost see the condescending sneer on my mother's face. It was on the tip of my tongue to remind her that, while her family could trace its lineage back to the Mayflower, she was still descended from immigrants.

"Anyway." My father picked things back up. "After

14

that incident, your sister decided she no longer wanted to listen to reason and was going to do things her own way."

I suppressed a laugh. I wasn't sure why that surprised them. Rebecca and I might've both been tall and had the same blond hair – hers dyed lighter while mine remained more golden – but that was where the similarities ended, physical and in personality. Her eyes were hazel while mine were a brown so dark they were almost black. I'd always toed the line while she hadn't cared what anyone said about her. The biggest difference was that I tried to be nice to people while Rebecca's idea of nice was a backhanded compliment and laughing behind someone's back.

"You worked so hard for that company, I can't understand how you can let her run it into the ground."

I sat up, my temper flaring at the attempt to manipulate me. "You guys used the company once to get me to marry Britni. I'm not letting you use it again. If Rebecca screws up, it's your own fault."

"You're the one who left, Reed." My father's voice was sharp. "You abandoned your family, neglected your responsibilities–"

"I'm going to stop you right there, Dad," I interrupted smoothly. "I've always done what you expected of me. I went to Columbia and got an MBA because that's what you wanted. I went to work for the family business right after I graduated because that's what I was supposed to do. I married Britni. I almost had a kid with her."

"But you fucked that up, didn't you?"

"Lawrence!" My mom sounded shocked and I had to admit that I was a little surprised. My father rarely talked like that.

"I made a choice," I said quietly. "I chose me. I've had enough of doing everything I've been told to do. I'm not a child."

"Then you should stop behaving like one," Mom snapped.

"Figuring out what I want to do with my life is being a child?" I asked. "It's not like you support me. I have my inheritance, but I've also earned every penny of it as well as the salary I've received these past five years. I've never asked you for a dime. I'm an adult, and I deserve the opportunity to figure out what I want out of life."

"And what is that?" Dad asked. "Sleeping your way through half of Europe?"

"Nice to know you have people keeping tabs on me," I said. It didn't surprise me. I had a feeling the hotels where I'd stayed had been reporting my activities to my parents.

"Come home and take charge of the company again while you decide what you want to do," Mom suggested.

It was tempting, I thought. It was a solid job. I liked the people I worked with. But I knew if I went back, I'd never leave again. Breaking free the first time had been hard. Leaving a second time would be virtually impossible. I had to stay away.

"I don't think that's a good idea," I said. "I need to be away while I figure this out."

"This discussion isn't over," Dad said.

It was for me, but I didn't say that. They'd figure it out when nothing they said worked.

"I'll talk to you guys later then," I said.

"We love you, Reed," Mom said.

"Love you too." And it was true. I did love them. I just didn't want to be like them.

I ended the call and headed for the bathroom. First on the order of business for today was breakfast. After that, I planned to check out a few places I hadn't seen yet. I did appreciate good art and Paris was the perfect place to enjoy that. I was thinking two more weeks and then I'd be ready to move on again. I didn't want to overstay my welcome. I hadn't yet decided where I wanted to go, but wherever it was, it sure as hell wouldn't be Philadelphia. Not anytime soon.

Chapter 3

Nami

Paris, France.

I'd never been allowed to come here alone before. I threw a glance over my shoulder and scowled. I supposed I wasn't truly alone now either, but at least the two hulking masses behind me weren't my overprotective parents. When my parents had told me I would be allowed to take a trip across Europe after my college graduation, I'd been thrilled, sure that I had finally earned my freedom. After all, I had spent twenty-two years being the dutiful daughter. I did as I was told, everything from what classes to take, to who my roommate was allowed to be. I had been a good girl and stayed in my room studying while others went to parties, flirted and drank. I had disobeyed only once and my parents didn't know about the night I'd snuck out to see my friend, Aaron.

I sighed as I thought of him. Aaron Jacobs. He'd been a friend since freshman year. Sweet, kind. The kind of man a normal girl would've been thrilled to take home to her parents. I hadn't allowed myself to become attached because I'd known that it would never work between the two of us. I'd been honest with him upfront, and he, in turn, had been honest with me. We'd become close friends, and my parents had been nervous until I

17

introduced them to Aaron's boyfriend.

Well, I supposed there was that one little thing that would've given some parents pause. Aaron was bisexual. I hadn't told my parents that though. Not because they would have freaked out about him being attracted to men, but because being bisexual would've meant he could've still wanted me. No, I'd simply made sure he had his current boyfriend present the first time I introduced him to my parents and they'd never worried about him after that.

I smiled to myself. They should have. I'd made it clear to Aaron from moment one that we couldn't have a relationship, but as graduation had approached four years later, I'd asked him for a favor. He'd been single at the time and I'd been adamant that I wasn't going to go home a virgin. My bodyguards had gotten a bit lax those last couple weeks, prompted, I supposed, by the previous four years of good behavior. Whatever the reason, I'd been able to get to Aaron's dorm, do the deed, and get back before my guards realized I was gone.

I didn't regret it, especially now. I scowled at my reflection, hating the face that looked back at me. I had my father's chin and nose, my mother's cyan eyes and figure. The dark brown curls and tanned skin were the result of combining my mom's fair coloring with my father's darker coloring. I'd been told more than once that, had I not been barely five feet tall and on the curvy side, I could've been a model. The exotic look was all the rage.

I almost wished I had been tall enough. I could only imagine the look on my father's face if I had told him I planned to be a model. My parents weren't completely old-fashioned, but there were certain areas where tradition still held a high bar, and my sex life was one of those areas.

I'd said that Aaron would've been the kind of boy a normal girl could've taken home to her family. The problem was that I wasn't a normal girl. I was Princess

Nami Carr, eldest child of King Raj and Queen Mara. My family had ruled the tiny island nation of Saja for thousands of years. No one had really ever heard of Saja. We pretty much kept to ourselves, didn't bother with world politics or anything like that. We didn't crave the spotlight or had any important natural resources to exploit. We had nice beaches and pretty waterfalls, but we didn't sell ourselves as a tourist trap. We were fairly self-sufficient and liked it that way.

I loved my home, and my family. I just didn't love being a princess. I knew there were millions of girls who'd kill to be in my shoes, but they didn't get it. I wasn't just another princess. I was the crown princess, which meant I was destined to rule one day. And that meant there were certain things I didn't get to do.

Like choose a career.

Fall in love.

Choose whom I would marry.

Which is what brought me back to my current situation. My parents' graduation gift had actually been more of a bribe, or at least a way to put me in a better mood for when they dropped that particular bombshell on me.

Once I returned from Europe, I would be marrying a man they had already chosen. There would be an official engagement announcement, of course, and some sort of party for us, but the betrothal was set and the wedding would follow shortly. Most likely within a couple months of my arrival. Everything but the dresses, color scheme and flowers will have already been planned by the time I arrived home. As the princess, those were the only things I had a say in. My attendants would be picked for me, members of other noble families who my parents needed to keep happy. The only one I could count on would be my maid of honor, my sixteen year-old sister, Halea.

The guest list would be carefully selected and pruned until every seat was filled and no one important was offended. The location would be the palace, naturally. Saja was a nation of myriad religions and my parents wouldn't want to insult any of them by seeming to favor a specific location or have one religion oversee the officiating. That would be my father's job. As king, he would conduct the ceremony to ensure that no one religion was shown preferential treatment.

The finest dressmakers in Saja would be on call when I returned to do any necessary alterations to whichever dress I picked. That selection would come from a small number of appropriate dresses chosen by my mother. The same would go for my bridesmaid's dresses and the flowers.

As for my future husband, I knew nothing about him. My parents had said only that he would be handsome and from a good family. That was what mattered to them. To his family, I knew what they would care about. Saja's ruling line was very clear. Eldest child to eldest child, regardless of gender. Ironically, I would one day govern the entire island, but until my father passed, I had no say in my own life. While my husband would be king in name, I would be the ruler. But, once I had his child, his family's bloodlines would be forever linked to the throne. That was why my virginity was so important. The family would want assurances that it was their son's child I bore and no one else's. His virginity and fidelity didn't matter to them. Even as king, no bastard of his would have a right to the throne. He could have as many of those as he wanted.

Maintaining my purity was the main reason Thug One and Thug Two – otherwise known as Tomas and Kai – had been assigned to me the moment I'd left Saja. On the island, everyone knew who I was and no one would dare put themselves in a situation where anything improper could even be insinuated. A lot of girls assumed that being a princess meant always having dates to events like dances and proms. Not for me. What guy was brave enough to approach a girl flanked by security and ask her to go out with him? The answer was none.

I'd graduated from Princeton with a degree in political science – my parents' choice – and a minor in classical literature – my choice – but had nothing else to show for my four years in America. No friends aside from Aaron, and I knew I'd never see him again. No adventures or whirlwind romances. I couldn't even claim to have had four years where I didn't have to think about my responsibilities. I'd hoped this trip would be that opportunity for me, even if just for a couple weeks. Instead, it was just another reminder of what was expected of me.

"Princess, are you ready?" Kai spoke from his position at the door. His accent was rougher than mine, denoting the part of Saja he was from. "Your dinner reservations are in thirty minutes."

Of course they were. I had a schedule to keep. Appearances to make. My parents had managed to turn my graduation present into a royal event as well. I was expected to be seen in all the right places. I'd gone straight to London after graduation and stayed there for three days. Now, it was a few days in Paris and then on to Italy where I'd have a couple days before going home. Today was my last day in Paris and I'd been to several museums, five-star restaurants and taken in some of the sights. And I'd been bored out of my mind. I supposed I wouldn't have minded as much if I'd had someone to enjoy things with, but my bodyguards were strictly professional. They spoke only when spoken to; offered no opinions save ones that had been given to them by the king. And, most importantly, made sure I behaved.

I turned away from the mirror. "No, Kai. I'm actually not feeling well. I think I'll spend the rest of the night in bed."

"Do you need for us to call a doctor?" he asked.

I shook my head. "I'll be fine." I walked back into

21

my bedroom and closed the door. I looked in the full-length mirror. I'd dressed the way I was expected to dress for a dinner out. My parents may have made a big deal about my virginity and modesty in dress, but they both understood fashion. The pantsuit I wore had been designed specifically for me for this trip and I looked poised, elegant, and like I was about to walk into a courtroom or board room. All business.

I wanted fun.

I stripped off the clothes and hung them over the desk chair. My heart was pounding as I picked up the bag I'd carefully hidden from my bodyguards. We'd gone shopping earlier today and I'd purchased several outfits of clothing appropriate for a princess...and one dress I knew my parents would have instantly vetoed. Tomas and Kai hadn't seen it because I hadn't modeled any of the clothes, but I'd had to give the saleswoman cash and ask her to ring the dress up separately, putting it in a small bag inside the other bag.

I opened the bag now and pulled out my small act of rebellion. I slipped it on and looked at myself again. Now I looked like a twenty-two year-old college graduate ready to enjoy Paris. It was a deep shade of blue that made my eyes stand out and flattered my curves. The hemline hit me mid-thigh, still modest but far shorter than anything my parents would've let me wear. The neckline was plunging, nearly revealing my bra, but still covered more than some of the things I'd seen the women here wearing.

I pushed my hair back from my face, tousling the curls into their usual haphazard mess. I'd cut it short my first day in London, butchering it purposefully so I'd have no other option than to go to a stylist and let her trim it even shorter. Tomas and Kai hadn't been happy about that and I knew they were dreading my parents' reaction. I didn't care. I was tired of being good and I knew that I had a lifetime of decisions being made for me or decisions made based on what was best for my people. For this short bit of time, I wanted to do things my way.

I glanced towards the balcony. So far, my rebellion had been little things. My hair would grow again. No one had to see the dress. Now, however, was the defining moment and I had the feeling that if I went through with it, things were going to change.

I walked over to the doors and opened them, stepping out onto the balcony. I was on the fourth floor, which meant it was too far for me to risk jumping, but I'd come up with a plan yesterday when I'd first started batting this idea around. When the family traveled, we always bought out the rooms on either side of where we stayed to ensure extra privacy. My parents had done the same thing when they'd made my reservations. The room on the right had a balcony too, only a couple feet away from mine. I'd slipped the maid some money this morning to make sure the doors to the balcony were unlocked. Even in this dress, I wouldn't have a difficult time getting to that balcony. Once there, I'd go through the room, into the hallway and off to freedom.

For a few hours anyway.

Chapter 4

Nami

I couldn't believe that it actually worked. Getting across to the balcony had taken some balance, but it had been easier than I'd hoped. The maid had left the door unlocked and neither Tomas nor Kai had come out into the hallway when I'd slipped out of the room. I made it down to the lobby without anyone seeing me and then gave the desk clerk a little nod and a wave like I wasn't doing something wrong. Even if he thought to call up to the room, it wouldn't do any good. I'd left the hotel phone off the hook.

I caught a cab without any problem and was then on my way. Free, for a few hours at least.

It was too early for the best clubs to be open, but I didn't care. I'd get there eventually. I was a bit overdressed for regular sight-seeing, but I ignored the funny looks I got when I walked into the bookstore I'd spotted yesterday. It, of course, hadn't been on the list of approved stores for me to visit, but now I could spend all the time I wanted browsing the titles. No one there cared how I was dressed.

It was nearing eight by the time I made it to a restaurant to eat, and I purposefully chose one that wasn't five stars. The food was great and the atmosphere noisy. I loved it. I relaxed in my corner table, enjoying my food, and watching the people. Like most of the people on Saja, I spoke my own native dialect as well as English. I'd also been taught French, Russian, Spanish and some basic Chinese and German. I had a bit of Italian too, but not much. That was one of the things my parents had mentioned I'd be learning when I got back. We might not have had much interaction with other countries, but we were always prepared. Most of the people in the restaurant spoke English or French, so I listened to snippets of conversation, appreciating the banality of it all. Ordinary lives fascinated me.

When I left the restaurant, I finally headed to a club. The driver assured me that this was the hottest place in the entire city, if I could get in. That wasn't a problem. I was fully prepared to flash my passport since it contained my royalty status, but I ended up not needing it. The man working the door immediately waved me through and I stepped into the pulsing chaos.

It took a moment for my eyes and ears to adjust to the lights and the music, but as soon as they did, I was in heaven. No one here was whispering about me. Looks were either admiring or dismissive. A bit of jealousy from a couple women, but I knew it was based on appearance only, nothing more. No one here knew who I was.

At college, I'd wanted to keep a low profile, and since there were a lot of other people from prestigious or famous families, I'd thought it would be possible. Then, during freshman orientation, a cute guy had decided to sit next to me and strike up a conversation. Tomas and Kai had put a stop to that, announcing to the entire group that I was a princess and off limits. After that, Aaron had been the only one with enough guts to talk to me. Even the girls who would've normally tried to suck up to me kept their distance.

I wove my way through the crowd, heading for the

bar. I had no intention of getting drunk, but I was strung tight and needed something to take the edge off. Ditching Tomas and Kai had been bad enough, but being here would piss my parents off to no end if they found out. I also had absolutely no clue how to behave. This was so far out of my element that, for a moment, I considered leaving, sneaking back into my room and curling up in bed like I'd told Tomas and Kai I'd intended to do.

"Bonjour, belle. Puis-je vous offrir un verre?"

A deep voice came from behind me and I turned towards it. His French was flawless, but I detected the American accent that marked him as not being a native.

"I already have a drink, but thank you." The words were out of my mouth before I stopped turning and I immediately regretted them as I found myself staring at one of the most gorgeous men I'd ever seen. Messy golden blond hair, eyes that looked black under the club lights. He was tall, easily over six feet, and lean, but not skinny. Features that were just a hint too masculine to be pretty, but close. Full lips that curved into an easy smile.

"You're not French," he said, leaning closer so he didn't have to speak so loudly.

I shook my head, but didn't expound.

"You don't sound American either," he said. His eyes narrowed like he was studying me, trying to puzzle me out.

"I'm not," I said. "Are those my only two options?"

His smile widened. "Reed Stirling."

"Nami Carr." I found myself returning the smile. There was something about him that appealed to me, and it wasn't just his looks.

When I'd first met Aaron, there had been this kind of click between us. I'd never experienced it with anyone before or since, until now.

"Let's dance."

Reed grabbed my hand and I gasped as a shock ran all the way up my arm. Based on the look of surprise on

27

Reed's face, he'd felt it too. I could've written it off as some sort of static shock, the kind a person got when they touched metal, but I didn't think that was very accurate. Heat burned its way across my skin from the point where our hands touched and I knew I was blushing. I never blushed.

He pulled me towards him as we reached the dance floor and then released my hand. I had a moment to be disappointed and then he was moving to the music. He had the sort of feline grace that sometimes came with someone of his build and I wondered how that translated into the bedroom. My blush turned to flame and I silently scolded myself as I started to sway in time with the music. I'd come here to let loose a bit, not hook up with some random American, no matter how hot he was.

Then he put his hand on my waist and it was like I could feel every cell in my body waking up. His fingers curled possessively around me, pulling me closer to him so that our bodies brushed together as we danced. The music thrummed around us, but despite the sea of people, my world narrowed down to just him and me. His eyes locked with mine, pools of warm darkness, and I couldn't look away. My pulse pounded against my chest, my heart in my throat. I'd never been as aware of someone as I was of him right now.

Without consciously thinking about it, I raised my hand and pushed his hair away from his eyes, the strands damp with sweat. My fingers traced down his cheek and I felt the muscles in his jaw tense. The hand on my waist slid around to my back and he drew me against him until there was nothing between us but our clothes. I felt the swell of him against my stomach and it sent a thrill through me.

Sex with Aaron had been good. He was attractive and had been the kind of lover that most women would want for their first time. He'd made sure I'd climaxed before him and I'd thoroughly enjoyed myself.

Afterwards though, I hadn't really had a desire for a repeat performance. In fact, sex hadn't really been something I'd thought much about. If my parents hadn't made such a big deal about me not doing it, I probably wouldn't have even slept with Aaron.

Now, with Reed's body flush against mine, his desire for me clear, I wanted it. I wanted him. Aaron had appreciated my body and he'd genuinely cared about me, but he hadn't wanted me. Not really. Not at a primal level. Reed did. I saw it on his face and my body responded. I knew it was a bad idea. A terrible idea, actually, but I'd never wanted anything as badly as I wanted him right now.

I was teetering on the edge of decision as we continued to move to the music. It didn't have to be anything more than a hook-up. For all I knew, that's all Reed wanted too. I wasn't looking for a relationship. I couldn't. But sex, no matter how many times people said it didn't, always came with strings attached. Both sides had to know what was expected or feelings would be hurt, accusations made. When I'd gone to Aaron to ask him to be my first, I'd laid it all out for him. What it would mean for us, for our friendship. What it couldn't be. I'd known him and trusted him. I didn't know Reed.

Would it be possible for me to have that same conversation with him? Tell him that all I could offer him was one night? Most men wouldn't have a problem with that, I assumed. Especially an American man in a Parisian club. This wasn't exactly the kind of place someone went to find a soulmate.

There was also the safety factor to consider. I didn't want to even think about it, but I had no way of knowing the kind of man Reed was. I could feel how strong he was, see it in the way he moved. If he wanted to hurt me, he could. I knew a little self-defense, but I'd never really needed to think about it. I'd always had bodyguards to protect me.

29

I couldn't do it. It would be reckless, irresponsible, dangerous, and a lot of other adjectives I knew my parents would've used.

Even as I opened my mouth to excuse myself before I got caught up in the moment, movement at the corner of my eye caught my attention.

Shit.

They'd found me.

Chapter 5

Reed

I'd fully expected to spend most of my night trying to decide who I wanted to take back to my hotel room, but I'd only been at the club for a few minutes when I saw her. She was beautiful, and not in a stick-figure model kind of way. No, she was all woman. Short, but not petite. Exotic coloring and the sort of confidence that could be spotted across the room. Without hearing her say a word, I could tell this woman was used to holding her own against anyone. Even better, she had a quick wit and the intelligence in her eyes was a welcome difference from most of the women I'd been sleeping with recently.

She wasn't French or American, I realized after she spoke. Her English was flawless, but there was a hint of an accent I couldn't quite place. That was okay though. I only cared what it would sound like when she was moaning my name. When we began to dance, I became more certain that I had to have her. She moved perfectly with me, the kind of instant synchronization that rarely happened and I knew it would transfer to how we'd move together in a far more intimate setting.

I was getting ready to ask her if she wanted to get out of here when she suddenly stiffened. I frowned, following her gaze. Did she have a boyfriend or husband who was going to come after me? Then I saw two absolutely massive men scanning the crowd.

Shit. Who was this girl?

I looked down at her. Myriad emotions ran across her face before she settled on something I recognized quite well: rebellious determination. She grabbed my hand and pulled me after her deeper into the dancing throng. I followed, too surprised by the gesture and how strong she was to argue about it.

We went out the back entrance and found ourselves in an alley that smelled a lot less pleasant than the club had. She made a face, but didn't stop until we stood on the sidewalk behind the club.

"Did you drive here?" she asked. "Rental car?"

I shook my head. "Taxi."

She looked up and down the street and then up at me. "Do you have a hotel room or are you staying with friends?"

I doubted I was misreading the signals, but I asked just to be sure. "I have a room. Would you like to go back there with me?"

She took a step towards me and wrapped her arms around my neck, pulling my head down even as she pushed herself up on her tiptoes. I slid my arms around her waist as her mouth met mine. Her lips were soft and pliant, molding around mine. As I traced her bottom lip with the tip of my tongue, her mouth opened eagerly and her tongue came out to meet mine. The two twisted together for a moment and then she was stepping back.

"This can only be tonight," she said. "I need that to be clear."

I grinned. A woman after my own heart. "Sounds good to me." I stretched out my arm and waved down a taxi.

"Where are you staying?" she asked suddenly, as if something had just occurred to her.

"Hôtel Maison Souquet."

A relieved look crossed her face.

"I'm guessing that's not where you are?"

She shook her head. "Hôtel San Régis."

My eyebrows went up. I'd known she'd had money just by the way she was dressed, but that was definitely one of the swankier hotels in Paris. It was also one that boasted discretion, more out of the way. People who went to clubs like the one Nami and I had just been at usually didn't stay at places like the San Régis.

She'd tensed again and watched me warily. For the first time, I realized that I wasn't sure what I'd gotten myself into. Huge guys like the ones back at the club didn't come looking for random girls. They were security somewhere or, if she was telling the truth about where she was staying, for someone. I smiled to put her at ease, but I kept watching her, trying to figure out if I'd seen her somewhere before. She was too short to be a model and too curvy, but she could've been an actress. Musician. And there was always the rich family option. As we pulled up in front of the hotel, however, I decided it didn't matter. Like she'd said, it wasn't like we were planning on starting a relationship. As long as she wasn't married, I didn't care about who she was.

As I held out my hand to help her from the car, I discreetly checked out her left hand. No ring, no tan line or faint impression. I supposed she could've taken it off or not have worn it long enough to leave any other mark behind, but short of ruining the mood by straight up asking her, it was all I had to go by.

I kept a grip on her hand as we walked through the lobby to the elevators. She didn't seem impressed by the opulence, lending further credence to my theory that she came from money. When we stepped into the elevator, I pushed all of that aside and concentrated on the only thing that mattered.

I backed her against the wall and claimed her mouth again, exploring it thoroughly. She made a little sound in the back of her throat that went straight to my cock. I grasped her wrists in my hands, pinning them against the wall as I ground my hips against her. The sound turned into a moan. Oh, she was going to be fun.

Before the door of my hotel room closed, we were kissing again, pulling at each other's clothes. I could feel the desperation in her touch and it fueled my own desire. By the time we reached the bedroom, we were both naked, our clothes leaving a trail behind us. It wasn't until we fell back on the bed that I finally moved my mouth from hers.

I leaned on my elbow as I began to kiss my way down her body, my free hand exploring her soft skin as well. She cried out as I flicked my tongue across her nipple, then made a louder sound when my fingers began to tease the other one. Her breasts were amazing. Firm, perfectly shaped and just the right size. Her nipples were a dusky rose color and, if her reaction was any indication, extremely sensitive.

I took one between my lips, looking up at her while I did it. Her eyes were closed and an expression of pure bliss had settled on her face. Damn. Either this woman loved sex or her previous lovers hadn't taken care of her nearly as well as they should've. I scraped my teeth across the tip of her nipple and her entire body jerked, her eyes flying open.

I raised my head. I may have liked things a little rough, but I wasn't about to assume that she did too. "Was that okay?"

"Do it again." Her pupils were wide, the thin ring of color around them dark.

I repeated what I'd done, a little harder this time, and she watched. Air hissed from between her teeth.

"Yes." She dropped her head back down onto the bed.

I took that as an affirmative and resumed what I'd been doing. She writhed underneath me as I began to

34

suck on her hardening nipple. The sounds that she made were like nothing I'd ever heard before. Half whimpers, half moans and, mixed in were words in a language I didn't know. I couldn't wait to hear what she did when I was buried inside her.

Reluctantly, I left her breast and moved further down her body. If I'd had more time, I would've loved to see if I could get her to come just from that alone, but I didn't know how long she planned to stay. As I settled between her legs, I looked up and saw her watching me again, something on her face that it took me a moment to place. Uncertainty.

"Do you want to stop?" I hoped to hell she said no because my cock was almost painfully hard, but I'd never forced a woman and I never intended to. For a brief moment, I remembered how I'd felt when I'd learned about my former brother-in-law nearly raping Piper and my stomach knotted.

"No."

Nami's voice brought me out of the past and back to the present.

"Please don't stop."

I kissed the inside of her thigh. "I won't until you come."

Desire flared in her eyes and then I turned my attention to what was right in front of me. She was already wet and I felt a surge of pride that I'd turned her on that much just from the little we'd done. When my tongue flicked out to taste her, she gasped. I used my fingers to hold her open, exposing as much of her as possible to my tongue. She cried out, her hands grasping the bedspread as I teased her clit.

I covered every inch of her, exploring this part of her body as thoroughly as I'd done her mouth previously. I felt her starting to tense and rubbed the flat of my tongue across her swollen clit, coaxing her towards the release I knew she had building. Suddenly, it hit her and her body stiffened. She made a muffled sound and I looked up to see her hand in her mouth, as if she couldn't bring herself to let it all go.

I was determined to see her lose control the next time she came. I wanted to hear her scream my name.

As she was coming down, I slid a finger inside her. Her pussy gripped it tight, still quivering from her orgasm. Damn she was tight. I looked up at her, hoping she'd answer my question in the negative.

"Are you a virgin?"

She gave me a smile that was half coy, half shy. "No. But I'm not very...experienced."

I nodded. I could work with that. I moved my finger slowly, letting her body adjust to the intrusion before adding a second one. She moaned as I stretched her, preparing her. I put my hand on her stomach, just below her bellybutton, holding her against the bed as I crooked my fingers, searching for that special spot inside her. A sound half like a squeal, and half like a wail came out as I found it. I pressed my fingertips against the spot, rubbing it until she came again. She tightened around me until I swore. I kissed her inner thigh, waiting for her to relax again.

As she began to come down, I slid my fingers out and went up onto my knees. I leaned over her, reached into the bedside table and pulled out a condom. By the time I'd opened it and rolled it on, Nami was staring up at me, pure desire written on her face. I put my hands on her knees and started to slowly slide them up her legs.

"There are so many ways I want to take you," I said as my fingertips teased along her thighs. "So many things I want to do to you."

Something flitted across her face, some kind of regret and I knew that we didn't have the time. Whatever was going on with this young woman, her decision to leave with me had been impulsive.

I leaned over her, capturing her mouth again as I

entered her. I groaned at the sheer heat of her and she responded by sucking my bottom lip into her mouth. Her body trembled beneath mine as I slowly slid into her and it took all of self-control not to bury myself into her with one thrust.

She wrapped her legs around me, pulling me in fast and hard. She cried out as I reached the end of her. Her body tightened and I pressed my face against the side of her neck. Every cell in my body screamed at me to move, to finish it, but I fought it back, wanting to enjoy this as much as possible. We fit together so well and her responsiveness was like nothing I'd experienced before. I couldn't wait to see what she did when I started to move inside her.

When I was sure I could move without embarrassing myself, I pulled back a bit and then surged forward. She cried out, her back arching up.

"Too much?" I asked. I could hear the strain in my voice.

She shook her head. "Please don't stop." Her accent had thickened.

I didn't hesitate, every nerve thrumming. I began to move, driving into her deep and hard. Her nails dug into my forearms as her body moved against mine.

"Fuck," I growled. If she wasn't experienced, how the hell did she know how to move like that?

I wrapped my arms around her, pulling her up onto my lap as I rocked back on my knees. I buried my hand in her hair, yanking her head to the side. She raked her nails down my back and I hissed as pinpricks of pain intensified the pleasure I was feeling. I scraped my teeth across her neck.

"No marks," she gasped.

I nodded and used her hair to bend her back. I freed a hand to grasp her breast, lifting it until my mouth closed around her nipple. I felt her still holding back even as our bodies moved together. I took a hard pull on the sensitive flesh and earned a bit of a whimper. Not good enough. She was close. I could feel it. I was too. I needed her to come, and I wanted her to come hard.

I bit down on her nipple, hard enough to hurt, but not to mark. The sound she made wasn't quite a scream, but it was close and all I needed. As her body shook around mine, I found my release. I held her tight, riding out our pleasure until we were both coming down.

Even as the sensations faded, I knew the awkward moment was coming. The decision of how long to let her stay, of what to say. But right now, it was still just us, just two people enjoying each other's bodies. I ran my hand down her spine. Maybe I could convince her to wait for another go around. I wanted to see her on top of me, those beautiful breasts bouncing...

My post-orgasmic brain was still hazy as it began to run through scenarios, but it cleared almost instantly when I heard someone calling out in the main room.

"Mr. Stirling, I'm so sorry, they just..."

Too many things happened at once.

The manager's voice trailed off as the bedroom door banged open.

Nami pulled away from me, rolling onto the bed and grabbing the bedspread as she went.

I turned towards the door to see two enormous men coming at me.

"Stop!" Nami shouted from behind me. She then rattled something off in what I assumed was her native language.

The men both froze, equally horrified expressions on their faces. Whatever Nami was saying to them, they didn't like it. What I didn't like was the way they were looking at me.

Who the hell was this girl?

Chapter 6

Nami

My hands were shaking so badly that I almost couldn't hold the blanket up high enough to cover my breasts. I hadn't expected Tomas and Kai to find me so fast. I certainly hadn't expected them to come busting in to Reed's hotel room.

Of course, their initial thought had been that he'd kidnapped me and was forcing me to have sex with him. I knew they'd think that from the moment I heard the manager yell from the main room. They'd stopped because I'd told them to, then they'd frozen because I'd informed them that I wasn't a virgin anymore.

Reed was looking back and forth between me and the men, completely baffled. I felt bad for him, but now wasn't the moment to explain. With as much authority as I could muster while sitting in a bed naked except for the hotel's bedspread, I quickly informed Tomas and Kai that should they deem it necessary to tell my father or mother about this, I would feel obligated to tell my parents that I had, in fact, actually lost my virginity back at Princeton while they were supposed to have been watching me. I saw the realization on their faces, the knowledge that no matter what they said, they were the ones who'd be screwed if this came out.

"Leave." I switched back to English for Reed's sake. Neither man moved, their eyes darting towards Reed and then back to me. "He's already seen me naked," I snapped. "You two don't get to. Out! Now!"

Their faces matching shades of red, they left, Tomas slamming the door behind him.

"Um, Nami?" Reed turned to look at me, his eyes wide. "What the hell was that about?"

"I am sorry, Reed," I said, climbing out from under the covers. I grabbed for my clothes, unable to look at him. "I wish things could be different. I wish I could spend tonight in this room with you."

I swallowed hard, myriad emotions choking me. I wished I could tell him all the other things I wanted. To be able to choose my own path, my own life. I couldn't say any of that though.

"I have to go. I have a train to catch in the morning." I fixed my dress and allowed myself a glance at Reed. He was watching me with those dark eyes, an unreadable expression in them. "I'm sorry."

I walked out without another look back. Tomas and Eli were waiting just a couple feet away from the door, their faces back in those expressionless masks they always wore. I didn't have to see what they were thinking to know it. They thought less of me for what I'd done. I kept my head up though. I had nothing to be ashamed of. A woman taking charge of her sex life wasn't something bad or wrong, and I wouldn't let them make me feel bad about it.

"How did you find me?" I asked as we stepped into the hallway. I held up a hand before either of them could speak. "Never mind. I don't care."

"Your father called," Tomas spoke.

I was always surprised at Tomas's voice. He didn't talk much, especially to me, but when he did, it always made me want to laugh because it was so soft and almost feminine. At the moment, however, nothing was funny.

40

"He did?" I tensed as we stopped at the elevator.

"Mr. Mikkels has been monitoring the media."

"Of course he has," I muttered. Mikkels was my father's PR person. He'd been adamantly against me going to Princeton, sure that I'd be a public relations nightmare. Even after four years of model behavior, he didn't like me. He'd hated the idea of me going on a trip to Europe, making it clear that he thought I'd go wild the moment I stepped foot in London. To my credit, I had at least waited a while before I ran off to a club.

"It seems that there was a model at the club and you were in one of the pictures a reporter took," Kai said.

Shit. That couldn't lead to anything good.

"Your father has decided that it is time for you to come home," Tomas said.

"I have a week of my trip left," I said, walking out of the elevator ahead of the men.

"King Raj was quite insistent that we take you to your train first thing in the morning. Once we arrive in Italy, we're to make sure you are on the plane immediately."

"Dammit," I muttered under my breath. Apparently me telling Reed I had a train to catch wasn't a lie after all. I caught Kai giving me a disapproving look at my use of language. "Do you have a problem?" I snapped at him.

"No, Princess," he replied stiffly.

I would've felt bad for getting smart with him if I hadn't been fuming about my father's orders. Tomas and Kai had been stuck with me for over four years, away from home and everyone they knew. Neither of them were married or had kids, but I knew that Tomas had a large extended family, including several nieces and nephews, and Kai's mother was elderly and sick. I suspected he'd taken the job to pay for quality care for her. Saja had only two nursing homes on the entire island and it wasn't easy getting someone in there.

A limo was waiting for me in front of the hotel. Kai

41

climbed into the passenger's seat while Tomas followed me into the back. The best thing about my bodyguards was that neither of them ever tried to strike up a conversation. That could be a bad thing if I wanted a distraction from the chaos in my head, but right now, I appreciated being able to think uninterrupted.

Well, not think so much as daydream. I didn't want to think about the future and what would happen when I got home. Right now, I wanted to enjoy the memory of my last vestiges of freedom.

While I'd had fun at the club, it hadn't been until Reed had approached me that I'd truly begun to enjoy myself. It had been crowded and loud, with people pressing all against me. I hadn't realized how much I'd gotten used to the little bubble of personal space that who I was had always accorded. Even at school, people hadn't tried to get close since Tomas and Kai had always been there, lurking in the background.

I wondered if Reed would've tried to talk to me even if Tomas and Kai had been there. Remembering the way he'd carried himself, the self-assured way he'd spoken, I thought he would have. He didn't seem like the kind of man who was intimidated by anyone.

I clasped my hands together on my lap, resisting the urge to run them over my neck, across my body, following the path his hands had taken. I could almost feel them, hot against my skin. The nipple he'd bitten throbbed, every movement chafing even as it sent a thrill through me. Aaron had been a good lover, at least I'd assumed so. He hadn't hurt me and I'd come with him, but it had been purely physical pleasure. There had been none of the fire I'd felt with Reed. When he'd been inside me, I'd felt like I had belonged there, with him, our bodies locked together.

I shook my head and swiped at the tears that had formed in my eyes. It was foolish to remember. Maybe later when I was alone and could touch myself, imagine that it was him, but not right now. Now, all I could think of was the way he looked at me, as if I was his only focus. I wasn't naïve. We had no commitment, nothing between us that suggested we would've been anything more than a one-night stand, but for that one night, he had been with me, only me. He hadn't been thinking of someone else, or using me for his own pleasure.

I could only wonder if the man my parents had chosen for me would be equally as attentive. The knot in the pit of my stomach said he would not. My husband would be chosen for his family, his bloodline, nothing else. My own desires were secondary to what was best for the kingdom, and I'd always known it would be so.

I was, after all, a princess.

Chapter 7

Reed

What the hell just happened?

I stared at the bedroom door as it closed behind Nami. I was still kneeling on the bed, buck naked, the scent of her still on my body long after she'd left with two guys who looked like they should be linebackers in the NFL. It wasn't until I realized that I hadn't gotten rid of the condom that I managed to move. I grimaced as I pulled it off and tossed it into the trashcan. Now I was standing in the middle of the room, still trying to figure out what had happened.

One moment, we'd both been coming down from insanely intense orgasms, and the next minute, I'd been sure I was about to be assaulted by two angry-looking men. I still didn't know what Nami had said to them, only that it had made them leave without hitting me. Not that I wasn't grateful, but it would've been nice to have had some sort of explanation other than the apology Nami had given me.

Who was she? Those men had obviously been her bodyguards, and I supposed it was possible they'd thought I'd been forcing her, but somehow, I thought there was more to it than that. A rich girl might have bodyguards, but I'd gotten the impression that she was more than just someone with money.

I shook my head as I walked into the bathroom and turned on the shower. Tonight had been one of the strangest nights of my life, and one of the best. Most of the other women I'd slept with since coming to Europe had been enjoyable, but Nami had been different. She had an innocence to her without being naïve. A rare combination. And she'd said she was inexperienced, but her body had definitely known what it was doing.

I hissed as the spray hit my back. I'd forgotten that she'd scratched me. From the feel of it, she'd gotten me pretty good. I smiled to myself as I wondered if her nipple hurt. I almost hoped it did. I actually wanted her to remember me, which was strange because every other woman I'd been with, I'd wanted them to forget as soon as they'd left. Hell, I'd wanted to forget them. I'd enjoyed the sex while we were doing it, but afterwards, I just felt empty, like a part of me was missing and no matter what I did, I couldn't fill it.

Nami, though, I found myself wishing that we could've spent more time together. And not just another go in bed either, which was strange. As good as the sex had been, it would've made complete sense for me to want to take her again, keep her here all night, fucking until neither of us could see straight. That wasn't what I was thinking, however. Well, not the only thing I was thinking.

I actually wanted to spend time with her. Talk to her. Learn what made her tick. Discover what she did for a living or if she was like me, living off of an inheritance. I thought an inheritance, but she'd struck me as the kind of person who didn't spend a lot of time partying. I'd watched her for a bit at the club before I'd approached, deciding if she was the one I wanted to take back to my room. She hadn't exactly looked like she'd been enjoying herself. It was like she was trying to enjoy being there.

As I washed my hair, I wondered what she was rebelling against. Parents? Society? What expectations had driven her to that club? To my bed? I frowned as I realized she might not have come with me because she'd wanted to be with me, but rather because I'd been the one dancing with her when she'd made the decision. I shouldn't have cared. We'd both gotten what we'd wanted: good sex. Okay, great sex. But still, I should've been relieved at the thought of her having only picked me out of convenience rather than actual attraction. I wasn't though. I wanted her to have wanted me. Wanted me as much as I'd wanted her.

And I had wanted her. From the moment I'd seen her, I'd wanted her more than I'd wanted anyone in a long time. Since Piper, as a matter of fact. I reached for my soap and told myself that if I was honest, I'd wanted Nami more than I'd wanted Piper. It had taken a while, but I'd come to see that what Piper had told me before had been true. I'd fallen so hard for her because of what had been going on in my life. I hadn't loved the woman I'd been engaged to and Piper had been there, warm and willing. She'd had a crush on me and we'd both let it convince us that we were supposed to be together. I'd thought I'd loved her, but I knew now that I hadn't. Not really. I'd loved the idea of her, of the freedom she represented.

The other women I'd been with since coming to Europe, they'd all been fun, and while they'd ranged in appearance and had run anywhere from twenty to thirty, they'd all been essentially the same. Sexual, physical beings. Some of them might've been intelligent, but that hadn't been a factor. I'd seen the same expression in all of their eyes. Lust. Whether for money, fame or my body, it didn't matter. They'd just wanted it, wanted me to fuck them, but hadn't wanted to know me. Nami and I hadn't talked much, but it hadn't taken more than a couple seconds with her to know that she was different. Or at

47

least I hoped she was. Hoped that she'd wanted me for me and not for what I could offer her.

I closed my eyes as I stepped under the spray. I needed to stop thinking about her. I was going to Madrid tomorrow morning, leaving France and everything here behind. Besides, she'd said that she had a train to catch in the morning as well. We'd never see each other again.

I dried off as I walked back into the bedroom, tossed the wet towel onto the floor and climbed under the covers. I could smell the two of us on the bedspread and I closed my eyes as my body responded.

As I rolled onto my side, something sharp and hard dug into my ribs. I swore as I sat up, reaching over to turn on the light. There, on the sheets, was a necklace. A thin golden chain with an emerald pendant. I wasn't an expert, but I was willing to bet both metal and jewel were real. An image flashed through my mind. The jewel hanging just above Nami's gorgeous breasts. The necklace must've fallen off when she'd scrambled to cover up when her goons had come in.

I sat there, holding the necklace in my hand and wondered what I should do with it. I had her name, but nothing else to go on, so it wasn't like I could just mail it back to her. I could leave it at the front desk here, but I wasn't sure her bodyguards would be pleased with me for making a public connection between Nami and myself. I knew where she was staying at least. I could go over and give it to the desk clerk there, have him call her room and tell her that someone had found her necklace. A little white lie about where and no one would have to know the truth.

The jewel heated up in my hand, reminding me of the way her skin had heated under my touch, how it had flushed a lovely dusky color. At first, I'd thought she'd just been tan, but when she'd been bare, I'd realized it was just her natural complexion. She was quite the exotic beauty, I thought. The skin and dark hair in stark contrast

48

to her eyes, those bluish-green pools.

I shook my head and flopped onto my back. Damn. Now all I could think about were those eyes, that body. The way she'd looked up at me when I'd been above her, inside her. The tight, wet heat of her molding around me. How our bodies had fit together so perfectly.

"Shit." I squeezed my eyes closed and tried to think of something else, but it was too late. My cock was getting hard at the memory of her. The way she'd tasted. The expression on her face when she'd come.

"Fuck!" I practically yelled it and had a moment to wonder if the room next to mine could hear me. If they could, they definitely would've heard Nami earlier.

I swore again. The memory of how she'd sounded when she'd come that last time made my stomach tighten almost painfully and my already hard cock throb with need. I could try to ignore it, will it to go away with thoughts of unappealing things. I could go to sleep, forget about Nami and head to Madrid in the morning as I'd planned. Leave the necklace with the desk here and not care about whether or not Nami got it back.

I sighed. I couldn't do it. I couldn't forget about her. I closed my eyes and she was there. Those lips, swollen with rough kisses. That neck I'd wanted to mark. Her breasts, full and perfect. Nipples so responsive to every little touch...

My hand was around my cock before I'd consciously decided to do it. With Nami's necklace in one hand, gem biting into my palm, I began to stroke myself. I thought of her, those silky curls I'd buried my hand in. The thin layer of coarser ones between her legs. Just enough so she wasn't completely bare, but not too much. The way her pussy had clamped down on my fingers when I'd made her come. Her body shuddering against mine when I held her close during her last climax. How it felt to be inside her. Wondering what it would be like to have been bare, skin sliding against skin. Emptying into her, filling her...

49

I came with a half-groan that was her name, cum spilling over my hand and onto the sheets. I was still breathing heavily as I looked at the necklace again. It was probably a mistake, but the necklace gave me an excuse to do it. After all, I couldn't let her leave without it. It was probably some sort of family heirloom or a gift or something.

My stomach clenched. Maybe a gift from a fiancé. No, I thought, she wouldn't have done that. She wasn't the type of woman who'd cheat. I pushed aside the thought that I'd done just that, slept with a woman when I'd been engaged to someone else. That had been different. A different set of circumstances. Besides, I thought with a wry smile, Nami was a better person than I was.

I clutched the necklace tighter as I rolled onto my side, away from the damp spot. I'd clean up in the morning. Right now, I needed to sleep. I had a busy day ahead of me. It would be a long-shot, but I had to try to find her. After all, she really did need her necklace back. Anything else would just be icing on the cake.

Chapter 8

Nami

I didn't sleep well at all. If I hadn't been dreaming up some way to get out of the whole arranged marriage thing I knew was coming up as soon as I arrived home, I was replaying every scintillating minute with Reed. Needless to say, I was both tired and frustrated when my alarm went off, and that was just the start of my day. Now I was on a train moving across France, headed for a private airport in Italy where a plane waited to take me back to Saja.

I'd tried calling my father as soon as I'd gotten back to the hotel, thinking I could at least talk him out of bringing me home early, but he hadn't taken my calls. The fact that he'd sent them straight to voicemail told me that he was angry with me, angrier than he'd ever been. He'd never refused to speak to me before.

"Not that it matters," I said out loud. No one else was in the private car so my musings were safe. "What else can he do to me? I already have my degree, so he can no longer hold college over my head. He's already set up my marriage so he can't threaten to marry me off early."

I was sure that the marriage was one of the things he was worried about. If my behavior caused a scandal, a chance existed that the man or his family would call off the engagement. I couldn't say that the idea didn't have its appeal. The fact still remained that it wouldn't matter if this fiancé bolted or not. My parents would simply turn to their second choice and the wedding would continue as scheduled. Someone was always willing to marry a princess, even if they themselves would never get to rule.

I scowled at my reflection in the window, watching the blur of scenery whipping by. Even though my parents wanted me to obey their rules and be the obedient daughter, they'd also raised me to be strong enough to rule the kingdom after they were gone. Part of that strength included not allowing my husband to override me. It was ironic, I thought, how one of the things they'd instilled in me from birth could be the same thing they were trying to suppress. I supposed their intent was for me to be strong-willed, but not against them. I may have been an adult, but to them I was still a child. I assumed it was the same for a lot of parents, but with mine, the difference was that I couldn't do the usual young adult thing of going off to do my own thing, knowing they might not approve but would accept it as a natural part of growing up. Abandoning my parents' wishes would mean walking away from my people, my country, my duty. I would be giving up a legacy that my family had upheld for generations.

And yet, I wondered if it would be worth it. Being able to choose what I wanted to do, how I wanted to live. My fingers touched my lips. Who I wanted to love.

I didn't love Reed. I wasn't a fairy tale princess, falling in love at first sight, but he intrigued me. Something about him called to me and I wished I had the opportunity to explore it.

I'd had that instant click with Aaron, but it had never been romantic, not even when we'd had sex. Sure, he was hot, but even the physical attraction had been different. With him, it had been more of an appreciation of his physique, an admiration. I could appreciate the muscles and his strong, masculine features. It had been that attraction that had made our sexual encounter pleasant, but we'd only ever connected as friends.

I didn't want to be friends with Reed.

I sighed and rested my forehead against the cool glass of the window. It wasn't like I wanted a relationship with Reed. Or maybe I did. I didn't know. But that was something a normal girl would be able to figure out, right? She would be allowed to take her time to get to know a guy she found attractive and amusing. See if he was the kind of man she wanted to be with. Find out what kind of sexual chemistry there was between them.

I snorted a very unladylike laugh and leaned back in my seat. I already knew the answer to that one. The sexual chemistry between us was explosive to say the least. I shifted in my seat, letting myself enjoy the dull ache between my legs. I'd heard the phrase "ridden hard" used when talking about sex, but I'd never had a clear picture of it until last night. Aaron had been gentle, and my body had responded. Reed had, most definitely, not been gentle and I'd enjoyed it even more.

My cheeks flushed at the memory of how he'd used his teeth on me. The first time, I'd been startled, but the zing of electricity racing through me had been something much different than pain, something more intense than any of Aaron's kisses or touches had been. All I'd known at the time was that I'd wanted more.

Now, I wondered how Reed had known something about me that I hadn't. How had this complete stranger been able to play my body with his fingers and mouth? How had he known that I would beg him to fuck me harder than I would've thought enjoyable? Reed had seemed like a man who had known many women, but Aaron had known both woman and men. Why had Reed been the one to truly show me what sex could be like?

I felt tears pricking at my eyelids and I rubbed my palms against my eyes. Now that I knew, could I be satisfied by anything else? What would I do if my future husband didn't understand me the way that Reed had? Would he allow me to teach him, show him what I liked? But would that reveal my secret? I could explain away certain biological things fairly easily. Saja wasn't so primitive that they would expect a woman's hymen to be intact, especially if that woman had spent a good part of her teenage years taking riding lessons. It would be the sworn statements of my bodyguards, my parents and myself that would be held as testimony to my virginity. But if I showed myself to be knowledgeable of what I liked, would my husband assume I had simply learned while pleasuring myself, or would he suspect the truth?

I couldn't be put in prison or executed for having lost my virginity before marriage. That wasn't how my country did things. Most Saja men and women engaged in premarital sex just as those in civilized places did. My virginity was only important because of what it meant to the man I was supposed to marry. If he – whoever he was – found out the truth, he could divorce me, and collect a hearty settlement for breach of contract, thanks to the papers we all had to sign. That was to say nothing of the scandal it would cause. Like the rest of the world, Saja citizens loved to gossip, especially about celebrities, and in my country, no one was a bigger celebrity than royalty.

I ran my hands through my short curls and nearly growled in frustration. Why couldn't I have been born somewhere else, to some other family? While I'd loved my time in America as well as what I'd seen of Europe, I'd never intended to stay away from Saja. I loved my home, my beautiful island. I loved my people. Unlike some royal families, we weren't kept quite so separate from everyone else, weren't taught that we were better than the common people. Sure, I'd had a bodyguard even there, but it hadn't been like college. They had been my people. No real danger there. But still, the line had been there, the separation of knowing who I was and who they were.

"Why couldn't I have been born to someone else? Some other family," I spoke my thoughts out loud, needing to hear them. Needing to hear myself actually wish that I wasn't me. "I could be normal."

I laughed softly. Normal. It sounded as funny out loud as it had in my head. Other girls dreamed about being princesses, but I dreamed about being other girls. But even as I said the words, I'd known I didn't really wish them to be true. That's why I'd needed to hear it. To let myself know how ludicrous it sounded. Wanting to be something I wasn't, shirking my duty.

Sometimes though, I did wonder if things would've been different if any of the three children my parents had lost between my sister and I had lived. One would have been a son, the other two, we didn't know. If I'd had a brother who'd lived, I supposed things might have been different. I would have had a choice then. I could have given up my position as the eldest to him, let him be king and have lived my life as a princess like my sister. Still not quite a regular person, but with more freedom than I currently had.

I supposed, technically, I could have abdicated the throne in favor of my little sister. Halea was only sixteen. She'd have years before my parents would make her marry, and she was a much more compliant child than I'd ever been. She would do as she was told.

And that was why I never could've done it. No matter how much I longed to be free of the responsibilities that came with being the crown princess, I would never have put my sister in my place. Not because I wanted the power, but because I knew what it would do to her. She wouldn't just be bendable to our parents' wishes, but also to whomever she married. She would be queen in name only. It would be too easy for a man to take over, and I didn't know of any man on Saja who could be trusted with that responsibility and honor.

No, I would do my duty. Return home without complaint. I'd take over the responsibilities required of me. I'd marry the man they chose. I would be queen, the strong queen that Saja deserved.

With the choice made, all I had to do now was wait. The train would be in Italy soon and it wouldn't be long after that, I'd be on a plane home. I closed my eyes and leaned my head back. Maybe I could get some sleep before it all happened.

I must have drifted at some point because I sat up with a start when the door to the car opened. I opened my mouth to ask my bodyguards what was wrong, but the words died before they came out. It wasn't Tomas or Kai who stood in the doorway.

It was Reed.

Chapter 9

Reed

It hadn't been easy, finding the right train. I'd ended up having to bribe someone to tell me what train Nami's tickets were for, and then I'd had to trade mine for Madrid for ones to Venice, all while watching the clock and hoping I'd be able to make it in time. I'd had to run, but I'd gotten there before the train had pulled out. Then it had just been a matter of finding the right car. I'd started at the far end of the train and worked my way up. I didn't think she'd be in any of the more public cars, but I wasn't about to miss her because I didn't search thoroughly enough.

At first, I'd told myself that I would just find her and give her the necklace. Then I'd apologize for freezing the other night and give her a proper good-bye. When I traded my ticket, I told myself that it was because I needed to get onto the train to find her. I didn't let myself think of anything beyond that.

When I saw the two big guys standing in front of the door to a private car, I knew I'd found her. There was no way either of those two would let me in, which meant I had to figure out a way to distract them. I wasn't sure what made me think to do it, but I stepped back into the dinner car and leaned over to speak to the man behind the bar. Two minutes later, a pair of men in suits hurried past me to investigate the possible terrorists I might have seen talking in the hallway.

I opened the door, and for a moment, thought I'd been wrong, that the car was empty. Then I saw her and my heart skipped a beat. She was sleeping for a split second before she sensed that someone was here and bolted upright. She opened her mouth and I thought she would say something or scream, but I watched the recognition dawn in her eyes a moment before they widened in surprise.

"Hi." That came out a lot less impressive than I'd imagined it would be.

"Hello." She recovered quickly. "I did not expect to ever see you again."

I leaned against the doorframe and held up my hand, letting the necklace drop. The emerald bounced on the end. "You forgot something."

Her cheeks flushed and my stomach tightened at the memory of that same flush covering her entire body. She started to stand and I held up a hand, walking towards her. When I was just a couple steps away, the car lurched and my confident swagger ended up with me tumbling onto the seat across from her.

I swore as I fell, face flaming. Could I look any more idiotic? I'd been prepared to give her the necklace and make a suave exit so that the last memory she had of me was a scorching kiss and not me kneeling on the bed, naked, and staring at the two massive, angry men who'd just burst in. Instead, she had her hands over her mouth, unsuccessfully attempting to stifle a laugh.

"Are you okay?" she managed to ask as I attempted to right myself.

I nodded. "Just embarrassed," I muttered. I got to my feet and held out the necklace. "Here."

She stood and smiled up at me, her eyes sparkling with humor. She took the necklace, her fingers brushing against mine. Electricity shot up my arm. Suddenly, the air felt thicker and I was aware of everything. The way her hair curled across her forehead. The curve of her breast and hip beneath her clothes. The clean, fresh scent of her.

"I–" The word stuck and I cleared my throat before trying again. "I'll be going."

I was two steps from the door when she spoke.

"Wait."

I stopped but didn't turn back to her.

"Do you have to go?" Her voice was soft.

"Well, um, it might be a good idea if I leave before your bodyguards come back." I glanced over my shoulder.

"Where did they go?" She sounded more amused than scared which told me the bodyguards weren't there for protection from a specific threat, but rather a lifestyle thing.

"Someone may or may not have reported two suspicious looking people lingering in the hallway, and may or may not have said they overheard something that sounded like a conversation about a bomb."

Her eyes widened and, for a moment, I thought she would go off on me. Instead, she laughed. "You really did that to them?"

I turned to face her, sticking my hands in my pockets in what I hoped was a nonchalant manner. "I may or may not have."

She shook her head and gestured towards the seats. "Oh, they will be angry, but they won't come in here. Not when they know I'm pissed at them for..." She blushed, but kept her chin up, "what happened last night."

"So, what you're saying is that I'm safer in here than I am out there?" I grinned. Whatever this spark was between us, I liked it.

"Most definitely." Her tone was serious, but her eyes were twinkling. "So why don't you sit and keep me company."

I took the seat across from her again, not wanting to presume what she meant by keeping her company. One part of my body was sure of what it wanted and I attempted to subtly adjust myself as I settled in the seat.

"We didn't really talk much yesterday," she said with a smile.

I was pleased to see that she looked as nervous as I was. "Well, there were plenty of words and sounds, but I don't really think that constituted talking."

Her blush darkened. "I didn't even get to ask where you were from."

I smiled. "Philadelphia. And you?"

Her face stiffened, smile freezing.

"Never mind." I quickly changed the subject. Since I was desperate for another subject, I said the first thing that popped into my head. "I have to ask, did you go with me last night because I was convenient?" I immediately regretted the question as soon as it was out of my mouth. "Sorry, didn't mean to put you on the spot. Again."

"No," she said. Her expression softened. "I went with you because I liked you."

I was surprised at how relieved I felt at that simple statement, but I couldn't stop myself from asking a follow up question. "You didn't know me. How did you know you liked me?"

She frowned and my curiosity piqued. "It's hard to explain."

"Try." I gave her my best charming smile and tried not to sound eager.

"Well, I thought you were handsome, of course, and an excellent dancer." She turned her head, like she couldn't continue when she was looking at me. "But it was the way I felt when you touched me."

"Like little sparks of electricity dancing across your skin?" I asked softly.

She turned back towards me, her eyes meeting mine.

"Exactly."

We were both silent for a minute and I supposed she was thinking the same thing I was, how this had suddenly become something more than a random hook up. I didn't know what it was, but it was something.

She leaned back, breaking eye contact. "So, Mr. Philadelphia, what brought you to Paris?"

I sat back as well. I didn't mind that she was deliberately moving the subject away from our connection. Whatever it was, it was intense, and I didn't blame her for wanting to dial it back a bit.

"I'm taking a vacation," I said. "A bit of a European tour."

She crossed her arms and raised an eyebrow. "Really? You don't have a job to go home to? A...family?"

The way she said it made it pretty clear she wasn't asking about my parents and siblings. I smiled and mimicked her posture. "I worked for my family business since I got out of college and I recently realized that I didn't want to do it anymore. Decided to take a bit of a break." I felt myself relaxing, enjoying the interaction. "As for my family, my parents aren't exactly pleased with me at the moment and my spoiled little sister is trying to prove that she has what it takes to fill my shoes." I tried to keep my tone light, but a slight narrowing of Nami's eyes told me that I hadn't succeeded as well as I would've liked.

"Parents can be funny," she said. The tone of her voice made me think that she wasn't talking about just mine. Her eyes flicked away and back again. "I have a younger sister too." She smiled. "But she's not spoiled."

I chuckled. "That's good. How old is she?" I was actually fishing for a hint about her own age, but didn't want to come out and ask it. Sometimes she looked like she was barely out of high school, other times she appeared years older.

"Sixteen." Her lips twitched in humor. "Six years younger than me. That's what you wanted to know, isn't it?"

I shrugged, grinning at her. "Aren't you going to ask me how old I am?"

She shook her head.

"So you're not worried you slept with an old man?"

She laughed. "You're not even thirty yet."

"Good guess," I said. "Twenty-seven." Something clicked for me as I did the math. "Is this a graduation trip?"

"Good guess," she echoed me with a smile. "Princeton."

"Nice," I said. "Columbia."

"Political science with a minor in classical literature."

"MBA."

"Let me guess," she said. "Parents?"

I nodded. "And yours?"

"Not the minor," she said. "That's all me."

"Well, you did better than me," I admitted. "I didn't manage to get a minor I liked."

"Maybe that's what I liked about you," she said. "It seems we're kindred spirits."

My stomach clenched at her words. It wasn't like she was saying we were soulmates or destined to be together forever, anything like that, which was good, but she was saying there was a deeper connection here.

"Well, there's one way to find out." This time it was me who guided the conversation away from the serious. "Favorite color?"

"Scarlet." She grinned.

"Cyan." The word popped out and I flushed as I glanced at her eyes. I'd always liked blue and green, but if I'd been asked before what my favorite color was, I would've said silver. I hurried to ask another question. "Favorite food?"

"Apple pie."

"Pizza. With extra cheese and pepperoni."

"My turn for a question." Nami's eyes were glittering with something I couldn't quite place. "Girlfriend?"

"No. You?"

"No girlfriend. Or boyfriend." Her tongue teased her bottom lip and my blood began to run south.

I tried to get my mind back to something more innocent and the back and forth conversation continued. Favorite song. Favorite movie. Childhood pets. School subject. It kept going until Nami stood up suddenly and walked over to the door. I thought she was going to look out and see if her bodyguards were back, but she didn't. Instead, she turned the lock.

When she turned back to me, her eyes were dark. "One more question. And please answer honestly."

I nodded.

"Do you want me?"

Chapter 10

Reed

Was she kidding?

Did I want her? There was no way in this life I didn't want her. All confusing connection shit aside, she was gorgeous and a great lay. I would've had to be dead not to want her.

I stood up as she walked back over to her seat. I reached out and grabbed her hand, stopping her from sitting down. "I want you." I traced along her jaw with my finger. "Do you really need to ask?"

A shadow crossed her face and I saw a hint of vulnerability in her eyes.

"You do, don't you?" I said softly. I brushed her hair back from her face and then ran my thumb along her bottom lip. She shivered and her response made my chest tighten. "How could I not want you? You're the singularly most exquisite thing I've ever seen. I haven't been able to stop thinking about you."

"I've been thinking about you, too," she admitted, her voice quiet, eyes down.

"Look at me." My tone was neither harsh nor loud, but she immediately obeyed, her eyes rising to meet mine. "Do you want me?"

She pushed herself up on her toes so that she could touch her lips to mine. It was barely even a kiss, but it sent a bolt of electricity straight through me. She put her hands on my chest and leaned her body into mine, the motion of the train causing us to sway together. "I want you," she whispered.

My hands went to her waist, holding her as I bent my head to give her a proper kiss. Her arms slid up around my neck as I parted her lips with my tongue, thoroughly exploring her mouth. I slipped my hands under her shirt, keeping one at the small of her back while the other moved up her spine. I paused at her bra strap but didn't undo it. I knew where I wanted things to end up, but I also didn't want to presume. Her fingers twisted in my hair and she pressed her belly more firmly against my hips until I moaned. I was already half-hard and the memory of what it had been like inside her was quickly changing half to full.

She stepped back, breaking the kiss, and I let her go. I'd be disappointed if that's all there was, but it had been a hell of a kiss. She grabbed the bottom of her short-sleeved shirt and pulled it over her head. While I was getting rid of my own clothes, she stripped off her jeans and undergarments so that by the time I was completely naked, she was too.

"Sit."

I did as she asked. No way was I going to argue with a beautiful naked woman.

"I wanted to do this last night," she said as she walked over to me.

I swallowed hard as she went to her knees, pushing my knees apart to make room for her. Her breasts brushed against my thighs and her nipples hardened at the contact. A surge of desire went through me. She was so beautiful.

When her hand wrapped around my cock, I groaned. Her tongue flicked against the tip, then circled it, making every nerve in my sensitive skin light up. As her lips closed over it and she took me into the moist heat of her mouth, I swore. She'd said she hadn't had much experience, but she definitely had some great instincts. Her tongue was moving around and across the part of me that was in her mouth while her hand stroked the several inches she couldn't take. I gripped the edge of the seat as she dropped further down, her lips stretching wide around me. When her free hand reached underneath me to cup my balls, my entire body jerked, pushing my cock even deeper into her mouth. She drew back as her fingers began to toy with me, rolling and massaging my balls even as she ran her tongue up and down my length.

Finally, I had to call her off. "No more." My voice was rough.

She glanced towards the door. "It's too bad we don't have hours more because I would very much like to taste you."

Fuck. I took her chin in my hand and pulled her up to me, sitting up to capture her mouth. I could taste the salt from my skin and it only fueled my desire. She climbed up onto my lap, her knees resting on either side of my waist. I grabbed her hips, wanting nothing more than to sink inside her, feel her gripping me tight, but safety always came first.

"Condom," I managed to say.

She caught my bottom lip between her teeth, nibbling at it before sucking it into her mouth.

Inexperienced my ass. This girl knew what she was doing. Either that or she had some amazing instincts.

"Got it," she said.

I gave her a questioning look as she tore open the packet.

"I took a couple from the hotel before I went to the club the other night," she explained as she rolled the latex over my throbbing cock. "I hadn't planned anything, but I figured it was better to be prepared."

"You would've made quite the Boy Scout," I

muttered. I circled one of her nipples with my finger. "Except the whole being a girl thing."

"Reed."

I looked up as she said my name.

"I want to see you."

I didn't have to ask what she meant because she started to lower herself onto me. Myriad emotions played across her face as she took me inch by agonizing inch until she was on my lap, every bit of me buried inside her. She rocked back and forth, her eyes closing, head falling forward. My fingers tightened on her hips until I was sure I would leave marks.

"Does it always feel like this?"

Her question surprised me, distracting me from the urgent need to move. "Like what?"

Her eyes locked with mine as she slowly began to rise. "I cannot put it into words." Her accent had thickened. "Do you not know what I mean?"

I did. I hadn't at first because her question had caught me off guard, but then I'd gotten it. Sex with her wasn't like sex with any of the other women I'd hooked up with during my trip. Our bodies moved together like we'd done this a thousand times before, but not in the way that it was old or something like that. More like a dance that we both knew the steps to and we moved at the same rhythm.

"No," I admitted. "It's not always like this."

I leaned forward, moving one hand to capture her breast. I squeezed the firm flesh as she picked up the pace. When I latched onto her nipple with my mouth, she cried out something in another language. Judging by the way her body tightened, I assumed it was positive. My tongue circled her nipple, teased the hard point of it. When I began to suck on it, her body jerked against mine, driving me deeper than I would've thought possible.

"Reed," she gasped my name. "Reed, please."

Her nails dug into my shoulders and I knew without her saying what she needed. I pulled her down on me hard, making her whimper, and then bit the delicate flesh in my mouth. I felt her mouth on my neck, her teeth in my skin even as she cried out, using my body to muffle the sound. I held her, thrusting up into her twice, pushing her through her orgasm as my own exploded through me. She wrapped her legs around me, our bodies still intimately joined as we rode out our pleasure.

I kissed the side of her neck as my hand ran up and down her spine. I'd answered honestly when I'd told her that it wasn't always like this, but I hadn't told her that I didn't know why, or that it scared me half to death. I could feel whatever this was between us growing. It didn't matter that we barely knew each other. This thing was completely out of our control, and I knew that if we didn't walk away soon, we'd have started something that neither of us had intended.

A knock at the door made both of us jump, ending the moment.

"What is it?" Nami called out, not trying to hide the annoyance in her voice.

"We are almost in Venice."

She looked at me and sighed. "Very well, Tomas." She climbed off of my lap, grimacing as I slid out of her. She spoke to me, her voice low, "You need to go."

I looked at the door and then back at her. "And how do you suggest I do that? I seriously doubt your buddies out there will let me walk out. It doesn't take a rocket scientist to figure what we were doing in here."

She frowned as she reached for her clothes. "You're right."

She opened a door, revealing a tiny private bathroom. She wet a washcloth and handed it to me before taking one for herself. We cleaned ourselves up in silence and dressed. We hadn't had the chance for this sort of awkward moment last night, but it wasn't as strained as I'd thought it would've been. I could tell she was thinking and I left her alone, my own thoughts preoccupied with what I was going to do now.

"Hide in the bathroom," she said suddenly.

"What?" I asked, surprised and wondering how that was a solution.

"Hide in the bathroom," she repeated. "I'll ask Tomas and Kai to come in and get my luggage, then take it to the last car and wait for me. I'll make up something about wanting to avoid the press."

"Press?"

The tips of her ears turned pink and I knew she wasn't just flushed from sex. She kept her back to me as she answered, "My father is making me come home early because the media took a picture of me at the club yesterday."

"You weren't allowed to be at a club? You're over twenty-one." I found myself wondering again who she was.

She took a deep breath and turned around to face me. "My parents have a very strict code of behavior that I am supposed to follow." She gestured towards the door. "They're supposed to keep me in line."

I grinned. "I don't think they've been doing a very good job."

"You have no idea." She didn't seem amused. "This trip was a graduation present from my parents. I was allowed to have fun, but only the sort of fun of which they would approve. Dancing at a club was not on the list."

"What do they have against dancing?" I asked. Was she from some sort of strict religious family?

"Nothing," she said. "But it is what might come after the dancing that is the problem." One side of her mouth tipped upwards in a half-smile. "What did happen after we danced?"

My eyes widened. "Sex?" Shit. What had I gotten myself into?

"Sex." She nodded. "Tomas and Kai's main job

70

watching me through college and on this trip was to keep me from having sex." Now she grinned at me. "As you can see, that didn't work very well."

"Will you be in trouble?" I asked, concern for her superseding anything else.

She shrugged. "Not if they keep their mouths shut, and since it would mean admitting they didn't do their job, I don't think they'll say anything. And it's not like I'll be in danger if my parents find out."

"Nami," I began.

She put her hand on my arm. "Don't worry about me, Reed. The worst that will happen is that I'll receive a lecture on proper behavior for...the way a lady should act."

I was pretty sure she'd been planning on saying something else, but I didn't push.

Her smile was sad now. "I just wanted a few days to do what I wanted, not what was expected of me."

I could definitely sympathize with that.

"I wanted to have fun without constantly having to wonder about what everyone else would think." She scowled at the door. "Without those two hovering over me every minute of every day."

An idea popped into my head. It was a bad one, possibly the worst one I'd ever had, and I knew I should just keep my mouth shut. But Nami looked so miserable and I couldn't help but compare her to me. She was where I'd been back in Philadelphia, bound by her parents' expectations without a hope of breaking free. I couldn't do anything about that, but I could offer her what she'd just said she wanted.

"Are you serious about wanting to have some fun?" I asked.

She looked up at me, a puzzled expression on her face. "Yes."

"And you want to get away from the linebackers out there?"

She nodded.

"You promise you won't be in any danger if you do something reckless?" I didn't want to risk this if it meant she would be hurt.

"I won't," she said. "My family has expectations, but they aren't violent if those aren't met."

"Then call them in here. I'll hide while you have them carry the luggage to the last car like you'd said. Except, instead of me sneaking out and away, we're going to go together."

Chapter 11

Nami

I stared at him, unsure if I was hearing him correctly. Surely he couldn't be suggesting that the two of us run away together. That was ludicrous. And yet a part of me was thrilled at the idea.

I immediately pushed the thought aside. He didn't mean for us to run away together. Not like that. Besides, I couldn't do it, couldn't leave my family. But...I realized what he meant. A little detour before going home. A chance to have what I'd wanted, at least a single day of freedom. A day to have fun without Tomas and Kai breathing down my neck, watching my every move.

"What do you say?" He held out a hand. "Want to have some fun before you head home?"

I couldn't begin to say all the ways this was a bad idea. The risk to my reputation, being out and about with a virtual stranger. The chance that my parents would find out. The ruining of the engagement.

Still, I couldn't help but think about what it would be like, to walk around Venice with Reed, like we were some couple on a romantic getaway. No eyes on me, no worrying about every little thing.

Before I could second-guess myself, I slid my hand into his. "Yes," I said. "I'd like that very much."

He raised my hand and kissed the back of it. "Then let's get started. We should be arriving in Venice soon." He released my hand and went into the bathroom, closing the door behind him.

I took a moment to collect myself and check to make sure my clothes were all on properly. I didn't want to risk them thinking there was anything strange going on. I needed them to think that I was still going along with my father's wishes. They wouldn't force me to do anything. It wasn't like that. But they would stay by my side the whole time, make sure I was never alone. Use their presence to intimidate crowds to move around us so that I could only go where they wanted me to go. They could call my father, tell him that I'd tried to slip away...again. He wouldn't hurt me or anything like that. What he wouldn't do was trust me again.

"Tomas, Kai." I opened the door and gave them each a quick smile. "Come here please."

They both looked angry and, if what Reed had said was true, they had good reason to be. Neither of them said anything though. They wouldn't. Being detained wasn't exactly the kind of thing security would be pleased to tell their employer. They came in without a word or a greeting, but that wasn't entirely unusual.

"I want to get off from the last car," I informed them. "Avoid the possibility of any media."

They exchanged looks that I recognized. They didn't generally like it when I took charge. They preferred to follow things like class schedules, itineraries, things like that. They were loyal though, understood their role when it came to who was in charge. They would do what I asked unless it went directly against my father's orders.

"Take the luggage to the car and wait for me there."

"But, Pr–"

"Are you really going to argue?" I cut Tomas off before he could call me by my title. I didn't know how much Reed could hear, but I didn't want him hearing that.

74

"It's a simple task. Take our luggage to the last train car and I'll meet you there when we arrive in Venice."

"Shouldn't we not wait until we arrive at the station, take our things then and go together?" Kai suggested.

I shook my head. "Do you really think it's a good idea to try to haul all of our luggage through crowded corridors while everyone else is trying to leave too?"

They exchanged looks again and this time I knew it was because I'd made a good point. I honestly hadn't even thought about it until I'd said it, but it actually made sense. It seemed that luck was on my side.

"Hurry up." I motioned towards the suitcases and then stepped off to the side to let them pass by. I backed up against the bathroom door so that neither of them would accidentally bump against it. Since it was one of the few places I could be out of the way, it didn't look suspicious.

I closed the door behind them as they left, but didn't tell Reed to come out yet. I wanted to be sure Tomas and Kai didn't come back for something they missed, so I waited a few minutes and then started to open the door. My hand was on the latch before I thought better of it. I didn't want to be rude. I rapped my fingers against the door twice.

"They're gone."

He slid the door aside and we were suddenly face to face. A mere inch apart, I could feel the heat of him, smell the scent of the train's soap mingled with the scent that I recognized as him. I looked up at him, my heart beating hard in my chest.

He cupped my chin, his skin burning against mine. I barely had a moment to register the kiss before his mouth was hard against mine. A shiver of desire went through me as my lips molded themselves to his. My body leaned against his and I could feel him getting hard against my hip.

His teeth scraped my bottom lip and I moaned. I

75

couldn't believe how good he made me feel. A single kiss and my knees were weak.

He sighed as he broke the kiss, but he didn't let me go. "I wish this was a much longer ride."

"Regretting your offer?" I teased. I knew what he meant, but I didn't want to go there. I was already pushing what was smart. There couldn't be anything between us and I could feel us getting closer the longer we were together.

"Getting cold feet, are we?" He smiled at me as he laced his fingers through mine.

"Not a chance." I smiled at him. "You're stuck with me."

His eyes darkened and he squeezed my hand. "Sounds like fun to me."

Silence fell between us, thick and tense with desire. How could I want him again? I'd slept with Aaron and enjoyed it well enough, but I hadn't wanted him a second time. With Reed, I'd had him twice and still, I wanted more. If I had my way, we'd be heading straight to a hotel and not coming out for a week.

Dammit. I seriously needed to stop thinking about sex with Reed. We weren't going there. We were going to be in Venice and I fully intended to see it.

"How do we do this?" I asked, breaking the moment. "Tomas and Kai will wait in the last car for a while, but I wouldn't put it past them for one to stay with the luggage and the other to come back and get me."

"Then I guess we'd better move then." He dropped a wink and opened the car door. He looked both ways, then pulled me out into the hall after him.

"Where are we going?" I kept my voice low, then flushed when I realized what I was doing.

Reed didn't seem to have noticed because he answered my question in a voice almost as quiet. "The dining car."

"Really?" I asked.

"We'll follow people out of there into one of the other cars and get lost in the shuffle."

"You think that'll work?" I gave him a doubtful look.

He shrugged. "Saw it work in a movie once." He frowned. "At least I think it worked."

I wasn't entirely sure if he was joking or not, but either way, I would go along with it. What was the worst that could happen?

As we made our way into the dining car and ducked into a booth, my stomach was in knots and my palms were sweating. I almost wanted to let go of Reed's hand, but I was more worried that I'd end up losing him in a crowd and then I'd be lost and by myself. I spoke several languages, but wasn't fluent in Italian. I hadn't realized how much I'd accepted the presence of my bodyguards until I thought about what would happen if Reed and I got separated.

"Are you okay?" Reed looked over at me, concern on his face.

I nodded.

"Because you're kind of hurting my hand."

I flushed and let go. He smiled at me as he flexed his fingers and shook his hand.

"Sorry," I muttered.

"Are you sure you're alright?"

"I was just...worried that we'd get separated."

Reed stood and held out his hand. "Don't worry. I won't let you go."

My stomach twisted at his words and I warned myself not to read too much into what he'd said. He was talking about right now, that was all.

I took his hand and let him lead me into the group of people who were heading back to their seats. Even though I knew the chances of Tomas or Kai finding me so quickly were slim, I couldn't stop myself from looking over my shoulder. I had a feeling that wasn't going to change until we were safely outside and deep in the city.

As we stood near the door, Reed pulled me closer to him. "Ready to have some fun?"

I smiled up at him. Despite the nerves, I was starting to feel a rush of excitement, the kind of rush that came from doing something I wasn't supposed to. The best part about all of this, however, wasn't what I was about to do, or even how attracted I was to Reed. The best part was that Reed didn't know who I was, what I was, and he wanted to do this with me. He wanted me for me. Maybe most of it was for my body, but I knew there had to be at least a little part of him that liked me for more than sex, otherwise we wouldn't be here. For the first time in my life, I wasn't a princess or an heir to a throne. I was Nami. Just Nami. And I had a feeling I was going to like it.

Chapter 12

Reed

I couldn't believe I made the offer, and I was even more surprised that she'd accepted. The words had just kind of popped out and then I had to figure out what we were going to do. Fortunately, I was able to put the time I spent in the bathroom to good use. By the time she told me to come out, I had an idea of what to do to get off the train without being seen by her bodyguards. Then she'd been right there and I'd kissed her. I'd needed to kiss her. It wasn't like anything I could explain, only that with her standing that close, I couldn't help myself. The scent of her, the heat of her body.

I shook my head to clear it. I believed Nami when she said her bodyguards wouldn't hurt her. I wasn't so sure they wouldn't hurt me, however. I had a feeling I'd just missed getting the shit beat out of me in my hotel room. I was quite certain it would be in my best interest to avoid them altogether, and to do that, I needed a clear head. Unfortunately, with Nami so close by, it wasn't as easy as I would have liked. I couldn't believe how easily she distracted me.

"When the doors open, just walk right out. Don't rush or keep looking over your shoulder. We're just two tourists coming in to Venice on the train." I kept my voice low.

"More knowledge from movies?" she asked. I could hear a bit of strain in her voice, but there was excitement too.

I couldn't deny that I felt the same. It wasn't like this was some sort of rescue or anything like that. I was just trying to give someone a day or two of freedom and fun because I knew what it was like to live a life for someone else. Part of me wanted to tell her to break free completely, to not wait as long as I did, but I reminded myself that I didn't know Nami's whole story. I couldn't assume that her situation was like mine. I had to trust her to do what was right for her.

Besides, I wasn't a hero. I allowed myself a wry smile. I was an unemployed rich kid making my way across Europe, sleeping with whoever I happened to find. I had no direction, no purpose. In fact, standing here with Nami, getting ready to sneak off a train and vanish into Venice for a day or so, was the first time I'd had a plan beyond the times stamped on my train tickets.

The doors opened and we followed the crowd out. It was almost noon and a beautiful May day in Italy. Nami was gripping my hand tight enough for it almost to hurt, but I didn't say anything this time. Excitement was quickly chasing away my nerves. I led us towards the front of the train, hopefully away from where the bodyguards would be coming once they figured out Nami was gone.

Still, we needed to get away from the station and out of sight. I'd been to Venice once on a business trip, and while I hadn't had time to thoroughly explore the city, I did know a couple places. The first thing we needed, however, was a boat. It wasn't that difficult to find a gondola. Once we settled in, I spoke to the nice Italian man smiling at us. "*Portaci al Museo Guggenheim, per favore.*"

"What was that?" Nami asked. "I caught part of it,

but Italian isn't my strongest language."

"I asked him to take us to the Guggenheim Museum," I said. I released her hand and put my arm around her shoulders, pulling her close to me. "Now let's just look like we're enjoying the romance of the city."

I nuzzled the back of her ear to make her laugh and it worked. I felt the last of the tension leave her as she turned towards me, her mouth covering mine. I made a sound of surprise as her tongue pushed between my lips. She turned her body towards me so that her breasts pushed against my chest, her kiss aggressive. My body began to respond and it was only the gondolier clearing his throat that kept me from taking things further.

"Young lovers?" His English was heavily accented but understandable. "From America, no?"

"Yes." I gave him a charming smile. No need for Nami to tell him where she was from. A pair of Americans wouldn't attract that much attention. If Nami was from some place exotic, it might.

"I feel like I'm in a movie," Nami said quietly as we settled back into more appropriate positions. "Something like *Roman Holiday.*"

"That's the one with Audrey Hepburn, right?" I asked. "I think I had to watch it in school once."

She rolled her eyes. "You Americans can't even appreciate your finest accomplishments."

I laughed. "Sorry. I'm a bit more of an action adventure kind of guy than the classics."

"Ah, like the adventure we are on now."

I kissed her nose. "Exactly."

What was I doing? Acting like this was some cute little date? I'd always come across as suave and sophisticated. I didn't get women by being goofy or silly. I was charming. Cool, collected. A bit cocky.

Except around her. I'd been all those things yesterday, but today, I'd lost it. I found myself at a loss for words. Fell over my feet. And she seemed to like it.

The odd thing was, I sort of did too. It was strange. I felt more relaxed around Nami than I had around any other woman I'd ever been with. Even Piper.

We pulled up next to the museum and I helped Nami up onto the sidewalk. We kept holding hands as we walked into the museum. I'd never been inside, but I figured this would be the best place to hide for a bit. Her bodyguards would have to search for her alone unless they wanted to make a scene by calling the cops and the impression I'd gotten from Nami was that no one wanted attention. Venice was full of places like this and the chances of them finding us right away were slim.

"You know," Nami said quietly. "If I wanted to tour museums, I could've done that with Tomas and Kai."

"Ah," I said. "But could they give you running commentary about European Abstractionism or one of Jackson Pollock's greatest masterpieces?"

She raised an eyebrow. "You learned about art while getting your MBA?"

"Nope." I grinned at her. "Learned it to impress girls. Did it work?"

She laughed, then slapped a hand over her mouth as the sound echoed. "I think that's one of the things I always hated about these places. I love the beauty of the art work, but I always feel like I'm in church, like I can't talk too loud or I'll be reprimanded."

"I know what you mean," I said, pitching my voice just as low. "And you know what?" I pulled Nami through a door that said 'Employees Only.' "It's always made me want to do something a bit...wicked."

I shut the door behind us and pulled her to me. I couldn't say what it was, but I couldn't keep my hands off her. My mouth was hard on hers and she made a noise that sent my blood rushing south. I cupped her breast through her shirt while the other hand moved down to her ass. She ground her hips against me and it was my turn to moan. The things this woman did to me.

She pushed me back against the door and moved her mouth from mine, trailing kisses down my neck, pausing at the base to lightly nip at the skin. Her hand slid between us and she pressed her palm against my cock.

"Dammit, Nami," I groaned. If she kept that up, I was either going to end up with a massive hard-on when we walked out of here or I was going to embarrass myself and come in my pants. Neither option was appealing.

"I think I should help you with this little problem." She grinned at me. "Or…not so little."

I stared at her as she went down on her knees. When I'd pulled her in here, I'd imagined making out, copping a feel over her clothes. Not this.

"What are you doing?" The question was ludicrous, but I couldn't stop myself from asking it.

"Having fun." She winked at me as her hands quickly undid my pants, pulling them down just enough for her to reach into my underwear and pull out my cock.

I was already mostly hard, but the moment her lips touched me, that changed. My hands curled into fists as she took half of me, letting me swell in her mouth until she had to release me.

"Nami."

"Shh," she said, her hand running up and down my length. "We don't want anyone coming in here, do we?" She looked up at me, hints of cyan peeking through her thick lashes. "Unless that's what you want." She flicked out her tongue against the tip of my cock and it twitched.

The mental image of what someone would see if they came in flashed my mind. This beautiful woman on her knees, hand and mouth on my cock. It was gone as quickly as it came, the wet heat of Nami's mouth driving away all coherent thoughts.

I put my hand on her head, not to control her, but needing to touch her. Her curls were soft against my fingers, the sensation adding to what I was feeling as she began to suck on my cock, deep, steady pulls of her mouth that had my knees weak and my pulse racing.

"Nami." I twisted my fingers in her curls. "I'm close."

She looked up at me as my cock slid from between her lips. "I want you to go in my mouth."

I swore. Where had this woman come from?

"Is there a reason why you shouldn't?"

I shook my head.

"Unless you don't want to?" Her voice was soft, uncertain.

I dropped my hand from her head and ran my thumb along her slightly swollen lips. "You have no idea how much I want to."

She took the tip of my thumb in her mouth, sucking on it hard before releasing it. I rested my hand on her cheek as she leaned forward to wrap her lips around me again. My eyes closed, head falling back against the door with a thunk. Some women had a natural affinity for things of a primal nature. Nami had to be one of those because the things she was doing with her mouth and tongue...

My entire body stiffened as I came. I bit down on my bottom lip to stifle the sounds I wanted to make. My cock pulsed in her mouth, emptying even as her hand continued to work over the base, milking out every last drop. I could feel her swallowing and forced my eyes open. I looked down to find her eyes already on me, watching as she licked me clean.

I reached down and grabbed her arms, pulling her to her feet a bit more roughly than I'd intended.

"My turn." The words were practically a growl and her eyes darkened at the sound.

I turned her so she was facing the door and quickly opened her pants. She gasped as I shoved my hand down beneath her panties. Her legs parted as my fingers slid between her folds.

"I wish you were wearing a skirt," I said, my voice

low. I pressed my mouth against her ear. "Because I really want my mouth on you."

My fingers began to rub over her clit as my other hand slid under her shirt, moving up to her bra and pulling a cup down so I could get my hands on bare skin. Her nipple hardened almost immediately as my fingers closed around it. She rested her forehead against the door, her breath coming in harsh pants as I drove her body towards climax. As much as I wanted to take my time with her, show her just how high I could take her, I knew this had to be fast, and there was something to be said for a quickie.

"You're so hot and wet." I traced the shell of her ear with the tip of my tongue and she shuddered. "So wet for me."

My cock rubbed against her jeans, the friction almost painful against my sensitive skin. I gave her nipple a sharp tug and she made a strangled sound, like she was trying to hold back.

"That's good," I murmured. "Don't be loud. Wouldn't want someone to come in here and see you about to come on my fingers. And that's what's going to happen, isn't it?"

She nodded, every muscle in her body tense. She was close. I could feel it.

I nipped at her earlobe and moved my fingers harder and faster, pushing her. She began to tremble and then came with a cry.

"That's it." I kissed the side of her neck, wishing I could mark her flawless skin as she shook in my arms. I kept my fingers moving slowly over her clit, coaxing out every last bit of pleasure I could. When I stilled, I kept my arms around her, my hand on her breast, until I was sure she could stand on her own.

She turned towards me, clothes still in disarray, her eyes shining. She reached out and took the hand that had been in her pants, raising it to her mouth. When she slid my fingers into her mouth, my stomach tightened. Her tongue moved over my skin, thoroughly cleaning each digit. My cock twitched and I knew if she kept it up, I'd be hard again in no time.

I pulled my hand away and leaned down to kiss her, tasting us both in her mouth. Her body pressed against mine and I wondered if there was any way I could get her in bed again before her day of fun was over. I didn't know why I wanted her so badly, and I wasn't going to take the time to try to figure things out. All I knew was we were both here and I was going to give her a day of freedom for her to remember.

Chapter 13

Reed

What happened in the storage room hadn't lessened my desire for her. If anything, it had made it stronger. As we made our way through the city, I found myself constantly wanting to touch her. My arm around her shoulders, at her waist. Hand on the small of her back. Fingers laced between mine.

I barely registered the beauty of Venice even as our gondolier took us on a tour. All of my attention was on Nami and her reaction to everything. She was delighted at the architecture, amused by the other tourists. She was the strangest combination of maturity with child-like joy.

As we went, we also talked and I was again surprised at how easy it was to open up to her. By mid-day, I was telling her things I hadn't discussed with anyone.

"My parents decided that I needed to marry the daughter of this business partner of theirs. Britni."

A shadow crossed her face, but was gone again before I could really be sure that I'd seen it. "Did you love her?" she asked.

I shook my head. "I barely knew her. She was a few years younger than me. I knew her brother was an ass, so that didn't make me more inclined to like the idea, but it was for my family." I looked down at my left hand where

I'd worn a gold band for the short time I'd been married. "I'd been okay with it until I met this girl. Piper. She was in my sister's class."

"The spoiled one?" Nami was smiling, but her eyes were guarded.

I nodded. "I screwed up everything. I thought I was in love with Piper, but I didn't think I could break off the engagement with Britni, so I went through with it."

"You're married?" Nami stiffened and started to pull away from me.

"No," I said quickly. I kept my arm around her, but didn't try to pull her closer, not wanting to be aggressive. "I did marry Britni, but it was the marriage and Piper that finally made me see how miserable I was." This was the first time I'd said all this out loud, I realized.

"What did you do?"

"Well, after I admitted it to myself, I knew I had to do something about it, but I wasn't sure what." I twisted one of Nami's curls around my finger. "Then my brother-in-law did something awful and when I saw how his family rallied around him, I knew I couldn't be a part of it anymore. I filed for divorce."

"And Piper?"

The words were flat and I looked down at Nami, wondering if I could read her thoughts on her face. I couldn't. I supposed I could've lied to her and told her that my divorce was the reason I'd come to Europe, but I didn't want to spoil what we had with a lie. Lies were what had gotten me into trouble in the first place.

"I went to her, told her about the divorce, but it was too late." It didn't hurt to think about it anymore, which is what made me realize I hadn't been in love with Piper after all. "She'd found someone else."

"I'm sorry," Nami said, her voice sincere.

"I'm not," I replied honestly. "She told me that the two of us had been drawn together because of circumstances, nothing else. We really weren't a good match."

"Is she why you came to Europe?"

"Part of it." I shifted in my seat and Nami moved with me, tucking her head against my shoulder. "My parents were furious about the divorce and threatened my job. That's when I realized I couldn't take it anymore. I was tired of doing everything they told me to do."

"And did they accept your decisions?"

I heard the careful tone in her voice and knew we weren't just talking about me anymore. "Not exactly. I quit my job and left. That was a couple months ago."

"And you haven't been back since?"

"No." My fingers traced patterns on Nami's arm. "But I've talked to them a few times."

"And are they okay with your choices now?"

"Not really," I admitted. "But I don't regret doing it. Quitting or divorcing Britni. I've spent too much of my life doing as I was told. It was fine when I was a kid, but I'm far too old to be toeing the line like they wanted me to. I need to choose my own path. Work, love, family. They have to be my choices."

Silence fell over us as our tour guide pulled us up to a spot where we could get off. I helped Nami out of the gondola and she put her arm around my waist, leaning her head against me. I was surprised, but wasn't about to complain. I put my arm around her shoulders and we headed for the *Palácio rosado*.

"It's so beautiful," Nami said softly as we made our way inside.

She was right. The outside had been impressive enough, but the interior with its ornate high ceilings and breath-taking architecture, was spectacular. The tour guide was talking but I didn't hear a word he said and I didn't think Nami did either. She seemed to be deep in thought and I didn't want to interrupt her. Neither of us spoke through the entire tour, but as we broke off at the end and started to walk about on our own, she broke the silence.

"My family has planned my life out." She was staring straight ahead and her voice was soft. I almost thought she might be talking to herself rather than me. "I told you that I majored in political science because it was what they wanted, but it's beyond that. I, too, am supposed to take over my family's...business."

We stood at the Bridge of Sighs, oblivious to everyone else around us. I didn't know what was going on with Nami, but she was clearly dealing with some difficult choices.

"It's been in my family for generations," she continued. "A legacy passed down to the eldest child, boy or girl, and we're expected to rise to it. We're trained for it from birth." There was a hint of bitterness in her voice.

"And what if you refuse?" I asked.

"I can't." She sighed and straightened, pulling away from me. "If my brother had lived, maybe I could have, but he died when he was only a few hours old."

"I'm so sorry," I said.

"I don't remember him," she said absently. "I remember when my mother miscarried though. Twice. How sad everyone was. My parents weren't going to try for another one. Halea was their miracle baby. Four weeks early and so tiny. Even when she finally came home, she was so small I was afraid to hold her."

I had the sudden, sharp memory of my mother handing me a squalling, red-faced bundle. Rebecca had been a handful from moment one, but I'd loved her then. I supposed I still loved her, but I didn't like her very much. I felt a stab of jealousy for what Nami and her sister had. Her parents might've been similar to mine, but she at least had Halea.

"You see, if I choose to step down from my position, it would go to Halea." Nami crossed her arms, rubbing them with her hands as we followed a group of people to see the dungeon. "And she couldn't handle it."

"Does she want it?" I asked. "I know you said she's sixteen, but some people know what they want to do when they're that age."

Nami shook her head. "It doesn't matter. She doesn't have the strength to do it, to deal with everything."

I wondered what sort of business the Carrs owned, but I didn't ask. I was getting the distinct impression that she would only offer the personal details she wanted, and nothing more.

"She wants to please people," Nami continued. "She hates conflict. Always the peacemaker."

I could see where that would be a problem in the business world. While compromise and negotiation always required a bit of flexibility, someone who always wanted to make peace would certainly get walked all over. To be good at being in charge, a person had to have the right combination of stubbornness and a willingness to consider others' opinions.

"There's no one else," she said.

I hated the tone of defeat in her voice. A wave of protectiveness washed over me, surprising me. I'd never been protective of anyone. Not really. I considered myself a gentleman and tried to look out for people, but it was never anything like this. I wanted to hold her and tell her that it would all be okay.

"Can't your parents just hire someone? I know it's not ideal for a family business, but surely there's someone who's been loyal enough to be considered family without being blood."

The smile she gave me said it all. "No, Reed. It has to be me. And I've made my peace with that. More or less, anyway." She reached over and grabbed my hand, squeezing it tightly. "That's why this means so much to me. When I go back, it's all responsibility."

I didn't say anything as I pulled her to my side, tucking her under my arm where she fit so perfectly. I hated this. I hated not being able to help her break free

91

like I had. I hated her parents for making her feel so trapped. And I hated how much I cared. I didn't know this girl. She was supposed to have been a fling, another in a line of hook-ups to help me forget the mess I'd left in Philadelphia and to distract me from the fact that I had no idea what I was doing. But it was more than that already, had been from the moment I'd met her even if I hadn't wanted to admit it then.

I told myself that I needed to stop asking questions, stop trying to figure out a way to help. I couldn't help. All I could do was listen and then let her go when it was time. But as I looked down at her, my heart twisted at the thought of letting her go, never seeing her again.

Dammit. I knew better than to do this, but I couldn't seem to stop myself. I didn't know who she was or what I was feeling, only that it was more than I should. I also knew that no matter what I did, things were going to end badly. For both of us.

Chapter 14

Reed

As afternoon turned into evening, I started getting hungry. With all the craziness that had been going on, I'd forgotten to eat today. I doubted Nami had eaten much either, so I steered us towards a place I'd heard of when I'd been here before. I hadn't eaten there, but it sounded like a good place to take her. I'd heard it had an amazing view of the gondolas. Nice and romantic...

I pushed the thought aside. Romance didn't matter. I wasn't trying to date her. I kept telling myself that as we walked up to Risorrante da Raffaele. Still, I couldn't help but think about what it would be like to take her someplace like this on a real date, as something more than just some girl I'd hooked up with. A girl I was just supposed to be showing a good time.

I could see how things would play out differently if we'd been here as a couple. We would've been planning the trip together, with the restaurant as part of it. I pulled out her chair for her, returning the smile she gave me. After we ordered, I decided to ask the question I'd been wondering for a while now.

"What would you do," I asked, "if you could do anything? If your family business wasn't a factor. What would you do?"

Nami looked surprised and I understood why. When a person was raised, groomed, to take over the family business, there was never anyone asking what we wanted to do, not seriously anyway. Our opinions, our wants, they didn't matter.

"I haven't given it any thought."

The reply came automatically. I recognized the sound of something that had been rehearsed, the kind of response a responsible older child was supposed to give when asked that question.

"Yes, you have." I called her on her lie. "I know you have because I always did."

She smiled, unapologetic about the deceit. "You did?"

"Of course." I smiled back. "I did the whole MBA thing and found out I have a knack for it, so my dreams changed, but they weren't always for business."

"What were they?" she asked. "When you were a child, what were your dreams?"

"If I tell you mine, will you tell me yours?" I teased as the waiter poured us both the wine I'd ordered.

She winked. "You first."

"All right," I agreed. I leaned back in my chair. "How far back do you want to go? Preschool?"

"You were ambitious even then?" She seemed amused. "Why does this not surprise me?"

"Oh, nothing so ambitious," I said. "I once wanted to be a police car. Not a policeman, but a car."

She laughed, a full, real laugh, not the kind that someone gave to be polite. "You wanted to be a car?"

I shrugged. "I was four. I didn't know that wasn't exactly an option." I took another swallow of wine. "I figured it out eventually."

"So did you want to be a police officer then?"

"No." I shook my head. "When I was older, but before I really understood what it meant for me to take over the family business, I thought I might want to be a lawyer. Not a prosecutor or some sleazy defense attorney. I wanted to go into family law, take care of kids."

It was funny how I thought of that now. I hadn't thought of it in years, not since I'd gotten into high school and my parents had started telling me what classes to take. Or, as they put it, 'strongly advising' me what would be needed for me to get into business. I'd been surprised that I'd felt protective of Nami, thinking that I hadn't felt that way before, but I had. I'd wanted to help people.

"You're quiet," Nami said, breaking into my thoughts.

"Just remembering," I said. "So there you have it. I wanted to be a lawyer and then went to business school."

"Is that what you will do now?" she asked. "Go to law school?"

I shook my head. "No, I've given that up. I don't think I'd be suited for law anyway. I actually do have a good head for business."

"So you will go back to your parents' business?" She sounded surprised.

"No." I leaned back as the waiter brought our appetizers. "I want my own business." I frowned. "I thought I had a good idea before, but now I'm thinking I might want something else."

"What?" she asked.

"I have no idea." I laughed. "None at all."

We ate for a few moments, enjoying the weather and the city itself. I had to admit, I was definitely enjoying this trip to Venice much more than my previous one. I looked across the table at Nami. There was no denying that it was due to the company.

"You never told me yours," I said as the waiter cleared away our appetizers and placed our entrees in front of us. "If family wasn't an issue, what would you want to be? What would you do?"

She flushed, piquing my curiosity. Whatever it was, it had to be interesting.

"Now you have to share," I said.

She pushed some of her food around on her plate and took a bite. I didn't press her again. She'd tell me when she was ready. I could see that she wanted to. After a couple minutes of us eating in silence, she finally spoke.

"I wanted to be a teacher."

"A teacher?" I was surprised, not because I didn't think she'd be good at it, but because it didn't seem to match her initial reaction.

"And a mother." She looked down at her plate.

Ah, that made sense now. Well, sort of. "Will your family's business keep you from being a mother?" The question popped out before I thought about it. "Shit. I'm sorry. That's none of my business."

"It's okay," she said, her voice quiet. "Let's just say that if I have children, because of my position, I'd most likely see very little of them. They'd be raised by nannies. Governesses."

"Couldn't your husband take care of them? If you've got such a good position, he wouldn't need to work long hours." Dammit. I kept putting my foot in my mouth, but I couldn't help it. I wanted to know more about her, how she thought, what she wanted. "That is, if you planned to get married. You wouldn't need to just to have kids. I mean, I just assumed since your family was so adamant about the whole sex thing..."

Shit. I sounded like such an idiot. Fortunately, Nami was laughing. It wasn't the same full laugh she'd had before, but it was real.

"Yes, Reed, I would need to be married." She was smiling, but it didn't reach her eyes. "My parents would not approve of children any other way."

I frowned as I took another bite.

"You do not approve." Her accent had thickened and I knew she was upset.

"Actually, I was just thinking of how well our parents would get along." That was half the truth anyway.

"My parents put an 'heir' clause in the business contract they drew up when Britni and I got married." I stabbed a piece of chicken with a little more force than necessary. "Kids are just pawns to my parents."

Nami reached across the table and put her hand on mine. I jerked my head up, startled as much by the gesture as I was by the touch itself.

"All we can hope for, then, is to do better for our children than our parents have done for us."

There was something in her voice that made me turn over my hand and squeeze hers, offering her comfort for whatever she was feeling. I raised our hands and kissed the back of hers.

"I'm sure you're going to be a great mother," I said sincerely. I felt a stab of jealousy at the thought of her with another man and immediately shoved it away. I had no right to be jealous. She wasn't mine. This was just a fun follow up to a great night.

"I don't think so." She pulled her hand away from mine. "My eldest will be forced to do exactly what I'm doing now."

I frowned. "But you don't have to do things the same way your parents do. You can let your kids do whatever they want."

She shook her head, but didn't expound. She went back to eating and silence fell between us again. When the waiter came back to ask if we wanted dessert, we both declined and I asked for the check.

"I'll pay," she said, reaching for her purse.

"No way." I picked up the check and handed the waiter my card. "My treat."

As the waiter walked away, Nami leaned across the table, her expression serious. "Reed, you do understand, this is not a date. It cannot be a date."

"I know," I said. And I did, intellectually. A part of me, however, still had a bit of hope that this could be something more. I didn't know what, because I wasn't letting myself think that far ahead, but something.

She shook her head. "No, you don't. You have to understand that I will have to walk away soon, and we will never see each other again."

I couldn't let her see how much I hated that idea. I stood and held out my hand. "Soon, but not now, right?"

I saw the emotions flit across her face but didn't say anything. She had to make this decision on her own. If she declined and said she needed to go now, I'd respect it. I'd take her wherever she thought it best to find her bodyguards and then I'd go find a hotel room. But I didn't want her to say no. I wanted her to take my hand and come with me somewhere we could be alone. Really alone.

She stood but didn't take my hand. I tried to hide my disappointment as I lowered my hand. This was it then. We were done. I barely registered the waiter returning my card. All I could think about was the best way to say good-bye. I wanted to kiss her one last time, feel her pressed against me.

"Soon." Her voice was low as she closed the distance between us. "But not now."

She stood on her toes and claimed my mouth in a kiss that went straight down through me. I could feel the want, the need, as her tongue curled around mine, her body moving against me in a way that wasn't entirely appropriate for public. I didn't care about anyone who might be watching though. All I cared about was the woman in my arms.

When she broke the kiss, she didn't pull away. "Take me somewhere we can be alone," she whispered.

"You read my mind." I brushed my lips across hers. "Let's get out of here."

Chapter 15

Nami

I didn't know what I expected, but it wasn't something like Hotel Moresco. It was absolutely gorgeous, and far too expensive for a few hours. I had no doubt that was all we would get. Tomas and Kai hadn't caught up with us yet, but I had no doubt that they'd find me soon. Even if they didn't, I would need to call them and meet. I'd missed the plane today, and we could make excuses for that, but if I put off going home for more than a day, I risked my parents finding out what I was really doing.

I should have left him at the restaurant, I knew that, but I hadn't been able to make myself walk away. I'd seen the look in his eyes when I hadn't taken his hand and it had reached something deep inside me, a part of me I hadn't known I'd had. All his talk of dreams and what I wanted had stirred up feelings I hadn't allowed myself to feel in a long time. I'd accepted my parents' will and resigned myself to my position, to marrying a man I didn't know or love. What I'd told him about children was true. I may have been inheriting the title of queen and the rule of Saja, but I was still expected to provide an heir. At least, unlike European monarchies, the gender wasn't important.

It had been that thought, that this was what I'd be doing to my own son or daughter, that had made me go with him. I needed to forget about what was to come, live in the moment, focus on nothing but him. I knew I'd gotten in too deep with him, cared too much, and it was that knowledge that would keep me sane during what was to come. It would be Reed's voice I would hear, his body I would see and feel when my husband came to me.

I'd heard a story once that a young English princess, when she told her mother that she was frightened shortly before her wedding night, was given the sage advice to close her eyes and think of England. I would not be thinking of Saja on my wedding night, gritting my teeth and getting through it. Instead, I would think of Reed. Imagine it was his hands on me, him inside me. My husband would never know that any sounds of pleasure I made were from the memory of the man currently at my side.

"Are you sure about this, Nami?" Reed asked. "I don't want you to do anything you don't want."

I squeezed his hand and led him onto the elevator. "I want you."

His eyes darkened as the doors closed and he backed me up against the wall. He cupped my face between his hands, and I waited for a hard, demanding kiss. I could feel the desire radiating off of him. Instead, his touch was gentle, his thumbs brushing along my bottom lip.

"The things you do to me," he murmured. He lowered his head and touched his lips to mine, the briefest of kisses, but enough to heat my entire body from head to toe.

The elevator dinged and we were on the fourth floor. Reed had gone for whatever room they had available, but I had no doubt that even the cheapest room here would be opulent. I wasn't disappointed, but I only cared about one thing.

I pulled him after me, the bed my only objective.

"Not that I'm complaining," Reed said as I pushed against his chest so that he fell back on the bed. "But I was thinking we could take our time."

"I intend to," I said as I stripped of my shirt and jeans. "I am going to take my time with you."

His eyes widened slightly. "Nami?"

I didn't speak as I pulled off his shoes before climbing onto the bed. I straddled his waist and took hold of his t-shirt. He raised up enough for me to pull it off, baring his sculpted, lean torso. I felt his eyes on me as I slowly ran my hands over his chest, down his arms and then back up before moving down to his stomach. I didn't look at him as I teased along the waistband of his jeans, memorizing the way the pants hung low enough to show off the top of those v-grooves that I knew pointed the way to a magnificent piece of flesh.

I leaned down, running my tongue over his abs, enjoying the moans my attention elicited. I traveled up his chest, kissing and licking my way across his skin. When I reached his nipples, I took my time on each one, licking and sucking until he had a hand on my head, fingers buried in my curls. Pinpricks of pain went through my scalp, making things low inside me heat up. I scraped my teeth across the tight skin and he swore. I smiled and bit down, worrying at his nipple until he was writhing beneath me, the friction doing wonderful things to me.

Suddenly, he was pulling me up and crushing my mouth to his. He bit at my bottom lip, sucking it into his mouth to soothe away the sting. His free hand pressed against the small of my back, pushing me even harder down against him, the only thing between us was my panties and his clothing.

"Could I make you come this way?" He paused in his assault on my mouth only long enough to ask the question.

I didn't need to answer because I was already coming. The pressure and friction from his jeans on my clit pushed me over the edge. I pulled my mouth away from his to cry out.

"I love those sounds you make." He sucked on my earlobe and I squirmed, sending new ripples of pleasure through me. "Want to see what else I can make you do?"

I pushed myself up on my knees. "Not yet. I'm not done with you."

He slid his hands up my sides. "Please. You're killing me."

"Maybe a peek." I smiled down at him as I reached behind my back and unhooked my bra.

"Fuck," he groaned as he cupped my breasts. "You have the most amazing tits."

My eyelids fluttered as his fingers found my nipples, rolling them hard and fast, almost painfully. He tugged on them and my head fell back, my body arching towards his touch. I put my hands on his chest, feeling the rise and fall against my palms, the beat of his heart.

His hips moved under mine and I felt his weight starting to shift. I shook my head and slid backwards, moving away from his hands.

"I'm not done with you yet." I positioned myself at his knees and got to work ridding him of his jeans. I left his boxer-briefs on, wanting to remember the sight of him like this. Long legs, trim waist. The way the cloth clung to him. His cock was already starting to grow and I licked my lips in appreciation, remembering the taste of him from earlier today.

I ran my hands up his muscular legs, the hair rough against my palms. I cupped his cock through the cloth and gave him a gentle squeeze, smiling as he swore. I hooked my fingers under the waistband of his underwear and he obliged by lifting his hips so I could pull them down and then off. His cock came free, thick and swollen. I sat back on my heels, letting myself enjoy the new view.

"You going to stare at it all night or do something

with it?" He was teasing, but I could hear the strain in his voice.

I didn't answer him, but instead reached out and lightly ran my fingers along the underside of his cock. It twitched and his hands fisted in the bedspread. He swore and begged, but I didn't let him hurry me. I let my fingers explore every inch of his shaft, never giving him enough pressure. When I was done with that, I moved lower, cupping his balls, rolling them between my fingers, feeling the weight of them, the soft skin holding them.

"Please, Nami, I'm dying here."

I smiled. My panties were soaked, my pussy throbbing. I was as desperate for him as he was for me. I shifted, pulling off my panties and tossing them on the floor. I started to rise on my knees, then hesitated. There was something I wanted, but I wasn't sure how to ask it.

"What is it?"

My eyebrows went up. I hadn't thought my face was that easy to read. Or was it just that Reed knew me that well?

"Nami." His hand touched mine as he sat up. "What is it? If you've changed your mind..."

"No," I quickly assured him. "I was just wondering if..." I could feel heat rising to my face, and it wasn't from arousal. "Never mind." I looked away.

"Hey." He hooked a finger under my chin and turned my face back towards him. "Whatever it is, you can ask me."

I wasn't sure if it was the look in his eyes or the fact that I knew this might be my last chance to have what I wanted, but I managed to force the words out.

"I want to feel you."

"Nami..."

"Only you." I saw him swallow hard. "Nothing between us."

His hand tightened on mine.

"I'm on the pill," I said. "But if there's a reason..."

"No." He shook his head. "I always...I mean, I'm clean."

"It's okay if you don't want to. I know some guys don't trust..."

"I trust you." His words were firm. "Is this what you want?"

I didn't answer right away. I knew it was risky. He said he trusted me, but the trust had to go both ways. I didn't think he was lying to me, so there was that.

I looked straight into his amazing dark eyes. "If you want to..."

His mouth covered mine, silencing the rest of my statement. I let him lay me back on the bed, let him take control. I wanted to feel the weight of him on me, the way his muscles bunched and moved under his skin. His tongue thrust into my mouth even as he entered me with one smooth stroke.

My back arched and I cried out. Painful pleasure went through me with a shock, electricity shooting across my nerves as he opened me. He swallowed every sound as he drove us both towards our release. He stretched me wide around him, rubbing against every bit of me. The base of his cock pressed against my swollen clit and I dug my nails into his shoulders.

His lips began to make a trail down my jaw and I could hear my moans, loud in the relative silence. I should've been embarrassed, but all I could think about was how amazing he made me feel and not caring who knew it. As his mouth traveled down my neck, I made another decision. I was so close and there was one final thing I wanted.

"Mark me."

He froze, raising his head so that our eyes met.

"My breast," I said. "So my parents won't see it."

He gave me a quick, bruising kiss and then buried his face against my breast. I gasped as he teased my nipple with his teeth, a sound that turned into a sharper cry as he began to suck on the skin next to it, drawing it into his mouth even as he kept steady, rhythmic strokes. His fingers raked through my hair, ran down my face, my sides. I was aware of all of it, every place he touched me. I was on fire, racing for a full-on explosion.

"Come, Nami." Reed's voice was ragged and I could feel him start to lose control. "Please, baby, come for me. I'm so close."

There was tenderness in his voice, something more than just lust. That did it, took down the last of what I was holding back. I let go, let him hear me call out his name, and then I felt him shudder, his cock emptying inside me. The warmth filled me, adding to the flames consuming me. I could feel the world starting to gray out, but I fought it back, needing to feel all of it. If this was the last time, I wanted to memorize every sound, scent and sensation. I would never see Reed again, but this would stay with me, warm me, keep me. No matter what happened.

Chapter 16

Reed

I couldn't breathe. My heart was pounding, my blood roaring in my ears. All of that, however, was secondary to her. Every place our bodies touched, my skin hummed. I was more aware of her than I'd ever been of anyone else in my life. I rolled us onto our side without pulling out of her. I wanted to stay as close to her as possible, keep us joined until I had no choice but to let her go.

It was foolish, I knew, to allow myself to get so attached. She'd made it clear that there could never be anything between us, that when she left, I'd never see her again. Drawing this out would only make it that much harder when she had to go. I couldn't help myself though. I'd told her that I wanted her, but that word seemed inadequate to describe what I felt towards her. She was a craving, an addiction. Every moment I spent with her just fed the habit. I couldn't be near her without needing to touch her. Despite that, it wasn't only physical. I wanted to make her smile, protect her from everything and everyone who would hurt her.

"You're thinking." Nami pushed hair back from my face. "I must not have been very good if you can think so soon after."

I took her face between my hands. "I'm thinking about you. Only you." I kissed her fiercely, trying to put all the things I was feeling into that one action. I couldn't tell her because I didn't understand it myself, but I wanted her to know.

A knock at the door interrupted us and I frowned. I rolled over, reluctantly leaving her warm embrace. I grabbed my pants and pulled them on, grimacing as the jeans chafed my cock. I headed out to the main area as I zipped up.

"Who is it?" I called as the person knocked again.

"Mr. Stirling, it's the hotel manager."

Well that couldn't be good. The only times I'd ever seen a manager come to a room was when someone had done something stupid or trashed it. Since I'd done neither, I had a feeling it could only be one thing. And, I guess, technically, I had done something stupid.

"Reed." Nami's voice was soft behind me. "Is it them?"

I glanced over my shoulder and saw that she had the bed sheet wrapped around her. My stomach tightened at the sight. She was covered, but I knew she wasn't wearing anything under that sheet. Nothing but the mark I'd left on her breast.

"Mr. Stirling, there are two gentlemen out here who wish to speak with you and your lady friend."

I could tell by his tone that he wasn't happy with me. He sounded polite enough, but I'd spent hours in hotels like this and could tell the difference between professionally polite and genuine cordiality, even in heavily accented English. I didn't answer, looking to Nami to see what she wanted to do.

"Let them in," she said. She straightened, shoulders back and chin up. The vulnerability she'd had with me was gone. Whoever her parents had brought her up to be, that's who she was now.

"Just a minute," I said as I turned back towards the

108

door. I took a deep breath and opened the door.

I stepped back so that I was at Nami's side, not touching, but close enough to make it clear she was with me. I knew she'd said that her bodyguards wouldn't hurt her, but I wasn't entirely sure I trusted them. The impression I'd gotten from Nami had been that she'd never really done anything like this before, which meant she couldn't know how they'd react, not really. And I'd be damned if I let anyone lay a finger on her.

The manager came in first, the expression on his face carefully blank. I had no doubt he'd seen much worse than this. Following him were Tomas and Kai. Even though they didn't really look alike – aside from their bulk – I didn't know which one was which. They weren't wearing blank expressions. They were pissed. I automatically took a step forward and to the side, shielding Nami. I caught a glimpse of surprise on their faces, but it passed quickly.

"It's okay, Reed," Nami said. She put her hand on my arm as she stepped up next to me. "Tomas and Kai won't hurt me."

My hands curled into fists, but I didn't argue with her. I'd let her believe it, but if either one of them came near her, they'd have to go through me first.

"We have spoken with your father." One of the men spoke to her as if I wasn't even there. His voice was surprisingly soft for such a large man. "We told him that we experienced some technical difficulties that delayed our flight." He glared at me. "But we must go. Now."

Nami slid her hand down my arm until she reached my hand. Her fingers threaded between mine. "And if I do not wish to leave right now?"

The other one spoke, his voice apologetic, but firm. "Then we will involve the police."

"The police?" Nami echoed. "What are you talking about, Kai?"

Kai looked at me, his gaze anything but friendly.

"We will tell the police that this American kidnapped you and violated you."

My mouth dropped open. Was he serious?

"You cannot do that." Her hand squeezed mine. "I went with him willingly. I will not support your story."

"You will have no choice." The one who must've been Tomas spoke up. "The media will pick up the story and your only options will be to confess the truth to the world or go along with the lie."

I found my voice. "I don't know who you two think you are, but I'm not some nobody. My family has money and influence too. I'll have the best lawyer in Venice on my side and I won't just refute the charges, I'll file lawsuits against both of you for defamation of character."

The look Kai gave me told me clearly that he thought me beneath him, no matter what I'd just said.

"Can I speak with you for a moment?" I turned my back on the bodyguards and looked down at Nami. "Privately."

She looked at Tomas and Kai. "Give us a moment." When they didn't move, her voice hardened. "Now."

Neither one of them looked happy, but they stepped back into the hallway and closed the door behind them. I had no doubt they'd taken up their post there, ready to do whatever was necessary to get Nami home.

"I'm sorry, Reed," she apologized. "I never thought things would go this far."

I made a dismissive gesture. "You don't have to go with them, Nami. I'll protect you. Let them try to get me arrested. I wasn't kidding when I said I could have the best lawyer in the city. And that's not counting the American lawyers my parents would send as soon as I called home." I took both of her hands. "I'm sure my family knows people here that will make a big enough fuss that nothing will happen to me."

"But they're right," she said. Her smile was sad. "If the press picked up the story, I would have only two

110

choices. One, to hurt you and lie, or two, tell the truth and ruin my family."

My heart gave a painful thud. "Admitting to being with me would ruin your family?"

She raised our hands and kissed my knuckles. "Admitting to what happened between us would. Maybe not ruin, but certainly harm."

"I thought you said your parents weren't that old-fashioned."

"You don't understand."

The words were gentle, but they sparked my temper.

"What do you mean I don't understand? I'm probably the only person who can come close to understanding. I know what it's like to have parents pressuring you to do what they want you to do. Mine forced me into an arranged marriage, for fuck's sake!" My voice was rising and I struggled to keep it down. I wasn't angry with her, not really. I was angry at the circumstances, the stupid little things that were keeping us apart. Her family. Her sense of duty.

"No, Reed." She pulled her hands out of my grasp and took a step back. She took a deep breath, a resigned look on her face. "You don't understand because my parents aren't some rich family with a business they want me to run."

I looked at her, confused. Had she lied to me? Was she trying to scam me? Get money from my family? A thousand possibilities ran through my head, each one worse than the last. Were my instincts with women that awful? Granted, Piper was as good as I'd thought she was, just not the right girl for me. Britni, I'd known she wasn't the kind of woman I wanted. Maybe it wasn't bad instincts, but rather bad luck.

Then Nami said the last thing I expected.

"Reed, I'm a princess."

111

Chapter 17

Reed

"Excuse me?" I had to have heard her wrong. I could've sworn she'd just said that she was a princess, but that couldn't be right.

Could it?

She spoke stiffly, formally. "I am Princess Nami Carr, eldest child of King Raj and Queen Mara, heir to the throne."

I stared at her. This had to be some sort of joke. A weird, twisted prank.

"Tomas and Kai are my bodyguards, my protectors," she continued. "But they were also sent to the States and Europe with me to make sure I didn't do anything that would embarrass my family...or cause problems with my betrothal."

"Betrothal?" This kept getting better. I was getting light-headed. "You're engaged?" The thought occurred to me that Piper would've appreciated the irony of me falling for someone who was engaged.

"Not officially," she said. "Like you, I was given no choice in the matter. My parents are in the process of selecting an appropriate husband for me. A man from my country who has a good name and a good family."

"And who wants to be king," I quipped, trying to make a joke out of it. This couldn't be happening.

"No." She shook her head. "I will rule. He will be king in name only. Our children will inherit the throne when I am gone. His bloodline will rule only because it is a part of mine." She stopped suddenly and waved a hand dismissively. "That's not important."

I sat down on the arm of the couch, not trusting my legs to hold me. "Right. The succession of monarchs isn't important."

She gave me a sharp look and I could see the hurt in her eyes. I immediately regretted my flippant remark.

"It's just a lot to take in, Nami...I mean, Princess."

"Don't call me that!" she snapped.

Her face was flushed, but I knew it wasn't because of arousal or embarrassment. She was pissed and I was pretty sure it was at me. And I deserved it.

"This is why I did not tell you when we first met." Her eyes were dark and flashing, the color of an ocean during a storm. "I have spent my whole life as Princess Nami, one day to be queen. Never knowing if someone wanted to be close to me for my title, for royal favor. I wanted only to be wanted for me."

Now I really felt like shit. I stood and crossed the distance between us quickly. She didn't move or reach out to me, her jaw set.

"I'm sorry," I apologized. I pushed back a curl from her forehead and let my fingers linger for a moment. "I was shocked and acted like an ass."

She relaxed a bit, but still didn't try to touch me. Her arms hung at her sides, her hands clenched into fists.

"Please, Nami. Forgive me." I went for quiet and sincere rather than charming. I put my hands on her shoulders, but didn't try to pull her towards me. If she came to me, it would be her choice.

Suddenly, her shoulders sagged and she leaned against me, her free arms sliding around my waist as she

114

rested her head on my chest. Her other hand clutched the sheet to her chest. I wrapped my arms around her, closing my eyes as I kissed the top of her head.

"I wanted to tell you," she confessed. "When you were telling me about your family and everything that happened. I wanted to share it all with you, but I didn't want you to look at me differently. I wanted to be seen as just me."

"There's nothing 'just' about you." I looked down at her as she tilted her head back so she could see my face. "And knowing who you are...it makes me admire you more. It took a lot of guts to rebel." I paused, and then tried to lighten the mood by adding, "The whole political science major thing makes a lot more sense now."

That got a faint smile. "Just one small step in the process that started when I was born. Training for the throne. Etiquette and language classes outside of my regular classes. In depth history of most countries. Knowledge of treaties and trade agreements." She sighed.

"And that's why you won't abdicate," I said, understanding. "Why you won't hand things over to your sister. You don't want her to have to go through all of that."

She nodded. "If my brother had lived, I could have turned things over to him and no one would've thought worse of me for it. There are plenty of countries we deal with who have issues with women in power."

"You're right," I said. "Your situation is definitely different than mine. My parents can hire someone to take over the company if Rebecca screws things up. You have an entire country relying on you."

"And that's why this meant so much to me." Her hand slid up and down my bare back as she turned her face and pressed a kiss over my heart. "Time to be me and not have to worry about my responsibilities."

"Because you have to go home and be the crown princess again," I said.

"Right." She flicked her tongue against my nipple and I bit back a moan. "And that means marrying a stranger. Bearing his children and letting another raise them. Even if I'm not queen yet, I won't be allowed to raise them the way a normal person would raise their children."

"And you don't want your husband doing it either." I wasn't sure how I knew it, but I did.

"I don't know him," she said. "What kind of man and father he will be. Maybe he'll be a good man and I will grow to love him."

I tried not to acknowledge the flare of jealousy that went through me at the thought of her loving another man. Of another man touching her. Making love to her. I clenched my jaw. She wasn't mine, I reminded myself.

"If that is the best I could hope for, I wanted to have something I could remember." Her fingers traced patterns on my lower back. "That's why I slept with my best friend in college, so I would not have my first time be with a stranger."

"And me?" I asked softly.

"You." She made a quiet sound that might have been a sigh. She pulled her arm between us so she could put her hand over my heart.

"I'm a stranger."

She smiled and pressed her lips against my chest, heating my bare skin. "But you wanted me. Not the princess or the chance to see your child on the throne. Me."

"And what was that about?" I asked, gesturing back towards the bedroom with my head. "Taking it slow. Wanting me to..."

I swallowed hard at the memory. I'd never done that before, not even with Britni. Even thought we'd been contractually required to try to start having kids shortly after marriage, I'd kept making excuses about why I wanted to wait just a bit longer. I'd never had sex without a condom.

Nami's face turned red and I thought she'd refuse to answer, but she didn't. I supposed since her big secret was out of the bag, there wasn't any point in hiding anything else.

"I wanted to remember you," she said. "What you feel like, smell like, sound like. When *he* is touching me, I wanted to be able to close my eyes and imagine it was you."

Fuck. My fingers flexed on her waist and I told my rebellious cock that it wasn't allowed to get hard again.

"We will be expected to start a family immediately," she continued. "And I wanted to remember what you felt like inside me, what it felt like to have nothing between us, to have you come inside me. I thought that if I had those memories, perhaps doing my duty would not be as unpleasant."

Yeah, my cock was definitely not listening to me. I closed my eyes and rested my forehead against hers. "I hate this," I admitted. "I hate knowing you'll be forced into a marriage you don't want. Into the bed of a man who won't know how to please you." I didn't add what I was thinking. A man who might hurt her. I pushed the thought away. I couldn't bear to think of someone harming her.

"You had an arranged marriage," she reminded me.

I raised my head and gave her a wry smile. "And you see how well that turned out. But at least I'd had an idea of who Britni was." I ran my fingers through the hair above her ear. "Besides, even though I didn't love her, both of us were willing. What he'll do..." My fingers curled into fists at her sides. "It's almost rape."

She shook her head. "Nothing will happen without my consent. No one will force me."

"Isn't that what your parents are doing?" I asked. "By making you marry this man, they're forcing you to sleep with him."

"I'm agreeing to the marriage," she said, reaching up

117

to put her hand on my cheek. "And I understand everything that goes along with it. It's my choice."

I wanted to ask if *he* was her choice, but I knew I didn't have the right to ask it. She'd told me that we could never be anything more than this, and I'd told myself I was okay with it. After all, I wasn't looking for a relationship. That was the last thing I needed right now. Especially a relationship with a princess.

"I have to go." She started to pull away from me. "I'm sure Tomas and Kai are getting restless. And they will make trouble for you." She reached up and ran her fingers through my hair. "Even if nothing came of it, I'd never forgive myself for causing you such problems."

I couldn't do it. Not yet. "Give me tonight."

She froze, still in my arms.

"One whole night," I continued. My pulse was racing. "Spend one more night with me. You can leave in the morning." I heard the pleading note in my voice but didn't care. I needed to have her one last time.

She looked at me for a moment and stepped out of my embrace. My stomach twisted into knots. She would leave and I would never see her again.

"Tomas. Kai," she called out loud enough for the pair in the hallway to hear her.

They came back in, looking just as pissed off as before.

"Call my father and tell him that we'll be leaving first thing in the morning." She glanced at me, but kept her face expressionless. "I'm spending tonight with Reed."

"Princess, we cannot allow it." Kai's voice was firm.

"You can and you will," she said. There was steel in her voice and I knew that was her queen voice, the one she would use to rule. "You know what will happen if word gets out about what's happened here. And I will make sure my father knows that you both failed in your duty to keep me...pure. More than once."

I couldn't believe she could sound so sure of herself

when she was wearing only a sheet, her curls mussed from sex. It was sexy as hell.

"You two will be solely responsible for the dissolution of my engagement. You will be dismissed in disgrace, unable to find employment anywhere. People may talk about me, but you will be the ones who are blamed."

Both men shifted uncomfortably.

"So, you will do as you are told. Call my father. Make preparations to leave tomorrow morning." She paused, and then added, "I give you my word. I will get on that plane tomorrow morning without complaint."

They exchanged looks, then nodded.

"Very good," she said. "Now go."

When the door closed behind them, she turned and looked at me. "One more night."

Chapter 18

Reed

A million things ran through my mind. All the things I wanted to do to her, and I knew I didn't have enough time. For a moment, I wondered if forever would've been enough for me to have my fill of her, but I pushed the thought aside. There was no need to think of things that weren't possible, especially when our time together was short.

Keeping my eyes locked with hers, I reached out and wrapped my fingers around her hand. Her fingers loosened as I pulled her hand back and the sheet covering her dropped to the floor.

"It's my turn to take it slow," I said as I ran my gaze down her body. "And not only because I want to remember every dip and curve, every magnificent inch of you." I took a step towards her. "I'm going to make sure you'll always remember me." I ran the tip of my finger down the slope of her breast. "That you'll never forget me."

"I don't think that is possible." She raised my hand to her mouth and slid my finger between her lips. As she sucked on it, my cock began to harden, remembering what it was like to have that hot suction surrounding me.

121

As much as I liked what she was doing, I'd meant what I'd said. It was my turn. I gently pulled my hand away and went down on my knees. There was enough of a height difference that I was able to press my lips against her stomach before bending down to taste more interesting parts.

She moaned as I ran my tongue along her folds, the skin still sensitive from what we'd been doing not too long ago. I put one hand at the small of her back to steady her and lifted her leg to hook it over my shoulder, opening her up to me. As I slowly licked every inch of her, her body danced and moved above me. I could taste myself on her, in her, and I savored our combination. I memorized every dip, the texture of her skin against my tongue. When I began to tease her clit, she buried her hands in my hair, my name coming in gasps. She was close and I wrapped my lips around her clit, sucking on it the way she'd sucked on my finger.

She came fast and hard, her hands tightening painfully in my hair. The keening sound she made sent a stab of pride through me. She'd been so quiet before and I loved that I could break through that. Part of me wondered if her bodyguards could hear her, and not a small part of me wished they could.

"Stop, stop," she begged, pulling my head away from her. "Too much."

I smiled as I eased her leg off of my shoulder and stood. "I'm just getting started." I cupped the back of her head and kissed her. Even in this I took my time, my tongue thoroughly exploring every inch. Her tongue curled around mine, sliding back into my mouth.

I ran my hands down her back, fingers tracing the ridge of her spine as they made their way down to her ass. I cupped the firm muscles and lifted her. She squeaked in surprise, but I swallowed the sound and held her body against mine, my cock brushing against her ass. Her legs wrapped around my waist and I walked us back to the

122

bedroom, not breaking the kiss the entire way.

My knees bumped against the bed and I lowered her to the mattress. Her body stretched out beneath mine, all soft curves and firm muscle. I ran my hands down her sides, over her hips, committing them to memory. My knee was between her legs and she ground down against me as I moved my mouth down her jaw to her throat. I placed open-mouthed kisses along her neck, tasting the salt of sweat, the tang of her skin.

Her body writhed under my touch and I imagined what she must've been feeling. My own skin felt like a live wire, like the slightest touch would set me off. I slid down her body, lips and tongue making a path across her collarbones and down between her breasts. I took them each in hand, memorizing the shape and feel of them, the weight of them. When I covered her nipple with my mouth, she made another of those delightful sounds. I wished I could spend hours seeing just how many different kinds of sounds I could coax from her.

My fingers attended to the nipple not in my mouth, rolling until it was as hard as the one I sucked on. I alternated my tongue and lips, teasing and suction, storing away every noise for the future. A future without her.

I put that aside. She was here, now, her body hot and needy beneath mine. That was all that mattered. I moved to the other breast, paying equal attention to it before moving further down her body. I ran the tip of my tongue down her stomach, pausing to tease her bellybutton until she squirmed.

When I settled between her legs, I looked up at her. "I'm going to make you come again." She took a shuddering breath. "One more time before I take you." I kissed the inside of her thigh. "And I want to hear you scream my name."

I didn't wait for her to respond. I put my mouth on her thigh again, pulling the skin into my mouth, worrying at it until I left a dark mark on her dusky skin. She'd told me I couldn't mark anywhere her parents would see. Unless she married when she stepped off the plane or decided to go swimming, no one would see this.

When I was satisfied, I turned my attention elsewhere. I knew her clit had to be sensitive, so I avoided it, circling her entrance with my finger before sliding it inside. She said something that I was pretty sure wasn't English, but it didn't sound like she wanted me to stop. I kept my strokes slow, easing her into another orgasm. I knew if I moved too hard, too fast, it would hurt and not in a good way.

Only when she stopped talking and started moaning did I add a second finger. Her body stretched to accommodate the digits and I worked them slowly before curling my fingers to press against that spot inside her. Her entire body jerked and I knew I'd found it again. I took a moment to marvel at how well I knew her body after just a short time together, and then I returned to worshiping it.

"Come on, baby." I brushed my thumb across the top of her clit even as I rubbed her g-spot. "Come for me."

"Yes!" Her back arched and her hips jerked, pushing my fingers deeper.

I nipped at the soft skin of her thigh and her body tensed, pussy gripping my fingers. I hissed, remembering what it had felt like to feel her tightening around my cock like that. I managed to move enough to keep pressure on that spot, driving her higher until she was pleading for me to stop.

I withdrew my hand and pushed myself back on my knees. My cock was hard, pressing painfully against my zipper. I almost wished I'd put my underwear back on when I'd gotten out of bed. I climbed off the bed, not taking my eyes off of her body even as I stripped off my jeans. She was glistening with sweat, her skin shining. Her body still quivered, her eyes wide and dark. I wanted to see her like this whenever I closed my eyes. She was the most beautiful thing I'd ever seen.

I wrapped my hand around the base of my cock, holding it tight. I needed as much time to regain my own composure as she did. Every fiber of my being was begging me to bury myself inside her, take her hard and fast, find my own release inside her. I wasn't going to do it though. This was our last night together, the last chance I had to make sure she remembered me. I wanted her to think of me when that other man kissed her, touched her. I wanted it to be my name she had to force back when she came.

"Reed." She held up a shaking hand.

I climbed onto the bed and knelt between her legs. I took her hand, brushing my lips across her knuckles before releasing it. I leaned forward, cradling her neck, tipping her head to give me easier access to her mouth. I took a long, deep drink of her, then moved back so I could watch her face as I slid home.

"Ahh." The long, drawn out sigh passed between her lips as I took her in one steady thrust. Her eyes were glazed, her body rising to meet mine.

I rested my weight on my elbows, keeping enough space between our bodies so that I wasn't crushing her, but I could still feel her skin slide against mine. I kept my strokes slow and steady, withdrawing almost the whole way before filling her again. Neither of us spoke as our bodies moved together. Without her saying it, I knew she was doing the same thing I was, committing each movement to memory. Registering every nuance, every sensation.

She raised her hand, tracing my face with her fingertips. My cheekbone across to my nose. My jaw and then over my lips. I darted my tongue out to lick the pad of her finger.

"I will never forget you," she whispered.

My heart clenched painfully in my chest. There was too much emotion in those words, too much for how little we knew each other, but I felt it too and it was my undoing. My body tensed as I began to come, but I thrust into her again, needing her to come with me, needing to feel her come apart. Her body jerked as the base of my cock rubbed against her clit and she stiffened.

"Let go." I scraped my teeth against her neck and that was it.

"Reed!"

It wasn't quite a scream, but it was my name and it was enough. I squeezed my eyes closed and pressed my face against her neck. She would remember me and I would remember her. We would never be more than this, but we wouldn't forget either. It would be enough. It had to be.

Chapter 19

Nami

I told him I wouldn't forget him and it was true. But probably not a wise thing to say. It was too much, too soon, but we wouldn't have anything else. I couldn't wait for a future moment because we didn't have one. This was it. He hadn't said it back to me, but I'd seen the look in his eyes when I'd said it. It had been enough.

It had taken all of my self-control not to succumb to the tears welling up in my eyes as Reed and I came. The finality of the moment hit me and I was thankful Reed wasn't looking at me. By the time he raised his head, I'd gotten my emotions under control.

He rolled us over and, as he slipped out of me, I felt a pang of loss. I wondered if it would feel the same when I slept with my husband. Would I wish he was still inside me or would I be grateful that he was done? Reed pulled me back against him, wrapping his body around mine. I snuggled back against him, grateful that I had asked for the whole night.

"Are you okay?" Reed asked, his voice low.

I nodded, not trusting my voice to speak.

"Get some sleep." He kissed my temple. "I'll be here when you wake up."

I pulled his arms more tightly around me. I didn't

think I could to sleep, but I had no problem lying here in his arms while he slept. I'd never shared a bed with someone, not even by accident. Tomas and Kai had been diligent about me never falling asleep when Aaron and I hung out. The night we'd slept together, I'd left almost immediately after it was over.

Now, with Reed's arms around me, I knew what I'd been missing. Warmth. Safety. I felt his heart beating against my back, the slow rise and fall of his chest. The faint stubble on his cheeks was rough as he tucked his chin against me. I could feel his cock against my ass, soft and still slick with the results of our union. The logical part of me said we should clean up, but I was content where I was and didn't want to go anywhere.

The last thought was sleepy and I was surprised to feel my eyelids starting to fall. I'd rest them, I decided. It wasn't like I could see Reed anyway. It was more about feeling him. I was still concentrating on the various places our bodies touched when I finally slipped under.

I didn't know how long I slept, only that morning light was peeking between the curtains. It was still early though and, like he'd promised, Reed was still there. He'd shifted at some point during the night. We both had. He was on his back and I was laying half on his chest, one of his arms wrapped around me, his other hand on his stomach. The sheet was low on his waist, barely hiding what I knew was underneath.

I looked up at him, enjoying the chance to see him in a new way. He looked much younger asleep, closer to my age than to thirty. His face was relaxed, with none of the worry I'd seen. Even when he'd been laughing or we'd been in bed, there had still been little lines on his face. Based on what he'd told me about the stress he'd been under back in the States, I supposed it wasn't surprising. Now, however, all of that was gone.

I shifted slowly, not wanting to wake him, but needing to see him better. His hand slid down my back,

128

coming to rest just above my ass, but he didn't wake up. I reached out, hesitating with my hand just above his face. I traced his lips with the lightest of touches, letting my fingers memorize their shape and feel. I could feel them now, the ghost of them on my mouth, between my legs, on my body.

Heat pooled in my stomach. I wanted him again. I wished I had more time. That I could take him in my mouth while he was still soft, feel him grow and swell as I licked and sucked the soft flesh. I hadn't gone down on Aaron that night. Reed was the only man I'd taken in my mouth and the memory of his taste was still thick on my tongue.

Before Reed, I'd never imagined I'd want to do something like that, but I'd loved the sounds he'd made, the way I felt. I loved that I could make him come apart, the look in his eyes when I'd swallowed every drop. I hadn't known what I was doing, but I didn't doubt I'd done well.

I was surprised at how easily sex had come to me. Things had been awkward with Aaron, but he'd assured me that first times were always like that. I wasn't sure that the difference between the first and second time was that drastic with everyone, but there hadn't been any awkwardness with Reed. It had felt natural, right. My body had moved with his in a way it hadn't with Aaron, and I didn't think it was simply because I'd done it once before.

His hair fell across his forehead and I gently pushed it back. I smiled at the mess it was. I could almost imagine him struggling with it before going in to work, trying to get it to lie flat. I wondered if it ever did, but as much as I tried, I couldn't quite picture him with neatly combed hair. In a suit, yes, but not looking like the hundreds of other businessmen I'd seen. My smile widened. It didn't matter what he wore or how he looked. Reed could never be like anyone else.

A lump rose in my throat and my eyes pricked with tears. I couldn't put it off any longer. I eased out from under his arm. I'd promised Tomas and Kai that I would leave with them, and I meant to keep my word. I wouldn't give them any excuse to burst back in. Reed and I'd had our perfect night together and I would keep that memory safe, untainted by a confrontation.

I climbed off of the bed as carefully as I could. I didn't want to say good-bye. Mostly because I didn't know how to do it. We'd already done the awkward one-night stand good-bye, but this time it was different. He meant more to me than just a single night. But I didn't know what that actually meant. I couldn't tell him that I hoped we'd see each other again, because that could never happen. If he woke up, I wouldn't know what to say.

And I couldn't say for certain that I'd have the strength to leave him if he did. One kiss, even a kiss good-bye, and I couldn't guarantee I'd be able to walk away. I didn't think clearly when I was with him, when he was touching me. The very fact that I was here was evidence to that. Before I'd met him, my rebellions had been little ones. I would never have dreamed of spending a day in Venice without my bodyguards, but he emboldened me, made me act more impulsively than I ever had before. Even my rebellions had been planned out.

I gathered up my clothes from where I'd left them and headed into the bathroom. I didn't take a shower, not wanting to waste the time or risk Reed waking. I cleaned up as quickly and as best I could, then dressed again. I scowled as I pulled on the clothes I'd worn yesterday. I hated the feel of them, but I didn't have any other options. At least one good thing would come out of having to go straight to the plane and home. No one would think it weird I wanted to shower, put on some clean clothes and sleep.

How different this would be if I'd just been some girl

he'd met in Paris. Someone with a normal family.

I shook my head and splashed cold water on my face. I couldn't think of that now. The time for flights of fancy and daydreams had passed. It was time to move on, to do my duty. I knew what it would mean and what was expected of me. I'd been raised for this. Born for this.

I took a steadying breath and walked back into the bedroom. I'd half expected Reed to be awake, but he was where I'd left him. More or less. He was on his side now, but he still appeared to be asleep. That was good. I didn't want him awake, but I also didn't want to leave without something to say good-bye. Reed deserved better than that.

On the desk was a sheaf of paper and a pen. A note would have to do. I stood there for a moment, wondering what to write. The words came more easily than I'd thought and it didn't take me long to get them all down. I folded the note and turned towards the bed. I set it on the end table and let myself have one final look at Reed. I leaned down and brushed my lips across his forehead. I couldn't stop the tear that trailed down my cheek, but I hurried out of the room before others could follow.

I'd wanted the time with Reed so I'd always remember him, but as I left the bedroom, I knew I couldn't hope for Reed to do the same. He needed to forget me. And that's what I'd told him.

My note had been simple.

Thank you for giving me what I needed. I can move on with my life now. I wish you all the happiness in the world.

And I did wish him that. I just wished that he could've been happy with me.

Chapter 20

Reed

I hadn't fallen asleep with any of the women I'd slept with since leaving the States, but it had felt natural to do so with Nami. Her body fit perfectly against mine, back against my chest, head tucked under my chin. I'd wanted to stay awake all night, knowing that I wouldn't have this chance again, but the lack of sleep the previous night and a busy day were a strong combination and I hadn't been able to resist. It was a deep, dreamless sleep and when I started to gradually wake it was that slow, thick waking, the kind that felt like swimming through molasses.

The first thing I knew was that she was no longer in bed with me. Her body heat was gone, but I could hear her moving around. I kept my eyes closed until I heard a door close. I opened my eyes and saw that she'd gone into the bathroom. I rolled onto my side, unsure of what I should do.

Would it be better to let her know I was up? Should I actually get up and dress so I could walk her to the door? Or would it be better to stay in the bed and say good-bye from here? That felt crass. But what would I say when she walked out of the bathroom? A simple 'good morning' felt trite, but I didn't think it'd be fair to expect anything else.

I didn't know how to do this. How to say good-bye. The other women I'd slept with had either left when we were done, or I'd been the one leaving. There hadn't been cuddling, sleeping, lingering. There'd been no expectations and no hard feelings. Before everything had gone to hell back home, I'd dated, but in those instances, the morning after good-byes hadn't been weird because I'd known I'd be seeing them again. With Nami, that wasn't the case. I had no clue what was appropriate.

I had another problem with not knowing what to say. It was less about appropriate and more about not being able to find the right words to either tell her what I felt or to hide it. Would it be fair to tell her that I didn't want her to go? Would she think it was a ploy, just me saying it to make what we'd done feel less like a hook-up?

And if she believed I was telling the truth, what then? It wouldn't change anything. Before she'd told me the truth, I might've thought she could do what I'd done and break away, but I knew now that wasn't a possibility. A family business was one thing. A kingdom was another. And telling her that I wanted to see her again would just be cruel to both of us. We both knew it wasn't going to happen.

The other option was just as unappealing. If I walked her to the door or stayed in bed, only telling her good-bye and that it had been fun, would she think I didn't care? Would she believe this entire thing had only a mere blip on my radar? Her words to me echoed in my mind. She said she would never forget me. I felt the same way. No matter where I went from here, I'd never forget her and the short time we had together.

I was torn, neither choice giving me anything to work with. Unless, the thought came to me, I didn't let her know I was awake at all. If she wanted to talk to me, she could wake me up. In that case, I could let her speak first and base my response on her words. And if she didn't, it would've been her choice not to say good-bye.

The doorknob turned and I made my decision. I closed my eyes and kept my breathing even. I heard her walking, then nothing for a minute or two. I risked opening my eyes a sliver. She was still here, standing at the desk and frowning at a piece of paper. As I watched, she wrote a few lines and set down the pen. I quickly closed my eyes and a moment later, I was glad I had. I felt more than heard her coming towards me and stop next to the bed.

The light brush of her lips against my forehead almost made me lose my resolve and then I felt a drip of liquid on my skin. My stomach twisted. She was crying. It took all of my self-control not to jump up and go to her. I hated knowing that I'd been the cause of her tears and the thought of her in pain made my own heart ache.

Dammit!

When I heard the main door close, I opened my eyes and stared at the ceiling. Had this been a bad idea? Should I have walked away at the club? Not gotten on the train? Not suggested we leave together? I'd had a dozen points where I could've walked away and I hadn't used any of them. Who knew how different things would've been if I'd done the smart thing. It seemed like all I did lately was second-guess my decisions.

I sat up. It didn't matter now. I made my choices and, for better or for worse, I had to live with the consequences. Unfortunately, one of those seemed to be a deeper attachment than I'd ever meant to have.

I swung my legs over the edge of the bed, ready to head into the bathroom for a long, hot shower. That's when I saw it. There was a folded piece of paper sitting on the table next to the bed. I didn't want to read it, but I picked it up anyway. It was brief and I read it three times before the words sunk in.

She planned to move on and she wanted me to do the same. She wished me all the best. I wished her the same. I

135

just wished it could've been with me. She was right, and I hated it. We had to move past this. It was the best thing for everyone involved.

She'd go back to her family and her country. Marry whoever her parents had chosen for her. Become a mother and a queen. I'd finish my trip and figure out what I was going to do with the rest of my life. We both might look back on these couple days fondly, but that's all they would be. Memories.

I ran my hand through my hair as I stood. It was time to let go. Time to do as she'd said and move on. Still, a part of me said to go after her, to tell her that we owed it to ourselves to see where this could go. I silenced the voice as I walked into the bathroom. Shower, then eat. After that, I'd move on with the rest of my life. Our time was up.

Exotic Desires Vol. II

Chapter 1

Reed

I'd spent the last two weeks trying to convince myself
that this was what I wanted to do, where I wanted to be.
I'd spent three more days in Venice, but that was mostly
because I'd forgotten my luggage on the train when I'd
run off with...*her*.

I could've bought new clothes, but I'd decided against
it in favor of spending the time drinking while I'd waited
for them to be shipped back. The next day, I'd bought a
new ticket to Madrid and left, hoping the memories
would stay in Venice.

They hadn't.

I'd partied in Spain, drinking enough that I'd spent
most mornings hanging over the toilet. After a week, I'd
moved on to Lisbon, Portugal. Two days ago, I'd given up

on the cities and headed to my family's villa in France. It was just outside of Marseille, perfectly located for a trip in to the city, to enjoy what it had to offer, but far enough away that I could have quiet if I wanted it.

I'd tried quiet yesterday. It had ended with me drinking pretty much everything in the villa and passing out on the floor until past noon today. Tonight, I planned to head into the city and see if I could find someone to take my mind off things. I'd been focusing on alcohol rather than sex, but I think that might have been why I couldn't stop thinking about her.

I ran my hand down my face.

Her. Nami Carr. Fucking Princess Nami. Meeting her had been chance, but everything that had followed had been choice. Hers and mine. I'd intended for it to be nothing more than a fling. A fun one, but a fling nonetheless. I'd had dozens of them during my trip, and none of them stood out. I could barely tell one from the other in my memory. Blondes and brunettes – no red-heads because I hadn't wanted to be reminded of Piper – they all blurred together. Some had been aggressive, liking it rough. Others had wanted me to be gentle. I remembered bits and pieces of what we'd done. The positions we'd fucked in, a little kink here and there.

Except for Nami. I could remember every detail of my time with her. How her body had felt beneath mine. The sounds she'd made...

I bolted off the couch and headed for the bathroom. There was no doubt about it. I needed to get laid. The lack of sex had to be the reason I couldn't stop thinking about her. I needed someone else to get my mind off of the pretty princess.

I splashed some cold water on my face, ran my hands through my hair and then headed into my bedroom to find what I wanted to wear. The villa wasn't as large as my family's home in Philadelphia, but it was big enough to have a bedroom for my parents, myself, my younger

138

sister Rebecca, and a guest room, as well as two bathrooms, a full kitchen, dining room and living room. My parents had bought it for family vacations. I hadn't been here in years though. Running the Stirling family business hadn't left much time for vacations. Hell, I'd even cut my honeymoon short.

I snorted a laugh. Honeymoon. The entire marriage had been a joke. I hadn't wanted to marry Britni Michaels and she hadn't wanted to marry me either. Sure, we'd slept together, but there'd been no passion, no real attraction. We'd done what we'd needed to do. I'd never asked who she'd been thinking of when we'd fucked, but I sure as hell hadn't been thinking about her. I waited for the familiar burst of shame and guilt but didn't feel it. For the first time since I'd left Philadelphia, I could think of the entire mess without any strong emotion. I was pretty sure that Piper had been right when she'd told me that what she and I'd had hadn't been real, and this was further confirmation of it. That was a relief. I wasn't in a hurry to rush home, but at least now I knew that when I did, I'd be able to handle it.

I gave myself a glance in the mirror, thought about trying to smooth down the mess of gold that was my hair, then decided against it. I knew I looked tired, but I also knew it wouldn't matter. I was a good-looking guy. I wouldn't have trouble getting a woman to come back with me. I looked away from the mirror before I could see the doubt in the near-black pools of my eyes. Not doubt about my ability to get a woman. Doubt about whether or not I really wanted to.

I pushed the thought aside and headed out to the garage. We had three cars here and our groundskeeper kept them all in excellent shape. I chose my favorite – the black Spyder – and drove in to Marseille to see what I could find.

A couple hours later, I had a bit of a buzz, but not so much that driving was a bad idea. I also had a tall, thin blonde wearing a dress that probably should've been classified as a handkerchief. Said handkerchief was currently riding up so that I could see the tiny string of red lace that made up her thong as well as her firm ass. I could see this because she was on her knees in the passenger's seat despite my strong objections that this was dangerous. Her breasts were pressed against my arm, her hand rubbing my half-hard cock through my pants. This was my compromise. She'd originally been trying to get her hand down my pants while promising to do things with her mouth that I was pretty sure were illegal in most places in the States.

When we got to the villa, she climbed out of the car, gave me a grin and pulled her dress over her head, dropping it onto the floor of the garage. She wasn't wearing a bra and her rose-colored nipples jutted out from her small breasts. Her thong barely covered more in the front than it did in the back, the sheer fabric leaving absolutely nothing to the imagination.

"Is this your car as well?" she asked as she turned to the car to our right. Her words were heavily accented, but understandable.

"My family owns all three cars," I said, looking across the top of the Spyder at her.

She cast a grin over her shoulder as she walked over to the Aston Martin and bent over the hood, giving me an even better view of her ass.

"What are you doing?" The question was stupid. It was obvious what she was doing.

"*Je veux que tu me baises ici,*" she said, wiggling her ass at me.

I wasn't going to turn that down. I walked over to her, taking the time to admire the view. As I reached her, however, I couldn't stop another image flashing across my mind. Nami in the same position, her hard nipples brushing against the cool metal, back arched in obvious invitation.

140

I frowned, pushing thoughts of Nami out of my head. I needed to focus on...shit. I couldn't remember her name. Now that I thought about it, had I even gotten her name? Oh well. It wasn't like I was planning some sort of relationship with her. *Ma chérie* would work just fine. There were three things people always needed to know how to say in other languages: Where is the bathroom? Do you speak English? And at least one endearment.

Thanks to her attention in the car, my cock was hard and ready, and as I slid my hand down her ass and between her legs, I found her soaking wet. I slid a finger inside her, then a second, earning a small moan. She pushed back against my fingers as I pumped them into her a couple times before pulling them out. She made a sound of protest, but I ignored it as I reached into my pocket and pulled out a condom. I'd make this one quick and then we could head inside and find out how long it'd take her to get me hard again. I doubted any of the things she'd talked about before were illegal here.

I opened my pants, pushing them down just low enough to get my cock free and rolled on the condom.

"Ready, *ma chérie?*" I asked as I pulled aside the flimsy fabric of her panties, exposing her bare skin.

"*Oui.*" She spread her legs even further apart. "Fuck me. *Se il vous plaît.*"

I rubbed the tip of my cock across her entrance, then pushed inside. She let out a string of French obscenities as I stretched her wide. I might've only been on the high end of average when it came to length, but I was thick and it always took a bit of work to get inside. By the time I was balls deep, her breath was coming in pants mixed with sounds of pleasure.

I slid my hands up from her hips, across her ribs and then around to cup her breasts. My hands covered them completely and I couldn't help but remember what Nami's had felt like, the weight of them. My grip tightened for a moment and then I began to move.

I started with a few shallow thrusts, letting my partner get used to the feel of me as I played with her nipples. The tips were long, perfect for me to tease, but they didn't feel quite right between my fingers. A flare of anger went through me. Anger at Nami for leaving. Anger at myself for not being able to forget.

I straightened, grabbing on to the girl's hips. The first time I slammed into her, she let out a surprised squeal. The second stroke was just as hard as the first and she swore, pushing back against me, wordlessly asking for more. All of the pent-up frustration from the last two weeks exploded and I began to pound into her, taking her as fast and hard as I dared.

She dropped to the hood of the car, working one of her hands beneath her to rub her clit. Her bare flesh squeaked against the metal, mixing with the moans falling from her lips. I barely registered any of it. All I could think about was the wet heat of her, the way she was tight around me. I needed to come, to lose myself in the oblivion that only an orgasm could give me.

I didn't last long. I felt her start to come, her muscles tightening around me, milking me and I exploded. I groaned, biting back the name I wanted to call out. I closed my eyes, wanting to see only darkness, but it was Nami's face I saw. I opened my eyes as I took a step back, panting heavily.

I didn't look at her as I pulled off the condom and tossed it into the nearby garbage can. I heard the click of her heels as she walked over to me and I forced myself to smile at her. Her fair skin was flushed, her nipples swollen. She was beautiful, but not enough to completely distract me. I needed something more than just a quickie.

"Would you like something to drink?" I asked as I tucked myself back into my pants. I didn't bother doing up the zipper or buttons, however. I wasn't planning on wearing them much longer. Either she'd be leaving and I'd head to bed, or we'd be fucking again. Neither option

142

required pants.

"Champagne?" she asked.

I nodded. "I think there's a bottle or two somewhere in the kitchen."

She smiled as she moved closer. Her hand slid down the front of my pants and I sucked in a breath as she cupped my sensitive flesh. She leaned forward and took my bottom lip between her teeth, lightly biting down before running her tongue across it to soothe away the sting.

"We fuck again, yes?" she asked as she took a step back, breaking our contact.

There was one decision made. "Yes," I said. "As many times as we can." I gave her a more genuine smile.

She smiled back and licked her bottom lip. "Good. I want to suck your dick next."

In spite of – or perhaps because of – her crude words, my cock gave an interested twitch as I thought of what it would feel like to slide into her mouth. Unbidden, the memory came to me of Nami on her knees in a storage room.

"This way." I reached out and took her hand.

A plan quickly formed in my head. The kitchen had counters that would be a perfect height for me to get my mouth on her. Then we'd head to the living room where she could return the favor while I sat on the couch. We could fuck there too. If I thought I could get it up again, we'd go to the bedroom.

As we walked into the kitchen, she spoke, "*En passant, mon nom est Cosette.*"

Cosette, I thought. Nice name, but I doubted I'd remember it. She was just another fuck, after all.

Chapter 2

Reed

The body next to mine snuggled closer to me, her arm flung across my chest, breasts pressed against my side. As I headed towards wakefulness, I kept my eyes closed, trying to cling to the fantasy that it was Nami stretched out next to me. The closer I got to being fully conscious, however, the more my brain registered all of the things that were wrong.

The woman at my side was too tall. Her head was at my shoulder, her feet even with mine. And she was too thin. I could feel her ribs under my palm as it slid across her side. Her breasts and hips were smaller, her hair shorter and not curly.

Right. The blond from the club in Marseille. What was her name again? I know she'd told me after we'd fucked in the garage, but by the time she'd had her mouth around my cock, I'd forgotten it. She hadn't seemed to notice though. She'd definitely been an enthusiastic lover. By the time we'd passed out, I'd lost count the number of times we'd come and the number of places we'd fucked.

I should've been able to get what I'd wanted: a couple hours where I wasn't thinking about Nami. Instead, no matter what we'd done, I'd kept comparing her to Nami.

How the two of them felt different. The sounds they'd both made.

I'd loved listening to Nami when we'd had sex. The moans. The little exclamations in her native language. How she'd cried out my name.

The blonde hadn't done that. She'd said things in French, but I'd understood the language almost as much as I did my own. Her cries of pleasure had been sharp, shrill. She'd said my name, but the accent hadn't been the same. She'd been adventurous and had clearly enjoyed the things I'd done to her, but I hadn't felt the responsiveness I'd gotten from Nami.

Claudia? I thought as I finally opened my eyes and looked down at her. No, it was something from a movie. Wait, not a movie, a play. A book? All three. Cosette. I'd had to take a couple shareholders to the theater once and we'd seen *Les Misérables*. I hadn't really cared for it, but I wasn't a big fan of musicals. The girl who'd played Cosette had been cute though.

I carefully extricated myself from under Cosette's arm and pulled the covers over her before heading across the hall to the bathroom. I turned on the shower and then, after a momentary internal debate, locked the bathroom door. I didn't want Cosette waking up when she heard the shower and deciding to join me. I didn't want to sound cold, but I was done with her. We'd had our fun and I'd let her use the shower when I was done if she wanted. I'd pay for her cab ride home and tell her I'd enjoyed our night together, but I didn't want her to think there was anything more to it than last night. The thought of her wet, naked body didn't turn me on now. It just made me tired.

I washed quickly even though I would've preferred to linger. I wasn't going to be an ass though and leave Cosette sitting in my room alone, wondering what she was supposed to do next. And I certainly wasn't going to make her think she had to call her own cab and pay her way home. I might not have been interested in her anymore, but I wasn't a complete cad.

I wrapped my towel tightly around my waist and wished I would've thought to bring clothes with me. I hadn't though, which meant I had to go back into my bedroom to find something to wear. Cosette was awake and smiled when I came in. She was still under the covers, and didn't seem like she was trying to seduce me, so that was good.

I spoke before she could say or do anything that would make this a whole lot more complicated. "The bathroom's free. Towels are in the little cabinet next to the shower."

Her smile wavered a bit, but she didn't get angry, so I kept going.

"I'll call a cab while you're cleaning up."

I saw a flash of anger in her eyes, and then it was gone. Without a word, she climbed out from under the covers and walked out. I breathed a sigh of relief that there hadn't been a fight. That was one of the reasons I usually didn't let my partners spend the night. Leaving right after sex was a lot less awkward than a morning-after conversation. I supposed it was something about the intimacy of literally sleeping together that made some women assume that there was more between us than sex.

I dressed quickly, unsure how long Cosette would be. She might take her time, hoping I'd change my mind, or she might be so pissed that she didn't want to be around me any longer than she had to. As soon as I pulled my shirt over my head, I called information for the number of the closest cab company.

Fortunately for me, the car arrived in record time and when Cosette came out of the bedroom, again dressed in her little handkerchief of a dress, I was able to escort her right out to the car. The driver gave me a knowing wink, but didn't say a word as Cosette climbed into the backseat, deliberately opening her legs so that I could see she wasn't wearing her thong. I really hoped she hadn't left it in my room, thinking she'd call about it later. I hated women who tried sneaky things like that.

I'd made no promises to her, no indication that I wanted a relationship. In fact, I'd specifically told her that all I wanted was a hook up. If she'd read anything else into it, it was on her. If she had left her panties in my room, they were going straight into the trash. As good as the sex had been last night – and considering how many times we'd done it, I couldn't really describe it as less than that – I was starting to have regrets.

As I watched the cab drive away, I ran my hand through my still-wet hair, sending droplets of water raining down on my shoulders. It was longer than I usually let it get. It was nearly impossible to tame unless I kept it short and, in those last couple weeks back home, it had been my private rebellion. Now it was a combination of that and just being lazy.

I went back inside. My stomach growled as I walked into the kitchen, but I couldn't find anything appetizing enough to eat. Finally, I grabbed a box of cereal and headed into the living room, fully intending to eat directly from the box and watch tv until I figured out what I was going to do now.

I thought I'd been lost before, drifting from one party to the next, one woman to the next. I'd had no direction, no idea of what the future held. That feeling had increased tenfold since I'd watched Nami walk out of my hotel room. I'd been living in the moment with her, but it somehow hadn't felt like that. If I was honest with myself, I'd felt more myself than I had...ever.

There'd been no plan, no schedule, but I'd taken charge, deciding what we were going to do, where we'd go. When we'd talked, I'd felt like I could share everything with her. She could have helped me figure out my path, I thought. She would've listened when I'd given her a list of ideas of what I wanted to do with the rest of my life, and she would've given an honest opinion. She

148

would have supported whatever decision I made.

I leaned my head on the back of the couch and closed my eyes. For the first time since she'd left, I gave myself permission to call up the image of her face. Dark brown curls, cropped short. Just long enough to bury my fingers in the silky strands. Dusky skin. High cheekbones and a straight nose. Cyan eyes contributed to her exotic beauty. Only…it was more than her appearance. It was the way her full lips had curved into a smile. The blue-green sparkle of her eyes when she laughed.

A pang of longing went through me, so sharp that it was an almost physical hurt. I missed her, I finally allowed myself to admit. I missed her body, her scent. The intelligence of her conversation. The way I'd kept making a fool of myself in front of her.

I opened my eyes and looked around. The villa was just as beautiful as it had always been, every piece of furniture and decoration carefully chosen by a well-paid interior designer to show off the proper mixture of wealth and taste. I'd never really cared about any of that before, but it had been more of a not caring brought about by being used to it. Now, I saw things differently.

What was the point of all this, I asked myself. Why have all this money if all I was ever going to be was miserable? I didn't know if my parents were happy with their lives, but I doubted it. I knew Rebecca wasn't. She'd always pretended to be, but no one that nasty could be anything less than miserable with themselves. And then there was me. I'd never really thought about happiness before. It was all duty and loyalty. I'd tried to be happy with Piper, but even that hadn't done it.

I was tired of this, I realized suddenly. All of it. Not only tired of traveling around Europe without any purpose, fucking whoever I got into bed, and then moving on to the next party. I was sick of being a Stirling, of the responsibilities my last name put on my shoulders. Or, more accurately, the responsibilities my parents thought being a Stirling meant. I was tired of being told what to do, who to love and how I should behave.

I wanted more out of life than one party after another, one faceless woman. More than the power and money that came with being in charge of the Stirling businesses. I wanted my own life, but not because I wanted to rebel against my parents. I wanted it because I actually wanted to be happy.

And I was sure I needed Nami for that. My time with her had been the best I'd had for as long as I could remember. Even when I'd talked about my parents and my life back in Philadelphia, it hadn't seemed as important as it had before. When I was with her, I wanted to be a better man, not to impress anyone or make my parents proud. I wanted to deserve her. And not because she was a princess, but because of the amazing person I knew her to be. She deserved every happiness, and I wanted to give that to her.

I just didn't know if I was part of the equation. For all I knew, she was happy back in her home country, preparing for her upcoming wedding, ready to take on the mantle of crown princess. Despite her assertion that she'd always remember me, I couldn't help but wonder if I'd already faded from her mind. The thought hurt more than I cared to admit.

Chapter 3

Nami

I'd lied.

I'd told my parents that I'd submit to their will when I returned from Italy, but that promise had lasted all of two days before I'd given up.

It wasn't that I didn't love Saja. My island home was just far enough into the ocean that we didn't have to worry much about people from the mainland disturbing our peace. Every once in a while, we had visitors, but we weren't a country that thrived on tourism. Actually, we mostly kept to ourselves. While we imported goods, we weren't reliant on any one country, which allowed us to stay out of political issues. The beaches were beautiful, some rocky, some sandy. Our capital was more of a town than a city, but it was the closest thing to a metropolitan area we had. All of our businesses were there. Banks, police department, all of that. And, of course, the courthouse. We were a monarchy, but we used a justice system similar to America and the United Kingdom. The king or queen – whichever happened to be the ruling monarch at the time – did have the final say, but appeals rarely went that high. Our crime rate was low, our economy flourishing, and everything was perfect.

Everything except my life. Saja was my home. I

loved it, just like I loved my family. King Raj and Queen Mara. My family had been ruling Saja for several generations, the crown past down from oldest child to oldest child, regardless of gender. And now it was my turn.

I was only twenty-two years-old, out of college for only a couple weeks, and my life was over. I opened my eyes, squinting against the early afternoon light. My head was pounding and my mouth was dry. There was a stale, nasty taste that told me, as much as the headache, that I'd drunk too much last night. Again.

When I'd left Princeton with my political science degree, I'd known what was coming next. An arranged marriage to a man of my parents' choice. Additional lessons in various foreign languages as well as ongoing updates on the political and economic situations in major world powers. Invitations to parties I didn't want to attend, mingling with people I didn't want to know. Basically, all the shit that came with me being the heir to the throne.

I hadn't been happy about it, but I'd accepted it as being just the way it was. I'd been thrilled with my parents' graduation gift of a European trip, but even that had been all about politics. Being in the right place at the right time. And, of course, behaving myself. I'd done my little bit of rebellion, though. Cut my hair...and lost my virginity. The first, everyone could see and my parents could brush under the table as some sort of fashion statement. The second had to be kept a secret.

Saja wasn't some backwards country where I'd be beaten or killed for having sex, but being the crown princess meant that my future husband would want to ensure that it was his child who would be next in line. That meant my parents, myself and the two bodyguards who'd been with me since I first went to America for college, all had to sign documents stating that I was a virgin.

I grinned despite the throbbing in my temples. That ship had sailed back in Princeton when I'd slept with my best friend. It hadn't meant anything though. My smile disappeared and I climbed out of bed. I didn't want to think about who I'd slept with next. I'd been trying to put those thoughts out of my head since I'd gotten back.

When I walked out of my bathroom, feeling a bit better after a quick shower and brushing my teeth, I noticed what I hadn't before. I hadn't been alone in my bed.

Fuck. I scowled. Who had I slept with last night? I closed my eyes, trying to remember. Most of the last two weeks was a blur. An intoxicated blur.

I'd played the dutiful daughter for two days, but then my parents had told me that they were down to their top three choices for my future husband. That hadn't been a surprise, but then I'd made the mistake of asking if I could meet all three and have the final say. I knew my parents loved me, but the look on their faces had made me hate them for a moment. It had been clear, without a word needed, that my marriage wasn't any of my concern.

I'd known that, of course, and if it hadn't been for what had happened in Paris, I might not have cared. I'd prepared myself. But then I'd met Reed and had experienced a glimpse of the kind of life I could've had. That taste of freedom had infected me and I couldn't seem to get back the same sense of duty I'd once had.

I wanted more out of life.

To my parents' dismay and disappointment, that meant I'd decided to have some fun. The first night, I'd only snuck out and gone to a club. I hadn't known until Kai and Tomas had shown up that my parents had a GPS tracker on my phone. Apparently, that's how my bodyguards had found me in Venice too, except the reception there had been so bad that it had taken them a while.

I pushed those memories aside. I didn't want to think

153

about Venice.

My parents had freaked about my trip to the club, but the family's PR person, Mikkels, had managed to keep it under wraps. Then they'd doubled my guard detail. I could barely go to the bathroom without tripping over one of them.

The body on the bed rolled over and now I could see his face.

Right. Ari. Now I remembered. Well, pieces of it anyway.

Ari was only a couple years older than me and my newest bodyguard. I smirked. He'd done a hell of a lot more than guard my body last night. The flashes of memory I was getting involved a couple bottles of Saja's finest alcohol and a very naked man.

I glanced at the clock. Tomas and Kai would be back shortly, and there was no way Ari wasn't fired. It had been his job to keep me from doing anything stupid. Unfortunately for him, I was smarter than he was.

Since I'd been put under virtual house arrest, I hadn't been able to get out, but I'd managed to find enough alcohol in the house to keep me pleasantly buzzed every night. When I'd met Ari, however, something snapped. I didn't just want to annoy my parents, I wanted to piss them off.

Ari tossed off the blankets, revealing a toned, muscular body. He was shorter than Tomas and Kai, just under six feet, and thinner than them, but he couldn't exactly be called lean. His hair was dark and thick, his shoulders broad. He had strong, masculine features, hazel eyes and didn't resemble Reed in the slightest.

Which is exactly why I'd wanted to have sex with him. I'd needed someone who didn't look like Reed. Someone who would help me forget him. I'd told Reed that I wanted to remember him, and a part of me wanted to hang on, but I'd also learned how painful remembering could be. It might've been easier if it had just been sex, but there had been a connection with Reed I simply couldn't deny.

While I still didn't want to even think about someone chosen by my parents touching me, fucking me, I knew I couldn't keep reliving the memory of my time with Reed. It hurt too much. I needed him out of my head if I could ever go through with this. With the marriage, with training to become queen.

I shook my head. Apparently, last night hadn't worked.

I looked at Ari again, letting my eyes moved down from his chest to where his cock rested on his leg. I was happy to see a used condom on the bed next to him – I hadn't been able to remember if we'd used one – but my attention quickly focused on the thick shaft slowly swelling as I watched.

"Good morning." Ari's voice was thick with sleep, drawing my attention back up to his face.

I smiled, but didn't say anything. It was clear on his face that he hadn't come to the realization he was completely screwed, and I didn't intend to change that. In fact, I was thinking I might want to at least give him something good to remember after he was fired. I walked towards him, putting a little extra swing into my step. I hadn't bothered to dress and his eyes watched the sway of my breasts as I walked towards him, his cock stiffening with each step.

His hand went towards it automatically and I watched him stroke himself as his cock grew. It wasn't quite as big as Reed's, but big enough to do the job. I climbed up the bed, enjoying the way his eyes were drawn to my breasts. I stopped between his legs and pulled his hand off of his cock.

"My turn." I grinned at him. I wrapped my hand around him and began to stroke, enjoying the feel of his skin beneath my palm.

"Princess," he groaned.

I saw something flicker across his eyes as he said the title and immediately tightened my hold. He swore and his eyes rolled back. At any moment he could realize this hadn't been a good idea after. I used my free hand to grab a condom from the side table and ripped it open with my teeth. I rolled it down his shaft, then moved up so I was straddling his waist.

His eyes darkened with lust as he reached up to my breasts. I waited for my body to respond to him the way it had done to Reed, but while his touch was pleasant, there was none of the heat I'd experienced before. I closed my eyes and sank down on his cock, letting out a breath as my body adjusted to him. His hips jerked as I settled and a ripple of pleasure went through me as the motion pressed him against that spot inside.

"Princess." His voice was strained.

"Shh." I shook my head. I didn't want to hear him talk, especially if he was going to call me "princess". I didn't want to be the princess. I wanted to be Nami.

I rocked back and forth, feeling the difference between Reed and Ari. I didn't know what it was, but it just didn't feel the same. I pushed the thought from my mind. I didn't want to think about Reed right now. I concentrated on the friction as I moved, the feel of his hands on my breasts.

As I began to move faster, Ari's hands dropped to my hips, not trying to move me, but just resting there. I opened my eyes, trying not to sigh in frustration. I couldn't remember if he'd been this passive last night, but this definitely wasn't doing it for me. I kept one hand on his stomach and moved the other to the place where our bodies joined. My fingers quickly found my clit and began the familiar back and forth motion I used to get myself off.

His fingers flexed on my hips and he groaned, his face flushing as I felt him come. Damn. I would've thought he'd had more stamina. I ground down against him, putting near painful pressure on my clit until the pressure burst inside me.

My nails dug into his stomach and he let out a gasp of pain.

"I'm sorry," I said, opening my eyes.

"It is quite all right, Princess." Ari panted. "I am here to serve."

The words hit me with an almost physical force. Here to serve. I was his princess. Even if he wanted me, I was still the princess first. Not a woman. Not a person. Just the princess.

I climbed off of him and went into the bathroom without a backward look. I knew when I came back out, he'd be gone, either fired or attempting to explain himself to Tomas and Kai. Either way, I wouldn't see him again. Not that it mattered. It hadn't worked.

I was keeping my promise to my parents even though the thought of doing so broke my heart. I wanted Reed.

Chapter 4

Reed

"Where the hell did you go, Nami?" I muttered to myself as I flopped back onto the couch.

One would think in the age of the internet, finding the king and queen of a country shouldn't be too difficult. I had no clue which country I was looking for, but I'd figured I'd start by searching the names she'd said. King Raj and Queen Mara. I'd found nothing.

Had she lied about who she was?

The thought had been circling in my mind for the past two days as I'd searched for her. I'd successfully ignored it up until now, but I'd known that I would have to face it at one time or another. Actually, I admitted, I'd hoped I wouldn't have to face it at all. I'd had this foolish notion that I'd be able to find her in just a few short hours, hop on a plane and go find her. The question would be unimportant.

But I hadn't found her. I'd gone to bed frustrated last night and it looked like I was going to do the same tonight. Now I had that question too.

Was the reason I couldn't find her because she wasn't a princess? Had she just made everything up in order to get rid of me? It seemed a bit extreme as far as plans

159

went. She could've just said she was married or something like that. Married to some rich guy who insisted on the bodyguards. That wouldn't have been so far-fetched. Claiming to be a princess...now that one was a bit extreme.

She had to have been telling me the truth. I just couldn't figure out why I couldn't find her parents. Maybe I wasn't going about it the right way. I frowned at the laptop. I was a businessman. I knew how to read stocks and the business page. I knew a bit about researching things, but that was pretty much limited to typing stuff into a search engine and spending hours wading through shit. I'd been a CEO. Stuff like that was why I'd had assistants.

I glanced at the clock on my computer. It was night here but still evening back home. I'd resigned my position at the company, but I still had a good relationship with a lot of people back there, including one of my former assistants. Louis had been with me since the beginning, my first hire when I'd taken over as CEO five years ago. He was a couple years older than me, but had never behaved as if I was too young to be in charge.

I pulled my cell phone out of my pocket and scrolled down to Louis's number. He answered on the second ring.

"Mr. Stirling!" He sounded surprised, but pleased. "How are you doing?"

"Good, Louis," I said. "And I'm not your boss anymore, so please call me Reed."

"You're just on a sabbatical, Mr. Stirling." Louis's voice was firm. "How can I help you?"

A sabbatical. That was interesting. It appeared my parents hadn't told them that I'd actually resigned. It made sense though. A lie like that would be the best way to keep our shareholders from getting too nervous with Rebecca in charge. It wasn't a surprise that I hadn't heard the story before. I hadn't looked at any business news since leaving Philadelphia.

I wasn't about to correct Louis's mistaken impression. Best to speak to my parents first. With Louis, I stuck with what I needed. "I'm looking for someone. Twenty-two. Princess Nami Carr. Parents King Raj and Queen Mara. I need to know where Nami is from. Which country her parents are king and queen of."

If Louis thought this was an odd request, he didn't say anything about it. "Is this personal or business, Sir?"

"Personal." I definitely didn't want him doing this on business time. The last thing I needed was my sister finding out that I was looking for someone, not to mention that, no matter what my parents said, I wasn't in charge anymore. "I know that cuts into the amount of time you can spend searching."

"I'll do my best," Louis promised. There was a moment of silence, and then he added, "Do you know when you'll be coming back, Mr. Stirling?"

"No." I kept the answer simple even though I felt bad about essentially lying to him. I didn't have a plan to go back any time soon, if ever.

"I'll keep you apprised of what I find," he said. "Good night, Sir."

I hung up the phone and tossed it onto the couch next to me. I had absolutely no idea what to do now. Should I keep on with my feeble attempts to search or had I pretty much exhausted all of those options? I wasn't even really sure what I was looking for, or what I planned to do when I found it.

If I managed to track down her parents and figure out what country she was from, what then? I had vague notions of some sort of romantic reunion where I'd show up and convince her to give me a shot. I'd charm her parents, show them that I was the right match for their daughter. I was the one who deserved to marry –

Fuck.

I sat up and put my head in my hands. What was I thinking? I didn't want to get married again, especially

161

not to someone I barely knew. I'd done that once and it hadn't ended well at all.

But Nami wasn't Britni. They were as different in personality as they were in looks, which basically meant night and day. Britni was spoiled, petty and arrogant. Nami wanted nothing more than to be a normal person, to live a normal life. She was kind and funny and sweet. She had a streak of steel in her too. A strength of which I didn't think even she knew the depth. I hadn't loved Britni, but Nami...

Dammit!

I slammed my hand on the coffee table. I wasn't in love with Nami. I couldn't be. Not after just a couple days. The problem was, I couldn't come up with another reason as to why she was constantly on my mind. It couldn't be explained away with only lust. I'd had other women who could've quenched it if that's all it was. Not that I didn't want her. It was stronger than lust though. I couldn't even rightly call it desire. It was a need, like food or water or air.

But it wasn't love, I told myself again. I'd thought before that I'd been in love and I'd been wrong. I wasn't going to make that mistake again. No, I'd wait until I found her, see if she was even willing to see if there was anything more to what we had than two nights of passion.

I was still arguing with myself regarding whether or not I was in love with Nami when my phone rang. I sighed when I saw the screen. Mom. I wasn't really in the mood to talk to her, but I'd ignored her previous two calls. Ignoring this one would just be rude.

"Mom." I tried to keep my voice flat. "How are you doing?"

"We're fine," my dad answered.

Right. Conference call.

"Reed, you need to come home."

My heart skipped a beat at the tone of my mother's voice. There was a hint of something that sounded a lot like panic.

"What's wrong? Is someone hurt? Sick?"

"It's Rebecca." The words were tight.

My heart constricted painfully. I might not have liked her very much, but she was my sister and I loved her for that.

"She's okay." My mom must've sensed that my father's terse statement made things sound bad.

"Physically," Dad said.

This couldn't be good.

"Your sister's in a bit of a...delicate situation."

I wished they'd just get on with it and tell me what was going on.

I heard my father's half-laugh at my mother's words. "Don't sugarcoat things, my dear. Reed, your sister's been having an affair with Benjamin Westmore."

My first thought popped out of my mouth. "Seriously? He's older than both of you."

"Not Senior," my dad said. I could almost hear him rolling his eyes. "Junior."

"Right." I felt stupid. "And he's married."

"Married with kids," Mom clarified.

"And to make matters worse, Westmore Senior has already sent us invitations to the wedding of his youngest son, Blayne."

I'd only known Blayne Westmore by reputation, but I had to admit that I was surprised he'd settled down at all. I also had the vague recollection that my parents had been trying to marry him to my sister. That would make tensions between the two families run a bit high.

"So don't go to the wedding," I suggested. "Send an expensive gift."

"We're not calling for advice." Dad sounded annoyed. "We want you to come home and take the third invitation. Go with us."

I stood up and began to pace. I couldn't sit still and listen to this. "You want me to fly all the way home for

163

the wedding of someone I don't know."

"We want you to show everyone that we're a united family and that we will rise above this little...incident."

My mom, ever the diplomat.

"I'll think about it." I couldn't bring myself to refuse outright. The sense of duty to family did run deep. "But I'm not making any promises."

"We'll have a ticket reserved for you on Friday if you're coming."

After a couple more moments of small talk, the call ended. I knew they were both frustrated that I hadn't made any promises, but I'd given them the best I could. Besides, I had Nami to think of. I needed to find her before it was too late and she was married.

I paused, sighing. If it wasn't too late already.

I had no idea how fast things like this moved in her country. For all I knew, she could've gone straight from the airport to her wedding. Time wasn't on my side.

However, I thought, being back in the States might give me more resources. I could hire a private investigator to find Nami, deal with him face-to-face instead of making calls from halfway around the world.

I would do it, I decided. I'd go home. Something inside me clicked. This was a turning point, I thought suddenly. Whatever happened, it was going to happen at home because once I'd found Nami – or was told that finding her wasn't possible – I would have to decide where to go from there. There would be no putting it off anymore. My weeks of fun were over and it was time to start looking towards the future. A future I hoped Nami would be a part of.

Because, no matter what I told myself, I was in love with her.

Chapter 5

Reed

When my parents had called to try to coax me into coming home, I'd thought they'd exaggerated how bad things were. By the time I arrived in Philadelphia a few days later, things were even worse. Rebecca had driven our company into the ground. Money was missing. Clients were jumping ship and the only thing that had saved the employees was Julien Atwood.

I could feel my parents watching me as my father explained that Julien had convinced his family into buying out the company at a loss. The papers had been signed yesterday. I knew why they were watching. It had been Julien, after all, who'd gotten the girl, but I didn't begrudge him Piper. In fact, I was happy for her, for them both. They'd been able to overcome so many obstacles to be together, not the least of which was their families and pasts. I could only hope to be so lucky.

"How bad is it?" I asked, pulling myself out of my thoughts.

My father frowned at his plate. "We have other assets," he said. "Other sources of income."

I knew what he meant. Stocks and real estate mostly. I also knew how lavishly my family lived. The business had been a steady source of income they'd been able to spend without risking their net worth.

"It's not only the money," Mom spoke up. "What happened with Rebecca and Benjamin, and then the Atwoods having to buy us out..." She shook her head. "Our societal standing has never been more precarious." She gave me a disapproving look. "And all because of that Piper girl."

I leaned back in my chair, no longer hungry. "I'm not with Piper, Mom," I reminded her.

"Do you think that makes it any better?" Dad asked. "The whole Brock scandal overshadowed what happened between you and Britni, but people didn't completely ignore the fact that you left the daughter of a prominent family for a whore. Now she's with the Atwood boy and you look like a fool."

"Piper isn't a whore," I snapped. I wasn't sure which part of that pissed me off the most. The fact that he'd referred to Brock Michaels being arrested for rape to be a 'scandal' or that his concern over Piper choosing Julien over me had nothing to do with whether or not I was hurting.

"Stripper, sorry." He gave me a hard look that said he wasn't sorry at all.

"Why didn't you liquidate other assets to save the business?" I hadn't intended to ask the question, knowing it would come across as accusatory, but my patience had all but disappeared with my father's statements.

His face flushed, a mottled red creeping up his neck. "I don't believe that's any of your business."

"You practically beg me to come back here and then tell me that it's not my business?" I crossed my arms. "What do you want from me?"

Both parents looked startled at the blunt question, but I didn't try to smooth it over. I was through waiting for and following their instructions like a good little puppet.

"Tell him." My mother's voice was soft.

Dad glared at her for a moment and then sighed. "I

suppose you do need to know." He folded his hands on the table. "We seem to have gotten behind on some of our property taxes." He shifted in his seat. "And made some bad investments."

"So when you said you had other assets and income...?" I let the question trail off.

"We won't starve," he said. "But we're going to lose the villa, the vineyard and maybe the apartment. All sold to pay our taxes."

"Are you asking to move back here full-time?" I asked.

The house here on Chestnut Hill had originally belonged to my parents, but they'd sold it to me a couple years ago when I'd decided I preferred it to an apartment in the city. The family used it occasionally and I didn't mind as long as I was given advanced warning. I valued my privacy, particularly from my family.

"It may come to that," Dad said. "But I was thinking more about the stock you own."

"What about it?" My eyes narrowed. I had a bad feeling I knew where this was going.

"You're not majority holder, but you do own the second biggest chunk. I want you to buy out everyone else and get the business back from the Atwoods."

My mom reached across the table as if she was going to touch me, then stopped and pulled her hand back. "You've done well for yourself, Reed."

She was right. I had. While I did enjoy the comforts that my family name offered and I had like being able to stay at the villa and the vineyard in Italy, I had money beyond the trust fund I'd inherited when I'd turned twenty-one. I'd invested well and, while I had splurged on occasion, I didn't spend excessively. I'd promised myself that I would never count on my inheritance or trust fund to support me.

"What would you do with the business if I got it back?" I asked.

167

"Well, you're back now," Dad said. "And the stock would be in your name, of course. We always intended for you to inherit the company. It'd just come a bit early."

And there it was. Like the past few months hadn't even happened. I was expected to come back and pick up as if I hadn't been away at all. I'd had my fun and now I was supposed to be the good son again, regardless of what I wanted.

"I have a lot to think about." I pushed my chair back and stood. "You said the wedding's at one tomorrow?" My mother nodded. "I'll see you when it's time to go then."

Before either parent could press the matter any further, I walked out of the dining room, heading for the stairs. I'd wondered why my parents had insisted I come to my house rather than meeting them at their place. Now I knew why. It was a not-so-subtle way of letting me know that if I didn't let them stay here, they could be homeless.

I was so caught up in my thoughts that I almost ran into Rebecca.

"What are you doing here?" The question came out more harshly than I'd intended.

"Hiding," she snapped. "I'm a disgrace, or didn't our parents tell you?"

"Sorry," I apologized automatically. "You just startled me. I figured you'd be at your place."

"My place." She barked a bitter laugh. "I don't have a place, Reed. When Mom and Dad found out about the affair, they stopped paying my rent and I didn't have any choice but to live with them."

I searched her face, trying to tell if she knew what was happening with our parents' finances, but I couldn't see anything other than outrage at the indignities she'd supposedly suffered.

"And now that the golden child is back, I'll fade into the background again."

168

I knew I should feel some measure of sympathy for Rebecca considering how she had always been overlooked when it came to a lot of things, but I'd been just as much a pawn of our parents as she had. She could've done things differently, chosen to make something of herself separate from our family.

"I don't know if I'm staying," I admitted.

She rolled her eyes. "And why wouldn't you? You have everything here." A cruel smile curved her lips. "Well, everything except Piper. I hear she and Julien are quite the couple."

"I'm happy for them," I said quietly. Her expression said she didn't believe me, but I was telling the truth.

"Are you thinking of trying to get Britni back then?" she asked. "Because that ship sailed too."

"What's that supposed to mean?"

The smug look on her face said she'd been holding on to this particular tidbit. "She's engaged. Or will be soon enough from what I understand. Rich, good-looking, and here's the best part...he's not in love with another woman."

My hands wanted to curl into to fists, but I forced them to stay open. "You do know I never loved Britni, right? If she's found someone who loves her, good for her." My voice was even.

Anger flashed in her hazel eyes. Apparently, my lack of reaction annoyed her.

"Love's for idiots." She folded her arms over her chest and squared her shoulders. "Men marry for lust or money and women marry for money or prestige."

"Oh really?"

"Come on, Reed. You can't still seriously be that naïve."

"Is that what you were doing with Benjamin Westmore?" I asked. "Trying to get him to pay you off as his mistress?"

Her cheeks flushed. "That was a mistake. I've learned

169

since then." She glanced at her watch, an expensive one I'd never seen before. "I have to go. Cecily's expecting me."

"Cecily Postman?"

Rebecca nodded. "We're spending the weekend together since I'm apparently not good enough to go to the Westmore wedding." She turned to start down the hall.

"Cecily's in London."

Rebecca froze. "What?"

"I saw her at the airport when I arrived. She was getting ready to board a plane to London and didn't say a word about you meeting her there." I took a step towards my sister. "Where are you really going?"

Her jaw tightened. "None of your business."

"Rebecca..." My voice held a note of warning.

"Let it go, Reed. It's my life."

Trying for the nice, protective older brother wasn't working, so I went for option number two. "Are you sleeping with Cecily's father?"

The stiffening of Rebecca's spine told me the answer before she spoke, "And if I am?"

"Then you're stupid, Rebecca. He's old enough to be your father. His daughter is your best friend, for crying out loud."

"Tell you what, Reed." She still didn't look at me. "You worry about your love life and I'll worry about mine."

"Well, I guess you get a point since this one isn't married."

She opened her mouth, then closed it.

There was nothing I could do but watch her walk away. She wouldn't listen to me, I knew. Rebecca never listened to anyone. She did what she wanted to do and that was that. I shook my head and resumed my walk to my room. I was seriously jet-lagged and if I didn't get some sleep, I wouldn't be even close to presentable for the wedding tomorrow.

It wasn't until my parents and I were in the car heading to the church when I realized I hadn't once thought about the fact that I was going to see Piper again. I'd been too preoccupied wondering if either Louis or the PI I'd hired had found anything on Nami. Once I was seated, however, I found myself scanning the crowd for Piper. Just before things got started, I spotted her with Julien. She looked at me and gave me a tight smile. I could tell, even from a distance, that she was worried how I'd react to seeing her with him. I smiled and nodded, then turned away, hoping she could still read me well enough to know that we were okay.

As soon as the wedding began, however, Piper was the furthest thing from my mind. I couldn't help but wonder if Nami was married already. Had her wedding been like this? When everyone turned to watch the bride walk down the aisle, I didn't see the tall blonde. In my mind's eye, it was Nami, expression politely resigned. Or had she been happy? Did her parents pick her a match she could love?

I wasn't sure which thought bothered me more. That Nami would be miserable with a man she didn't care for, or that she would fall in love with him. I barely heard the ceremony as I tortured myself with thoughts of Nami and her unknown betrothed. At their wedding. Holding hands. The kiss. Dancing. The wedding night.

I let out a breath. I had to believe that she wasn't married yet. It would be hard enough to convince her to break an engagement. She'd never divorce her parents' choice.

By the time I found myself at the same table with Piper and Julien, I'd all but convinced myself that it wouldn't matter what I did. I'd lost Nami the moment I'd let her walk out of the hotel. To my surprise, Piper seemed genuinely concerned for me and I found myself telling her and Julien everything. Part of me did it because I wanted Piper to know that I understood what she'd said when she'd chosen Julien over me and there were no residual feelings. Another part of me needed it for another reason. I had to tell someone about her, about what I was feeling.

When I finished, Piper leaned forward, her dark green eyes kind. She put her hand over mine in a sincere and platonic gesture. "Do you love her?"

I didn't let myself overthink it. "Yes."

"Then fight for her, Reed." She squeezed my hand. "If what the two of you have is real, don't you dare give up. You deserve to be happy."

I smiled at her and thanked her, but in the back of my head, I couldn't help but wonder if she was right. Did I deserve to be happy?

Chapter 6

Nami

After my little fling with Ari, I'd given up on using a man to make me forget what I'd lost. Actually, I'd given up forgetting at all. I'd worked so hard to remember Reed that it was impossible to erase him now. That realization had depressed me enough that I'd spent the last two days in bed, getting up only when necessary. Like to use the bathroom and find more alcohol. I knew my parents had forbidden anyone to bring me anything, but I had enough blackmail on Tomas and Kai now that they were willing to help me out in exchange for a promise that I wouldn't try to sleep with anyone else. Neither one of them had been happy that they'd had to fire Ari and make up a lie to tell my parents.

The door to my bedroom banged open, making me jump, then wince at the bolt of pain that went through my head.

"Enough!" My father's voice was loud and stern, neither of which did anything to help my headache.

I grabbed the covers and pulled them up over me even though I was fully clothed. "Ever heard of knocking?" I muttered.

"Nami!" My mother chastised me. "You cannot speak to your father that way."

I sighed and climbed out of bed. The room wavered a bit, but didn't spin, so I was able to stay on my feet. I considered that to be quite the accomplishment. "Sorry." I couldn't leave it at an apology though. "Just figured a warning might've been nice. I could've been changing my clothes."

"Considering you have not changed clothes for more than two days, I did not believe that would be an issue." My father raised an eyebrow.

He had a point.

"This behavior of yours must stop," Mother said. "It is not befitting any member of a royal family, much less the heir."

I looked from one to the other. I could see bits and pieces of myself in both of them. Halea looked nearly identical to our mother, but I was a blend of them in personality as well as physical appearance. I'd also inherited a stubborn streak from both of them.

"I'm staying inside," I said. "But don't worry, I'll make sure I'm presentable for any public stuff." I swayed and put my hand on the bedside table to steady myself. "And that's what matters, isn't it? The face we present to the public. It's not like I'm making any major decisions or anything."

"You are the crown princess," Father spoke through gritted teeth. "It is your duty to learn all these things regarding the rule of Saja."

I resisted the urge to roll my eyes. I was already testing my father's patience and I had a feeling it would've been the last straw. "Like I said, I'll make sure I'm the picture of perfection when we interact with the public. Let me have the privacy of my own room to do as I please."

"Namisa Persephone Carrmoni."

I flinched at the sound of my official name. Within the family, we never referred to each other by our birth names. Those were for public face only. All Saja royalty had two names, the one that went on records and treaties, that the media used, and the one we used within the privacy of our home and when we were moving about unofficially. I'd taken that a step further when I'd shortened my last name for school. Four years away at school as Nami Carr, I'd almost forgotten that other name.

"This will stop. Now."

I recognized my father's tone. It was the one he used when he was having the final say in something. Like he was now.

"There will be no more alcohol save for wine or champagne at official functions. You will not become intoxicated, either publicly or privately."

My hands curled into fists as he continued.

"You will retire to your room at a respectable time unless busy with state or family business. You will wake no later than seven, bathe, dress and make an appearance at breakfast. All attire will be from your approved wardrobe, and you will not deviate from that."

There was a moment of silence and then my mother spoke, her voice soft. "I know this is difficult to accept, Nami, but you are the princess, and it is your duty to take on these responsibilities. You have always known this would be the way."

I *had* known, but there was a difference between being a child, or even a teenager, thinking of being in my early twenties as so far away, and being here and now.

"I understand how difficult this is for you."

It was on the tip of my tongue to snap at her that she didn't know. She had married in to the throne. I had been raised for it. The only person who could've understood was my grandmother, my father's mom. She had ruled before him. But I couldn't ask her for advice or guidance. She'd passed away when I'd been only seven. I didn't say anything to my mother though. It would have been bad manners to remind her that she was royal by marriage, not blood.

"It was a mistake to allow you to go to America for school," Father said. "There is a reason all Saja royals remain on the island for their schooling. Your roots are here, Nami, not out there."

"I know," I said softly. My headache was fading away, as were the other effects of what I'd drank, and a resigned depression was starting to sink in.

"So we are agreed?" Father asked. "No more of this foolishness?"

"We are agreed." I looked down, not wanting him to read on my face what I was feeling.

"Good," Mother said. "Now, make yourself presentable and join us in the receiving room. Wear the blue dress at the front of your closet."

I stiffened. I knew which dress she meant, and I knew why it had been purchased. "You've chosen?"

"We have," Father said. "Dress and join us. You will be meeting your future husband within the hour."

I watched them leave without any of us speaking again. When the doors closed behind them, I sank to my knees, all the strength running out of my legs. Here it was. My engagement. The fork in the road. Accepting this would mean I could fight it no more. My fate would be sealed.

I would've laughed at that if I could've ensured I wouldn't cry instead. My fate had been sealed the moment I'd been born, then again when my brother had died. I didn't have a choice other than how I would enter in to this. I could drag my feet, fight it tooth and nail, and still lose, or I could be gracious and hope that the man my parents had chosen was good and kind.

But first, I had to take a shower, because there was no way I was going to meet my fiancé smelling like someone who'd been sleeping off a bender under a bridge. Then I would dress and go to the receiving room to meet the man with whom I'd be spending the rest of my life.

The blue dress my mother had purchased while I was

away was a little loose even though it was technically my size. I frowned. I must've lost weight over the past couple weeks. Not surprising. I hadn't really been consuming much real food recently. I smoothed it down, making a couple little adjustments here and there until it fit well enough. I smoothed down my curls. They were still damp, but presentable. I went with minimum make-up and a pair of heels that gave me a couple inches but were still considered decent.

I gave myself one last look in the mirror. I could still see faint bruise-like smudges under my eyes, but they were only visible if someone paid close attention. I doubted anyone would notice. I took a deep breath, cleared everything else out of my mind and headed down the hallway. The receiving room was at the front of the palace, allowing us to bring people into our home without bringing them into the part where we actually lived.

When I walked inside, my parents were already there. Standing with them were three people. I recognized two of them as part of a fairly wealthy family. I couldn't remember their name, but it didn't surprise me that they were the ones my parents had picked.

"May we present our eldest daughter, Namisa Carrmoni," Father spoke in our native language.

I bowed my head a bit, enough to indicate respect, but without making it seem like they were above me. The woman curtsied, but I saw her pale eyes watching me. There was no doubt in my mind that she was wondering how long it would be before I'd give her a grandchild to assure her bloodline on the throne. Her husband bowed and kept his head down, his face carefully guarded. He was smart. I wasn't sure if that was a good thing or a bad thing.

I let my eyes turn to the third person now. He'd bowed, but not as low or as long as his father, and he hadn't kept his head down. His eyes were a clear blue, the kind that had the potential to be as cold as a glacier. Right now, they were unreadable as they met mine. He smiled, but it didn't reach his eyes. He was handsome, with jet black hair and chiseled features. When he straightened, I saw that he was about average height, a bit under six feet tall, and muscular, with wide, broad shoulders. Most women would've been attracted to him. If I hadn't had Reed on my mind, I might've been too.

"Princess Namisa, meet Machai and Naomi Nekane, and their son Tanek." Mother's voice was stiff and I wondered if she hadn't been as fond of this match as my father. "Tanek is your betrothed."

I'd figured as much, but hearing it said out loud like that still made my stomach flip, and not in a good way.

Tanek stepped forward as I extended a hand. He took it, bowed slightly and kissed the back of my hand. "Princess." His voice was low and cultured.

"Tanek."

Something dark passed across his eyes at my use of his first name. I tightened my jaw and lifted my chin. Too bad if he didn't like it. He didn't have a title and, until we were married, he wouldn't. Even then, I would still be above him. Others would be required to address him as prince, and then king, but I would still be the leader.

"We have decided that a short engagement would be best," Father said.

Mother turned to me, her expression tightly polite. "We have a lot to do, my dear, so we'll be spending every day until the wedding planning for the event."

I heard what she wasn't saying. I would have no chance to screw this up. They'd made their decision and now I had to live with it.

Chapter 7

Reed

Piper was right, I decided. I deserved to be happy and that couldn't happen until I knew where things stood with Nami. Even if she didn't want me, if she'd already married her guy, at least I'd know.

And no matter what happened, I was done here. Not just done with my family's business – which didn't belong to my family anymore – but with Philadelphia, with the obnoxious high society people, with everyone, related or not.

I wasn't going to do what my parents had asked and buy the company out from the Atwoods. Besides the fact that I wasn't interested in being in charge again, I didn't trust my family to do right by the people who worked there. I trusted Julien to though.

I laughed at that and shook my head as I looked down at the list I'd made. I was almost done. The last thing I had to do was tell my parents, and I was putting that off until I knew where I was going. I would eventually tell my parents, but I wanted to wait until I was ready to leave before I said anything. Give them less time to try to talk me out of it.

The first thing I'd done was pay ahead on property taxes for two years, and then sign the house over to my

179

parents. It wasn't as hard as I thought it would be, giving away the place that had been my home pretty much my entire life. I guessed that was because it hadn't actually felt like my home. Not just mine. Even at my age, I'd always felt like I was still at my family's house, not mine. Now it was theirs again. I just hoped it would give my parents enough time to get their feet under them because I wasn't planning on bailing them out with anything else.

I'd had to pull quite a few strings to get everything together on a Sunday, but the Stirling name wasn't complete mud, especially when it was linked to my first name. Granted, people knew about the whole Britni thing, but the Michaels weren't exactly bright shining stars in Philly at the moment and business people were more likely to overlook an affair versus bad financial choices. It helped that what I was asking for had to do with money, and I had plenty.

Everything that was under my name was being turned into cash. I wouldn't be able to get it all today, but I'd set things into motion to have everything split into several different accounts at different banks. I'd taken a loss on some art work and on a couple other possessions, but getting this taken care of quickly meant more to me than a couple hundred thousand dollars. I wanted to be ready to go at a moment's notice.

I looked around the living room, realizing for the first time how nothing here was mine. The furnishings had changed a bit over the years, but I'd hired the same decorator my parents had used. There were family pictures on the wall, but they were all portraits or identical prints of ones in the apartment. I'd kept very few mementos over the years and none of them were displayed.

I didn't have anything I wanted to take with me. The knowledge that I could leave at any point with just my wallet and passport filled me with a sense of relief and a thrill of excitement.

A knock at the door pulled me from my thoughts and I got up. I wasn't sure who it could be. Rebecca was going to come visit me, but it might've been my parents. I didn't really want to see any of them, but I couldn't think of anyone else. Unless Piper and Julien had decided to stop by, but while we'd gotten along fine at the wedding, I didn't think we were at the 'drop by for a visit' stage.

When I opened the door, I almost slammed it shut again. The only thing that stopped me was the fact that I couldn't move. My feet were frozen to the spot and I was pretty sure my mouth was hanging open.

"Hey, Reed." Britni grinned up at me, her light blue-gray eyes sparkling. "Heard you were back in the city."

"Britni." I found my voice, and was relieved to hear it sounded normal.

"Aren't you going to invite us in?" Britni asked.

It wasn't until then that I realized she wasn't alone. The man behind her was about average in height and build. Sandy brown hair and pale green eyes. He was good-looking, I supposed, in an average sort of way. I assumed this was the new fiancé.

"Come in." I stepped out of the way and let Britni and her guy walk on by.

"This is Jeremy MacKenzie, by the way," Britni called over her shoulder. She waved her fingers at me, a giant diamond glinting in the light. "My fiancé. He just asked me tonight."

"Nice to meet you, Jeremy." A strange, surreal feeling had come over me. "And congratulations."

Britni went straight into the kitchen and started rooting around, coming up with a bottle of wine a few seconds later. Without asking permission, she pulled a couple of glasses out of the cupboard and poured us each a glass.

"I think we need a toast," she said, raising her glass. "To true love."

I was glad she hadn't said it after I'd taken a drink. I

probably would've choked on it. As it was, I barely managed to swallow it despite how good it was. What the hell was she doing here?

"This is good, Reed." She gave me another smile. "Then again, you always did have good taste."

Jeremy gestured around the kitchen. "Did you hire someone or do it yourself?"

"Hired someone," I said. "But I don't think she did much in here. Looks pretty much the same as it did when I was a kid."

"You grew up here?" he asked.

I nodded. "On and off. We lived in the city too."

"Well, while you two are getting to know each other, I'm going to visit the restroom." Britni set down her glass and breezed out of the room.

"Is this as awkward for you as it is for me?" Jeremy asked, pitching his voice low so that Britni couldn't hear.

I let one side of my mouth curve up in a half smile. "I imagine so."

"I told her we shouldn't come," he said. "Especially not without calling first."

"Britni gets what Britni wants," I said wryly.

"She didn't get you," he observed.

"She did for a while," I countered. I grinned at him. "But I got away."

"Rumor has it there was another woman involved." Jeremy slid closer, his voice taking on a conspiratorial tone. "A stripper?"

I rolled my eyes. "Not exactly the whole story."

"I didn't think so." He reached over and put his hand on my arm. "Arranged marriages usually have secrets. I know mine does."

I stared at his hand, my mind reeling. Was this seriously happening? I had to be reading into it, right? This was one of those platonic bromance moments, right?

"But when you have an understanding..." His hand slid up my arm and around the back of my neck.

182

Oh, shit.

I took a step back. "Sorry, Jeremy. I didn't mean to make you think..."

"No problem." He took a step back and held up his hands, palm out. "My mistake. I just assumed..."

"You two getting along?" Britni said as she came back into the kitchen. "My two boys?"

"I'm not your boy." I gritted my teeth. "What are you doing here, Britni?"

"And that's my cue to take a look at this beautiful house." Jeremy drained the last of his wine and walked out of the room.

"All right," I said as Jeremy disappeared. "Talk to me."

"Can't a girl just want to see her ex-husband?" Britni gave me wide, innocent eyes.

I raised an eyebrow. "Do you really want me to replay the night I told you it was over?"

Her expression tightened for a moment, then relaxed. "I've had time to think about what happened between us and I want us to be friends."

"Friends?" I echoed. This had to be a dream. Some sort of weird, abstract dream.

"Of course." She moved in close, backing me against the counter before I knew what was happening. "Friends with benefits." She put her hand on my chest and slid it down between us.

I jumped to the side as she cupped my cock through my pants. "What the hell, Britni?!"

"Jeremy's parents want the same thing yours did. An heir. And as I'm sure you've already figured out, I'm not exactly his type."

"So get artificially inseminated," I snapped. "Because I'm not an option."

Britni gave me one of her pouts. "Come on, Reed. You can't say that we didn't have fun together."

"Fun?" I raised an eyebrow. "I don't know what your

183

definition of fun is, but nothing I experienced during our marriage was fun."

She reached for the zipper at the front of her shirt and pulled it down, exposing bare skin. "You didn't have any fun? That's disappointing." She opened her shirt and flashed her breasts. "What do you say we try again?"

"Zip up your shirt and tell me what the hell you're really doing here, because I know it's not because you want to fuck."

"Actually," Britni said. "It is." She walked towards me. "I want a baby. Your baby."

My eyes narrowed suspiciously. I hadn't heard much about the Michaels family since Brock went to jail, but what had happened couldn't have had a positive effect on their finances. Pieces fell into place, but I was hoping I was wrong. I didn't want to think Britni could be that manipulative and cold, but it made sense. If I got her pregnant, she could claim that the two of us had some sort of random night of passion. A simple paternity test and I'd be paying a hefty amount of child support. And she knew I wouldn't argue with it because I would never let a kid suffer.

"I think you need to leave."

She yanked up her zipper. "Are you fucking kidding me? After what you did to me? You owe me."

"I owe you? I signed the divorce papers and gave you more than the prenup allotted." My temper was rising and I fought to keep it down. "We're done, Britni. In fact, I'm done with this whole fucking thing."

"What are you talking about?"

"I'm leaving," I snapped. "Everyone in this town is fucking crazy." So much for my carefully thought out plan to reveal my plans only after I was going. Oh, well. In for a penny... "I'm leaving Philadelphia, and once I'm gone, I'm not coming back."

She laughed, a shrill, brittle sound. "Sure you are. Everything you know is here. You're not going

184

anywhere."

"Yes," I said firmly. "I am. "I've made all the arrangements. I'm just waiting on a call and then I'm gone."

"Darling." Jeremy spoke from the doorway. "I hate to be a bother, but my parents are expecting us so we can make the official family announcement."

Britni glared at me for a moment longer before fixing a fake smile on her face and beaming it at Jeremy. Based on his expression, he wasn't fooled. I had a moment to wonder what he was going to get out of this marriage. It wasn't like he really had to worry about getting outed. Being LGBT friendly was quite popular among our social circle and I hadn't heard that his family was overly religious.

"Let's go. I'm done here." Britni gave me another dirty look before stalking out of the room.

I followed them to the door to make sure they left and when it closed, I stayed there, resting my forehead against the door for a moment. If I hadn't been certain that I was going to leave Philadelphia and not look back, what had just happened clinched things for me.

I really hoped someone found Nami soon, because if I had to stay here much longer, I was going to go crazy.

Chapter 8

Reed

I looked down at her as she kissed her way down my body, her mouth leaving a hot trail across my skin. They were wet, open-mouthed kisses, teeth and tongue alternating to sting and soothe. When she dipped her tongue in my bellybutton, I laughed and was immediately rewarded with a nip to my stomach.

I groaned. "You're killing me here, Princess."

Her hands slid up my thighs, fingers massaging the tight muscles there. I wondered how it was physically possible to feel tense and relaxed at the same time. Then again, it seemed like it was only during sex that it happened, and so many impossible things were possible when two people came together.

"Stay still," she whispered as she moved her head lower. She put her hand on my stomach and my muscles bunched and jumped under her palm.

How the hell did she expect me to stay still when her touch was like electricity? Whenever I was near her, it felt like every cell was trying to find a matching one in her body, its other half. The pull was beyond magnetic, beyond anything I'd ever felt before.

I sucked in a sharp breath as her tongue darted out

to taste me. Her fingers danced over my swollen flesh and it twitched in response. My eyes wanted to close so I could focus solely on the sensation of her hot breath as she lowered her head. I forced them to stay open, wanting to watch her take me in her mouth.

Her lips slowly closed around the tip and I felt her tongue tease the skin there. I reached down and put my hand on her head. Her hair was like silk between my fingers and I wondered what it would feel like long, how the curls would brush against my thighs when she went down on me. Maybe I could talk her into growing it out.

My cock slid over her tongue as she took more and more of me. Her lips stretched impossibly wide as she neared the base. I couldn't take my eyes off her. She looked up at me as the head of my dick bumped against the back of her throat. I waited for her to gag, withdraw, and use her hand as she took the first couple inches again. Instead, she took a slow breath and let me slide down her throat.

"Fuck!" My back arched and it took all of my self-control not to thrust harder into her mouth. One hand tightened in her hair and the other grabbed on to the sheets.

Her nose brushed against my pelvic bone and she stayed there, my cock engulfed in the soft wet of her mouth. One hand moved beneath me, cupping my balls, then rolling them in her hand. After what felt like years, she raised her head and my cock fell out of her mouth with a near obscene plop. She used her free hand to stroke me as she ran her tongue along the underside of my shaft.

"Nami," I moaned her name as she took one of my balls into her mouth. The hand on my cock didn't miss a single stroke and I could feel my orgasm building deep inside.. I was so close. Her hands and mouth were doing such wonderful things that I never wanted her to stop, but the end was coming...

188

I jerked awake, disoriented for a moment as I tried to remember where I was and what I was doing. Right. I was at home. Or, at least, at the house on Chestnut Hill. That was home for now.

My phone rang again and I realized that's what had woken me. I fumbled for it, my brain and body still thick with sleep. I managed to get it just before it went to voicemail.

"Hello?"

"Mr. Stirling?"

I frowned at the familiar voice. I should know it, but couldn't quite place it. "Yes?"

"It's Louis."

Right, my former assistant. "Of course. Good morning." There was a reason he was calling me, but I couldn't for the life of me figure out what it was.

"You asked me to look into finding someone for you."

I sat up, all traces of sleep gone. "Did you find her?"

"I spent the weekend working with your PI like you asked and I'm pretty sure we found her."

My heart was pounding so hard against my chest that I thought Louis might be able to hear it. This was it.

"You said her name was Nami Carr, correct? And her parents were Raj and Mara, King and Queen of some country you didn't know."

"That's right."

"What we found is a Princess Namisa Carrmoni, daughter of a King Amir Rajada Carrmoni and Queen Persephone Mara Carrmoni."

I crossed my legs and rested my elbows on my knees. She hadn't given me a complete alias in an attempt to make it impossible for me to find her after all.

"From what Mr. Stiles and I found, the Carrmonis are the royal family of a small island country called Saja. The family name has changed over the years since it seems like they don't follow a traditional monarchy of the

189

eldest son taking the throne..."

"I don't want a history lesson, Louis," I said dryly. It took a great amount of self-control not to just yell at him to tell me how to get to Saja.

There was a moment of silence before Louis continued. "I've emailed you a picture of Princess Namisa. I'm confident this is the young woman of whom you spoke."

"And you said the name of the country is Saja?"

"It is."

"How do I get there?" I climbed out of bed and headed into the living room where I'd left my laptop on the table.

"I've included those instructions in your email as well, Sir," Louis said. "I took the liberty of finding several flight possibilities."

"Thank you, Louis," I said, sincerely grateful. "You have no idea how much this means to me."

"No problem," he said. There was a pause, and then he spoke again. "You're not coming back are you, Mr. Stirling?"

"No." I didn't want it to become public knowledge yet, but I owed Louis at least this much. "Are the Atwoods treating people well?"

"Yes," he answered. "But you are missed, Sir."

"I'm not your boss anymore," I said as I turned on my laptop. "Call me Reed."

"This is good-bye then."

"It is," I said. "If you ever need anything, you call me. Money, a reference, a call to some connection. Anything." I fully intended to send him a nice check for the work he'd done, but I wasn't going to tell him that. He'd argue.

"I'll do that."

I could almost hear the smile.

"Good luck with your young lady, Mr. Stir – Reed."

"Thank you, Louis."

190

I had a lump in my throat when I ended the call. Louis and I hadn't been close friends, but he'd been one of the few people I'd always been able to count on. I hadn't realized just how much until now. I'd already made my peace with leaving my family, but saying good-bye to Louis somehow made things seem more final.

I pulled up the email he'd sent and opened the attachment. My heart did a strange twist when I saw her. She was dressed formally, but there was no doubt in my mind who she was. "Princess Namisa returns from European vacation." The caption put the picture as having been taken shortly after she'd left me. She had a smile on her face, but even in a picture, I could tell it was forced. I'd smiled like that before, after all. I'd worn it for my engagement announcement. My wedding. Pretty much every public appearance with Britni. I could tell Nami was miserable.

I tore myself away from the picture and scrolled down to the travel information Louis had sent. It seemed there were only three airports in the entire world that flew to Saja and none of them were in the US. The one in Italy had the shortest flight time, but there were also flights out of an airport in India and one in Switzerland. Louis had already made calls and, if I was lucky, I could get on a flight to the Swiss airport today, then fly out of Switzerland and make it to Saja by tomorrow evening.

It wasn't even a question.

I called the airline and made the arrangements as I grabbed something to eat from the kitchen. It was going to be a long flight and airplane food wasn't exactly my favorite thing in the world.

Once I finished, I collected my laptop and went into my bedroom to pack. Two suitcases and a carry-on were all I planned on taking with me, which meant anything I left behind, I wouldn't see again. Fortunately, I'd already figured out which things I wanted and what I could live without, which turned out to be almost everything.

I quickly packed what clothes I could into the suitcases, then put my laptop in my carry-on with a few other necessities as well as the paperwork I'd done yesterday. Everything was set up, but I wanted to have the papers with me in case some question came up. I'd been serious when I'd said that I wasn't planning on coming back.

I looked at the clock once I'd finished. Twenty minutes before I needed to leave. I could've called my parents or sister, let them know I was leaving, but I had no way of knowing the conversation would end when I needed it to. Better to send off an email right before I got onto the plane. After that, I could turn off my cell phone and not have to worry about returning their calls until I was waiting for my plane in Switzerland.

I picked up my bags and headed out to the town car I'd called. No point in leaving a car at the airport when my ticket was one-way. Plus, I'd already sold mine. As I got into the car, I looked up at the house, expecting to feel a twinge of regret or of sadness. Instead, all I felt was exhilaration. I was going to see Nami and start a new life. The old life fell away and I didn't look back as the town car pulled away from the house. Out with the old and in with the new. No matter what happened from here on out, my life at least would be driven by what I wanted rather than my parents. My life was mine again.

Chapter 9

Reed

I wasn't entirely sure what I'd been expecting when I walked out of the tiny airport, but I was positive it hadn't been this. The sun was on its way down, but the air was still warm for the first week in June. Saja didn't look like Sicily or any of the other European tourist islands I'd been to over the years. It didn't look like Hawaii either, despite the beach I could see from where I stood.

Taxi cabs lined the space in front of the airport and I quickly grabbed one. The driver accepted the Euro I gave him, then shot me a sharp look when I asked him to take me to the palace.

"Why you want to go there?" His English was more heavily accented than Nami's had been, but I could immediately tell they were the same.

I gave him my best charming smile. "I'm an American tourist. We don't have palaces in America."

That seemed to ease his suspicions, but I still got the impression that he wasn't sure how he felt about my request. They didn't seem to have many visitors here, I observed as we drove into the capital. I hesitated to call it a city. I'd grown up in Philadelphia, spent a lot of time in New York and DC for business, traveled to LA, Dallas, Chicago and Miami. Those were cities. This looked more like a town.

Still, it was a nice little place. I saw businesses that had signs in both English and the native language. A couple bookstores and electronics stores. One or two furniture places. Half a dozen clothing stores. I even saw a law firm and a hospital. Granted, they were a fraction of the size of anything in Philly, but it seemed that the little I'd been able to find on Saja had been right. They were fairly self-sufficient.

The car pulled up in front of a pair of massive iron gates. Beyond them, nearly hidden from view by trees, was a massive house that couldn't be anything but the palace. I paid the driver and told him not to wait. It wasn't until I had my suitcases and carry-on on the sidewalk next to me that I realized I hadn't entirely thought this out.

I couldn't exactly walk up to the gate, knock and ask for Nami. Aside from the fact that what I was about to do was most likely against royal protocol, I doubted she'd told her parents anything about me. If I showed up saying that I'd met Nami in Paris, I could get her in trouble, and I still didn't know for certain what that would mean. Saja seemed like a fairly modern place, but when it came to things like the princess's virginity, I wasn't about to take any chances. Not with Nami.

I needed to figure out a way inside without attracting attention. I was at least lucky that I didn't stand out physically from the people of Saja. While the majority of the people seemed to have darker complexions and hair, there had been enough people with fair skin and lighter hair that I didn't stick out like a sore thumb. Passing for a native, or at least a resident, however, wouldn't be enough.

I took my luggage and headed down the sidewalk, circling around the side of the massive fence as soon as it curved away from the sidewalk. The path next to the fence was worn, as if walked often. The fence was overgrown with something that resembled ivy, shielding the view, but it also provided me a place to hide my suitcases and bag.

I felt like an idiot, but I knew I had to see Nami before her parents met me, and that meant I needed to sneak in and find her. I couldn't do that while carrying my things around and I didn't want to waste my time checking into a hotel. It'd be night before I'd be able to make it back here. I couldn't wait that long. The need I'd had for Nami had gotten stronger the closer I'd gotten to her. I had to see her, needed to know that she'd missed me as badly as I'd missed her, that she still wanted me.

I covered my things and looked around to make sure I'd be able to find them again. Satisfied that I'd recognize the hiding spot again, I walked a little further down the path, looking for a place I could sneak in. I had a vague recollection of making fun of the scene in *Romeo and Juliet* where he snuck into the Capulet garden to see Juliet, and smiled to myself. I was probably too old to be making romantic gestures like that, but I was considering this to be more practical than romantic. Or at least that was what I told myself as I found a place where the ivy was thinner, offering me a better look at the grounds.

I was near some sort of service entrance and, as I watched, a smaller gate swung open and a small cart pulled out. I flattened myself against the fence and hoped the ivy would cover me. The cart went the opposite way and I decided to take a chance and quickly slipped through the gate just before it closed behind me.

I could hear people laughing and carrying on inside. The smell of dinner made my stomach growl. I ignored it and moved to the back of the palace. I had absolutely no clue where I was going, a fact that was made abundantly clear when I looked up at the three story building sprawled across several acres. My heart fell. There was no way I'd be able to find Nami before someone spotted me and I got kicked out, or arrested for trespassing.

I could hear Piper's voice in the back of my mind

telling me not to give up, but I argued back that she hadn't foreseen this. I'd almost convinced myself to turn around and sneak back out when I heard something. Or rather, someone.

Nami.

"I'm fine, Halea." Her voice was tired, but I knew it. "Go back to your room and get some sleep. You have your English lesson tomorrow."

I followed the sound, arriving in time to see a girl walking out of a door. She was in her teens, with light brown hair, a fair complexion and a petite build. She had only the faintest resemblance to Nami, but I had no doubt this was Nami's sixteen year-old sister, Halea.

I waited until the girl was out of sight before I walked to the door. I didn't want to open it in case there was an alarm, but I wasn't sure knocking was the best idea either. Unfortunately, I had to do one or the other unless I turned around and left.

I knocked.

I heard Nami talking, "Halea, I told you..."

Her voice trailed off as she opened the door and saw me. Her eyes widened, her face going pale. She recovered quickly, holding a finger to her lips as she shifted so she could partially close the door.

"Gentlemen," she spoke to someone behind her without taking her eyes off me. "My sister and I need to speak in private."

"We're under orders not to leave you."

I recognized Kai's voice.

"I want to talk to my sister without you thugs hovering over me," she snapped. "Run and tell my parents if you want to, but get the hell away from me."

I knew the moment they left because she grabbed the front of my shirt and yanked me towards her, going up on her tiptoes to press her lips against mine. I was so surprised that it took me a moment to respond, but when I did, my arms went around her waist, my mouth opening

196

to let my tongue tease against her lips. She made a sound, crushing her body against mine so that I could feel her full breasts, soft against my chest.

When she finally broke away, she put her hand on my cheek. "What are you doing here?"

"I came for you." I ran my thumb along her bottom lip.

She glanced over her shoulder. "I don't know how long they'll give me, but it should be enough."

I barely had a moment to register the hallway she pulled me down, but then we were at a door.

"This is the quarters where my personal maid usually stays, but she's not there yet. Walk through the bedroom. There will be a small kitchen and living space. On the other side is another door. It's usually kept locked, but I have the key. It leads into my room." She put her hand on my chest over my heart. "Will you come to me?"

I brushed my lips across hers. "Always."

Her fingers flexed against my chest, and then she turned and hurried away. I opened the door and went inside. It took me a moment for my eyes to adjust, but I was standing in a small alcove. Based on the coat rack, I assumed this was where the maid would've left her shoes and coat before going further into her quarters. I followed Nami's instructions, my body thrumming in anticipation. Waiting until I heard the key turn in the lock was pure torture, but then the door opened and she was there.

I didn't remember closing the door behind me or taking off my shirt, but then her warm hands were on me, fingers tracing over my chest, nails lightly scraping my nipples. I made a sound in the back of my throat as I slid my tongue into her mouth, thoroughly exploring the familiar territory, relearning it.

My hands moved across her back, then down to cup her ass, pulling her tight against me. She moaned into my mouth as she ran her hands around to my back and then down to my ass. I kept one hand on the firm flesh and the

197

other pulled up the back of her shirt, giving my fingers access to her soft skin.

As we tumbled onto the bed, our mouths came apart. Her face was flushed, hair mussed, full lips swollen, and she was the most beautiful thing I'd ever seen. Before I could rid her of her clothes, she pulled her shirt over her head and tossed it to the floor. She wore a strapless bra that barely contained her ample breasts and, as I watched, she reached behind her and undid the clasps, sending the bra to the floor with her shirt.

"My memory didn't do you justice." I cupped her breasts, savoring the weight of them.

I lowered my head to taste her, circling her nipple with my tongue, first one then the other. She buried her fingers in my hair and held me to her breast. Her grip tightened when I took her nipple into my mouth, keeping the suction light at first, then increasing it until she was writhing against me.

When I raised my head, she was breathing heavily, her pupils blow wide with desire. "How quiet do we have to be?" I asked.

She shook her head. "I gave the guards permission to lock me in so they could leave."

I gave her a questioning look. "Why would they need to lock you in? Aren't they here to protect you?"

She grinned at me, her eyes glinting with that wild streak I'd seen in Venice. "In theory, but lately, it's been more about baby-sitting me. I haven't exactly been the best-behaved princess lately."

My hands went into fists as something occurred to me. Had she been with another man? I looked down at her and saw a shadow on her face as she read my expression. I didn't want to know. After all, I'd been with what's-her-name during the time we'd been apart, and several others. We'd agreed to move on. I couldn't blame her if she'd done the same thing I had.

"It doesn't matter." I kissed her forehead. "As long as

198

you want me now." I looked down at her again, suddenly uncertain.

She kept her eyes locked with mine as she took my hand and slid it under her skirt. Our hands moved between her legs until my fingers were pressed against the crotch of her panties. Her very wet panties.

I took her mouth again, laying her back on the bed as my fingers slipped beneath the crotch of her panties finding her hot and ready. She cried out as I slid a finger inside her and I moaned in response, my cock throbbing at the feel of her pussy clenching around my finger.

I made my way down her throat to her breast, taking her nipple between my lips even as my finger pumped into her, preparing her. I added a second finger as my thumb rubbed back and forth across her clit.

"Please," she begged. "Inside me. Please."

It had been too long. I couldn't wait anymore. I'd go slow later. Right now, I needed to be inside her. I undid my pants even as I pushed her skirt up and climbed between her legs. I shoved my pants down just below my ass, lifting my mouth from her breast so I could see her face as I shoved into her. Her nails dug into my shoulders as her entire body stiffened. I swore, squeezing my eyes closed as she came.

She was still quivering around me when I gathered myself enough to start moving. My thrusts were jerky as I fought my body to put off the inevitable. The pressure inside me was nearly unbearable, the feel of her around me, under me, almost too much.

"Reed."

I opened my eyes when she said my name.

"Let go."

She lifted herself up enough to press her lips against my throat. As I buried myself deep inside her, she bit down on my neck, sending a sharp spike of pain straight through me and pushing me over the edge. I clutched her to me as I came, my body trembling with the force of my orgasm. She wrapped her legs around me, holding me to her, inside her.

It didn't matter that we hadn't seen each other in weeks. It didn't matter that her family had plans for her and that I had no clue what I wanted to do next. Nothing mattered but the fact that we were together, our bodies one. I loved her and that would be enough to overcome any obstacle that came our way. I wouldn't lose her.

Chapter 10

Nami

We made love two more times, and I knew that's what it was, not simply having sex or fucking. No man would've come half-way around the world just for good sex, and especially not a man like Reed. Gorgeous, rich, sweet, charming...he was everything a woman could want, and that wasn't even throwing in how amazing he was in bed. Granted, I didn't have a lot of prior lovers to compare him to, but I had heard people talk enough to know that what I experienced with him wasn't normal. I felt a stab of jealousy at the thought of him being with other women and pushed it aside. I had no right to be jealous. Especially not now.

I could feel him behind me, the heat of his body warming me. I'd left the air conditioning on high through the night and the room was almost chilly. I was glad though because I wanted to enjoy this moment for as long as possible. I'd never thought I'd have this again. I didn't know what it meant for us, for me, but I was trying not to think about it.

"Mmm." He made a sleepy sound, his arms tightening around me. "Good morning."

I opened my eyes, but didn't look up at him. "How did you know I was awake?"

He kissed my temple. "Because the only time you're completely relaxed is when you're sleeping."

How was it he knew that about me? We'd spent all of three nights and one day together. But he was right. I could feel my body tense up the moment I woke. Well, partially right. "Not the only time." I pushed my bare ass back against him and heard him suck in a sharp breath.

He laughed, but there was an edge to the humor. His hand shifted until it was covering my breast. I closed my eyes as desire twisted low in my belly. How could I want him again? My entire body ached from last night, but I didn't care. I just wanted to beg him to take me again. From behind, on top, it didn't matter, so long as he was inside me.

"What time is it?" He kissed the hollow under my ear and I shivered.

I looked at the clock and groaned, but not in pleasure. "It's nearly seven. I need to get up." The last thing I needed was someone bursting into my room to find out why I wasn't awake yet.

"Just a couple more minutes." He squeezed my breast and I felt his cock start to harden against my hip. "We can be quick."

My pussy gave a throb at the thought of it. It would be so easy to say yes, to feel him slide into me. I wondered how different it would feel to have him take me this way. I could imagine his fingers on my clit, bringing me to climax as he spilled inside me...

I sighed. No. It was too risky. Reluctantly, I disentangled myself from his embrace and climbed off the bed. I didn't look at him as I headed into my bathroom. I knew he was smart enough not to leave and risk being seen, so I took my time cleaning up. I needed to think, compose myself.

He'd caught me off guard last night, and once I'd kissed him, that was it. I didn't know what it was about him, but when I touched him, it was like my brain short-circuited. I couldn't think clearly. The fact that I'd brought him into my bedroom when my fiancé and his family were in the guest quarters was proof of that.

Tanek.

Shit.

I pulled on my robe. I definitely couldn't do this naked. It was going to be hard enough with him naked. I had to do it though, no matter how much I hated it. I took a slow breath and let it out, then stepped back into the bedroom.

Reed was sprawled on his stomach, the sheet only half covering his ass. I flushed as I saw the long, red furrows I'd made in his back. He hadn't complained. In fact, if I'd correctly interpreted the sounds he'd been making, he'd liked it.

For a moment, I thought he was sleeping and that I had a bit of a reprieve, but as I walked closer, he rolled over and smiled at me. I didn't smile back. I couldn't. My chest was tight and there was a knot in my stomach that felt like ice. His smile faltered and he sat up, thankfully pulling the sheet across his lap as he did.

"What's wrong?"

I sat on the edge of the bed, but didn't reach for him. "Last night was a mistake."

I felt him tense and his face instantly became a hard mask, unreadable.

"A mistake." His voice was flat.

"I'm engaged, Reed," I said softly. "I told you that my parents would be choosing a husband for me. They have. I have no choice but to marry Tanek."

I stared at her. "You have a choice. There's always a choice."

I could hear the note of desperation in his voice and it hurt my heart.

"I was where you are, and I made the wrong choice," he continued.

"You weren't in the same position," I countered.

"This is different. You were worried about letting down your family. I have an entire kingdom to think about."

I stood. He might not have been touching me, but he was still too close. I walked a few steps away and then turned towards him. I couldn't meet his eyes though, and focused on a spot just over his shoulder.

"Just because I don't have a whole country doesn't mean I don't understand responsibility."

I shook my head. I couldn't listen to him. He'd support all of the things I'd been feeling and I'd walk away from my family, my duty...and I'd never forgive myself.

"You're not one of us, Reed." I saw him flinch and forced myself to finish it. "Tanek and I are getting married this weekend. This is my choice. My future is here on Saja with him, not with you."

Chapter 11

Reed

This couldn't be happening. Not after everything I'd done to find her. And I knew it wasn't because she didn't want me the way I wanted her. It wasn't just because we'd slept together again either. I'd seen how she felt, heard it in her voice when she'd called my name. She loved me, I knew it.

But she wasn't choosing me.

Her words hung in the air between us. There was no question about the meaning.

I couldn't look at her as I climbed off the bed and began looking around for my clothes. Something about hearing this while she was clothed and I was naked made it feel all the more humiliating. I winced as I bent down, the skin on my back stretching the marks she'd made. I'd enjoyed it when she'd scratched me, and I'd enjoyed even more the thought that I'd be remembering this encounter for days while we made our plans. Now, the pain made my temper rise.

"You should've told me that when I first showed up," I snapped as I pulled on my pants. "Instead of kissing me and then inviting me back to your room. Making me think there was a chance for us." I grabbed my shirt and pulled it over my head, suppressing a wince as the fabric slid over the scratches. I hoped they'd heal quickly. I didn't want to remember this.

"You're right," she said, her voice infuriatingly calm. "I should have told you then and sent you away."

I turned towards her, bristling at her word choice. "Sent me away? What, like I'm some servant to be dismissed when I've served my purpose?" My hands curled into fists and I fought to keep my voice low. No matter how I felt, I didn't want Nami's bodyguards bursting in to find me here.

Her expression hardened. "Do not presume to understand my thoughts or feelings on the matter."

"Oh, I'm sorry, *Princess*." I spat the last word out as I shoved my feet into my shoes. "Should I be thanking you for letting me fuck you?"

I felt a stab of mingled guilt and satisfaction at the hurt I saw in her eyes.

"Do not speak to me that way." Her posture was stiff, unyielding, her eyes cold.

"Excuse me if I'm a little pissed." I walked around the bed to stand in front of her. Pain overrode my anger for the moment. "Do you have any idea what I gave up to come be with you?"

That was what hurt the most, I thought. She was behaving as if she was the only one who had something to lose here. As if I'd just happened to meander onto her property by happy accident and I could leave now and everything in my life would just go back to normal. No harm done.

"I've been looking for you for over a week. Hired investigators to try to find you because I couldn't stop thinking about you. I liquidated all of my assets, signed over all of my property. I told my family that I was never coming back to the company and left Philadelphia with no plans to return." My voice shook and I paused for a moment to steady it. "I did all of that so when I found you, I would be free to go wherever, be whoever you needed. I gave up everything for you, Nami."

She started to raise her hand like she wanted to touch me, but then dropped it. "I can't."

"Damn you!" I spun around, wanting to hit something. Anything. But I knew it wouldn't be smart. Anything sounding remotely violent would alert whoever was guarding her door. And with the way things were currently going, I'd be lucky if I didn't find myself arrested for rape.

"Reed," she started to speak.

"No!" I turned back towards her, my hands almost shaking with the force of my emotions. "Don't. Don't you dare say my name or make some excuse. It's not that you can't. You won't."

"I have to do what's best for my country." There was a note of pleading in her voice, pleading for me to understand.

I shook my head, refusing to try to see it her way. "No, you're doing what's best for you. What's easy."

"You think this is easy?" Her eyes sparked angrily. "Do you think I wish to be sold off like some prize to the highest bidder? Married to a man whose only interest in me is that I put his child on the throne once I'm gone?"

"I think it's easier to hide behind tradition and duty than it is to follow your heart." I ran my hand through my hair and glanced at the door. We were tempting fate, arguing like this, but I couldn't let her go without a fight. "And I know that your heart is with me." I walked towards her again, this time stopping only when we were mere inches apart. "Tell me I'm wrong."

She looked up at me and, for one terrifying moment, I thought she'd say it. That I was wrong about how she felt about me. That she'd played me this entire time. After what I'd done to Piper, I supposed I would've deserved it.

"It doesn't matter what I think or feel," she said softly. Her eyes slid away from mine.

"Of course it does." I grabbed her chin and held her

face in place. "Look at me, dammit!" She did, but her expression was guarded. I forced myself to speak quietly. "What you want matters, and no one who cares about you is going to say otherwise."

She took a step back. "What I want is to marry Tanek on Saturday, as my family desires."

Everything inside me turned to ice.

"Okay, then." I nodded. I couldn't look at her. "If that's what you want."

"I do."

I should've felt pain at those words, knowing she'd be saying them again in only a few days, saying them to bind herself to another man. The man she wanted more than me. The man she'd be with forever. The thoughts piled onto each other until it was hard to breathe, but, still, no pain. I was numb. Every part of me, as if I'd been shot through with Novocain.

"I won't bother you again." The words sounded hollow.

I stepped around her and walked over to the door I'd used the night before. I knew I'd need to be more careful sneaking out than I had been sneaking in, but even the thought of being caught and arrested for trespassing, or whatever else they could throw at me, couldn't spark anything in me. I thought I heard her say my name as I stepped into the maid's chambers, but I didn't stop or turn around. I needed to go, because I knew that once I felt again, it was going to be bad, and I couldn't be here when that happened.

I had enough sense to peek outside rather than just walk out, but everything seemed distant, like I was viewing it from some other place. My brain processed the grounds, the people, but none of it seemed real. I couldn't even feel the door against my fingers as I held it. This entire thing felt like a nightmare, the kind that seemed to go on for years.

I needed to leave. Now. The words prompted no

208

urgency, but I moved anyway. There was a box on the step next to the door. I had no clue what was in it, or if it was important, and I didn't care. I didn't care about anything at the moment. I stepped outside, picked up the box and headed towards the same entrance I had used last night. I didn't know if my attempt at a ruse would work, but it was all I had. Hopefully, everyone would be so busy with wedding preparations that no one would think twice about a stranger carrying a package away from the house.

I passed by a few people who didn't even glance my way and then I was free. I stepped out onto the little side street, dropped the box, and began walking towards where I'd hidden my bags. I didn't know what to do now. Everything I owned was in these two bags. I'd had no plans besides finding Nami. No hotel reservations, no idea of where to go or what to do. I had money and the ability to get even more with a simple phone call and a new bank account.

What good would any of that do me, I thought. I could get a room, but to what end? Saja was beautiful, no doubt, but I had no purpose for being here. No purpose at all, in fact. I was worse off than I'd been when I'd left Philadelphia after Piper.

Piper. I almost laughed. She'd chosen Julien over me and had then told me not to give up on love. Great advice. Love was a joke. It didn't matter, and what was worse, I should've already known this. Duty and honor. Some people respected those. More respected money. Maybe that's what I should do. Find good investments. Make myself even richer than I already was. I'd have women hanging all over me. Gold diggers, but at least I'd know what they were.

I trudged down the sidewalk, ignoring the taxi that passed by. I'd been so sure that when I found Nami, everything would magically fall into place. We'd run away together and plan our future. Whatever she wanted was what I would want.

Only she'd said what she wanted, and it wasn't me.

I felt a faint crack in the numbness. The pain was coming soon and I didn't think anger would be enough to keep it at bay much longer.

Chapter 12

Nami

I heard myself say his name, but there was no conscious thought to it, only my need for him. It was something deep and primal, instinctual. He was in pain and I wanted to go to him, help him, take it away, but I was the cause of that pain. And I had my own to deal with. It was deep and excruciating, like I was tearing apart. The need to go to him only made it worse as I resisted it.

But I had to resist. If I went to him now, I wouldn't be able to give him up, no matter the cost. I'd follow him anywhere, go wherever he wanted. I would leave my family, my home, my responsibilities. The would-be marriage would never happen. My sister would take my place and what would be, would be. Saja would prosper, just as it always had. My parents were young and healthy. They would continue to rule for years. Who knew, maybe, in the future they'd accept my choice and things could be different.

I couldn't risk it though, no matter how much I wanted to. I couldn't take the chance that my parents would try to mold Halea, marry her off as soon as she turned eighteen. It was less than two years away, not enough time for me to convince my parents to change centuries of tradition. And it wouldn't be enough time with Reed. I knew that as soon as I heard the announcement of Halea's engagement, I'd come back. Every moment more I spent with Reed, the harder it would be to leave him if I had to. Better to make a clean break now.

As he walked out of the room and out of my life, I continued to tell myself that I'd done the best thing possible for both of us. Reed needed to forget me, forget that any of this had happened.

Involuntarily, my eyes dropped to the bed. The sheets were still in disarray, the evidence of what we'd done clear. I suddenly needed to be elsewhere. I couldn't stay in this room, the scent of sex and Reed thick in the air. I forced myself not to run. The maids would come in to clean and I couldn't risk any of them figuring out what I'd done.

I went through the motions automatically. Making the bed, straightening things. Lighting a few scented candles. I walked around the room, focusing on the least little thing that might give away my secret. The tension inside me was building, coiling me tighter and tighter until I needed release.

I pulled my robe more securely around my waist and knocked on the door. A moment later, I heard the lock click. Tomas opened the door and stepped aside, letting me out into the hallway. I didn't really want to be in the palace, but if I'd gone out to the grounds the same way Reed had, someone would figure it out and I wouldn't be able to use that particular exit if I really needed it in the future.

I almost laughed as I walked out of the room. I wasn't sure what I thought I'd use it for. Sneak out for another night on the town? I wasn't going anywhere soon. I didn't even get to have a honeymoon like a normal person. The Princess of Saja spent her honeymoon touring the country with her new husband, meeting the people.

The marble was cool beneath my feet and I could hear the footsteps of the guards behind me. Even in my own home, they were there, following. Watching. I wondered how many would come on my honeymoon. I supposed I should be thankful that Saja tradition no longer dictated that there be witnesses for the consummation of the marriage.

I turned down a short hallway and went into the bathroom. I didn't actually need to use it, but it was the only possible way for me to get rid of my bodyguards. I stayed inside for a minute. I didn't know where I wanted to go or what I wanted to do. Only that I wanted to do it alone.

I slipped out of the other door and cut through the library. I wanted to be outside. There was something about fresh air and sunshine that spoke of freedom more than the richest palace in the world. And freedom was what I craved. Freedom to love and be myself, to make my own choices. I wouldn't ever have that freedom, but I could at least, for a short time, have the illusion of it.

The palace gardens were quite beautiful, perfectly maintained and lush with exotic flowers that were both native to Saja and ones brought in from around the world. My parents often took people into the gardens to impress them. That wasn't where I wanted to go though. What most people didn't know was that there was a small alcove just off of the garden where nature had been allowed to take its course. Wild roses native only to Saja covered the stone walls and the paths were overgrown. I'd often gone there as a child when I wanted to be alone or when I was upset.

Although, I had to admit, my childhood fears and hurts were nothing like what I was feeling right now. I'd never had a broken heart before, not even a childhood crush like most children had. I'd had my fair share of hurts and slights. Even being a princess hadn't kept me from the cruelty of gossip and fake friends. If anything, being who I was had made it worse. But still, nothing could compare to what I was feeling now.

Leaving Reed in Venice had been insanely difficult and it had hurt, but it was nothing like this. I'd been able to tell myself that it had been a simple one-night stand, a crazy fling that I'd get over soon enough. And then he'd come for me. I couldn't brush aside what that had meant. Something had shifted between us.

I didn't know if it had happened when I'd opened the door and saw him or when I'd kissed him, but I did know that by the time I let him into my bedroom, every touch meant more. Neither of us had said anything about it, but I'd known he'd felt it too.

He'd been right. The moment I'd seen him, I should have made him go. Told him about the engagement and sent him on his way. I would've been sad, I knew, but I wouldn't feel like my heart was being ripped from my chest. It was crazy to feel so strongly for someone I barely knew, but I couldn't deny it.

"Princess Nami."

I jumped, stepping off the path and nearly crushing a few bright yellow flowers. I put my hand on my chest, feeling my heart pound against my palm.

"I apologize if I startled you."

Tanek stepped out of the shadow of what I thought was a fruit tree of some kind. The paths through the garden were the same, but the flora had changed since I'd last been here.

"Sorry, I was lost in thought." I managed not to stammer, but it was a close thing. "A lot on my mind."

"I imagine so," he said with a charming smile. "A wedding and a honeymoon are no small feat."

I nodded and stepped back onto the path. I wasn't entirely sure what to say to him. He was going to be my husband and I didn't know how to talk to him. He held out his arm. I didn't want to touch him or have a discussion. All I wanted to do was be alone and cry.

But, I was a princess and princesses rarely got what they wanted, contrary to what most people thought. I smiled at Tanek and hooked my arm through his.

The height difference between us wasn't as much as it was between Reed and I, and I found myself able to look up at Tanek without getting a crick in my neck. I tried studying him objectively, seeing him as I would have if last night, if Venice, hadn't happened. He was handsome, with fairly rugged features. That was good. The people would subconsciously trust him more than they would a 'pretty boy', as the girls in America might say. Even if I was ruler, they would want someone who appeared strong at my side.

"May I ask a question?" Tanek asked, breaking the silence.

"Of course." We went along the curve of the path, away from my private garden. Tanek would share my bed and my life, but I would keep at least one thing for myself.

"Why are you out in the garden in your robe?" His voice was pleasant, but something in me squirmed.

"I woke up and was in the mood for some fresh air." I stopped as the path took us between a small copse of trees. "I missed the gardens while I was away."

"That is right," he said as he released my arm and stepped in front of me. "You attended college in America."

"I did." I resisted the urge to step away, to put some distance between us. I had to get used to it at one time or another, and considering the wedding was in a couple days, it'd probably be a good idea to do it sooner rather than later.

"Did you enjoy your time there?" He reached up to twist a curl around his finger.

When his knuckles brushed against my cheek, it was all I could do not to flinch. His touch was unfamiliar, I told myself. That was all. But Reed's touch had once been the same and I'd reacted differently from that first moment. I'd wanted his hands on my body, his arms, his lips...

I gave myself a mental shake and tried to remember the question. "Yes," I said. "I enjoyed myself."

"I thought so." He took another step towards me, something darkening his eyes. "How much did you enjoy yourself, I wonder?"

My heart thumped painfully against my ribcage. My instincts screamed at me to run, but I was a princess. The future queen of Saja. I did not run from anyone. I squared my shoulders.

"What, exactly, are you implying?" I made my voice as cold as possible.

He put his hand on my waist. "How far did the American boys get?" His hand slid up and grasped my breast.

I jerked back and my palm cracked against his cheek. "How dare you! How dare you speak to me in such a manner, touch me without my permission!" My face was flaming, my temper flaring back to the surface from where it had retreated under hurt. "I am the princess. *Your* ruler."

Tanek's cheek was red, but his eyes were blazing. Before I could react, he grabbed my arm and jerked me towards him. I opened my mouth to scream. I'd have him in jail for this. His fist sank into my stomach, driving the air from my lungs so that all I could do was gasp.

"You are a princess, but you do not rule me." He hissed, his face an inch from mine. "I am to be your husband and you will learn your place."

He shoved his hand between the folds of my robe, groping my breast. His fingers twisted my nipple cruelly, sending pain shooting through me. I cried out, but it wasn't much of a sound.

"Perhaps what you need is to know what it means to

216

be a wife." He released my breast and pushed his hand between my legs.

I fought against him, pressing my thighs together. He let go of my arm and buried his fingers in my hair, yanking my head back. He pulled at the belt of my robe as he dragged me off the path and threw me to the ground.

"How many?" He asked as he pressed his knee into my chest. "How many men did you take, whore?"

I glared at him, hitting at him, for all the good it did. I could barely breathe and my blows were weak. I felt the adrenaline racing through my veins, but it didn't do me any good without oxygen.

"First I shall make you mine." He began to unbuckle his pants. "Then I will punish you for allowing someone else to take what is mine." He wrapped his hand around my throat and leaned down so that his lips were next to my ear. As the world began to go gray, he whispered, "I will be your king and you will obey me."

As he shoved my legs apart, I prayed that the darkness would come and keep me.

Chapter 13

Reed

The capital of Saja, it turned out, had several nice hotels in varying price ranges, all located within walking distance of one of their beautiful beaches. It was the kind of place people would visit and call paradise. The kind of place men would take their wives on their honeymoon, on special anniversaries.

I snorted a laugh and turned away from the window. I'd gotten the best room at the best hotel, almost out of habit rather than any real desire to have a nice room. I hardly noticed it, processing main room, kitchenette, bathroom, bedroom. No details. No appreciation for anything around me.

I walked into the bathroom, stripping as I went. I was exhausted physically, emotionally and mentally. Between the jet lag and the lack of sleep last night, I would've been half-dead on my feet even if I hadn't been through hell emotionally. I stood under the shower spray, barely registering if the water was hot or cold. I was still wrapped in that numb cocoon, but I knew it was like an eggshell, fragile and ready to break at any moment.

I toweled off, dropping it at the foot of the bed before I climbed under the covers. I didn't care that it was still morning, I just wanted to sleep. I supposed I should've been thankful for the jet lag and lack of sleep since I was too tired to overthink anything, then I sank down towards the darkness. For a moment, I saw a flash of Nami's face, of her eyes, and had a sudden, sharp fear that vanished as I fell asleep.

I woke up hours later, with no idea of how much time had passed, only the strange disorienting feeling that came with sleeping during the day. I rolled over and squinted at the clock. Four o'clock. I was never going to get back on the right schedule if I didn't get up now. I could still manage to get to sleep tonight, even if it wasn't until late.

I sat up, rubbing my eyes. My stomach growled and I remembered that I hadn't really eaten much of anything over the past two days. I wasn't hungry in the sense that I wanted to eat, but I knew I needed to. I didn't want to try to figure things out or try to make any sort of decision when I wasn't thinking clearly.

I picked up the phone and called down for room service. Fortunately, I didn't have to wade through native cuisines as they had plenty of other options. I picked a roast beef sandwich and some random sides because they seemed to be the easiest rather than caring anything about appetizing. It also seemed to be a fairly quick preparation as they knocked less than fifteen minutes later. I was halfway to the door before I realized I was naked and had to stop and grab my towel. I wrapped it around my waist, accepted the cart and settled on the sofa to eat.

I didn't really taste anything, more focused on not thinking than I was on the food. I should be thinking. The thoughts were there, buzzing at the back of my mind like bees, but not the nice little honey bees we were supposed to like. No, these were angry bees, ones that wanted to sting and kill.

I sighed and put down what was left of my sandwich. As much as I didn't want to, I needed to figure out what I was going to do now. I'd spent my time in Philadelphia thinking about getting here, and not much about what came after. I'd assumed Nami and I would figure things out when it came time for that. I'd never even considered what I'd do if she didn't want me. Sure, I'd known that was a possibility, but I'd put it up there with the possibility of my plane crashing on the way here. Something that could happen, but a remote possibility.

The thing was, I really didn't believe she didn't want me. Granted, she'd told me to leave, but she'd also said this was her duty. That meant she wasn't making the decision based on her feelings for me. I just didn't know what to do with that information.

If only I had more time, I was certain I could convince her that I was the right choice for her. The realization hit me and I swore under my breath. I didn't need to convince her. I needed to convince her parents.

Nami felt that it was her duty to marry who her parents chose because that person would be the best for the country. I'd been thinking all this time that I needed to take Nami away from here, that she needed to escape Saja as much as I had Philadelphia. She loved her country and her family though. She didn't necessarily want to get away from them or not be queen. She could still do that and be with me.

If I could convince her parents to let her have a choice in the matter.

I wasn't exactly some pauper bent on marrying her for her wealth or title. I wasn't royalty or anything like that, but my name did mean something back home. With my liquidated assets, I had plenty of money to bring to the table, enough to prove that my interest wasn't financially motivated. I could tell them that I'd fallen for her before I'd known she was a princess. I'd never reveal that we slept together, but I'd at least be able to tell them that we'd spent time together and that I loved their daughter.

I could also tell them how my parents had forced me into a loveless marriage and how badly that had ended. If her parents truly loved her, they would see that they needed to change their traditions and allow her to choose a husband. And if she chose me, I'd agree to sign whatever they wanted. Hand over my assets. Pledge my loyalty. Renounce my citizenship if it would mean Nami and I could be together. They couldn't fail to see my dedication to Nami if I did all of that.

There was no guarantee it would work. No way of knowing if they'd even care that I loved her. In their minds, doing what was right for the country might be what was right for Nami. Securing her position as future queen, giving her a husband who would have the support and backing of the people. I had to consider that as well. Perhaps they wanted to be able to let Nami choose but knew that if she chose poorly, the people wouldn't follow her.

She'd been right when she'd said that I didn't understand, that I wasn't like her. I didn't know the people of Saja. I'd done as much research as I could while on the plane over here, but there wasn't a lot of information. It was an isolated country with no prominent citizens in any particular field. For all I knew, this isolation caused the people to be suspicious of outsiders. I'd gotten no feelings of animosity, but I appeared to be a tourist. A rich American here to spend money and strengthen their economy. Would they feel different if they knew I wanted to be a member of their royal family? Not to rule them, but simply because I loved one of them. Would love make a difference to them? Just because they were progressive enough to accept a female monarch didn't mean they would allow an outsider in.

There were hundreds of questions, thousands of possibilities, and no way of knowing without trying. Nami had told me to leave, that she was choosing Tanek, but I'd come too far to completely give up without even an attempt.

First thing tomorrow, I told myself. I'd go back to the palace, but not to sneak in this time. I'd ask to see the king and queen. I hoped they'd be intrigued enough at the idea of some random American man wanting to talk to them that they'd overlook the fact that I didn't have an appointment. Once there, I would tell them who I was and what I wanted. If they threw me out, at least I'd know I'd tried.

And what if they agreed? What if they said Nami could choose without losing her birthright? Was I willing to stay in Saja, a king in name while my wife ruled? Yes, I thought, I would do that. I didn't care about the power and I'd already made up my mind that I wasn't going back to Philadelphia anytime soon.

Then there was the alternative. What if her parents allowed her the choice, but she didn't choose me? What if, once she'd met Tanek, she'd fallen for him, realized that what she felt for me was nothing more than the thrill of the forbidden, that she wanted a man of Saja at her side, someone who understood her world. I wasn't sure my heart could take another blow like that, especially not with Nami. I'd run to Europe to escape the pain when Piper had chosen Julien over me. Where could I go if it happened again? Where else could I run?

I had a sudden and laughable flash of me in Australia with surfers and kangaroos. I didn't laugh though. Nothing about this was funny.

Time crept by, each agonizing second worse than the last. I was torn between elation at my plan and the certainty of success, and depression at the thought that it would fail miserably, that I'd end up adrift again, no future, no plans, no hope. Logically, I knew it was foolish to put all of my hopes and dreams into a woman, but this wasn't exactly a normal situation. Everything hinged on what happened tomorrow.

I'd always loved the Robert Frost poem about the two

roads and taking the one less traveled, mostly because I'd never done that myself. I could honestly say that, until I'd met Piper, I'd never actually felt like I was at that fork. I'd screwed things up with her, no matter how I ended up feeling about her, but I wasn't going to do that now. I didn't know what would happen tomorrow, but I knew that, no matter what, I'd be on one of two paths that I'd never even considered before.

I stayed up until midnight before heading to bed again. This time, my busy brain was louder than my need for sleep and I spent hours tossing and turning. Some of it was the time difference, but enough was my inability to turn off my thoughts. It was well into the early morning hours before I finally fell asleep. I woke a few hours later, still tired, but at least coherent enough to think straight.

I showered and shaved, scraping off two days' worth of stubble, and then went about the task of figuring out what to wear. I had a suit and a tux in my bags, but I wasn't sure if I wanted to appear in either one. I didn't know enough about Saja practices and customs to know if too formal was bad. Would they see the suit as me trying to impress them? It was an expensive one. Or, would they take it as a sign that I respected them, understanding their position? The tux was definitely too much.

In the end, I decided that a suit and a humble attitude would be the best possible combination. I'd show her family that I had money, but that I didn't care about it. Some guys couldn't pull that off, generally because they were lying, but since I really didn't care about money, I could do it. It was a fine line to walk. That was good though. It gave me something to concentrate on besides worrying about what could happen. And that, at least, I had some control over.

By mid-morning, I was ready to go. Well, at least physically. I was dressed and looked like my old self, the CEO who'd been managing his family's company for years. The son of a prominent Philadelphia family. I wasn't conceited, but I knew that I was considered quite the catch back home, and if my time in Europe was any indication, I wasn't exactly considered unappealing outside of the States either. But I wasn't trying to impress Nami. I needed to impress her parents, and I had a feeling that my normal charming self might not be up to the task.

I pushed aside the negative thought and headed down to the front of the hotel to catch a cab. There weren't very many cabs on the island, but it was easy enough to find one here. I got the same strange look as before when I asked to be taken to the palace, but he didn't pry, which was good because I didn't have any idea what I'd say.

When I got out at the gates, my heart was hammering and my mouth was dry. This was it. I could either get back in the cab and give up or I could do what I came to do. I took a breath as the cab drove off. I didn't really have a strategy here, so I figured the most obvious thing was my best bet. I walked up to the gate and hit the buzzer.

A minute later, a heavily muscled guy with what looked like a very big gun on his belt approached. He wasn't smiling, but he also wasn't pointing the gun, so I took that as a good sign.

"Hello." I was tempted to put my hands in my pockets but I didn't want him thinking I was reaching for something. I had to approach this place like I was walking up to the White House.

"American?" The guard seemed mildly amused, which I supposed was better than angry or wary.

I nodded and grinned. "My name's Reed Stirling and I'm from Philadelphia. I'd like to speak with the king and queen."

His eyes widened and, for a moment, I thought he was going to call the cops. Instead, he laughed. "And for what reason should I tell them you are here?"

Shit. I hadn't thought about that. I couldn't exactly tell this guy that I was in love with Nami. He'd either call someone to lock me up because I was crazy or think I was a threat. Besides, I had a feeling that wasn't something her family would want getting out, even if they did end up accepting me. I'd definitely have to be part of some big PR thing. I could, however, tell a partial truth.

"I met their daughter." I almost called her Nami and then remembered that wouldn't be how she was known here. "Princess Namisa. While she was in Paris. Saja sounded wonderful, so I came to visit, and I'd like to pay my respects."

He looked skeptical, but he didn't tell me to leave. He picked up his radio and said something in his native language. After a minute, someone answered back and the guard came over to the gate and punched in a code. The gate slid open and I stepped through. I stopped, letting the guard pat me down.

"The king and queen will see you in the receiving room."

Chapter 14

Reed

My first thought as I walked into the receiving room was that I was glad they hadn't taken me to their throne room – if they had one. This room was intimidating enough. I was rich and I'd seen the best of Philadelphia's best, but I was impressed. Expensive furnishings, beautiful artwork. I didn't even see the people for several seconds.

A pair that I felt confident assuming were the king and queen sat directly across from the door. They weren't on thrones, but I was willing to bet the chairs were at least a couple hundred thousand dollars. Their clothes were even more expensive than mine.

"May I present Mr. Reed Stirling of Philadelphia, Pennsylvania?" A man I couldn't see announced me and I stepped further into the room.

And that's when I saw her.

Nami was sitting at her father's other side, back straight, face carefully expressionless. A man sat next to her. He had black hair, ice blue eyes and an arrogant look that made me want to hit him. Then I saw his hand clasp Nami's possessively and my fingers curls into fists. If I hadn't suspected who he was before, I knew it now.

Tanek.

Nami's fucking fiancé.

I'd not really thought of him at all except in the vague idea of the engagement, but now I realized I hated him. Marrying Nami might not have been his choice any more than he was truly hers, but the way he was holding her hand said that he was staking his claim. He didn't know who I was, I was sure of it, but he was making sure I knew what his position here was.

"Mr. Stirling, I present King Amir, Queen Persephone, their daughter Princess Namisa and her betrothed, Tanek Nekane," the same man spoke again.

I gave a bit of a bow, feeling awkward as I did it, but based on the expression on the king and queen's faces, it had been the right thing to do.

"We do not find many Americans willing to make the appropriate gestures to royalty," King Amir spoke.

I gave a smile and a slight nod. I wasn't sure if they were the kind of monarchs who'd take offense with someone looking at them directly, but I figured I'd risk it. I wanted to see what I could of them, see what of Nami I could find. The physical part was easy. She looked like both of them. The personality was harder. I wondered from which she'd gotten her stubborn streak.

"You mentioned you met our daughter in Paris?" Queen Persephone spoke. Her tone was polite, but empty. She would've done well in business...and poker.

"I did." I risked a glance at Nami now, expecting to see her worried that I would give her away. She didn't look concerned though, or at least from what I could see. She wouldn't meet my gaze.

"And may I inquire just how that occurred?" King Amir asked.

I was on dangerous ground here, and I knew it. Anything I said to her parents could possibly hurt her, but with Tanek sitting right there, it could do even more damage. I opened my mouth to give them some sort of lie about how I'd met Nami, but I didn't get a chance.

228

"Mr. Stirling was on the train with me," Nami said. "From Paris to Venice. When the train was delayed, the two of us talked to pass the time."

The smile on my face felt fake, but I knew it looked fine. I'd had a lot of practice at home. I nodded as if in agreement. I would've preferred to keep it as close to the truth as possible, but she knew her parents. If this was the best transition into my declaration, then I'd go along with it. I just wished Nami's fucking fiancé would stop staring at me. I was nervous enough about proclaiming my feelings without him giving me the evil eye. I'd hoped to talk to the king and queen only, to convince them and then surprise Nami. But, if this was my only choice, I would do what needed to be done.

"Mr. Stirling is the head of his family's business in America," Nami continued. Her tone was pleasant, but there was no warmth in it. Nothing to let me know what she was thinking. "I believe he mentioned something about coming to Saja to determine if he might find business opportunities here."

"So you have come to introduce yourself and present us with a business proposal?" King Amir asked.

I kept my eyes on Nami for a few seconds longer, willing her to look at me, to show me what she was feeling. Was she saying this because she knew my real reason for being here and didn't want me to do it? Who was she more worried about me speaking to, her parents or her fiancé? Or did she think I'd tell too much?

I looked back at the king and queen. "I don't have a business proposal ready, your Majesties. I simply wished to meet you and establish an acquaintance in the hopes that we may someday have a working relationship."

I chose each work carefully. When Nami and I told them the truth, at least about what we meant to each other, my words could be interpreted different ways so they wouldn't think I'd been completely dishonest.

"That is quite enterprising of you."

229

I couldn't tell if Nami's father was impressed or being sarcastic in that subtle, annoying way that only members of high society – and apparently, nobility – could manage.

"Thank you," I said, giving a bland smile that he could either take as genuine or as me letting him know that I knew how he meant it.

"Now, Mr. Stirling, if you will please excuse us." Queen Persephone stood. "As a visitor, I am sure you have not heard, but Princess Namisa will be married on Saturday, and we have much planning to do."

"Of course." I resisted the urge to look at Nami again. The way the queen was looking at me made me think it was possible she suspected there was more to the story than we were saying. I didn't think that was a good thing, particularly based on what she'd just said. Nami's expression hadn't changed, and she still wasn't looking at me.

"Tomas and Kai will show you out," King Amir said.

Fuck.

The pair came towards me, their faces blank, but their eyes clearly said that if they had their way, they'd be throwing me rather than showing me, and making sure I had a few 'accidents' along the way. I smiled towards the king and queen one last time before turning around to allow myself to be escorted from the room. It took everything I had not to look at Nami again, but I could feel the tension radiating off of the two bodyguards and knew they were looking for any excuse to teach me a lesson.

We walked down the hallway towards the front doors, the guards half a step behind me so they could react if I tried to move. I wasn't dumb enough to run. Nami's parents would never accept me if I disrespected them in such a manner. I did need to see her though, talk to her alone. I needed her to know that I was willing to fight for her if she'd let me.

230

As we reached the front of the palace, another man opened the door, his face professionally blank. I stepped through the door, stopping as Kai grabbed my arm. His voice was low in my ear, but the volume didn't detract from the sincerity or the menace in his words.

"Stay away from the princess. If I see you again, I will present your balls to the king."

I didn't make any indication of acknowledgement, but he didn't seem to need one. He released my arm with a bit of a shove and I walked down the stairs. The front gates opened and I walked through them, turning the corner so that I was hidden from sight. I needed to figure out what I was going to do. I hadn't been able to complete my plan, so I didn't know where to go next.

I wasn't sure if it was smart to try for the other entrance again, so I began to walk in the opposite direction, hoping I'd be able to spot some way in. The security I'd seen had been good, but not fool-proof. It was clear that, while the royal family warranted protection, they weren't expecting some sort of attack. From what I'd read about Saja, it made sense. They were a peaceful country. Barely any crime at all, and only a small portion of it violent. Most of those were mild, like fist fights over stupid things, often while drunk. Saja had only one prison, and it had never been filled to capacity. In a country like this, excessive security would've been perceived as either a barrier between the people and their sovereign, or as a show of mistrust.

I fully planned to take advantage of that.

As I rounded the corner and headed along a quiet side street, I spotted something several yards ahead. A gate, barely big enough for one person to fit through, was opening. Covered with plants, I never would've known it was there, and based on how loudly it squeaked, it wasn't a commonly used entrance.

I wasn't sure if I should hide or hurry towards it and I stopped, caught in indecision. Then I saw a familiar figure step out onto the sidewalk.

"Nami." I breathed a sigh of relief and jogged towards her.

As I grew closer, I saw more than I had in the throne room. Her expression wasn't just impassive, but rather guarded, like there was something she didn't want me to see. Something else seemed off too, but I couldn't figure out what it was. She looked different, as if in the short time since I'd last seen her, something had changed.

"Why did you come, Reed?" Her voice was soft and she fixed her gaze at a point over my shoulder.

I reached for her hands, but she didn't respond, her fingers staying limp and cold in my hands. "I came for you. I want us to be together. I know you don't think it's possible, but I think I could convince your parents to give me a chance."

Now she did look at me, a moment of surprise flitting across her eyes before they went blank again. "Give you a chance?"

I nodded, sliding my hands up her arms until I was grasping her shoulders. "I'm not nobility, or from Saja, but I'm not from some poor, backward family. We're well-respected in Philadelphia." I didn't bother to add that our position in society was in a bit of peril at the moment. It wouldn't help things and I had no idea how long that trouble would even last. Rich people were easily distracted even if they never truly forgot.

She started to shake her head, but I kept going before she could protest.

"I have money so it's clear I'm not after that. I know how to behave around high society so I wouldn't embarrass you. I'd sign any sort of paperwork they asked. Renounce my citizenship and become a naturalized citizen of Saja. Whatever it would take to show your parents that I'm serious."

Her voice was soft. "It's too late."

My smile faltered. "No," I said. "I refuse to accept

232

that."

"Contracts have been signed." She lifted her chin, but didn't meet my gaze. "The wedding on Saturday is a mere formality. For all intents and purposes, Tanek is my husband."

"No," I repeated, my tone harder in disbelief and denial.

I closed the distance between us, reaching out to cup the back of her head as I lowered my mouth to hers. Her lips parted with a gasp of surprise and I slid my tongue between them. For a brief, wonderful moment, her body relaxed into mine, her mouth pliant as my tongue explored. She was mine.

Then her hands were on my chest, pushing rather than pulling. The kiss broke, leaving me gasping, my body aching. I stepped back, hands clenched at my sides. I wanted her so badly, but her actions had said to stop, and I did.

"What's done is done, Reed." She folded her arms across her middle as if hugging herself. "Go home. There's nothing for you here."

She stepped back through the hidden gate and I heard it latch behind her. I stayed there for a long time, but she didn't return. It was over.

Chapter 15

Nami

The white silk whispered against my legs as I followed him into the bedroom. It had been a beautiful wedding, the kind most girls would dream of. Flowers had been everywhere, each one chosen specifically for the occasion. Their scents had been perfectly blended so that the effect wasn't overwhelming. The palace ballroom had been decorated in sprays of white and gold, every inch of the place cleaned so that it had shone. The gold bridesmaid's dresses had been simple, elegantly cut for each bridesmaid to flatter the different figures. After all, a royal wedding wasn't about the bride.

Through it all, however, I hadn't been able to stop thinking about the wedding night. Ancient traditions would have stated that at least one of my parents, or a selected member of nobility be in the room as the marriage was consummated, but, fortunately, that practice had been discontinued generations ago. My father's great-grandfather had been the last to follow that particularly embarrassing scenario.

Tradition did still, however, require my parents, the wedding party and certain select guests, to escort us to the bridal suite. Last night had been my final night in my childhood bedroom. Those quarters were now being emptied and cleaned in preparation for a nursery. My new quarters would be with my husband.

As the doors shut behind us, I didn't even see the beauty of our room, the candles that had been lit to offer us dim, romantic lighting. All I saw was him. He turned towards me and I realized my hands were shaking.

It was silly of me to be nervous. This wasn't my first time, or even our first time. I already knew his body, knew the pleasure it could give me. But this wasn't like other times. We were married. When we came together tonight, it would be not only with my parents' blessing, but with that of the entire country. He would be my king, the father to my children.

He came towards me, his dark eyes nearly black in the dim light. He reached out and carefully removed each of the decorative pins that had kept my wayward curls manageable. With each one, he let his fingers graze my skin, sending a blaze of heat through me. By the time he was finished, the shaking in my hands came from an entirely new place.

I pushed his jacket from his shoulders, letting it fall to the floor as I moved on to his shirt. The desire inside me grew with every inch of skin revealed. He was so beautiful, his body a work of art.

It wasn't until both of us were naked that he finally kissed me, one hand buried in my hair, the other at the small of my back. I pressed my body against his as our tongues twined together, my nipples hardening with the friction. His cock was half-hard against my stomach and I could feel it swelling even as my own body responded.

I dimly wondered if it would always be like this, if I would always want him so badly that it hurt. It wasn't just the physical desire, the aching to be filled. It was him and being close to him. Our bodies joined, souls coming together. I'd always considered myself a complete person before, but with him, I knew I'd been only half of myself.

He laid me on the bed and propped himself up on one elbow to give his free hand the chance to explore. He started at my face, his fingers tracing each eyebrow, then down to my cheekbones. When he ran his finger along my lips, I parted them, darting out my tongue to touch his skin.

"Do you have any idea how beautiful you are?" he asked as his hand continued its journey, sliding down my throat, then across my collarbone, before dancing between my breasts.

I reached up and pushed back his golden hair. "You're beautiful," I said sincerely.

He smiled, a full smile that made his entire face light up. He caught my hand, holding it in place as he turned his head and kissed my palm. When he released my hand, he lowered his head to my breasts, placing light kisses across the skin. My eyes wanted to close, but I kept them open, wanting to watch him take my nipple between his lips.

I gasped at the heat of his mouth, then swore as he began to suck on the overly sensitive flesh. His hand caressed my thigh, adding to the heat already pooling in my belly. My back arched, wanting more. When he raised his head, I made a sound of protest.

"Shh, baby." He shifted his hand to my stomach, his thumb making small circles on my skin. "We don't have to rush. No one's going to stop us." He kissed my neck, my jaw, my lips.

He was right, I knew. We were married. The matching platinum bands on our fingers said that we were going to be together forever. We weren't going to be interrupted by Tomas and Kai. There would be no panic over whether or not we should be doing this. No rush to hurry because we had limited time. It wasn't just that it was no longer wrong, but rather that it was expected.

I was pulled out of my thoughts by the feeling of Reed's hand sliding around to my inner thigh. My eyelids fluttered as his tongue slowly circled my breast, moving up my golden skin to my nipple. As his fingertip ghosted over my lower lips, I finally let my eyes close.

The sensations surrounded me, overwhelmed me. There was the scent of him, spicy and masculine. Something so uniquely him that I would know it anywhere. The feel of him. His skin. The shape of his hands, his mouth. The heat from his body and mouth.

I moaned as his teeth scraped my nipple. How did he know that I needed those little pinpricks of pain? That my body craved an intensity that gentle caresses couldn't give me.

A finger circled my entrance and I squirmed. He chuckled, the vibration moving down through my breast even as he slid his finger inside.

I moaned, but I needed more. My eyes opened and I reached over to clutch at Reed's shoulders.

"Please." The word became a cry as a second finger joined the first. He curled them and my entire body went stiff.

Even while I was still in the midst of orgasm, I felt him shove his way inside me, stretching me, opening me. I wanted to scream, but it was as if all the air had been pushed from my lungs. The intensity of what I was feeling, physically, emotionally, it was almost too much.

Our bodies rocked against each other, friction and heat. My nails raked his back and his teeth worked over my skin. My world was narrowed down to our two bodies and where they were joined. He was mine and I was his, our hearts, minds and bodies made one. The rings didn't make it so. We'd been this way from the first moment we'd come together.

"Mine," I whispered possessively in his ear.

"Yes," he said. "Yours. And you are mine."

"I am," I agreed. I could feel another climax building. "Forever."

My muscles began to tremble...

I jerked awake, my body flushed and shaking with the force of the dream. I'd woken just before coming, leaving me bereft and tense. For a moment, I thought that was what had woken me, my body not able to take a second orgasm and still stay asleep. Then I realized that wasn't it at all.

Someone was in my room.

My heart leaped into my throat as I saw the shadowed figure sitting on the edge of my bed. Reed had come back. He'd known how I felt, the feelings I'd refused to name or think about, and had come to me.

The light next to the bed suddenly switched on and I swallowed a scream.

"Tanek." My voice came out more breathless than I wished it would have. I grabbed my blanket, pulling it up to my neck. I saw something flicker in his eyes and knew it had been the wrong move.

"You seemed to be enjoying your dream," he said.

"You should not be in here." I straightened, trying to regain my composure. My heart was pounding, the adrenaline racing through my system making me hyperaware of everything.

I'd scrubbed my skin nearly raw, but I could still feel every place he'd touched me. I hadn't wanted to look in the mirror this morning, but I'd forced myself, knowing I'd need to make sure I chose clothes that would cover the bruises. Tanek had either been lucky or he'd known what he was doing. He hadn't made a mark on my face and the ones on my neck were faint enough to be covered with make-up. The rest of me was another story.

I resisted the urge to pull my legs up. Aside from the fact that I didn't want Tanek to see another gesture made in response to him, I also knew it'd hurt enough to show on my face. He hadn't been satisfied to take me only once. I refused to think about the things he'd done to me, not knowing if I'd be able to maintain my composure if I remembered.

"I do not believe you should be telling me what I should or should not be doing." Tanek's voice was low and threatening. "On Saturday, I will be your husband and I will do as I please."

My temper began to rise, pushing through the fear and the hurt. Who the hell did he think he was? I'd agreed to marry my parents' choice because it was the right thing to do for Saja. I hadn't said anything to them today about what had happened, because I was still trying to figure out the best way to do it. Just going to the hospital and reporting an assault wasn't exactly an option for me.

"Get out of my room." I spoke through gritted teeth. "And I want you out of my home."

I expected anger, violence, outright refusal. What I didn't expect was laughter. A sharp, sardonic chuckle that managed to both piss me off and frighten me.

"I will leave your room...when I am ready." He reached over and grabbed my wrist, squeezing until I winced. "And I will not be leaving this house. MY house. I will be king and Saja will be mine."

He leaned closer and I could smell the alcohol on his breath. He wasn't drunk, but he wasn't entirely sober either.

"I will tell my parents what you did," I threatened.

"No," he said. "You will not, or I will tell them you were not a virgin when I took you."

My eyes narrowed. "They will not believe you."

"Don't be so sure about that," he said, his eyes cold. "But it doesn't matter. You will never say a word about what happened to anyone. Remember, accidents happens. It wouldn't surprise me if suddenly an accident happened that would leave me free to wed another. A real virgin."

I felt like I'd been punched in the stomach. He wouldn't.

"Your sister, Halea, is a virgin, I am certain. For now." He smiled. "I will spend the next two years teaching her how to please me, and then I will marry her.

240

She will be queen in name until she gives me a son, and then she will join you."

"Keep your fucking hands off of my sister!" I put as much venom into my voice as I could, but the words fell flat.

A sharp pain shot through me as I felt his strong fingers dig deep into the skin of my arm. He hissed in my face. "Then you better do everything I fucking ask of you. Pretend all you must, but you *will* obey me, bare my children...my son, our future king. It's you or Halea. Your choice."

He would do it, I knew. He would kill me, rape Halea, force her to marry him and most likely kill her too. I'd seen it in his eyes. He was capable of anything.

Before, I'd chosen to marry him to protect Halea from our parents forcing her onto the throne. Now, I knew I had to choose Tanek to save not only my life, but my sister's.

Chapter 16

Reed

I should've left Saja right after Nami had rejected me...again. The entire island was buzzing about the wedding. Even staying in my hotel room didn't keep me safe. The staff was cheery and constantly asking if I'd heard the wonderful news. Looking out the window was just as bad. The entire capitol was getting ready. There were flowers and streamers and all sorts of other things I might've found interesting if they hadn't meant the woman I loved was about to marry someone else.

Maybe that was why I'd stayed. To punish myself for what I'd done. For what I'd failed to do.

I ran my hand through my hair. I'd spent Friday pacing and trying to avoid the view while smiling politely at the people who brought my room service. I hadn't slept at all Thursday night, and last night hadn't been much better. Now, it was just after dawn and I didn't know what to do.

There would've been flights yesterday. Not many since it wasn't a big airport, but enough to get me out, especially if I hadn't cared where I was going. But I hadn't gone yesterday. Even though today was a Saturday and most airports ran on Saturday, today was a holiday of sorts. Nothing was open. Even the hotel had informed me that, during the wedding, no services would be available.

The palace was huge, but not big enough to support all of Saja's citizens, so the whole thing would be broadcast on Saja's only local station.

I wasn't planning on watching it. Or, at least, not on TV. I'd had a very bad idea that had woken me before the sun had come up, and I was currently arguing with myself about it.

I should go home. Back to Philly with my tail between my legs. My parents would be more than happy to let me take over again, no matter how I'd left things. The last time I'd seen Piper and Julien, it had been a bit awkward, but I'd gotten the impression that they wouldn't have been against a real friendship. And no matter what Piper had told me, I knew she'd understand why I'd given up. I could pursue Nami to the ends of the earth, but if she didn't want me, there wasn't anything I could do about it.

The thing was, I still didn't entirely believe that she honestly wanted Tanek. Something had happened after I left her. Something had changed that had made her choose to not believe in me. I didn't know what it was, but a part of me still didn't believe it. And I was pretty sure I wasn't going to believe it until I saw that ring on her finger...maybe not even then.

That was why I had to go. I couldn't just sit in my room and watch it on television. I had to actually be present, in the room, hear her say her vows. I needed to know that she was going to follow through, that she had gotten the life she wanted. I had to see that she didn't hesitate during any part of the ceremony, see that she meant what she said.

It would be painful. Awful. One of the worst things in the world to watch, especially if she went through with it. It would take all of my willpower to stay silent if they went with the traditional question about anyone speaking

244

up if they knew why a couple shouldn't be married. I was also pretty sure that I'd get in some serious trouble if any of the royal family, the bodyguards or the fucking fiancé saw me.

But I had to go.

I knew it deep down in my gut, and I'd known it all day yesterday. If she was going to stop the wedding, I had to be there to stand with her when she did it. If she went through with it, I had to be there to see it happen so I could move on. I still wasn't entirely sure how I would manage to do that, but I figured I should probably take things one step at a time. After all, I was about to do something so stupid it could land me in Saja's only jail if I was caught.

My plan was pretty simple. I already knew where the service entrance was and I also knew rich people. They didn't really look at the help. I didn't have anything that could let me pass for kitchen staff or something like that, but I did have a tux that I could wear and pretend to be one of the staff hired for inside the house. Most of the time, it wasn't about the clothes anyway. It was the attitude.

A couple hours later and I was standing inside the ballroom of the Saja palace. I'd gone through the open service gate with a huge vase of flowers, then spent the rest of the time before the wedding letting myself be ordered around by some high-strung woman in a serious-looking peach business suit. I'd waited until the last possible minute and managed to slip into the back of the room. Huge statues stood around the edges of the room and I tucked myself into the shadows. I knew I'd be practically invisible now, and that was what I wanted.

The bridesmaids came first. I recognized the girl I'd seen that night, the one I knew had to be Halea. The girl Nami was sacrificing her own happiness for. I had to admit, when I looked at that sweet, innocent face, I couldn't blame her. I didn't even know the girl and I wanted to protect her.

I turned with the rest of the crowd to watch as Nami walked in. Her dress was simple and elegant. White silk fitted to complement not only her coloring, but her figure as well. There was no veil or elaborate train, and the dress itself was relatively unadorned. I wasn't really paying much attention to the dress, however. I was too busy watching her face.

She was staring straight ahead, eyes fixed on her destination. While she was smiling, I could tell it was fake. She didn't look at her fiancé the entire way and, as I glanced towards Tanek, I saw that he wasn't looking at Nami either. He might've been turned in that general direction, but he wasn't watching her.

I didn't understand how they could do this. It was clear that neither one of them loved the other. Hell, they barely knew each other. How could Nami agree to marry this guy? Him, I got. Nami was rich and would be the queen someday. By marrying her, he'd be king and his kids would get to rule Saja one day. And if what Nami had said was true, he could fool around as much as he wanted because his bastards wouldn't have a claim on the throne. Nami's line was the one that mattered. So long as he got her pregnant, it wouldn't matter who else he knocked up.

My hands clenched at my sides. I didn't want to think about Nami conceiving a child with him, with anyone besides me. The realization hit me hard enough that I physically felt it. It wasn't that I just didn't want her to sleep with him. Yes, I hated the thought of him touching her, kissing her, being inside her, but it was more than that. I could picture her in my mind's eye, her stomach swollen with a child, and I knew that I wanted it to be my child.

I'd never really thought about kids before, not in any real sense. With Britni, we'd been expected to have a child, but I'd never imagined it, and certainly had never pictured Britni pregnant. I'd always wanted kids, but the idea had been far off, in a distant future, no matter how the years had passed. I hadn't even thought about them with Piper. Even though I'd insisted that I was in love with her, I'd never once imagined a future beyond a wedding. I hadn't considered what it would be like to grow old with her, what kind of mother she would've been. I knew she'd be a good one and when I thought of her and Julien having a child, I liked the picture I saw in my head.

I didn't want just a few more days or months with Nami. I wanted forever and everything that came with it. I wanted the strange food cravings and being yelled at in the delivery room. I wanted late night feedings and irritability from lack of sleep. I wanted the terrible two's and teenage rebellion. I wanted all of that as long as she was at my side. Dark curls streaked with silver. Aching bones and fading eyesight. All of the things that came with old age, they didn't scare me when I thought of going through them with her.

Her voice drew me back to the present. She was reciting her vows, repeating words similar to the ones I'd said not too long ago. I supposed it was hypocritical of me to question her choice, or to assume that her fiancé was only after the power and money. Hadn't I been there, marrying a woman I didn't love because it was what my parents expected of me? How could I fault either of them when I'd made the same choice? I would have regretted it now if it hadn't been for the fact that, had I not married Britni, Piper never would have chosen Julien and I wouldn't have left Philadelphia in the first place, which meant I never would've met Nami.

I had sometimes wondered if I hadn't married Britni, if Piper and I would have lasted. I knew we would've at least been together for a while because we'd had a true physical attraction to each other and had enjoyed spending time together. What I didn't know was if it would've led to a life in happiness or if she would've come to the same conclusion, that we really didn't love each other, not in the way we needed to.

As Nami and her fiancé joined hands, my heart twisted. It was almost over and Nami hadn't stopped it.

Had it been this way for Piper, I wondered. Had she felt sick to her stomach? Like her heart was being ripped from her chest? Like she couldn't get enough air into her lungs? I'd thought a lot about my wedding day over the short time Britni and I had been married. I'd thought about what would've happened if I'd stopped the ceremony, told Britni that I couldn't do it. If I'd walked down the aisle and claimed Piper right then. I'd never once tried to imagine what she must've been going through during the ceremony.

Was there a difference though? She'd said herself that we weren't truly in love. What I felt for Nami was real. I knew it in every fiber of my being, every cell. I'd never believed in soulmates or true love, even with Piper. Nami made me question everything I'd ever known. I wasn't whole without her. She was the one. The only one.

I missed the pronouncement, but looked up just in time to see Tanek kiss her. It was a fairly chaste kiss, but I could see the possessiveness even from where I stood. Tanek was making it clear to everyone present that Nami was his.

I leaned against the wall as the couple were presented to their people. I no longer trusted my legs to hold me. The pair walked down the aisle, Nami's arm looped through Tanek's, their stride evenly matched, as if they moved in perfect sync. Neither of them looked at anyone in the crowd and I was glad. I didn't want Nami to see me, and more than that, I didn't want to see her face, meet her eyes. I didn't think I could bear it if I saw her look at me with pity.

The wedding was over and the reception would begin shortly, so I knew I needed to leave. I forced my legs under me and began to walk out the way I'd come. I wasn't nearly as careful, but I wasn't seen. I wouldn't have cared if I had been spotted. Nothing mattered anymore. It was over.

Chapter 17

Nami

I wasn't entirely sure what I was expecting from my wedding day, but I did know that, as a child, when I'd pictured getting married, I'd always thought I would at least be happy. I'd always known that I wouldn't be allowed to choose my spouse, but when I was young, I'd dreamed that the man my parents chose would still, somehow, be the man of my dreams. He'd be worthy of the title prince, and later, king. A fairy tale in which the couple has a happily ever after.

Of course, as I'd gotten older, I'd realized that those kinds of things didn't exist. Still, I'd hoped for a marriage like my parents at the very least. Theirs had been arranged, but I knew they cared for each other. I didn't know how deep that ran or what kind of love they had for each other, but I knew they had been faithful and I'd seen them share affection. If I could not marry the man of my choosing, at least I could take comfort in the fact that my parents had married the same way and had spent the last thirty years in a good marriage.

Not once had I considered the nightmare to come. Saja had a low crime rate and laws that quickly and harshly punished violent offenders. Domestic violence and child abuse were treated the same as any other violent crime. We had always prided ourselves on how safe our country was, for visitors as well as citizens. Even if I hadn't been a princess, I wouldn't have ever thought my future husband capable of hurting me. As princess, the idea had been ludicrous, unthinkable.

And yet, I'd had to carefully apply make-up on my arms and neck to cover the fading bruises. Even as I walked down the aisle towards Tanek, I experienced twinges of pain from his assault. It wasn't so bad that I let it show. Aside from not wanting anyone present to know how he'd hurt me, I refused to give Tanek the satisfaction of knowing I still felt it.

The thing was, I knew I wouldn't be able to avoid it later tonight. It was my wedding night, and consummation was expected. It didn't matter that he'd already fucked me, or that I hadn't been a virgin when he'd done it. We'd be expected to have sex, and there to be proof of it on our sheets tomorrow morning.

After the ceremony, there would be a reception where we would be expected to greet our guests and pretend to be content, if not happy. Even the regular people in Saja knew that the marriage was arranged, though I was sure most of them thought it was something romantic. The other high society people at the wedding would better understand the truth, but I would still be expected to play my part.

I pushed aside thoughts of what was to come and tried to focus on the now. I didn't exactly want to think about where I was now, but it was better than what was coming. I forced myself to focus on repeating the words my father said, a mix of the standard vows of several different religions. I didn't particularly care about any of them. I said what I had to say and that was enough.

When my father asked for anyone who protested the marriage to speak up, I tensed, half-expecting to hear Reed's voice declaring that I couldn't marry Tanek. I could imagine him saying he loved me and we were supposed to be together. I'd accepted my fate, but in that moment, I knew that if Reed had indeed shown up, I wouldn't have been able to turn him away.

I missed what my father said next, but I didn't need to hear it to know it had been him telling Tanek to kiss me. It was all I could do not to pull back and slap him as his mouth came down on mine. It was a fairly chaste kiss, the kind most would expect from a couple who barely knew each other, but it hadn't been our first. I hadn't been able to forget the feel of his lips, hard and demanding, his tongue nearly choking me.

I managed to get through the kiss without gagging and then took his arm as my father announced us. I allowed myself a quick moment to scan the crowd and my heart skipped a beat. Golden hair. Reed? Was it him, lurking in the shadows? Why would it be, though? I'd told him I'd made my choice. He'd probably been on a plane back to America that same afternoon. In fact, he was probably in bed with some gorgeous blonde right now, forgetting all about me.

Pain laced through me at the thought, but I kept a smile on my face. It wasn't a real one, but it was good enough to fool the people, if not my parents and my husband. Husband. I didn't even want to think the word, but I made myself dwell on it. I had no right to be jealous or hurt over anything Reed had done. I'd been the one who'd sent him away, who'd broken his heart.

Or maybe I was overestimating what we'd had, how he'd felt. Perhaps his heart had only been bruised alongside his ego. Perhaps I only wanted to think that he felt the same way I did, like my heart was being torn to shreds, every beat sending a new wave of pain through me. I'd felt like that from the moment I'd told Reed that I was choosing Tanek over him, and it had only gotten worse when Reed had showed up at the palace the next morning. Now, it was constant, a familiar presence that

I'd almost become accustomed to. I wondered if I'd become numb to it after a while, and if that would be a blessing. Would not feeling anything be better than feeling what I felt?

Time began to move in jerky leaps and bounds as I found myself being moved from one table to another, shaking hands, kissing cheeks. The wealthiest and most influential of Saja's people were here. Some I knew well from seeing them at various functions over the years, others were strangers in all but name. It didn't matter though. They all wanted the same things: make sure the king and I both knew that they were present. The king for now, me for the future.

I danced and smiled, saying all the right things and behaving in a perfectly pleasant manner. I let Tanek put his hand on my arm and shoulders, pretending that I didn't find being near him repulsive. I smiled at my parents, pretending that I didn't hate them for what they were doing to me. I supposed I'd eventually forgive them, but at the moment, all I felt towards them was anger, and even that was not a strong enough word.

As evening turned into night, my father announced the end of the party. A few select guests were asked to stay, among them, my new in-laws. My already knotted stomach tightened even more. I knew what was coming next.

"We shall escort the new couple to the bridal suite," my father announced.

I allowed Tanek to take my arm and I curled my fingers under to keep anyone from seeing how badly my hands were shaking. My parents walked on either side of us, Tanek's parents slightly behind them. The others my parents had asked to stay were back there too, but I didn't look at them. The only positive thing I could feel was gratitude that Halea had been allowed to leave and not be a part of the processional.

When we reached the doors of what was to be our

new room, Tomas and Kai were waiting. Bodyguards outside the bridal suite on the wedding night was another tradition, to ensure that no one interrupted the consummation. I had a suspicion that my parents had put them there as much to make sure I didn't run off. I wouldn't though. I still had Tanek's threat ringing in my ears. Even if I told them now what he had done, I didn't know that it would make a difference. They wouldn't believe me. Besides, my parents had already shown that they put the country above me. A divorce would tear things apart.

I lifted my chin. It didn't matter. It was done and I'd made my choice. This way, Halea would be safe and I would live with the consequences.

Tomas and Kai opened the double doors, bowing slightly as Tanek and I passed. As was tradition, the parents of the one marrying into the family walked over to the bed and, together, pulled down the covers. According to our history, it was done so that the parents could see that the sheets were pure white before the act. Tomorrow, they'd be removed from the bed and be packed away with all those nice bodily fluids that went along with consummation, kept as proof should there ever be a question of the marriage's legitimacy.

"May all higher powers, nature and the universe bless this union," my father said.

I really hated the way he tried to cover all his bases. I knew for a fact he was an atheist who liked to mock other religions in private, but to the country, he always tried to make it sound like he was open to everyone. That was his public face, the one I knew I'd have to put on someday. I didn't know what I believed, but I promised myself that whatever it ended up being, I wouldn't pretend otherwise. In one area of my life, at least, I'd be myself.

"May their union bring forth many children." Tanek's mother gave the appropriate response to my father's statement.

I didn't look at Tanek as our families and the others turned and walked out. I waited until the doors closed before I took my arm from Tanek's. The room was lit with candles, giving me an eerie feeling of dejá vu. I remembered my dream. The way my heart had raced, my hands shaking. My pulse was beating fast now, and my hands trembled, but it wasn't the same. Before, it had been all about desire, passion, the need to join with him, to be complete. Now, it was fear and anger, each one warring for dominance.

Before either one could win, Tanek's hand was buried in my hair, pain shooting through my scalp. I let out a pained yelp and he twisted my neck around.

"Silence!" he hissed. "Your guards will remain outside the door all night and I do not think you would like what will happen if they interrupt."

I swallowed any other sound I might have made. I didn't know what exactly he would do, but I knew it wouldn't be good. Any hope I'd had that tonight wouldn't be painful for me had vanished, but at least Halea would be safe.

I clung to that thought as Tanek dragged me over to the bed. I couldn't completely suppress the pained moan when my knees struck the floor, but it wasn't loud enough to be heard. Cool air caressed my thighs as Tanek pushed my dress up around my waist.

"It is our wedding night," Tanek said as he yanked down my panties. "And I will have your virginity."

My mind didn't process his meaning until he spat and I felt his finger inside of me…not where I expected.

"I assumed you were not *that* much of a whore to your American men, and it seems I was right."

I grabbed the sheet and shoved it in my mouth just in time to stifle my scream.

Chapter 18

Reed

The white silk robe perfectly complemented her dusky skin, but she was even more beautiful without it than she was with it. I watched as the material slipped from her shoulders, revealing the body that had been haunting my every waking and sleeping moment.

"Why are you staring?" she asked as she sauntered towards me. "You have seen many women naked before, including me."

"Just enjoying knowing that you're mine."

One arm went around her waist, pulling her towards me. The other cupped the back of her head. Her mouth was soft and sweet under mine. She tasted of peaches and cream. Her breasts pressed against my chest, nipples already hard.

I slid my hand down to her ass, cupping the firm cheek. Her tongue curled around mine and I pulled her more tightly against me. My skin burned everywhere it touched hers and I walked her back to our bed.

Our bed.

Our room.

I loved the word.

I loved her.

I kissed the top of her head and brushed a few curls

from her face. My family. Nami and our children. They were all that mattered. I didn't care if I lost everything else, as long as I had them...

I woke slowly, rolling towards the far side of the bed, arm outstretched. For a few beautiful seconds, I thought I could feel her next to me. My wife. And our children would be waking soon, running in to see if we were already up. Beautiful children with the perfect blend of Nami and myself. Each one unique and amazing. The family I'd always wanted.

My eyes opened as my fingers found the space next to me cold and empty. With the sight came the truth, hitting me hard enough that I struggled to breathe. Nami was married, but not to me. She would bear children, but not mine. The life I'd imagined, the family in my dream, neither of them were real. Pain shot through me, and I turned my face towards my pillow. The future I'd thought I would have had disappeared hours ago when Nami had spoken her vows. All I had left now were dreams, and the taste they left in my mouth was bitter.

For the first time, I wished I'd never met Nami Carr.

***

I considered staying in my hotel room and drinking alone, but knowing that Nami was probably, at this moment, preparing to go to bed with her new husband, I felt like drinking by myself would be an entirely new level of pitiful. I didn't feel like trying to find a club, mostly because it would remind me of how Nami and I had first met, but also because I didn't particularly want to be around people. I snorted a laugh. I was too proud to drink alone, but I didn't want anyone around either. A club was usually where people went to interact with others. I wanted to be left alone, which meant a bar.

I considered leaving the hotel and having a cab driver take me somewhere, but in the end, I didn't feel much like that either. Fortunately, the hotel had a bar and that was just a short walk from the elevators. I made my way down there after a shower and dressing. If I'd stayed in my room, I wouldn't have bothered with either.

I took a seat at the bar, as far from the television as possible. I didn't want to see all the news stories about this morning's festivities, or worse, speculation about what was occurring right now. I didn't want to think about what she was doing.

"Give me shot of the hard stuff and keep the bottle close by," I said to the bartender when he came my way. "The best you have."

He nodded and went for the top shelf stuff. I tossed back the first shot without even tasting it, but it burned on the way down and that was what I wanted. I went slower with the second, sipping at it and trying to savor the flavor. It was good, much better than I'd expected, and it wasn't anything I'd tasted before. When the bartender came back to fill my glass again, I asked him what I was drinking.

"Saja's finest rum," he said in thickly accented English. "We do not have much variety made here, but our quality is excellent."

"Yes, it is," I agreed. Judging by the pleasant buzz now going through my head, it was strong too, and at the moment, that's what I cared about.

I had a fairly high tolerance for alcohol. Not quite as much as some of my friends from back in college, but I could hold my own. People were often surprised at how much business was conducted with the assistance of alcohol, and the last thing anyone wanted to do was sign a contract while drunk.

Tonight, however, I didn't have any business to do, no reason to stay sober. I'd only been truly hammered a few times in my life, and none of them intentionally. Well, not until recently anyway. No matter why I'd done it, I hadn't particularly liked it, and I definitely hadn't liked the results the morning after, but I knew I was about to do it again. Despite knowing that I'd most likely spend all next morning hugging the toilet, I wanted the oblivion that only alcohol could offer.

I was a couple steps past tipsy and heading towards slurring and staggering when a tall, dark-haired woman sat down next to me. I blearily glanced at her out of reflex, but then turned back to my drink.

"American or European?"

Her voice was lower than I would've expected, husky in that sexy kind of way that I was sure made men sit up and take notice. Or at least had a similar effect on a specific body part.

I turned back towards her. It took my eyes a moment to focus and I knew I was pretty close to plastered. The alcohol didn't stop me, however, from appreciating a pretty face, or a killer body. She had to be at least five ten, but with curves rather than skinny. Her hair was black, not brown as I'd first thought, and long. Dark eyes and tanned skin. She was the sort of woman who men would fall over themselves for just a chance to get her in bed.

And apparently, my previous disinterest had intrigued her.

"American," I answered her question late, but she hadn't taken her eyes off of me since asking it. "Reed."

"Lona." She held out her hand, palm down to let me know that she didn't want to shake.

I grasped her fingers and brushed my lips across the back of her hand. Good for me, I could still be smooth when I was drunk. She leaned towards me, giving me a good look at her ample cleavage. She was dressed sexy, but not slutty. I supposed there was still a possibility that she was a hooker working the hotel bar, but I was going to go with believing she found me attractive.

"Are you here on business?" She touched my knee. "Or pleasure?" Her fingers moved up my thigh.

I laughed and she gave me an amused look. "It wasn't business, but it definitely hasn't been a pleasurable trip either."

That wasn't entirely true, I knew. Images of Nami flashed into my head, memories of her beneath me, of her expression when she came. Until the moment she'd sent me away, the trip had been very much about pleasure.

"Perhaps I can change that," she said. Her hand curved around my thigh, her fingers brushing against my crotch.

I cocked my head and squinted at her, trying to figure out if she was hitting on me, or negotiating her rate for the night.

"I know what you are thinking." She slid her hand over and cupped my crotch. "And the answer is no."

"No?" I raised an eyebrow, spreading my legs open a bit more to allow her better access. Her fingers felt amazing.

"I am not asking for money." She stood and put her lips against my ear. Her breasts pressed against my arm.

"Then what is it you want?" I asked. She smelled like flowers and my nose twitched, wanting to sneeze.

"This." She squeezed my cock and teased my ear with her tongue.

"You just randomly come up to strangers in a hotel bar and grab their dicks?" The words came out a bit more directly than I'd intended, but then again, I hadn't really meant to say anything to begin with. I blamed the alcohol.

She grinned at me. "When my friends bet me that I cannot get the handsome American into bed, I do."

I returned the smile, wondering if it was as goofy as it felt. "I wouldn't want you to lose a bet on my account."

"I have a room," she said.

"You're a tourist?" I asked, surprised. I'd thought her

261

accent sounded like Nami's.

"Not precisely." She shook her head as she took my hand. "I am from the other side of Saja. My friends and I came for the wedding and did not want to drive home late."

My stomach lurched. "Wedding?"

"Ah, yes, you are not from here. The princess of Saja was married this morning."

"And you were invited?" Shit, that sounded rude. Still, I was more worried about keeping one foot steady in front of the other.

"I am a journalist," she said as we walked onto the elevator. "A small, online magazine, but all of Saja media was invited."

I grabbed her around the waist, spinning us so that her back was against the wall. The spinning wasn't good for my head, but the thought of having to listen to her talk about Nami's wedding was worse. I covered her mouth with mine, swallowing whatever else she was going to say.

She tasted like tequila. Her tongue danced with mine and she ground against my thigh, moaning at the friction. I moved down her neck, nipping at the skin there, biting and sucking until Lona's fake nails dug into my back hard enough to make me gasp.

The elevator doors dinged open and I pulled back. "This isn't my floor."

"No," she smiled. "It is mine."

Right. She'd mentioned a room. I let her lead me down the hallway, stealing a look down at her ass when she stopped in front of her door. Damn. She had all the right curves and an ass I could bounce a quarter off of.

For some reason, that idea struck me as funny and I barely suppressed a laugh. I didn't think Lona would be too happy if I started laughing like an idiot when I should've been concentrating on getting her out of her clothes.

When we stepped into the room, I quickly realized that wasn't going to be much of a problem. She apparently hadn't been expecting me to take off her clothes at all. She'd barely gone a few steps before she stripped off her dress and revealed that she hadn't been wearing anything underneath it.

Her skin was smooth and unblemished, her nipples a deeper shade of brown. She had the kind of body most men only dreamed of. And then she went down onto her knees.

"Fuck," I breathed.

"Yes," she said. "But I would like to taste you first."

Her hands made short work of my pants, tugging them down around my thighs and taking my underwear with them.

"Very nice," she said approvingly.

"You ain't seen nothing yet." If I'd been a bit more sober, I would've thought the statement inane. Now, it just seemed witty.

She wrapped her hand around my cock. Even soft, I was bigger than average. She worked her hand over my shaft for a couple strokes, then leaned forward and took the head between her lips. I closed my eyes, trying to concentrate on the feeling of her mouth, the wet heat, the suction.

I couldn't just focus on the sensations though. It wasn't what I wanted. Lona knew what she was doing. Her hands and mouth did all the right things. But I didn't want someone who was skilled. I wanted passion, not just for my body, but for all of me. I wanted different hands, a different mouth. I could imagine Nami, the sight and feel of her, but my body didn't respond because I knew it was fake.

I sighed and opened my eyes. Lona was still lavishing attention on my cock, but I knew it wasn't going to work. I was half-hard, but that was purely physical. Between the alcohol I'd consumed and the thoughts of

Nami, I wasn't going to be able to do this. I didn't want to do it.

I reached down and took Lona's arms, raising her to her feet. "I'm sorry," I said. I managed an embarrassed smile. "Too much to drink tonight."

I tugged myself back in, made a hasty exit from Lona's room and moments later I was heading back to the bar. I fully intended to continue drinking the rest of the evening. I would make sure by the end of the night I'd consumed enough alcohol so I wouldn't remember this mortifying day.

Chapter 19

Reed

I was a glutton for punishment. Stupidly masochistic. A moron bent on self-destruction. Basically, a fucking idiot.

For a reason that was still escaping me, I'd actually been in Saja for a week. A mother-fucking week. I should've left as soon as Nami told me she was choosing Tanek. But I'd stayed. Then I should've booked the first flight after I'd seen her go through with the wedding. But, no, I'd decided to stick around. Of course, any normal person with common sense would've grabbed any available seat to anywhere but here after the disastrous night I couldn't get it up.

As I'd already proven, however, I wasn't a normal person and I most certainly didn't have common sense. I used to. In fact, I had always considered myself to be the sensible one, the person who always made the right choices. Or, at least, I had been.

What had happened to that guy? I felt like every decision I've made lately had been the wrong one. When had I started fucking everything up? A part of me wanted to say that the bad choices had started here, or maybe in Europe, but I knew that I'd been making a mess of things before that. Had it been when I'd chosen Britni over

265

Piper?

Or maybe I was lying to myself completely. Did I only think I was sensible before because I'd always made good business decisions? Because I'd always followed what my parents had told me to do? Was that why I kept fucking up my own decisions? Because I'd never learned how to make the right ones?

I squinted against the sun as I stepped outside the hotel. I squinted, pain spiking in my temples as I put on my sunglasses. I'd basically spent the entire past week hungover or drunk. I'd started Monday morning by buying some beer and heading down to the beach where I'd made my way through a six pack while checking out the gorgeous women who were sunbathing there. I'd eaten practically nothing, but had gotten another six pack for the rest of the day. I'd flirted with a couple women, but hadn't let it go any further than flirting. When the sun had begun to set, I'd headed back to my room, eating something from room service, then finished off whatever alcohol I'd had left.

Despite the way my head had pounded the next day, I'd decided that I'd liked what I'd done the day before. Things sort of blurred together after that. I would spend the day drinking and flirting on one of the most beautiful beaches I'd ever seen without caring about the view. I had people all around but, aside from the few women who'd come by to hit on me, no one talked to me. It was a great combination of being alone and being with people. I didn't have to worry about condemning looks while I drank, probably because everyone assumed I was on vacation. One of the things I'd learned while in Europe was that people didn't expect much of Americans in general, and even less of those on vacation.

I supposed I technically was on vacation. I wasn't working, after all. Could I really consider it a vacation since I'd quit with plans to start my own business? Or did the fact that I had absolutely no ambition at the moment

266

and no concrete idea of what I wanted to do negate my original intentions?

I paid the clerk for my beer and tried to forget about the real world. I had plenty of money. Even staying here, it would take me years to burn through what I had. Unless, of course, I did something stupid. I'd known kids back in Philadelphia who'd blow thousands of dollars in a single night gambling or at a strip club. Then there were impulse buys like cars, but I wasn't in the mood to spend money on random things.

I found my usual spot on the beach taken and decided to head a bit further down. There was space here, but it was crowded enough that I didn't want to stay. Since it was a beautiful Saturday afternoon, I figured there'd be a lot of people on the beach, but it was even more crowded than I'd expected.

I sighed as I trudged through the sand, a beach towel under one arm, my beer under the other. The sun was overhead and I could feel the rays beating down on me. Sweat glistened on my skin as I made my way around scantily-clad men and women sunbathing, kids playing catch and a few families eating lunch. The sandy beach was starting to turn into an area that was a bit more rocky, and therefore less desirable, but there were still people setting up.

I crossed over to a large boulder that sat against a gradually rising cliff and decided this was far enough. I didn't care about getting to the water, so the rocks between me and the ocean weren't a problem, and the breeze that blew in was strong and cool.

I spread the towel at the base of the boulder and sat down, leaning back against the cool rock. The cliff offered only a small bit of shade, but it was enough. I cracked open a beer and settled in to people watch. Or, more accurately, stare at the ocean and pretend that I cared about life in general. Little thoughts would sometimes creep in, whispers asking what I was going to do next, reminding me that I couldn't exactly stay in Saja indefinitely. I was a tourist, not a citizen, and I'd eventually have to leave. Whenever any of those thoughts occurred, I'd take another drink.

I had a bit of a buzz going on by mid-afternoon, but I was still sober. Sober enough to be interested when I heard a murmur going through the crowd. I stood up and began walking towards the noise. I didn't know what was going on, but it sounded like it would be a good distraction and that's what I really needed.

I was at the back of the crowd, trying to see over a throng of heads, when I heard someone say a word I recognized even though it wasn't in English.

"...Namisa..."

My stomach flipped and I suddenly wished I'd eaten something this morning. The beer I'd drank was sloshing around, threatening to make a reappearance. It couldn't be true, I told myself. Nami was on her honeymoon. Someone must've just been talking about the wedding and it had nothing to do with the commotion I was hearing. Even if she was back from her honeymoon, she wouldn't be here, on a beach. She'd be off with her new husband doing wife things or queen preparation or whatever the hell it was someone like her did.

Then the crowd parted and I saw her.

Bodyguards surrounded her, moving people out of the way both by their presence as well as physically when some didn't move fast enough. I didn't see Tomas or Kai, but I supposed they were probably enjoying their time at home since they'd been gone for so long. If anyone deserved a vacation, it was those two. I wasn't particularly fond of either of them, but they'd spent years with Nami, almost constantly on duty. It couldn't have been easy.

The new guards – or at least new for me – weren't as big as Tomas and Kai, but they weren't exactly little either. Still, I could see Nami in the center.

I could tell something wasn't quite right just by the way she was walking. Shoulders hunched forward, arms around her waist. Her head was down, eyes on the ground. As she drew closer, I could see other physical differences. She was wearing a classically cut dress, a bit too fancy for the beach, I would've thought, but definitely something appropriate for a princess when she was out and about with her subjects. I knew it had to have been made specifically for her, but I could see now that it didn't fit right, as if she'd lost weight since she'd last worn it. The color should've been perfect for her too, but her skin was pale, as if she'd been ill.

I felt a flash of concern. Was she sick? It would explain everything, but I couldn't figure out why she'd be walking on the beach if she was ill. Surely the royal family had private physicians who would've made sure she stay in bed until she recuperated fully. And even if he or she had recommended exercise, I doubted this would've been the place to go. The palace had beautiful grounds she could've walked around.

She was almost directly across from me and I could see the bags under her eyes. She hadn't been sleeping well. A pain went through me. Of course she hadn't. She'd been married for a week. She and her husband had probably been busy trying to get that all-important heir to the throne. The thought of it made me want to throw up.

I started to turn away, not wanting to risk her seeing me. The last thing I needed was for her to realize I'd stuck around like some love-sick loser. As I started to go, however, I saw something else out of the corner of my eye. No one else would've caught it because no one knew her body like I did. I'd memorized it, dreamed of it.

On her upper arm, not quite covered by her sleeve, was a bruise. She'd used make-up on it, but I could still see it. As she shifted, her sleeve moved and I could clearly identify the shape.

Fingers.

Rage filled me, driving away everything else I'd been feeling. It all made sense now. Her appearance, the way she held herself. Why she'd seemed distant, different. The bastard was hurting her, and there was nothing I could do to stop him. Or was there?

Exotic Desires Vol. III

Chapter 1

Reed

I was aware that there were people around me, jostling to get in a better position to see their princess, but I barely heard or felt them. Every ounce of my attention was focused on her.

On the finger-shaped bruises on her arm.

It didn't feel real, like I was imagining things. Like my subconscious was making me see things that weren't really there, trying to convince me that Nami's marriage wasn't just one of obligation, but one of violence.

She was Princess Namisa Carrmoni, the next queen of Saja. She had fucking bodyguards whose entire purpose was to put themselves in harm's way for her. How the hell was her husband hurting her?

And I knew it had to be him. Tanek Nekane. The very thought of him made my already hot blood boil. I

271

could picture the first time I'd seen him, sitting next to her, curling his hand around hers as if to tell me that she was his.

I couldn't just stand here and let her walk by, let her go back to *him*.

I didn't care that she had chosen him and that their marriage was none of my business. It didn't matter that we were on a public beach or that Nami was surrounded by bodyguards. I had to get to her.

I hadn't realized that I'd made the conscious decision to move until I was only a few feet away. I could see even more clearly how much she'd changed since the wedding. Her eyes, normally a warm, sparkling cyan, were dull and listless as they focused on the beach in front of her. Her skin was surprisingly pale under its normally golden shade. Pale except for the place on her arm where her make-up didn't quite cover-up the bruises. I doubted anyone else could see them unless they were looking closely, and even then, they didn't know her body the way I did.

I swallowed hard. She'd rejected me, married another man, but none of that changed how I felt about her. God help me, I loved her.

"Nami!" I called out her name as I took another step towards her, reaching out a hand.

I knew she heard me. I saw her body stiffen, her shoulders tense. She started to turn when one of the bodyguards said something sharply in their native language. I didn't get the chance to say anything else, to ask her to talk to me, because another bodyguard had decided he didn't like the American tourist being so friendly with his princess.

One large hand grabbed my arm, spinning me around so that I met the other hand as it was coming. The fist collided with the side of my face and pain exploded along my jaw. The blow made me spin around, tears welling up in my eyes. I shook my head to clear it, anger quickly overriding the pain.

I let myself complete the turn, let it give me extra momentum as I made a fist. He hadn't expected me to fight back so my punch caught him off guard. Still, he was solid and possibly military. A fist to the stomach didn't do more than make him double over for a moment before he rushed at me.

Maybe hitting him hadn't been my best idea.

Before he tackled me, I caught a glimpse of Nami's shocked expression before I landed on the hot sand. The bodyguard was shouting something, but it wasn't English so it didn't really matter. What did matter was keeping my arms up to cover my face and my knees up to my chest. I knew how to fight, in general at least, but I also knew how to protect myself when fighting back wasn't an option.

I heard Nami's voice, sharp and commanding. The man hitting me stopped and it didn't take a genius to figure out it was because of what she'd said. I waited for her to come over to me, but she didn't. I heard people talking, walking, but no one came near. After a moment, I opened my eyes. Nami was gone. A few people were staring at me, but there were no cops, no guards. Only my total embarrassment and the bruises I could feel already starting to form.

I winced as I straightened my legs and got to my feet. Sand stuck to my sweaty skin and my knuckles throbbed. I could feel the side of my face swelling. I needed to get out of here. I staggered back up to where I'd left my things, but left the beer in the sand. Someone would come along and claim it most likely. They were welcome to it. I'd had enough alcohol for today.

I made my way back to the hotel on foot. Air-conditioning and getting off my feet sounded good, but I preferred to get strange looks from people on the sidewalk rather than trying to explain my appearance to a cab driver. The desk clerk did a double-take as I came into the lobby. That, I supposed, proved more than anything else that while Saja did have its fair share of tourists taking advantage of the beautiful island, it wasn't a typical tourism kind of place. Somewhere like Las Vegas, they wouldn't have looked twice at someone stumbling in like me.

I made it up to my room without anyone else seeing me and headed straight for the bathroom. I didn't wait for the water to warm or even bother to undress, but rather stepped inside still wearing my shorts. I sucked in a breath as the cold drops hit my skin. It wasn't until the sand started to slough off that I remembered I'd taken a shirt down to the beach, but I didn't remember carrying it up here. I sighed and reached for the shampoo. At least it hadn't been a good shirt.

My overheated skin began to cool off just as the water warmed up. I didn't linger long enough for it to get hot. I was sure a hot shower would feel good later tonight or tomorrow, but for now, I just wanted to be clean and get some ice on my face.

I didn't bother with clothes or even wrapping a towel around my waist as I headed into the kitchenette. There was ice in the freezer and I dumped some into a couple paper towels before going into the bedroom. I was tempted to take some alcohol with me, but I didn't. I was in pain, but my head was actually clearing and I needed that more than anything.

I stretched out on top of the covers, groaning at the pain in my arms and legs. I hissed as I put the ice pack on my face. I'd be lucky if I didn't have a black eye tomorrow. I gingerly probed at my teeth on that side. Nothing felt either cracked or loose. That was good. My parents had paid a lot for this smile.

I stared up at the ceiling. Part of me wanted to turn on the tv, fill the room with meaningless noise. I could find something to watch, nurse my wounds and feel sorry for myself like I'd been doing for the past week. It was tempting. Losing myself in drink and whatever I could find to watch. I wanted it. Wanted oblivion.

But I couldn't want it. Not now. Now that I knew the truth.

I'd hated the idea of Nami married to someone else, loving someone else. It had been agony to lose her, to lose a future I hadn't even known I wanted until I'd met her. But I'd comforted myself with the thought that she'd have a good life, a husband she could love. Then, at the wedding, when I'd seen that she didn't love him, but she was still willing to marry him, I'd told myself that she'd made her choice. If she wanted to live in a loveless marriage for the sake of her country, then that could keep her warm at night. I knew how miserable that kind of marriage was, but my sense of duty had been limited to family. Perhaps hers would be enough. Perhaps she could even grow to love him. It happened.

Now, though, I knew the truth. Tanek wasn't just possessive of her. There was no way that glimpse of a bruise was the only one. If it had been an accident or the result of overly enthusiastic sex – I'd occasionally left bruises on a lovers' hips or wrists when I was caught up in the heat of the moment – she might've tried to cover them up, but she wouldn't have looked the way she had. Her pale skin, weight loss, the dark circles under her eyes, they were all physical signs of her body being under prolonged stress. But it was the look in her eyes that had convinced me. I'd only seen a quick glimpse of them, but it had been enough.

I'd seen eyes like that before. I'd pushed that memory down for years, boxed it up, but now I let it come forward. I needed it now to give myself the strength to decide where to go next.

I'd been twelve when my friend, Nick, had invited me over to his house for the weekend. We'd been planning on going camping with his family, but, at the last minute, his father had gotten angry at something and started fighting with his mom. Nick and I had gone to his room and listened to the arguing from below. It hadn't been like when my parents had fought. A little bit of shouting, maybe a tearful complaint or hissed insult. No, I'd heard screaming and name-calling, the sound of things breaking. Nick's face had been pale, but he hadn't said a word. We'd played a video game that neither of us had really cared about and had waited for the noise to stop.

When it had stopped, Nick hadn't wanted to go downstairs, but I had. I'd wanted to call my parents and go home. I'd known that my family wasn't perfect, but they hadn't been like Nick's family. I'd crept downstairs and headed into the kitchen to use the phone.

And that was where I'd found her.

Nick's mom hadn't been dead yet, but known she wouldn't make it. She'd had that same bleak look on her face that I'd seen on Nami's face today. She hadn't responded or even seemed to care when I'd told her I was calling for help.

I'd found out later that there'd been dozens domestic violence calls to Nick's home, dozens of hospital visits for his mother. His father had been convicted of second degree murder and Nick had gone away to live with his grandmother in Texas. We'd stopped talking after that day. My parents had made me go to therapy, of course, and my psychiatrist had made me talk about my feelings for a while, and after a year, I'd stopped thinking about it.

Now, I needed the reminder. Every day Nami spent with Tanek was dangerous. He would kill her eventually. Maybe the same way Nick's father had killed his mother, in a violent outburst that had gone too far. Maybe it would be the culmination of injuries over the years. Or maybe Nami would finally give up and end it herself. Intentionally or by drinking herself to death. It didn't matter which scenario won out, they all ended the same way. With Nami dead.

No matter how hurt I was by her rejection, I still

loved her, and even if I didn't, I wouldn't have wished that life on anyone.

Well, maybe on the abuser, I thought grimly. I wouldn't mind seeing Tanek getting a taste of his own medicine. I clenched my fist. I wouldn't mind giving it to him.

That wasn't what I needed to be thinking about though, I reminded myself. Tanek being punished had to be secondary to getting Nami out of that situation. I didn't know yet how I would do it, but I'd made the decision not to sit around and feel sorry for myself anymore.

I was going to save Nami. Even if she didn't want to be with me any longer, I would make sure no one ever hurt her again.

Chapter 2

Nami

I hadn't really noticed much of anything as the guards and I walked along the edge of the beach. I hadn't had any specific plans about where to go today. As part of mine and Tanek's honeymoon, we'd been expected to survey the country. We'd gone along the far side before circling back so that we were in the capital after only being gone for a week. I preferred this arrangement with my husband. He would be off doing his thing, leaving me to spend some time away from him.

Not that I could ever actually get away from him. The ring on my finger – Tanek's mother's – was the clearest visible reminder and I'd already perfected the art of not seeing it, despite its size. I was even able to push aside the weight of it. Not thinking about it should've been easy. The bruises were starting to fade and I barely felt anything from Tanek's wedding night assault. I could almost pretend that the pain was from other types of exertion, hiking, walking, sight-seeing.

The people of Saja, however, wouldn't let me completely forget. They wanted to congratulate me on my marriage, offer advice. Some of the more superstitious ones offered blessings, sometimes accompanied by gifts of flowers and rocks – sorry, crystals – sometimes even potions. I wasn't entirely sure what to do with those until my mother told me that she had an entire closet full of these sorts of things. Reminders of a time gone by when magic was as real as anything else. Usually, I loved that Saja still retained that in some places, but now it was just one more reminder.

I was polite and smiled at each citizen, staying well-within the circle of bodyguards Tanek had insisted on me taking. New ones. I'd been grateful for them at first. I'd always had to be careful being out on my own, hoping that I wouldn't be recognized, but I hadn't realized how much higher my public profile would be after my marriage.

I'd assumed the new contingent of bodyguards had been to replace Tomas and Kai with ones I'd never met before. Ones who didn't have a direct personal connection to me. Tomas and Kai had never exactly crossed the line between employer and employee, but they'd kept my secrets, become my link to home when I'd been away. Moving them from being my personal guards to my sister's had been a smart move on Tanek's part. There wasn't anyone I trusted more to keep Halea safe. I just wasn't sure that even those two would be able to protect her from Tanek if I broke my word and turned him in.

I'd been thinking about all of these changes when we reached the beach. I wasn't sure why I'd decided I wanted to take a walk on the beach, only that I'd felt drawn here. Clean, fresh air. The tang of salt from the ocean. The breeze. It was beautiful, but I knew it wasn't the beauty that had put it in my mind.

As I walked along the waterline, I was forced to admit the little voice in the back of my head might have been right. I'd overheard a seemingly innocuous remark yesterday about an American who spent a lot of time on the beach, drinking beer. I had no real way of knowing if that American was Reed, but there weren't usually that many Americans on the island to begin with, and the woman's description had been of a tall, handsome man with golden hair and black eyes. I knew Reed's body well enough to build the image even without a more detailed description.

When I first started down the beach, I was sure it was just some sort of whim. A last ditch effort to catch a glimpse of the happiness I might've had. By the time I was halfway down the beach, I'd realized it had been a crazy idea. Seeing Reed again wasn't going to help anything, no matter how much I wanted it. Seeing him would only serve to remind me of what I'd given up and what I would never have.

A crowd was starting to form and I struggled to keep my chin up. It was surprising how quickly I'd learned to make myself invisible, hunching my shoulders, looking down. I couldn't let that carry over to my professional appearances. I had to appear as the same Princess Namisa that Saja had always known. Chin up, confident, ready to take on the world.

I didn't know how much longer I could keep up the facade. I was a strong person, but I could feel the wear already. It wasn't just physical, it was mental as well. Mental, emotional...every bit of me was exhausted. I didn't want to be out here. I used to love being around my people, talking to them, listening to their problems. Now, I felt the difference between us even more than usual. It wasn't just the extra bodyguards either. It was the way they circled around me, preventing anyone from even getting close or talking to me. I was apart. Different.

"Nami!"

I froze. None of my people would ever call me by that name. It was a personal name, a family name. One that we used among ourselves or used as an alias. There was only one person I knew who would call me that name in that particular accent.

Reed.

The name pierced my heart. I wanted to grab onto the hope that sprung up, but I pushed it down instead. This had been a bad idea. I had no room for that sort of hope in my life right now. All I could truly hope for was survival and that my sister would be okay. The moment I'd allowed Tanek to put a ring on my finger, I'd given up the right to hope.

It didn't stop me from wanting to see him one last time, no matter how painful it would be. Even as I turned, I heard a scuffle and I watched as one of the new men tackled Reed to the ground. I opened my mouth to yell at him, to tell him to stop, but the words stuck in my throat. I watched in horror as my bodyguard hit Reed again, then kicked him.

Finally, I found my voice and called out a harsh command. After so many years of speaking primarily English, my native language felt strange in my mouth. I hadn't forgotten how to command though. They might have been hired by Tanek and were more loyal to him than to me, but there was still enough respect for the Saja monarchy that, unless it went against Tanek's wishes, my word was law.

The man beating Reed stopped, his face flushed, breathing heavy. He looked annoyed at having been told to stop, but he didn't argue. Instead, he followed the rest of the men as they crowded back around me. They were closer this time than before, making me move at a faster pace until we were off the beach.

I went with them, resisting the nearly overwhelming urge to look back and see what had happened to Reed. It didn't matter that I still loved him. He wasn't my responsibility anymore. I couldn't think about his welfare. I had to think about my people, my family, my sister.

This past week had been like living in some sort of nightmare, one that didn't end when I woke up, but only began. Sometimes, I wasn't sure which was worse, the nightmares about losing Reed or waking up to the reality of what my life had become.

I'd hoped the honeymoon would give me the time to figure out a way to get Halea far enough away from Tanek to be safe. Once she was safe, I might be able to convince my parents of the truth. Instead, I'd been subject to public appearances where I had to pretend to love him, to be happy with my marriage. When I was worn out by them, we went back to whatever hotel we'd checked into for that day, and I'd be subject to Tanek's...affections. I'd stopped fighting him, but that hadn't meant he'd stopped hurting me. At least he'd refrained from hitting me as much.

And every night, before he fell asleep, he reminded me of what would happen if I dared to tell anyone about his treatment.

When we returned to the palace early, he cited an illness on my part, using the excuse to have me confined to my room for a couple days while he wormed his way even more deeply into my family. By the time I was deemed fit enough for a walk outside, Halea was only too excited to tell me just how much she'd been enjoying spending time with Tanek.

I should've had Halea on my mind as we made our way back to the palace. She should have always been the first thing on my mind, the only thing. I should have been thinking about how to get her away from Tanek, how to keep her safe.

The problem was, even with my eyes open, the only face I could see was Reed's.

Chapter 3

Reed

I didn't end up with a black eye, but the side of my face did turn some rather interesting colors. Fortunately, I'd spent enough time on the beach that I'd gotten a tan and the bruises weren't too obvious. My arms and legs were sore from where I'd blocked other hits, but overall, it wasn't too bad. The hangover was actually worse. Still, I refused to lay around in bed. I'd been moping for too long. I needed to get up and do something productive.

I spent most of Sunday trying to figure out the best way to approach the problem. I knew I had to do it from a logical standpoint rather than allowing my emotions to get involved. Whenever I thought of Nami being hurt, I couldn't think clearly. I wanted to go to the palace and demand to see Tanek, beat the shit out of him or challenge him to a duel or whatever it was people on Saja did when something like this happened. I considered lurking outside the palace until Tanek showed his face and then dragging him into an alley for a bit of turnabout.

As much as the idea appealed to me, I knew I couldn't do it. Not that I wasn't capable, but I knew that it would do more harm than good, not the least of which would be humiliating Nami. I couldn't do that to her, not on top of everything else. Plus, there was always the chance that she'd deny it all anyway and I'd end up in jail for assault. Tanek had to have something on her to have kept her from fighting back.

My next option would be to go to Nami's parents. I knew neither of them were very fond of me, but I also knew that they'd look poorly on anyone who risked tarnishing the family name. I had no doubt that Nami was hiding the truth from them as well.

The thing was, I didn't know which they'd consider the bigger scandal; that Tanek was beating their daughter or that someone was going to expose it. Parents who'd arrange a marriage to someone like that...I wasn't sure I trusted them to care more about Nami's well-being than they did about their good name.

I knew my own parents had cared more about the business part of my marriage to Britni than they had about whether or not I loved her, and that was bad enough. I liked to think that if I'd been in physical danger, my parents would've chosen me over business, but, in all honesty, I wasn't sure. If I was that uncertain about my own parents, I didn't think I could risk it with Nami's, especially when it would most likely be my word against Tanek's.

I needed proof. Evidence of some sort. I knew Nami. If she decided that she wasn't going to admit what was going on, she'd stick with it, no matter what. That meant she'd come up with some sort of excuse for any bruises. With her supporting whatever Tanek said, I'd get thrown out of the palace at the very least. Kai would make good on his threat at the worst. Instinctively, my hand went to my crotch. I had no doubt the bodyguard would indeed cut off my balls if he caught me talking to Nami again.

The first thing I had to do was discredit Tanek so that my own accusations would have more credence. That meant digging into his past. If I was lucky, I might even be able to find something bad. The problem was, I'd already proven that I was completely inept when it came to online research. This time, however, I couldn't involve any outside help. I had to do this on my own and discreetly.

That meant asking around.

Fortunately, I was able to play the ignorant American, fascinated with the whole concept of a monarchy. For the next few days, I made my way through various establishments, carefully asking about the new prince. I started at the hotel, asking members of the staff what they thought of Tanek. I didn't get much from them, but I hadn't really expected it. Employees at a place where discretion was certainly prized weren't likely to talk badly about members of the royal family. I had, however, seen the way several of the maids' eyes had flickered as they'd told me about the fairy tale life being lived by their princess. I hadn't been able to tell if it was jealousy or something more like worry.

The people of Saja were loyal, especially when it came to an outsider like me, but not all of them were skilled at keeping their feelings off their faces. By the middle of the week, I didn't have anything solid, but I did have a feeling that Tanek wasn't well-liked among most people. That, however, wouldn't be enough. Dislike of someone who'd been able to marry into the royal family could've easily been chalked up to jealousy. And even if it wasn't because he'd married Nami, Tanek's family was rich. I knew all too well how easy it was to hate people who'd been born into money. There'd been plenty of people in Philadelphia who'd hated my family just because we'd been wealthy. Well, I admitted, that might not have been the case with my entire family, especially my sister. Rebecca wasn't exactly a likable person.

Thursday evening, I found myself in a bar where I hoped alcohol would help people's opinions flow a little more freely. I started with asking about the king and queen, setting up my American curiosity. As I had everywhere else, I got the impression that the people of Saja genuinely liked their rulers. Unlike other countries, Saja had never really experienced any sort of true rebellion against having a king and queen. Their history was relatively peaceful and solitary. Nami's parents were just another in a long line of respected rulers.

When I turned my questions to the princesses, careful not to seem overly interested in one more than the other, everyone expressed similar sentiments. They believed Namisa would carry on the tradition of great queens and that Halea was a sweet and kind princess. I was able to edge into questions about Tanek, feigning ignorance over how the mantle of ruler was passed down on Saja.

Even with the alcohol, no one came out and said that they didn't like Tanek, but people were less enthused about him than about the Carrmoni family. More than one person commented along the lines that they were grateful Tanek wouldn't be their king. While no one was willing to cite specific instances, the general consensus was that Tanek Nekane wasn't exactly a nice person.

Not exactly news to me.

I assumed the king and queen had done their own research into Tanek's background, but I wondered if that had included talking to people. One would think that they'd want to know as much as possible when it came to the man marrying their daughter, but I'd seen enough people fool themselves simply because the alternative would mean they wouldn't get what they wanted. Also, there was always the likelihood that people wouldn't dare to say anything wrong against the man their king and queen had chosen for the princess.

It was past midnight when I finally headed back to my room, more discouraged than I had been all week. I'd really thought I'd get something at a bar. Something solid that I could take to the king and queen. Now, I saw how stupid that had been. Why had I thought I'd find something that the king and queen hadn't been able to find? Sure, there was a good chance that the people of Saja wouldn't have wanted to tell their king and queen what a horrible man their son-in-law was, but I didn't know what had made me think they'd tell someone who wasn't only a stranger, but an American to boot. The people weren't hostile, but it was clear that a line existed between natives and visitors. Even if I could've told them that I loved Nami, I'd still be an outsider. She'd been right when she'd said that I couldn't understand.

I collapsed onto the bed after a quick shower and was fortunate enough to fall asleep right away. Most of the week, I'd been restless, waking every hour or so from strange and disturbing dreams, most of which consisted of me chasing something I couldn't quite get my hands on. I didn't need Freud to tell me the meaning behind that. This time, however, I slept straight through, not waking up until I heard someone knocking at my door.

I glanced at the clock, surprised to see that it was already past nine, and climbed out of bed. I'd gotten in the habit of sleeping naked over the past couple weeks simply to cut down on the need to do laundry, so I had to grab a pair of pants and pull them on as I headed to the door.

I assumed it was housekeeping or room service even though I hadn't requested either, but when I opened the door, the young woman who was standing there wasn't anyone I'd seen before, and she wasn't wearing a uniform.

She was about average in height and build with dark hair and eyes. Pretty enough, I supposed, but I could only view her clinically since my own standard of beauty was pretty much skewed forever. Even the most drop-dead model wouldn't make me look twice.

"My name is Ina." Her voice was soft and heavily accented. "I have heard that you are asking about Tanek Nekane."

I kept my face blank and didn't answer the implied question. For all I knew, she'd been sent in by Tanek or the royal family to determine what I knew.

She continued after a moment's pause, "You will want to hear what I have to say."

I looked at her for a moment, weighing my options. Curiosity and desperation won out. I had nothing on Tanek and if what Ina said didn't have any worth, I wouldn't have lost anything more than a bit of time. I couldn't risk sending her away if she had information that could help me.

I stepped back and gestured for her to come into the room. She stepped past me, careful not to look at me, and that's when I realized I'd forgotten a shirt.

"Excuse me," I muttered, embarrassed as hell. I hurried into the bedroom, grabbed the first shirt I saw and pulled it on. I was pretty sure it was dirty, but it didn't smell, so that was what counted at the moment.

I came back into the main room and found Ina still standing there.

"Please," I said. "Have a seat." I sat on the sofa and she took the chair.

It wasn't until she sat down and started twisting her hands together that I realized how nervous she was. I leaned forward, all traces of sleep gone. Either she was here to try to trick me into something or she had something real. My gut said it was the latter.

"When I was seventeen, I went to work for the Nekane family as a maid," she began. She kept her chin up, eyes on me even though I could tell she wanted to look away while she told the story. "Tanek paid a lot of attention to me and I tried to discourage it. I told him I had a..." she struggled for the word "a suitor. That I was engaged. He did not care. It became so bad that I began to request a different schedule so that I was sure Tanek was out of the house, but that did not last long."

I had a bad feeling that I knew where this was going and it wasn't anywhere good.

"When I was nineteen, Tanek forced himself on me."

290

The words were clipped, as if she had rehearsed them enough times that they no longer had any meaning, though the look in her eyes told me they hurt just as much now as they had the first time she'd said them. "I did not tell anyone the first time, or the second. Who would believe me?" The words were laced with bitterness. "He left shortly after the second time, going on a trip of some kind. I tried to find another place of employment before his return, but it soon became apparent that it would not matter."

She took a slow breath and reached into her pocket, pulling out a small rectangle. I took it as she spoke again. "I was pregnant."

The little girl in the picture looked to be about three years-old and she had dark hair like her mother. The eyes, however, were the same clear blue as Tanek's, though the girl's were warm.

"I went to his parents with the truth, telling them exactly what I told you, and they fired me, giving me two week's wages and a caution that I should never speak of this. When Tanek returned and discovered I was gone, he came to find me. He took me by the throat and pushed me against the wall. He told me that if I ever told anyone about what he had done or ever made claim that the child was his, he would kill me and our child."

A chill washed over me. I'd known Tanek was an abusive bastard, but I hadn't let myself imagine that it would be this bad. A sick feeling settled in my stomach as I wondered if he had forced Nami as well. I pushed the thought away. I couldn't dwell on it, not if I wanted to keep my composure.

"When I saw the announcement of his engagement to Princess Namisa, I considered going to the king and queen, but I was afraid," she confessed. "I would risk my own life, but not that of my daughter."

"Why come to me now?" I asked, surprised at how calm I sounded.

"I was at the beach," she said softly. "I saw the princess and I knew that he was hurting her. And I saw you. When I heard that you were asking about Tanek, I knew you would fight for the princess."

I found myself nodding without conscious thought. "I will," I said. I stood and crossed the few feet between us before going down on my knees and taking Ina's hands in my own. "I will save the princess and I will make sure that Tanek can't hurt you or your daughter ever again."

It was a wild promise to make, I knew, but I wouldn't be able to live with myself if I got Nami away from Tanek and left Ina here to face his wrath. Whatever I did, I would make sure it made things safe for Ina and her daughter as well. I didn't love Ina, but it was the right thing to do, no matter how much harder it would make things. If I was going to be the man Nami deserved, it was the only thing I could do.

Chapter 4

Reed

As I made my way down the road that ran alongside the palace fence, I couldn't help but wonder if someone should tell the security guards about the ease with which a person could sneak onto the palace grounds. I'd gone in through the front door when I'd come to see the king and queen in the hopes that they could be convinced to allow Nami to choose her own husband. The first and last times I'd come in through a side entrance. The last time had been the day of Nami's wedding and I'd pretended to be one of the many people hired to work the event. No one had paid attention to me. The first time, I'd basically walked in through the gate, though not as bold. Somehow, I'd thought it should be more difficult to gain access to a royal family.

It was dusk as I approached the gate and I hoped that someone would be using the service entrance. The one thing I hadn't needed to do was climb over the wall and I didn't want to have to try it. I also didn't want to have to come back tomorrow. After what Ina had told me, it had been hard enough to not rush down here immediately. I'd needed to make preparations though. I couldn't just run in without a plan about what to do if Nami agreed to leave with me.

Not if, I told myself. When. She had to come. She couldn't just stay where she was and let Tanek beat on her until he finally went too far. As it was, I couldn't believe she hadn't left. I knew she had a sense of duty to her family and her country, but I never would have imagined that she would ever let a man hit her. If anything, I'd always thought she'd be the kind of woman who'd hit back. Then again, I'd never been able to imagine hitting a woman myself. Even Britni, at her worse, had never tempted me. Rebecca...well, we'd fought as kids, but that'd had nothing to do with her gender and everything to do with her being a bratty younger sibling. My gut told me, however, that something else was keeping her here.

I pushed aside thoughts of my family and everything else. I needed to pay attention. Getting caught trespassing wasn't the best way to get to Nami. In fact, it seemed like a pretty good way to get kicked off of the island, and I couldn't risk that.

As I got closer to the gate, I heard voices. I couldn't make out the words, or even if they were speaking English, but that didn't matter because I could hear the gate starting to creak open. A minute later, a man stepped out and I pressed myself into the ivy, praying it would hide me. He didn't even look in my direction as he turned and walked the opposite way. I didn't know if he was doing some sort of patrol or if he was leaving for the night, but it didn't matter. The door was starting to close and it was my only chance.

I darted around, muscles tense as I waited for a shout to signal I'd been spotted. Instead, the shadows of the falling night kept me from being noticed. I sidled along the inside of the wall, keeping my eyes on the guard standing by the small security booth. His back was to me as he studiously examined something on the ground, but even from a distance, I could tell that diligence wasn't high on his priority list. If this had been the only time I'd come through, I might've thought he was new or just bad at his job. As it was, I thought his behavior was about on par with everyone else's. From what I'd read of Saja's low crime rate, I supposed I shouldn't have been surprised.

I headed towards the door to the maid's quarters. The first time I'd been here, Nami had used it to sneak me into her bedroom. I didn't know if she'd since hired a personal maid or if Tanek would be in Nami's bed, but it was the best shot I had at finding her. If she wasn't there or if something kept me from getting inside that way, I would have to improvise and, while I'd enjoyed living for the moment when Nami and I had first met on the train, when it came to something like this, being spontaneous didn't seem like the best idea.

As I neared the door, however, I heard something. A low, sad sound that I instantly knew to be Nami crying. I wasn't sure how I knew it was her, only that the sound struck something inside me, pulling and twisting my guts. I abandoned my original plan to follow my instincts and immediately followed the wall to the left. Only a few feet away from where the building curved was a low garden wall. Even if it hadn't still been light enough for me to see glimpses of trees and flowers, the fragrance coming from behind the wall would've told me it was a garden.

The sound was coming from inside, so I made my way along the wall until I found an entrance and hurried inside. What little light I'd had was fading fast and the garden was shadowed. I could still make out a path and I kept to it until I found myself at a place where the path went to the right and Nami's cries came from the left. I stepped off the path and then realized that I was still on one, just one not well-worn. A few more steps and I found myself in a different part of the garden. The plants were wild here, made even more so in the waning light. I supposed it would've been quite beautiful in the daylight, but I only had eyes for the figure tucked behind what smelled like a rose bush.

"Nami?" I said her name softly, not wanting to startle

her, but she jumped anyway. Her face was pale and I caught a glimmer of tears on her cheeks. Only now did I wonder how, if she'd been trying to hide, that she'd cried loud enough for me to hear her. I didn't take the time to try to figure it out though. It wasn't important.

I took a step towards her and she flinched. I stopped, pain and anger mixing with enough intensity to make my hands shake. "Nami," I said her name again, as gently as possible.

"Who's there?" Her voice was strong despite her tears.

"It's me." I shifted to the side so that the rising moon could at least give me a little light.

"Reed?" She pushed herself up onto her knees. She shook her head. "What are you doing here? You can't be here."

I closed the rest of the distance between us and crouched in front of her before she could move away. "I know and I've come to take you away."

"Know what?" The words were sharp.

I wanted to grab her, shake her, ask her how she could let someone hurt her like that, but I knew I wasn't truly angry with her. I was angry with myself for having let this happen. I should've seen Tanek for what he really was. I should've fought harder for her. I never should have let her send me away.

I swallowed all of those feelings. Blaming myself or wishing that I'd done things differently wouldn't change anything. "I know that Tanek is hurting you."

She stood up, anger flashing across her face. "Get out."

I stood as well, but didn't step back from her. "I saw the bruises on your arm at the beach. That's why I was trying to talk to you. I know you saw me."

"I saw you," she said. "And there was nothing for you to see. I'd been on the beach for hours. I had dirt smudges on my skin. That's what you saw."

"You don't love him," I kept going. "Why are you protecting him?"

She shook her head. "I'm not protecting him. You don't know what you're talking about. And I have accepted a marriage without love, not that it is any of your business."

"It is my business." The words came out more harshly than I'd intended. "I love you, Nami, and I'm not going to let him hurt you anymore."

She stared at me and I realized what I'd said. I'd admitted it to myself, but I hadn't said it to her. I set my jaw, refusing to apologize or try to dismiss it.

"Reed..."

"I tried not to," I continued. "I told myself that you and I came from two totally different worlds and that it would never work. I tried to convince myself that it wasn't real, and when that didn't work, I told myself that if I truly loved you, I'd want you to be happy." I ran my hand through my hair. "I do want that, Nami. I want you to be happy, but I'll be damned if I didn't say that I want you to be happy with me."

"You can't love me." Her voice was small, broken.

I cupped her face in my hands and felt her entire body trembling. "I do," I said firmly. "I fought it because I didn't want to be in love, especially not with someone who I knew would only break my heart, but I couldn't fight fate." I wiped the tears from her cheeks. "We're meant to be."

Her face crumpled with a sob and I drew her against me. I didn't understand why she was crying, but she was in my arms, clinging to me rather than pushing me away, and I wouldn't fight her on it. She would speak when she was ready. It was dangerous for us to be here like this, but if she was going to leave with me, she had to come to terms with it.

After a few minutes passed, she began to talk and I realized that it wasn't the idea of leaving the palace that

297

had made her cry. Haltingly, she told me everything that had happened from the moment she'd told me to leave her bedroom. How Tanek had raped her, beaten her and threatened her sister. My arms tightened around her as I fought for control. I could feel the bile rising in my throat, threatening to choke me. I swallowed hard. If she could stomach telling me, I could stomach hearing it. One thing was for certain though. If I saw Tanek tonight, I wasn't sure I'd be able to keep from killing him.

When she finished, she looked up at me, face streaked with tears again. "I am so sorry."

"For what?" I smoothed her hair back from her face with one hand, my other arm still wrapped around her waist.

"I should have known...stopped him..."

I put my finger against her lips and the words died off. "No," I said. "None of what he did is your fault." I ran my thumb along her bottom lip. "If it's anyone's, it's mine. I should have fought harder for you."

She shook her head. "I told you to leave. I said that I'd made my choice."

"And I should have gone straight to your parents, told them how I felt and then beaten the shit out of Tanek for good measure." My voice darkened. "I should do all of that right now."

"No," Nami said. She reached up and put her hand on my cheek. "You can't do that."

"I know," I said reluctantly. "But I can do what I came here to do."

"Which is?" She was looking down now, as if she wasn't sure she wanted to hear what I was going to say.

I hooked my finger under her chin and tilted her head towards me. "Look at me," I said quietly. I waited until she did before answering her question. "I came to ask if you would leave with me."

Her eyes lit up and she raised herself on her toes, pressing her mouth against mine. I closed my eyes as my lips molded themselves to hers, pulling her body even more tightly to me until I could feel every line of her fitted along me. We were still in danger and there was so much more we needed to do, but for the moment, everything was right and I was going to enjoy it for as long as I could. Even if things went to hell when we opened our eyes, I had this to hold onto.

Chapter 5

Nami

My broken heart was coming together and swelling with love so fast that I was sure it would explode. The physical pain I'd been through for the past two weeks had been nothing compared to the emotional pain. Part of it had been because of my own hurt, my own longing for Reed and for a life I knew I could never have, but more had been because I'd known how badly I'd hurt him.

For two weeks everything had been a giant loop. Tanek and his abuse, both what had been done and fear for what he would do. Fear for Halea and the knowledge that I had to stay quiet. The words I'd said to Reed and the expression on his face when he'd left.

Almost as bad were the memories of our times together. I'd told Reed at one point that I'd wanted to memorize everything about him so that when I was with my husband, I could remember Reed's touch, what it had felt like to have Reed inside me. After the first time Tanek had raped me, I'd known I could never allow myself to taint the memories I had of Reed by thinking of him when I was with Tanek. Instead, I'd held my memories of Reed close, but hadn't let them surface, not wanting the reminder of what I'd given up.

I'd told myself I'd accepted my life, that until I could figure out a way to make sure Halea was safe, I would bear whatever atrocities I must. Deep in my heart, I knew it was killing me, but I held on, my love for Halea the only thing keeping me going. I didn't have the hope of a rescue. I hadn't even allowed myself to hope when I'd first realized that the man in the shadows was Reed. He'd come for me, but I'd known that once he knew the truth, he would leave. I was broken and weak, not the woman he thought he knew.

Then he'd said he loved me. I'd known how I felt about him, even if I hadn't wanted to admit it, and I'd suspected that his feelings for me ran deeper than physical attraction or 'caring'. I'd told him everything then, face burning with humiliation as I'd admitted out loud for the first time that Tanek had forced himself on me. I'd made myself say it, with enough disgusting detail, that it would push him away for good.

Except it hadn't. He'd been furious, but not with me.

And he wanted to take me away.

As I kissed him, I let myself see it. Sneaking out of the garden and through the service gate. Following Reed wherever he wanted to go. Someplace in Europe. Back to Philadelphia. Somewhere else in the States. It didn't matter where, as long as we were together and free.

I knew it couldn't be, but for that brief moment, I let myself believe, and then I stepped back.

"What's wrong?" Reed asked, confusion plain on his face.

"I can't." It killed me to say the words, but I had to.

"Yes," he said firmly. "You can. We've had this discussion before and I'm not having it again." Some spasm of emotion passed over his face and then was gone again. "It doesn't matter if you don't feel the same way about me. I'm not letting you stay and be hurt."

"If I don't..." My voice trailed off as I stared at him.

Was that really what he thought? His expression was

guarded, but I could still read it. He really did think that my feelings for him weren't as strong as his were for me. I took a step towards him again. Even if I couldn't leave with him, I wouldn't send him away with a lie.

"I love you, Reed Stirling." It was the first time I'd spoken the words and they sent a thrill through me. "And if I could, I would walk out of here with you, and never look back."

"Then do it." He reached out and grabbed my hand. "Please, Nami, just come with me. Your parents and your people can't want you to live like this, and if they do, they don't deserve you."

"I'm not staying for them," I said. Reed deserved to know the whole truth. "My duty to my family and my country might have kept me in a loveless marriage, but it wouldn't have kept me in an abusive one."

He frowned, but didn't interrupt.

"After Tanek...the first time..." I swallowed hard. "I told him to leave the palace." I looked down at my hands for a moment and then back up at Reed. I squared my shoulders and set my jaw. "He threatened to hurt my sister if I told anyone what happened. He said he would arrange for me to have an 'accident' and then request that his marriage contract be transferred to Halea. Anytime he thinks I might say something, he tells me, in detail, what he would do to Halea. Sometimes he shows me."

Reed looked like he was going to be ill. "That bastard," he muttered. His fingers tightened almost painfully around mine. "I'm going to kill him."

"Do you understand?" I asked, hearing the note of desperation in my voice. "I want to go with you, but I cannot leave Halea to the mercies of that man. I was willing to sacrifice my happiness to keep her from being miserable, but it's so far beyond that now."

"Go get her."

"What?"

"Your sister," he said. "I wouldn't leave any woman

303

to Tanek, and certainly not your little sister. But I'm not leaving you here to take the abuse either. If your parents won't protect you both, then I will."

I wanted to argue with him that it wasn't a matter of my parents not caring enough to protect me. Instead, there was no way to guarantee Halea's safety while Tanek's case was decided. It would be my word against his and my parents already knew that I hadn't wanted to marry him to begin with. That was one of the things I feared, that they would see this as another aspect of me rebelling against what they wanted and by the time I could convince them of the truth, it would be too late.

"Hey." Reed squeezed my hand again. "I'm serious. Go get your sister and the three of us will get out of here."

"And go where?" I asked. "Do what? Halea's a minor. My parents could have you arrested for kidnapping."

He pulled me towards him and wrapped his arms around me, holding me so tightly that it almost hurt. "I don't care." He kissed the top of my head. "I have to do it."

"If you get arrested, it won't do us any good," I said as I leaned my head against his chest. I hadn't realized how much I'd missed the sound of his heart beating until I heard it again.

"I'll take you two someplace safe," he said. "And then I'll come back to talk to your parents."

I looked up at him, eyes wide. "You can't do that, Reed. If you go in and tell them that you took us..."

His near-black eyes were serious as he looked down at me. "I'm going to tell them everything, Nami."

I started to shake my head. "You don't understand..."

"If I'm willing to take the risk of telling them everything, then maybe they'll believe me when I tell them what Tanek's done." He twisted a curl around his finger. "It doesn't matter how much trouble I get in if it means Tanek's out of your life."

"Yes, it does," I insisted. "You can't risk it."

One corner of his mouth tipped up in a half-smile. "Nami, I'd risk anything for you. Without you..." He shook his head. "The only way I could live without you is if I knew you were safe."

I went on my toes again so I could brush my mouth against his. I could see I wouldn't be able to talk him out of this. "What do we do now?" I asked.

He looked around. "Where's the safest place for me to wait while you go get Halea?"

I thought for a moment. "The maid's chambers. They're still empty."

He nodded. "All right. Get her and try not to be seen. We'll go out the service gate and then to my hotel. Tomorrow, we'll figure out the best way for me to approach your parents."

"They won't be here tomorrow," I remembered suddenly. "They left this morning on some diplomatic trip to Greece. They wanted me to go with them, but I told them I wasn't feeling well." My stomach twisted. "I didn't want to leave Halea alone here with Tanek."

Reed pressed his lips together in a flat line and I could see the anger in his eyes. I let it warm me, give me strength. He'd meant every word he'd said. He would fight for me, no matter the cost to him. I didn't want him to be hurt on my account, but now his protection extended to Halea as well. For her, I'd risk everything. Even the man I loved. And knowing he understood that made me love him even more.

"When will they be back?" Reed asked.

"Wednesday night," I said. The thought of having to stay here with Tanek until then made me sick.

Reed nodded, but didn't say anything. His arms were still around me, but I could see his expression was far away. I didn't ask any questions, giving him the time to think things through while I allowed myself to relax in his

305

embrace.

"We do this tonight," Reed said finally. "We'll still go back to my hotel room. Tomorrow morning, I'll make arrangements to get us out of the country."

"As soon as Tanek realizes we're gone, he'll be looking. He'll check the airport."

"Then I guess we'll have to rent a private plane to take us somewhere in Europe and we can decide where we want to go from there."

I started to shake my head. "He'll be monitoring my bank accounts and credit cards."

"Who said you were paying for any of it?" Reed gave me a small smile. "I may not be a prince, but I can take care of my princess." He kissed my forehead and then released me. "Let's go. The longer we wait, the more dangerous it becomes."

He was right and I reached out to take his hand as I led him out of the garden. We went back the way he came. Besides being quicker than going the other way, it also meant I didn't have to walk past the place where Tanek had attacked me. I moved cautiously, keeping an eye out for the new guards Tanek had assigned to me, but they weren't anywhere around. Over the last few days, as long as I was in the palace, Tanek hadn't insisted I be followed. He'd known I'd never leave as long as Halea was in danger.

Reed slipped into the maid's chambers and I gave his hand a quick squeeze before leaving him. My insides twisted as I walked away, but I reminded myself that this time was different. I was coming back and then we'd leave together. I wouldn't lose him again.

Chapter 6

Reed

Waiting for Nami to come back with Halea was one of the hardest things I'd ever had to do. Now that I knew the full extent of Tanek's abuse, every moment of Nami being gone was agony.

Scenarios kept running over in my mind. Everything from Tanek beating her until she gave me up to Tanek hurting Halea because of me convincing Nami to run. I kept seeing her face, bloodied and bruised, her body being used...

I shook my head and began to pace. The main room wasn't very large so I counted off steps to further distract me. If I didn't concentrate on something else, I would go after her and damn the consequences. The only thing that kept me from doing just that was the knowledge that if I did, I'd be putting both Nami and Halea in even more danger. If Tanek caught the two of them together, most likely he'd just guard them more closely. His control over Nami only lasted as long as her sister was safe. If he hurt Halea for small infractions, his secret would be harder to hide and from what I'd learned, Tanek hadn't gone this far without being arrested by making stupid decisions. He was cruel, but calculatingly so.

I was starting to imagine all of the various ways I

wanted to hurt him when the door to Nami's bedroom opened. I froze. Just because I was expecting it to be Nami didn't mean it would be. A moment later, I let out the breath I was holding. Nami smiled at me as she came into the darkened room. Behind her was a young woman who looked so much like Nami's mother that I could see what the queen had looked like as a teenager.

"Halea," Nami said softly. "This is Reed Stirling. He's going to get us out of here."

Halea's face was pale, but I could see the same steel in her that I'd seen in Nami. The girl held out her hand. "Nice to meet you."

I shook her hand and then turned to Nami. "Did anyone see you?"

"No," she said. "Not as far as I know." She glanced at her watch. "But we need to go before someone realizes we're missing." She walked past me towards the outside door. "I'll go first."

I opened my mouth to protest, but she gave me one of those looks that I knew she'd use when on official business.

"I'll check to see if anyone's out there. There'll be questions, but I'm not a stranger," she said. "Halea follows me and you come behind her to make sure she's safe."

I glanced at Halea, wondering just how much Nami had told her sister about why we were sneaking away. Judging by the stubborn set to Halea's jaw, it had been enough to convince her. I just hoped Nami had spared Halea the details. I couldn't imagine how guilty she'd feel if she knew Nami had stayed with Tanek to protect her.

Nami opened the door slowly and peered out through the crack. After a moment, she opened it wider and stepped outside. A few seconds ticked by and she motioned for us to follow. We stuck to the shadows as we went, but most of the guards seemed to be centered around the front of the palace. A few were patrolling along the fence, but they were easily avoided. When we reached the gate, however, we encountered a different problem.

The gate was closed. Before, I'd just waited until someone had needed to use it before sneaking in. That wasn't an option right now though. There were three of us and, any moment, someone could realize that the girls were gone.

We needed another option.

"I'll get him out of the booth," I said softly. "You two open the gate and get out. I'll follow as soon as I can."

To my surprise, Nami rolled her eyes. The gesture seemed so casual, especially considering our present circumstances, that it almost made me laugh.

"I thought we might need a distraction," she said. She held up a hand-held radio.

There was a hint of a smile on her lips and I felt a wave of relief go through me. I'd been worried that I would lose her to what had happened, but now I could see that she was still in there. We could get through this.

She pressed down on the button and said something in her native language. I caught 'Namisa' and that was about it. Before I could ask her, Halea spoke in a soft voice, her English as perfect as her sister's, though her accent was thicker. Nami had spent a few years in America recently.

"She asked for the name of the guard at the security booth and then told him that she did not receive a package she was expecting. She is telling him now to go look at the end of the street to see if it was left there."

"Thanks," I whispered. I gave her what I hoped was a reassuring smile.

This had to be completely disconcerting for the poor girl. One minute, her life is fairly normal, and the next, she finds out that her sister's being abused and they have to leave with someone she doesn't know, going somewhere unknown.

I didn't have much more time for speculation as I heard the gate creak open. The security guard in the booth was walking towards it. Nami held up her hand, cautioning us to wait. It was funny. I'd thought I was coming to rescue her and now she was the one responsible for actually getting us off the grounds. Then she glanced back at me and I saw the fear in her eyes. She was absolutely petrified that this wouldn't work, and I didn't need her to tell me to know that the only thing keeping her together was Halea.

Nami took a few steps out of the shadows and looked around before gesturing for us to follow. Halea and I followed Nami over to the gate and then out. Instead of turning towards the street, however, Nami turned the other way. As we went, I remembered Halea saying that Nami had sent the guard to the street to look for her non-existent package. Smart.

Nami led us down another side-street and then back up to the street that ran in front of the palace. As soon as we reached it, she stopped and turned to me.

"Where to now?"

Her voice was strong, but I could see the weight of it all in her eyes. I reached out and took her hand. I wanted to take her in my arms and kiss her, tell her everything would be okay. I couldn't do that with her sister here, not without making Halea either embarrassed or nervous. I didn't know how much Nami had told her about me, after all. Instead, I settled for squeezing her hand and letting her see on my face that I was taking over. She didn't have to be strong anymore. I saw the relief on her face, but she hid it quickly. She would still be strong as long as Halea could see her.

"We're going back to my hotel," I said. "This way."

I hated the idea of making the women walk, especially since both of them were wearing shoes that were more conducive for walking around a palace rather than walking down the sidewalk, but Saja was a small country and their royal family well-known. No one on the island would not recognize either princess. We couldn't take that risk. At least walking, they could keep to the shadows.

When we arrived at the hotel, I put myself between the desk clerk and the women, advising them to turn their faces away as we came in. I supposed the clerk would think I was bringing prostitutes back to my room, but as long as he didn't realize who Nami and Halea were, I was fine with that. My reputation wasn't exactly foremost on my mind at the moment.

Halea's and Nami's reputations, however, were my concern.

"Bathroom's right there." I pointed. "Bedroom's through that door. You two can share it. I have some clothes in there you can use until tomorrow."

Halea and Nami exchanged one of those sibling looks. I didn't know what they communicated in their silence, but after a minute, without a word, Halea walked into the bathroom.

As soon as the door closed, Nami turned to me. I took one step towards her, my arms open, and she fell into them.

"Thank you." The words were muffled as she buried her face against my chest. I felt the tension flow out of her body and she sagged against me. "Thank you for saving her. For saving me."

"Always," I promised.

I wanted nothing more than to keep her in my arms, take her into the bedroom and make love to her until every bad memory was banished from her mind. But I knew it wasn't only Halea keeping me from doing that. I loved Nami and I wanted her, but I would let her initiate all physical contact. I would do whatever it took to make her feel safe again.

"Sleep tonight, my love." I smoothed down her curls. "You're safe here."

I had Nami bring me out a pair of shorts and waited until the sisters were in the bedroom with the door closed before I went into the bathroom and changed. I left the light on and the door cracked so that if either one needed to use the bathroom in the middle of the night, they would be able to see that I was still asleep on the couch.

I wasn't sure when I'd ended up falling asleep, but the soft shuffle of feet on carpet woke me some time later. I looked up to see Nami standing at the end of the couch. I sat up, immediately looking around for the threat.

"What's wrong?" I pitched my voice low, not wanting to alarm Halea if she wasn't already awake.

Nami walked around to the side of the couch and I could see now that she was wearing one of my t-shirts. It hung down to mid-thigh, nearly as long as some dresses I'd seen. My stomach tightened as I wondered what she was wearing underneath. I immediately pushed the thought away before my body could respond even more than it already was.

"Nami." I started to sit up, but she shook her head. "What...?"

Whatever question I'd intended to ask was lost as Nami pulled my blanket off and dropped it on the floor. I swore softly as she straddled my waist, her hand hot on my stomach as she steadied herself.

"You don't have to..." I groaned as she grasped my cock through my shorts.

"Please." Her voice was soft. "I need to remember that it can be good."

My heart twisted at her words and I felt a surge of hate for Tanek, for what he'd done to the woman I loved.

Suddenly, she moved her hand and turned her face away. "I understand," she said, her voice empty. "I am not..."

I sat up so quickly she gasped, losing the rest of her sentence.

"Don't." The word came out harsher than I'd intended

and even in the low light, I saw her flinch and hated myself for it. I softened my voice and cupped her face as gently as I could. "I want you so badly," I confessed. "But I don't want to hurt you."

She let her weight settle more firmly on my lap and I knew she could feel my cock hardening against her ass. Her eyes locked with mine and she slid her hand across my chest. I put my hands on her hips, fighting the urge to take control. I'd told her the truth, but mere words weren't enough to convey the depth of what I felt for her.

"I need you inside me." Her nails scraped across my nipples and I hissed. "Do you need...?"

She didn't need to finish the sentence. I knew what she wanted. I wanted it too. I shook my head. "What about...?"

Her face hardened for a moment. "The one thing I can say is that even if he has been with others, he would not dare risk the health of a possible child. He's healthy and has been faithful." The last word held more venom than I'd realized she could possess.

I reached up to run my fingers down along Nami's cheek. "Are you sure? I would never ask you to do something you don't want."

She flexed her hand, digging her nails into my chest. "I want."

There was a ferocity in those two words that sent blood rushing to my cock so fast that it almost hurt. She leaned forward and our mouths crashed together hard enough to bruise. She pushed her tongue between my lips and my hands bunched the fabric of my t-shirt. I wanted to feel her skin so badly that my hands were shaking.

I broke the kiss, my chest tight. "I need to know..."

She froze in my arms.

"I need you to tell me what to do." I kissed her jaw and she relaxed. I looked at her and realized what she'd thought I was going to ask. "I will never ask you to re-live any of that," I said, tucking a curl behind her ear. "I'll

313

be an ear if you need one, but will never ask."

She nodded.

"Now." I kissed the corner of her mouth. "Tell me how you want me."

"On top."

My eyebrows went up at that. I'd thought for sure she would want to be in control. Not that I would complain. I didn't care how she wanted me, only that she did. "Are you sure?"

She nodded.

I wrapped my arm around her waist and managed to turn us over without either one of us falling off the couch. As I settled between her legs, I slid one hand up over her thigh and hip, venturing under the t-shirt to answer my previous unspoken question. My hand found nothing but skin beneath the cotton.

Nami's hands pushed at the waistband of my shorts and I could feel the shift in the air between us. There was an urgency now that hadn't been there before. An edge of desperation to the need that we both had.

"Inside me." Nami's breath was hot against my ear. Her hand slid around my hip and wrapped around my cock. "Now."

I covered her breast with my hand even as I surged forward, burying myself inside her. Her back arched and I saw her bite her bottom lip to muffle her cry. My entire body shook with the effort to stay quiet. I rested my forehead against hers for a moment, struggling for control.

"I love you," I whispered. My hand tightened around her breast.

"Then love me." She rested her heels against the back of my knees.

This wasn't the tender, gentle love-making I'd imagined she would want. This was something deeper and our bodies moved against each other with an almost primal need. My fingers moved beneath her t-shirt,

314

rolling and tugging on her nipple as soft, whimpering sounds fell from her lips, mingling with my own harsh breathing.

It wasn't long before she began to gasp and moan, the sounds of pleasure that I'd been dreaming about. I could feel my own climax coming and fought it, determined to feel her come around me before I let go. I leaned down and pressed my face against her neck. As I nipped at her throat, her nails dug into my shoulders and we came together, her pussy tightening around my cock as it pulsed inside her.

"Thank you," she whispered.

I could feel hot tears against my skin as Nami held me to her. I hated the circumstances that had brought us back together, hated what had happened, but I loved having her back in my arms. For her, I'd thought I'd left behind my home, but I knew now that wasn't the case. She was my home.

Chapter 7

Reed

I was deep in the best sleep I'd had in weeks when a loud bang jerked me out of it. For a brief moment, I couldn't remember where I was or what was going on, but then I saw the men coming into the room and immediately reacted.

I rolled off of the couch, hearing Nami make a noise but not looking at her. She was safe at the moment and I had to keep her that way. I needed to get between her and the men. I barely even registered the fact that I was naked.

It was only after a few seconds that I realized the men were cops and they had guns pointed at me. I automatically put my hands up, but I didn't move from my place in front of Nami.

I heard her suck in a breath as Tanek came into the room and it was only knowing that I was shielding her that kept me from going after him.

"Down on your knees!" one of the cops shouted.

"Not until he leaves." I jerked my chin at Tanek. "You get him out of here, keep him away and then I'll get on my knees."

I wasn't sure where things would've gone from there

because the bedroom door opened and Halea stepped into the room. Before I could move or speak, Tanek was there, grabbing Halea and pulling her towards him.

As soon as I heard him speak, I knew what he'd done.

"Please tell me he did not harm you as well, dearest."

My jaw dropped, my attention caught for a split second, just long enough for the cops to move. As I was thrown to the ground, my arms yanked behind my back, I managed to get out a question. "What are the charges?"

"Kidnapping." The cop jerked on my wrist and a sharp pain shot up my arm.

"And rape."

Tanek's voice cut through the chaos and I heard Nami gasp at his words.

"I am so sorry, my darling," Tanek continued. "That I did not arrive in time to stop him."

One of Tanek's personal guards came into the room and Tanek pushed Haley toward him. "Bring this innocent child to the car and wait for us. She shouldn't witness this horrible crime scene."

As soon as they'd left, I was pulled to my feet and one of the cops grabbed my shorts from the ground, roughly forcing me into them. Nami was on her feet now, the blanket wrapped around her. Her face was pale and I could see the panic on her face. She didn't know what to do.

"It's okay. Let me handle this." I mouthed the words and prayed she would understand them.

I didn't want her to think that I expected her to refute the charges, or that I would be hurt that she didn't tell the truth. I knew why she had to stay silent. I didn't want Halea in Tanek's custody any more than she did, and if it meant that my reputation had to suffer for a little while, then that was a sacrifice I was more than willing to make.

Her eyes met mine and I saw the pain in them. She understood, but it didn't make her hurt any less. My own heart twisted inside me and I wanted to go to her, wrap

318

my arms around her, take her pain away. I hated seeing her this way and I hated even more that I had to leave her, but my only other option was to put Halea at risk and, as much as I loved Nami, I couldn't do it. In fact, it was because I loved Nami that I couldn't speak the truth.

If it had been Nami's honor at stake, I would've kept myself quiet and waited until we could come before the king and queen to set things straight. With Halea being in Tanek's custody, however, Nami was at his mercy and I knew that we didn't have time. Once he had them alone, he would most likely release Halea, but I knew he would take out his anger on Nami.

I pushed the thought aside as the cops started to drag me toward the door. I couldn't think about what Tanek might do. If I did, I wouldn't be able to think straight. It would be a toss-up between trying to kill someone and trying not to throw up. Neither one would help Nami.

I kept my eyes on her as long as I could, forcing the cops to physically pull me from the room. I didn't care about how my arms were hurting where they gripped me or how my shoulders felt like they were going to be pulled out of their sockets. I didn't care about the people staring at me as I finally began to walk down the hall.

My head was swimming, thoughts racing. I couldn't get them in any order, couldn't make sense of them. And yet I knew I needed to focus. I had to figure out how to get out of this and save both Nami and Halea. At the moment, though, the only thing that was clear to me was that I'd failed them; I'd failed *her*.

Chapter 8

Nami

This couldn't be happening. It had to be some awful dream, some nightmare that I couldn't seem to wake up from. I'd been dreaming about the events of last night, reliving every wonderful moment from my reunion with Reed in the garden to falling asleep in his arms after we'd made love. And then I'd heard a loud bang and jerked out of my lovely dream to the horror that unfolded in rapid-fire images that I couldn't stop.

Reed putting himself between me and the men pouring into the room.

Grabbing for a blanket to cover myself and wondering, for one sleep-addled moment, why half a dozen cops were pointing guns at Reed.

Tanek.

My blood turned to ice and I couldn't think.

And then the worst possible thing. Halea came out of the bedroom.

I knew what would happen, but I couldn't stop it. Tanek grabbed her and handed her over to his guard. I barely heard what he said, but then the cops were throwing Reed to the ground and my brain finally registered the answer to his question.

Kidnapping and rape charges. I stared at Tanek in horror. I'd known he was a vile man, but I'd never imagined that he would have Reed arrested for rape. Tanek wasn't stupid. Having an American arrested was bad enough. The kidnapping charge would've been easy to dispute without any repercussions and Tanek could claim ignorance. No harm done.

Or, I realized, it would have been if the cops hadn't caught Reed and I naked on the couch.

This was all my fault.

Halea in danger. Reed arrested.

All of it was my fault.

There was no way this could end well. If Tanek had Reed formally charged, then all of this would go public. This could go two ways. I'd be forced to tell the truth, ruin my reputation, and be responsible for Tanek assaulting my sister in revenge. Or I would have to lie under oath and condemn the man I loved. Either way, I would be in disgrace, whether publicly or privately. Even worse, it would all have to be done in front of my parents. The Saja judicial system was similar to many other's, save that capital crimes such as kidnapping, rape and murder were always tried in front of the king and queen. They couldn't recuse themselves. They would have to hear every detail, whether real or made up.

I watched, helpless, as they dragged Reed from the room.

"We must take the princess to the hospital. She need to be examined by a doctor." The police officer speaking with Tanek was slightly older than my husband, but it was clear the man was out of his depth.

"No," Tanek said firmly. "If the princesses go to the hospital, someone will talk. We need to keep this quiet."

I could feel his eyes on me.

"Princess Namisa is my wife and I would not have her dishonored this way."

I ground my teeth together and prayed for the self-control I needed not to rush at Tanek and attack him. With Haley in the hands of Tanek's guard I couldn't do anything, for now at least.

"What do you wish us to do, Prince Tanek?" the officer asked.

"You may secure this as a crime scene regarding the charge of kidnapping. Let people think it was for money."

I almost laughed at that. I hadn't looked into Reed's family, but I knew they were wealthy. All he had to do was hire a good lawyer who'd submit his bank statements and it would be clear that Reed wasn't after money. Then I remembered what he'd said about having given up much to be with me. If that had included his family's fortune, Tanek might be able to sell the kidnapping charge.

"I will take the princesses back to the palace," Tanek continued. "From there, I will summon a discreet physician who can examine my wife."

I risked a glance now. Tanek wasn't looking at me. The cop, however, was. He looked nervous and I didn't blame him. It was clear that he wasn't entirely sure what to do. He knew protocol and he wanted to protect his princess. He just wasn't sure how. I gave him a slight nod and saw the relief in his eyes.

"Very well, Prince Tanek."

"And, Officer?" Tanek spoke as the cop was about to walk away. "Make sure your men know not to breathe a word of the secondary charge. I am sure the king and queen wouldn't look too kindly on those who disparaged their daughter's reputation."

"Yes, Sir."

I felt a faint stab of vindictive joy at the anger on Tanek's face at not being referred to as 'your Majesty'. It was bad enough that he could demand to be called Prince. As heir to the throne, I was referred to with the same honor as both of my parents. Tanek would be unable to demand that title until I became queen.

And I didn't intend for him to be at my side when

that happened.

"Princess Namisa." Tanek turned to me, eyes still flashing at what he considered to be an insult. "You should get dressed before we leave."

I nodded and hurried into the room and grabbed the clothes I'd been wearing yesterday. After a moment's hesitation, I took a t-shirt from Reed's bag and pulled it on over the camisole I'd been wearing. I could claim modesty and Tanek wouldn't argue, not in front of anyone. I closed my eyes and allowed myself a moment to feel the soft cotton on my skin, to breath in Reed's scent. It calmed me, and I opened my eyes.

When I walked out into the room, I kept my shoulders hunched, my arms crossed against my stomach. For all intents and purposes, I was the victim. As long as I played my part, my sister was safe. Tanek would know that it wasn't real, especially when he realized I was wearing one of Reed's shirts, but that didn't matter.

"Are you ready to go home?" Tanek made his question seem friendly, concerned, but I knew the truth.

"Yes." I allowed him to take my arm, stifling a wince as he dug his fingers into my flesh.

The police officers all bowed their heads as I walked past and I knew it wasn't only a sign of respect, but an acknowledgement of what they thought had happened to me. I kept my eyes straight ahead as we came out into the hallway. The hotel wasn't very full, but what few guests they had on this floor were in the hall, wanting to know what was going on. I could feel their eyes on me, hear whispered rumors. As we reached the elevators, Tanek shifted, putting his arm around me instead. I guessed he wanted the gesture to look comforting, but he still managed to situate himself so that his fingers could pinch my waist.

Outside the hotel, I was relieved to see no reporters, only a car. The driver opened the door and Halea was there. She looked concerned but thankfully, unhurt. No

324

matter what happened to me, I was determined to protect my sister. As we settled in the car, Tanek pulled me close, sliding his hand under the t-shirt and grabbing my breast. I made a small pained sound as his grip tightened and that seemed to satisfy him for the moment because he didn't make it worse.

He pressed his mouth against my ear, pitching his voice low so that Halea couldn't hear him. "You will pay for what you did."

My stomach flipped and I twisted my fingers together to keep my hands from shaking.

"Your parents are gone until Wednesday. They do not know anything about what happened, so they will not be coming home early to rescue you from your punishment."

I pressed my lips into a flat line, refusing to give him the satisfaction of another sound.

"Every night from now until they return, I will beat you until you learn your place. If my fists cannot convince you, then perhaps I will borrow a whip from the stables." His fingers grasped my nipple, twisting it painfully. "Once I have finished with that part of your lesson, I will use you in whatever way I please." He switched from our native language to English. "Your mouth. Your cunt. Your ass. You are mine. You will bear my son and he will make this country great."

I had no doubt that he meant it all, or that once I gave him a son – I knew he wouldn't be satisfied with a mere daughter – my life would no longer have any importance. What I feared was that he would become impatient if pregnancy proved as difficult for me as it had been for my grandmothers and my mother. Would he simply get rid of me and take Halea? It wasn't something likely to happen soon, but I had a feeling that he wouldn't wait very long, probably only until Halea turned eighteen.

All of our guards came to greet the car and I wondered how Tanek's men had explained the escape. I was actually surprised to see them all there rather than in jail or beaten to a pulp. Tanek couldn't have been happy when he'd discovered Halea and I were missing.

"Kai, Tomas, take Princess Halea to her room."

Both men glanced at me as they gestured for Halea to come with them. I avoided meeting their eyes. They couldn't know what Tanek had done to me. They would either kill him or go to my parents. While the first would relieve me of my problem, it would also put them in prison, no matter what their reasons had been. The second would put Halea in more danger.

"Claudel."

A tall guard of French descent stepped forward. He was a grim-looking man, the kind that would've looked more at home lurking in a dark alley than he did here.

"Escort Princess Namisa to our chambers."

Claudel gave Tanek a sharp nod.

"Keep the princesses in their rooms. Lock them in if necessary. They are not to leave."

What was Tanek doing, I wondered. Was he going to lock me in my room for hours, letting me imagine all the things he planned to do to me?

He switched to English as he answered my unasked question. "I will be going to the police station to deal with the criminal who dared kidnap our princesses." He glared at his guards. "And I will expect, upon my return, a competent explanation of how this happened, who is to blame and what is being done to prevent it from happening again." He threw a glance in my direction before returning to the guards. "Punishments will be dealt out when I return."

He got back into the car and Claudel came over to me.

"Princess," he said stiffly as he offered me his arm.

He wouldn't be violent if I refused, I knew, but I also knew that word would get back to Tanek and this small act of rebellion didn't quite seem worth the price I knew I would pay.

I took his arm and let him lead me into the palace and through the corridors to the room I shared with my husband. As the doors shut behind me, I sank to the floor and wrapped my arms around my knees.

What had I done?

I rested my forehead on my knees. "Reed," I whispered. "I am so sorry." Hot tears slid down my cheeks. "I'm sorry."

Chapter 9

Reed

I was actually surprised that I hadn't had the shit beaten out of me. Sure, the cops had shoved me around a bit more than had been necessary and I'd probably have some bruises from the manhandling, but I'd had worse rough-housing with friends growing up. Hell, I thought with a pang, I'd been hurt more by Nami's nails and teeth during sex.

Shit.

I looked down at my bare chest. There were faint half-moon indentations where she'd dug her nails.

I stood up and walked the few steps to the small mirror above the sink. I wondered if they realized it wasn't smart to have glass in a cell or if crime was so low they'd never had to consider what would happen if they'd put a truly violent criminal in here. I pushed the thought aside and studied my reflection. I wasn't looking for bruises, but rather for any mark Nami had left that could be taken as her having fought me.

I didn't have any scratches on my face, neck or chest. As far as I could tell, there weren't any on my back either, just a couple more of those half-circles near my shoulder blades. I flushed as I remembered her grabbing my ass at one point and wondered if I had the same marks there. I wasn't about to look though. The last thing I wanted was a cop coming in and catching me staring at my ass in the mirror. I had no clue what they'd make of that.

I went back to the bed and sat down. I rubbed at my wrists where the handcuffs had chafed. This was not how I'd envisioned things when I'd first come to Saja, or when I'd decided to save Nami yesterday. I had, however, known that this was a possibility when I'd taken both princesses back to my hotel room. Well, maybe not to this extent, but jail nonetheless. In my head, however, the kidnapping charges would be easily dismissed once I was taken before the king and queen and Nami told them she'd gone with me voluntarily.

But, of course, things couldn't be that simple.

It was my own fault, I knew. I shouldn't have slept with Nami last night. I should have just told her it wasn't a good idea and held her. Then again, what would've been the chances anyone would've believed that? Now, though, they had evidence, at least of a sexual encounter. I was actually surprised they hadn't taken me straight to a doctor to get swabs and take pictures and all that.

Fuck. I ran my hands through my hair. Was that what they were doing to Nami right now? Forcing her to get a rape kit done?

"Oh, baby, I'm so sorry," I whispered.

I'd never thought she'd have to be subjected to this sort of humiliation. It was only now that I wondered if I'd left marks on her. Had I bitten her? I knew I hadn't been gentle. She hadn't wanted me to be. And now, even if she was able to feel safe enough to say that the sex had been consensual, people would know some of her preferences. That sort of thing was awful enough for someone not in the public eye, but for a princess...I could only imagine what she was going through.

I closed my eyes, my head resting in my hands. What was I going to do? I wasn't too worried about myself. I had the money to hire a good lawyer and the connections back in the States to put some pressure on Saja if I needed to. But Nami and Halea, what was I going to do about them?

"Piece of shit American."

I looked up even though I didn't need to see him to know Tanek was the owner of the voice. He stood on the other side of the cell door, a smug look on his face. I stayed where I was, not trusting myself not to do something stupid...like smash his face against the bars repeatedly until he was unconscious.

"Did you know that, in Saja, kidnapping can be considered a capital crime? If royalty is involved, the death penalty is almost always added to the charge." His pale eyes glittered, giving me a glimpse of what Nami faced every day. "Add rape onto that and I believe that an execution will not only be requested, but required."

I fought to keep my voice calm. "Threatening an American with the death penalty, particularly for actions that you know to be false, sounds like a good way to start an international incident."

Tanek shrugged. "The United States has executed plenty of people who are innocent." His eyes narrowed. "And we both know I have evidence that can be used to prove your guilt."

I slowly stood up, keeping my eyes locked on his face. I knew his type. He was the kind of man who took pleasure in bullying people, trying to prove that he was a man by pushing around whoever he could. I might be the one in jail, but I wasn't about to let him think he could bully me.

I kept my voice even, but didn't bother to try to hide my anger and disgust. "What we both know, Tanek Nekane, is that, of the two of us, only one is guilty of rape."

His face twisted and he snapped something over his shoulder in Saja's native language. It didn't sound nearly as beautiful as when Nami spoke it. Then the door slid open and he was coming inside.

I knew what would happen and that I had only seconds to make a choice. I could fight back, probably get in a few good blows before someone came in. But even if he started it, I was the one who'd be charged with assault and, unlike the other two charges, I would be guilty of this one. I wasn't sure what the penalty would be for assaulting a prince, even one who married in, but I was sure it wouldn't be good for me.

That left me with the alternative. Take it.

He wouldn't kill me. At least, I didn't think he would. A trial and a death sentence would be bad enough. If he beat me to death while I was in police custody, even being the prince wouldn't protect him. A small part of me had the fleeting thought that if that happened, at least Halea and Nami would be safe.

And then he was there and I realized I'd already made my decision. I turned as he swung and his first hit caught me in the shoulder. I might not fight back, but that didn't mean I was going to stand there like an idiot. I kept my hands up, palms out. Tanek was angry, but he didn't fight stupid. Considering how well he'd been able to hide his actions, I had expected nothing less. I managed to block and dodge two more swings, but the third one caught me in the temple.

Stars burst in front of my eyes and I staggered back. Tanek hit me again, this time in the stomach and all the air rushed out of my lungs. A kick to my leg put a knot in my calf and I went down on my knees. I saw where the next kick was aimed and twisted so that it caught my hip. Pain flared through the muscle and I curled up, protecting my head and stomach as Tanek kicked and hit me. My ears were ringing, head swimming, and then I realized I wasn't being hit anymore. I risked a glance up and saw one of the cops pulling Tanek back out of the cell. I waited until the door closed before I uncurled, wincing at the pain. I'd barely healed from the last beating I'd gotten and Tanek had managed to catch a couple of the still tender spots.

The pair were speaking in their language, but based on the way the cop was glaring at me, I had a feeling that whatever Tanek was saying wasn't very complimentary. I tasted blood on my lip and could feel it swelling. Damn. Anger flared as I thought of him going after Nami like that and I stood, ignoring the pain.

"Tanek." I spit some blood into the sink. "I gave you that. Next time, you'll find out what it means to pick on someone your own size."

Tanek glared at me, but I didn't look away. After a moment, his face paled, then flushed again, an angry mottled color.

"I am going to make you an offer," Tanek said. His voice was shaking now, but I was pretty sure it wasn't because he was scared. He might've been a coward, but at the moment, he was an angry coward.

"Why would you want to make a deal with me?" I asked even though I already knew the answer. Things were under his control right now, with just a few people knowing what had happened. He knew I had money, and probably suspected that I had connections. He didn't want to risk me using either of them to expose the truth.

"I am sure you do not want to put the princess through the humiliation of a trial."

I scowled and tasted fresh blood.

"Here is my deal. If you confess everything, I will convince the police to drop the charges. You will be deported and never allowed in Saja again."

"I think I'll take my chances in court," I said dryly. There was no way the king and queen would force Nami to go through with testifying.

"Is that so?" Tanek scowled. "If that is your decision, I will make sure that Namisa must testify, confess every little detail of what you did to her."

"You wouldn't." I took a step forward.

"I would," he said. "And I will ensure that the lawyer asks the most awful questions. How she felt with you inside her. If you made her climax while you raped her."

I felt the blood draining from my face. He would do it. He would force Nami to lie under oath, and not just lie but be humiliated as she did it. Even though I knew she would be doing it to save Halea, I knew how she would hate herself for doing what she felt like would be a betrayal.

"And the best part," he continued. "Is that, with such a small judicial system, and the king and queen having to oversee everything..."

Fuck. I hadn't realized that Nami's parents would have to be a part of it, much less in charge of it.

"It would be at least a year before you would have a court date." Tanek's eyes gleamed. "And you would be here the whole time. Wondering what I am doing to the princess in your absence..."

Damn him! My hands curled into fists.

I hated the idea of confessing to something I didn't do, especially something as hideous as rape. I hated that anyone would think I could hurt Nami that way, and I had a bad feeling Tanek would use it as another bit of blackmail, but it was much better than the alternative.

If I confessed, I'd be sent to the airport and then home to the US. I'd hire the best attorney possible and come back to Saja to fight the charges and save Nami and her sister. While I didn't want to leave Nami with Tanek for another minute, it would still be less time than if I refused to confess and she was with Tanek until the trial. I shook my head. Even then, here'd be no guarantee I'd be free then either. In fact, if Nami lied – and with Halea at the mercy of Tanek, I had no doubt she would – I was almost certainly going to be found guilty. And most likely killed.

I just had to steel myself to do the lesser of two evils.

Chapter 10

Nami

I didn't want to take a shower and lose the lingering scent of Reed on my skin, but as soon as Claudel closed the door behind me, I headed straight for our bathroom. Tanek had said he would call a doctor to examine Halea and me. I didn't think he was lying about that. I wasn't sure how far he would go with these accusations against Reed, but I knew he'd want as much 'proof' as possible to hold over my head, and Reed's. The most obvious evidence would be Reed's DNA on and in me.

I scrubbed myself thoroughly, cleaning every inch until I was certain nothing of Reed lingered. As I stepped out of the shower, I wiped the fog off the mirror and forced myself to look. I needed to make sure there wasn't anything else on my body that could incriminate Reed. On the side of my neck was a small bruise, edged by what I knew were teeth marks. Heat flooded my body as I remembered the feel of him biting me. It wasn't too deep though and I doubted it would be enough for any sort of proof.

I touched it lightly and closed my eyes, letting myself remember Reed's touch, the feel of him on me, inside me. I knew Tanek would be back soon. Taunting

Reed would keep him occupied for a bit, but I knew it was me he truly wanted to make pay. I had absolutely no delusions about what would happen when he got back.

The memory of Reed and what we'd shared last night would keep me strong, keep me sane. I opened my eyes. I just couldn't afford to spend too much time in my head. I needed to dress and then try to figure out what I would do next.

I couldn't just be passive about this anymore. I had to do something to save not only Halea, but myself. It wouldn't be tonight. I knew that. I'd resigned myself to what was going to happen to me, but I refused to think about it. Instead, I was going to start being proactive.

I dressed simply, knowing no matter what I wore, Tanek would be pissed. At least if he drew blood, it wouldn't ruin something good. I sat in a corner chair so I could see the door, not because I thought I'd be able to escape when it opened, but because I didn't want to be caught off guard. Now, it was time to plan.

By the time the door slammed open, a couple hours had passed and I wasn't any closer to figuring out what to do. I'd gone through all of the protocols I knew, all of the passages in and out of the house. Every person who might help me. Every time though, I couldn't figure out a way to make sure Halea was safe while I came up with the evidence to show my parents.

When I saw Tanek's face, however, an idea popped into my head. It was a bad one. Possibly the worst one I'd ever had. But it was all I had.

"Come here, you little bitch." Tanek was already moving towards me even as he spoke. He didn't want to give me a chance to obey.

I climbed off of the bed and, as he reached for me, I saw his knuckles were already bloody and bruised. "What did you do?"

He grabbed my hair, yanking my neck back far enough to make it hurt. "I did to him what I am going to do to you." He added, "Except fucking. I am not a pervert."

I didn't even bother to argue with the hypocrisy of a sadistic rapist referring to homosexuality as perverted.

He let go of my hair and I could see on his face that he was daring me to run, to try to get away. He wanted an excuse to hurt me more. I refused to give it to him.

He grabbed the collar of my shirt and tore it straight down the center. I was definitely glad I hadn't put Reed's t-shirt back on. I'd hidden it so it would be safe from Tanek's rage.

"Not even wearing a bra." Tanek grabbed my breasts, squeezing hard enough to make me gasp. "How long did it take before you spread your legs for him?"

One hand moved up to my throat, not squeezing tight enough to leave marks, but enough to keep me in place as he shoved his other hand down the front of my pants. His fingers were rough as they probed between my legs.

"Was he the one who took your virginity?" His fingers found my clit and pinched. "Was he?" he shouted.

I shook my head.

"Did you offer him your cunt in exchange for him taking you and your sister?"

I shook my head, tears coming to my eyes as he twisted the delicate bundle of nerves.

The hand in my pants came out and made a fist before I could think. He drove it into my stomach, but I couldn't bend over, held in place by the hand around my throat. His fingers tightened.

"Careful," I gasped when I finally had some breath. "Don't want to leave marks where my parents can see them."

He grinned at me. "That is the beauty of this punishment." His hand tightened again and I began to choke. "I can and will mark you wherever I please. I do not need to be careful. The doctor coming tomorrow will want to see all of them. After all, we must have a clear

337

record of the injuries you sustained when you were assaulted by that horrible American."

He released my throat a moment before I passed out and I fell forward, gasping and coughing. I'd thought if I could get him to beat me, I could show my parents the marks as proof and have Tanek arrested before he could get to Halea. Now, I saw he'd already thwarted my plan, even without knowing it.

I barely realized Tanek was pulling off the rest of my clothes until he was pulling me up again and throwing me against the dresser. I collided with the side of it, the corner driving into my ribs. I felt blood running down my side, but didn't look down to confirm that the skin had broken.

"The police, the guards, Halea, they all know I was unmarked." I knew it was a stupid thing to say, but I had to try. I wasn't trying to avoid the beating, but reminding him that people knew the truth. I couldn't tell the doctor Reed had hurt me if there were those who could dispute it.

Tanek undressed as he stared at me, dropping his clothes to the floor. His belt, however, he kept in his hand. "Police officers and security guards can have tricky memories if enough incentive is given."

My insides were trembling at the sight of that belt, but I didn't let him see it.

"As for your sister." He cracked the belt. "If she knows what is good for her, she will keep her mouth shut."

My eyes narrowed.

"And you will tell her that tomorrow when you see the doctor. You will convince her that she is to confirm everything you say."

I didn't say a word or make a sound as he brought the strap down on my side.

"You should also know that, should you ever attempt to run again, you should remember that I employ a great number of people who are my eyes and ears."

I turned as he brought the belt down two more times in quick succession, pain bursting across my back and ass.

Suddenly, he was there, pushing me against the dresser, his cock hard on my ass. He kicked my ankles apart as he grabbed my hair again, twisting my head so he could speak directly in my ear.

"And some of those employees are very well trained in finding missing people. Trust me, they would search to the end of the world in exchange for a piece of your sister's virgin pussy."

I froze, then dropped my head. It was over then. Even if I managed to get Halea away, we would never be safe. I barely flinched when Tanek thrust into my ass even though the pain tore through me. He was right. He could use me however he wanted without regard for how it looked tomorrow. In fact, the worse, the better.

He didn't last too long, but I knew that didn't matter. If he couldn't manage to go again, he'd use something else. He was far from done with me.

The belt came again, hard enough to leave welts. Once, he hit my cheek and I cried out. That's when I heard the door open.

"Princess..."

I barely had enough presence of mind to try to cover myself as Kai and Tomas stepped into the room. I watched their eyes go from me to Tanek and back again. The expressions on their faces, more than how I felt, told me how bad I looked.

"Leave," Tanek hissed. "Return to your duties with Princess Halea, or I swear I will kill Namisa and claim I saw you two do it."

They looked at me and I knew they would do whatever I said.

It wasn't even a question.

I needed my sister safe.

"Go to Halea," I said. My voice was hoarse. "Keep her safe."

They left, but not before I saw the anger in their eyes.

The interruption seemed to have taken the majority of Tanek's anger and he tossed the belt away. "Slut."

I heard more than felt him spit on me, and then the door was closing and I was alone.

I wanted a shower, but I didn't want to move. I never wanted to move again. For the first time in my life, I actually considered how much easier it would be to just kill myself. I could almost feel it, a razor across my wrists, up my forearms. Blood pouring down my arms, releasing me, freeing me.

But then I remembered what Tanek had said he would do if I wasn't there. If I died, he would take my sister.

A felt a new kind of cold spread through me, something I hadn't felt before. This wasn't like ice. This was steel, hard and unbendable. The kind of cold I would need if I was going to protect Halea. The kind of cold I would need to kill Tanek.

Not in self-defense, not in a heat of the moment kind of thing. I was talking something calculated. Planned. First degree, cold-blooded murder. The kind of thing that could get me executed if I managed it. But it would mean Halea would be safe and I would be free.

My entire body pulsed with pain, but I pushed myself up, first onto my hands and knees. I stood, first leaning on the wall for support, and then managing it on my own two feet. First, a shower, and then, I would start figuring out the best way to kill my husband.

Chapter 11

Reed

I would've written my bogus confession right away if the cops had brought me a pen and paper. As it was, I didn't get either until mid-day on Sunday. I was pretty sure Tanek had told them to make me wait until then, wanting me to have to spend at least one night in jail. If I hadn't been so worried about Nami, I actually wouldn't have cared. The bed wasn't the most comfortable thing I'd ever slept on, but it wasn't too bad. I was alone in my cell, probably because Tanek didn't want me talking to anyone about what had happened, and I was unselfconscious enough that I didn't care about taking a piss out in the open.

But here I was, and that meant I spent Sunday writing out the most miserable piece of filth I'd ever seen. I tried being vague, simply writing that I'd met the princess in Paris, come to Saja and when I found her married, I'd kidnapped her. Halea had walked in so I'd taken her too. We'd gone to a hotel and I'd forced Nami to have sex with me.

I was sick to my stomach when I handed the paper to the officer, and then even more so when he gave it back.

"Prince Tanek was very clear. You must provide a detailed motive as well as be specific as to what you did to the princess." The cop looked almost as ill as I felt and I would've felt sorry for him if he hadn't been following the orders of a complete ass. At least it seemed like he thought he was doing the right thing.

I went back to the bed and sat down again. This time, I elaborated as to why I'd come to Saja, using at least some form of the truth in that regard. I said I'd fallen for the princess and wanted to court her. Then the lies started again. I said that when I found out she was married, I tried to make a pass at her and she rebuffed me. I was angry and decided that I would have her no matter what. I took her and Halea when the latter interrupted us.

I had to stop when I reached the part where I was supposed to elaborate on what I'd done to Nami. The moment I thought of putting pen to paper and coming up with lies as to how I'd violated her, my stomach heaved. I tossed the papers aside and barely made it to the toilet in time for my breakfast to come up.

I sat there for a few minutes, eyes closed, waiting to see if I was going to throw up again. I didn't want to do this, but I knew I had to. If I didn't do it exactly how Tanek wanted, he'd find some way to motivate me, and I didn't even want to think about what that would be. Plus, I knew the longer I was in jail, the more time he had to hurt Nami.

I stood, flushed the toilet then went to the sink and rinsed my mouth out. I splashed water on my face and looked in the mirror. One whole side of my face was swollen and bruised from where Tanek had hit me. It wasn't bad enough that I couldn't see clearly, but it wasn't comfortable either.

"Pull yourself together," I told my reflection. "You know what he's doing to Nami, and the only way you can help her is if you lie. Stop being such a pussy."

With that pep talk, I went back to the task at hand. As I began, I remembered how Nami had related Tanek's assaults to me, and I used what she'd said. When she and

Halea were safe, I'd make sure this confession was brought out and the truth told about who had really done these things. Nami might not have filed a complaint against Tanek, but her experiences would be written down.

I finished and handed the confession over to the officer. He skimmed it and I watched the disgust and anger grow on his face. I wanted to tell him that it hadn't been me, that I'd never do anything like that to any woman, much less Nami, but I kept my mouth shut. My reputation wasn't important right now. Once the princesses were away from Tanek, I would consider everything else.

Finally, he nodded. "This will do. A car will be here in the morning to take you to the airport."

Tomorrow. One more day and I'd be out of here and on my way to figuring out how to save Nami.

I went back to the bed and stretched out. I knew I wouldn't sleep well tonight either. My brain was already buzzing with a thousand different plans, each more unlikely than the next. At least I had the rest of the day with uninterrupted silence to think.

When the cell door opened the next morning, I'd managed only a couple hours of sleep, none of it restful, and I wasn't any closer to figuring out what to do than I had been when I'd first started.

"Time to leave."

One of the cops who'd arrested me came into the cell, the expression on his face telling me that he fully believed the charges. He looked like he wanted nothing more than to finish what Tanek had started, but I wasn't about to give him an excuse to hit me. I stood and put my hands in front of me, making sure he could see that I wasn't going to try anything.

He grabbed my arm and yanked me towards the door. I wanted to pull back, but I refrained. Just a little bit longer and I'd be free. A black town car was sitting in front of the station and the cop gave me a shove towards it.

"I pray you come back to Saja," he said. "It will give me great pleasure to make you suffer."

I was off to a great start, winning the hearts of Nami's people. I only hoped that when all was said and done, people like this police officer would understand why I'd done what I did.

I climbed into the back seat of the car, realizing for the first time how completely grimy I was. I was still wearing only the boxers they'd let me put on before leaving the hotel and I hadn't showered. I assumed this had been another way of Tanek trying to humiliate me. I grimaced at the smell. I couldn't get on a plane like this. If nothing else, I at least needed a shirt.

"Hey." I tapped on the black glass separating me from the driver. "I need to go to my hotel room and get my things."

No response.

"I at least need some clothes. They won't let me on a plane like this."

The window didn't come down, but I felt the car turn and slow.

Oh shit. A stab of panic went through me. I'd really thought that Tanek had meant to let me go. Having me put on trial or killed while in police custody would've caused some serious international relations with America. My godfather was a retired Congressman who still had clout in Washington.

However, if I should happen to be found dead in a seedy part of the city – even in a place like Saja, there had to be some unsavory parts, right? – the victim of a robbery, it would be sad, but officials could say that they were doing everything in their power to bring the killers to justice. Even better, if they made it look like I'd been involved in something illegal – gambling, prostitution, drugs – they could almost guarantee that the US would

344

stay out of it.

I heard both the front doors open and my heart began to pound. This was definitely not good. One person, I might be able to fight off, but not two, not on as little sleep as I'd had. Still, I tensed as the back door opened. I wouldn't give up without at least trying.

A familiar face looked in at me though it took me a moment to place it since the expression was actually friendly.

"Out."

I climbed out of the car, wondering why Kai and, I saw as I straightened, Tomas, had been chosen to escort me to the airport. Kai shut the door behind me and tossed me a shirt. My shirt, I saw with some surprise.

"Tanek has all of the family's cars under surveillance," Tomas said.

I pulled on my shirt. I would've felt better with pants too, but at least this was something.

"We know you are innocent of what Tanek says."

I stared at Kai. "What?"

"We have been assigned to Princess Halea, and she told us the truth of what happened," Tomas said. "The night the princesses returned, we went to see Princess Namisa, to ask her what she wished us to do in regards to Princess Halea's claims."

Kai's face tightened as he continued from where Tomas left off. "Tanek was beating Princess Nami."

My hands curled into fists.

"We wanted to stop him," Tomas said. "But he said he would kill the princess and frame us for the murder."

"Still, we would have tried," Kai insisted. "But Princess Nami told us to go to her sister."

I didn't doubt that. Even if she was being attacked, Nami's thoughts would've been to keep Halea safe.

"We spoke with the police," Tomas said. "And they told us you had written a confession. This was Tanek's doing?"

I nodded. "He said if I didn't, he'd make sure Nami had to testify to all sorts of horrible lies in front of her parents, and that I'd be waiting for a trial for a year, knowing that he was hurting her the whole time."

Tomas and Kai exchanged a look. It was Tomas who spoke, "Will you answer us honestly?"

I probably should have asked what the question was first, but I nodded instead. I was starting to suspect that Kai and Tomas wanted to protect Nami as much as I did.

"We know that you slept with Princess Nami in Paris and in Venice," Kai said.

"I did," I admitted, hoping this wasn't the part where they decided to kill me to avenge her honor. I didn't think so, but I could've been wrong.

"But then you came here for her," Tomas said.

"I did."

"Why?" Kai asked.

"Why?" I echoed.

"Why did you come here?" Tomas asked. "Paris and even Venice made sense, but lust does not inspire a man to come halfway around the world for a woman. Nor to risk what you have risked for her."

"I love her," I said. "I came here because I love her and I want to marry her."

"You have already put your freedom in jeopardy because of her," Tomas continued. "And now you have a free pass to go home. If you would like, we will drive you to the airport, as per our instructions."

"And if I don't like?" I asked.

"Then we would ask for your help," Kai said.

"Help with what?" I needed to hear the answer from them.

Tomas answered, "Help getting Princess Nami out of the country and away from Tanek."

Relief flooded through me. I wouldn't to have to do this alone. First, they had to know all of it. "We need to take Princess Halea too. That's how Tanek has been

346

keeping Nami quiet. He's threatened to do to Halea what he's been doing to Nami." The words almost choked me.

The fury on the guards' faces made me take a step back.

"Tomas will take the car to the airport as planned," Kai said. "And then drive it back to the palace." He looked at me. "He will then meet us at my apartment where we will be planning." He pointed towards an older car sitting at the other end of the alley. "That is my car."

Tomas walked to the back of the car and opened the trunk. Inside were my bags. He pulled them out and set them on the ground next to me. "You will need proper clothing for us to do this." He frowned at me. "And a shower."

I sighed. "Tell me about it." I picked up my bags. "All right, let's do this."

Chapter 12

Reed

We didn't have a lot of time to plan, I knew, because as soon as Tanek realized I wasn't on the plane, he would know that Tomas and Kai were helping me, and there wouldn't be any doubt as to what they were helping me do. The last thing we needed was for Tanek to either call the police or to add more security around the girls. I was pretty sure he wouldn't do the former, not now that I had Kai and Tomas helping me. He knew they'd seen what he'd done to Nami and since they'd been her long-term bodyguards, their word would carry a lot more weight with the king and queen than mine would. In fact, if the king and queen had been in Saja, I would've been tempted just to go to them, but they wouldn't be back until Wednesday and we couldn't wait that long.

While we waited for Tomas to join us at Kai's apartment, I took a shower and changed into clean clothes. When I came out of the bathroom, Kai had food waiting. By the time Tomas arrived, I was feeling relatively alert, though I gratefully accepted one of the energy drinks that Kai handed out as we settled around his small kitchen table.

Tomas took a drink and then spoke, "Shortly after

the wedding, Tanek removed Kai and me from Princess Nami's detail. He convinced the king and queen that it would be better if Kai and I moved to protect Princess Halea as she would be coming of age. We assumed Princess Nami asked to have us moved because..." He hesitated and then shrugged. "Because of you and everything that happened when we were in Paris and Venice."

"Oh." I grimaced. "Sorry."

He shook his head. "We see now that it was not the princess. Tanek replaced half of the guards with his own men. I can see now that Tanek knew he would not be able to harm the princess while she was under our protection."

"You may have been able to arrange time alone with the princess," Kai said. "But we knew that was because she wished it. If she did not, we would have stopped you."

"And we would have stopped him," Tomas said.

"We'll stop him now," I said.

The men nodded.

"And you two being Halea's guards is going to work in our favor." A plan was slowly forming. "We need to get her away someplace safe before Nami will even consider leaving. If I have the two of you taking care of Halea, then I can just worry about Nami."

"It will not be enough to simply remove them from the palace," Tomas said.

"Yeah," I said dryly. "I figured that one out all on my own."

Tomas glanced at Kai and then looked at me. "One of the reasons we thought you would be able to help us is that you have resources that we do not."

Ah. Right. Money. A lightbulb went off. Not just money, but connections outside of Saja. I had the resources to get the princesses out of the country.

"I might need some help with connections, but I think I have an idea." I leaned back. "I know there's the

350

one airport, but does it deal with private planes?"

They both nodded.

"Then here's what we're going to do," I said. "I'll pay for a private plane to be ready this evening. You find some excuse to get Halea out of the palace and get her to the airport. I'll follow with Nami. Once we're on the plane, you two can do whatever you can to make yourselves safe until we can get Tanek put away." I looked at Kai first and then at Tomas. "You know he's going to come after you."

"We know," Kai said.

"But we promised to protect the princess and we failed," Tomas said. "We will not fail this time."

I nodded. "Can you come up with something that won't make Tanek suspicious?"

"We will tell Halea that we're taking her someplace safe. She knows enough about what's going on to understand that the palace is not safe for her or her sister. We will have her tell the other guards that she wishes to go shopping for the king's birthday next week," Tomas said. "They will not wish to do that, so we will take her."

"That's good," I said. "What about Tanek? How do we make sure he doesn't interfere?"

"Most Monday evenings, Tanek spends the evening drinking the king's finest wine." Kai didn't even bother to try to disguise the contempt in his voice.

"Good," I said. "So we don't have to wait. While you two are getting Halea out of there, I'll go for Nami. I can get into her room."

Kai raised an eyebrow and my cheeks grew hot.

"She showed me that I can get in through the maid's quarters."

"I knew we should have locked those quarters up," Tomas said with a sigh. "But it does not matter. She is no longer in that room."

"What?"

"She and Tanek were moved to the bridal suite after

the wedding." Tomas looked down, as if suddenly realizing that I might not want to hear that.

"Where's that?" I asked, my chest tightening. I didn't want to think about what had been happening in that room.

Kai stood and walked across the small apartment to a cluttered desk in the corner. He rummaged through some things and came up with a piece of paper and a pencil. He brought it back to the table and began to draw.

"A map will probably be easier than trying to give you directions," Kai said. A few minutes later, he slid the paper across the desk.

"Nice." I had to admit, I was impressed. This wasn't just some stick figure equivalent. Kai had added in enough detail that I felt confident I could get from the maid's quarters to Nami's new bedroom without much difficulty. Well, at least without getting lost. "Now, what about the guards?"

"Tanek has been keeping both princesses in their rooms, with guards posted at all times," Tomas said. He leaned over and pointed to the room Kai had marked. "The guards are usually stationed here. What they and Tanek do not know is that there is a side entrance that the servants use." He gave a hard smile. "Tanek does not care enough to pay attention to what the servants do, and the guards are new enough that they have not yet learned all of the palace." He traced a line around to where Kai had made an arrow. "This is where you will want to enter."

"Do I need a key?" I asked. "The last thing I need to happen is to get stuck outside her room because the door's locked."

Tomas reached into his pocket and pulled out a key. "This is the servants' key. It will open all of the side doors."

"All right," I said. I looked down at the map. I could have this memorized by this evening, no problem. There were two other things we needed to talk about though. "Is the service entrance still available for a way out?"

Tomas shook his head. "Once Tanek figured out that you used it to escape Friday night, he ordered double the guards and a sign in sheet to be used every time the gate is opened."

"Okay." I sighed and ran my hand through my hair. "So how do I get on and off the grounds without being seen?" That probably should have been my first question.

"They do not search my car," Tomas said. "I will drive us in and you will be in the trunk."

Oh, that sounded like fun.

"Instead of meeting at the airport, you will meet us in the garage," Tomas said. "You and Princess Nami can ride out in the trunk."

Both he and Kai looked mortified at the thought of putting me and Nami in the trunk. I wasn't sure if it was more the idea of the princess or the two of us being together that they thought was worse. It was a good idea though. More than that, it was the only idea we had.

"All right," I said. "I assume Nami can get us to the garage without any problem?"

Tomas nodded. "She knows more hidden doors and passageways than anyone."

That didn't surprise me.

"One more thing," I said. "I need to know how we're going to get rid of Tanek after the girls are safe."

"We will need evidence," Tomas said. "The king and queen will not merely accept the word of a foreigner, especially once Tanek presents them with the kidnapping and rape charges. The fact that you have the princesses again will support that."

"What about you two?"

"Tanek will claim that we are angry at being moved from Princess Namisa's detail," Kai said.

"So what we need is someone else who'll support what a horrible person Tanek is." Another idea popped into my head. "And I think I know exactly who we can

353

call."

Forty minutes later, a familiar face showed up at Kai's door. She gave the bodyguards each a look and then turned her attention to me. We sat down and I quickly explained to her what I needed her to do.

"Let me see if I understand," she said once I'd finished. "You wish for me to approach the king and queen when they return to Saja and tell them what Tanek did to me?"

"Yes." I didn't see any point in trying to sugarcoat it.

"He will kill me and our daughter."

"No, he will not," Tomas said. "Kai and I will escort you to the king and queen personally and you will bring your daughter with you."

I reached over and put my hand on Ina's. "If you do this, we will make sure Tanek can't hurt anyone ever again." I paused, and then added, "And I will hire a lawyer to ensure that Tanek and his family pay child support for your daughter until she comes of age."

Ina's eyes narrowed. "Do you believe I can be bought?"

"No," I said calmly. "I think it would be a way of me showing my gratitude for your help and you getting what you deserve."

"And we will make sure Tanek gets what he deserves," Kai said.

We fell silent as we watched her think and consider her options. Then, finally, she nodded. "I will do this." There was a stubborn set to her jaw that told me she wouldn't go back on her decision. "And I will bring my...how do you say this in English?" She looked at Tomas and said something in their language.

"Insurance," he said.

"Insurance?" I asked.

Ina gave me a hard smile. "Yes, insurance. The papers that prove Tanek is my daughter's father."

For the first time since I'd been handcuffed, I felt true

hope. This could work. This could really work. I had one more call to make. I just hoped that I truly did have at least two real friends left in Philadelphia.

Chapter 13

Reed

Ina gave Kai and Tomas her address and then headed home. They would, we decided, go from the airport to Ina's house. Tanek would never think to look for them there. By the time he figured out what was happening, it would be too late. The princesses and I would be safe in Philadelphia. Kai and Tomas would protect themselves and then they would protect her as they took her to the king and queen. She would tell them the truth about what had happened between her and Tanek, and then Kai and Tomas would share the rest. Once Tanek was arrested, Kai and Tomas would tell the king and queen where we were.

I just hoped they didn't get in trouble for not giving up that information right away. We didn't need the two of them in jail. Then again, I was sure that if it happened, Nami would be able to straighten things out once we got the Tanek situation taken care of. I had to force my thoughts away from what would happen after. I needed to think only about what would be coming one step after another. If I tried to push too far ahead, I'd lose focus and that could be bad.

The sun was starting for the horizon when I climbed

into the trunk of Tomas's car. It was nicer than Kai's, so I was glad it was the one we were using. Kai's car would be left a few blocks from the airport so that he and Tomas could use it to get closer to Ina's house before walking the rest of the way. Tomas's car would remain at the palace while we took one of the town cars to the airport. As I curled up in the trunk and Tomas shut the lid, I did allow myself a moment to think about what it would be like to be tucked into a trunk around this size with Nami curled up next to me.

I felt us stop at the gates and thoughts of anything other than getting onto the grounds fled. I didn't realize I'd been holding my breath until I let it out as the car started to move again.

All right. I took another breath, slow and deep despite the musty smell all around me. The guys would pull into the employee garage which was around back and then they would head to Halea's room and I'd follow the directions I'd memorized. It was going to work, I told myself. It had to.

I blinked against the bright florescent lights as the trunk opened. Kai gave me a terse nod and then they were gone. I climbed out of the trunk and looked around. The garage was small and they'd parked near the main door so I didn't have to go far. When I opened the door, I found myself about half a dozen yards from the door I needed to get to. Fortunately, we'd timed things well enough that it was that perfect time between afternoon and evening, when everything was shadowed but the night lights hadn't yet come on. It was also the time when the day time staff were leaving and the night staff arriving. I'd thought this would mean double the number of people to avoid, but Kai and Tomas had told me that it was the opposite when the king and queen were gone. Things were more lax, and that would definitely be good for us.

I took advantage of that and managed to get to the door without being seen. Walking into the maid's quarters was starting to feel far too familiar, but I tried not to let it distract me. I went through the door using the key Tomas had given me. I managed to keep myself from looking at the bed when I passed it. I couldn't afford to be distracted by memories, either bad or good. I went through the door and down the hall, hating how slowly I had to move, staying close to the wall and checking constantly to make sure I was alone.

I didn't know how much time had passed by the time I saw the guards standing outside the doors I knew led to Nami's room. My heart was pounding so loudly that I knew the guards had to hear it and my shirt was sticking to my back, damp with sweat. I was so close.

I took a step forward, then froze as one of the guards started to turn towards me. Shit. I flattened myself against the wall as close as I could and prayed it would be enough. After several terrifying seconds, the guard turned again and I heard them talking. I heard Nami's name, but couldn't understand anything else. It didn't matter though. As long as they weren't talking about a plan to free the princesses, I didn't care. And considering they weren't getting on their radios and panicking, I felt pretty safe in assuming they didn't know I was there.

Once I was sure they weren't going to look at me, I went around the corner and down the short hallway to where the servant's door was tucked away. My hand was shaking as I took the key out of my pocket and I realized that I was scared. Not of being caught, not of being arrested again. No, I was terrified to see Nami again and have her think that I'd failed her. I couldn't bear to look her in the eyes and see that she was disappointed with me for not being able to save her before, knowing that every pain she'd endured since I'd been arrested was my fault.

I took a slow breath and my hand steadied. As I put the key in the lock, I heard a thud from inside. I frowned. Had Nami dropped something? It hadn't really sounded like that though. Not a sharp sound. More dull. Almost like...

My heart leaped into my throat and adrenaline dumped into my veins. Another thump, this one accompanied by a sound of pain.

Nami.

I didn't even think about the guards or my own safety. I shoved the door open and stepped inside.

Tanek held Nami against the wall, gripping her arm with one hand, fingers buried in her flesh. The other hand was in the air, ready to hit her again. She had a red handprint on her cheek, but I could see bruises from where I stood. She was covered with them. The thin nightgown she was wearing did nothing to cover them. Not the ones on her arms. Not the welts on her shoulders that I knew had come from a belt.

I was going to kill him.

Chapter 14

Nami

I'd thought I'd get a reprieve from Tanek tonight. With my parents gone, he could raid the best of my father's alcohol without the risk of being caught. He had done that, but had apparently decided that he preferred coming to me rather than passing out wherever he'd sat down to drink.

Evenings at the end of June were warm and I'd finally turned on the air conditioning just enough to take the edge off. I'd chosen a fairly thin cotton nightgown, believing that I would be alone. I hadn't looked in the mirror though. I'd made the mistake of doing that yesterday morning when I'd gotten out of the shower. The memory was enough to make me cringe and I'd never been so glad not to have inherited my mother's fairer skin.

Tanek had staggered into the room just a few minutes ago, his face flushed. I'd considered running since he didn't look sober enough to come after me, but I'd known that would end just as badly because the guards would catch me, even if Tanek couldn't. The thought had flickered through my mind then that this was the time to fight back. I wasn't sure if I could do it though, and I knew that if I was going to kill Tanek, I had to be sure. I couldn't go halfway or I'd be the one dead.

Despite him being drunk, Tanek was still taller than me and outweighed me by enough to make a difference. I couldn't do it now. It had to be planned, not impulsive, or it would never work.

"Surprised to see me?"

I didn't say anything. It didn't matter how I answered him, he'd take it as an insult or find some fault in it. Nothing I said would stop him if he wanted to hit me, and he always wanted to hit me. Sometimes, I was actually glad that he wasn't one of those men who acted sorry afterwards and apologized. If he continued to abuse me, I preferred he just be a bastard all the time.

"Who are you wearing that for?" Tanek sneered. He grabbed my arm and gave me a shake. "I know it can't be for Reed. He left this morning."

I pressed my lips together to keep from asking the question I knew he wanted me to ask.

He answered anyway, still too drunk to manage English, "I offered to let him go if he confessed. Didn't even take him long to decide."

My stomach fell. I should've been happy, I knew. Reed was free. He was on his way back to America where he would be safe. I couldn't help but feel a pang of betrayal that he'd been so easily swayed.

He smiled. "I've got the written confession right here. Handwritten and the only copy, of course. We don't need anything out there for nosy reporters to see...unless I want them to." He patted the pocket of his pants. "Do you want me to read it to you?" He thought for a moment. "No, better that I act it out first so you can be surprised. I'll read it to you after so you can relive the whole thing."

I glared at him but didn't say a word as he spun me around, shoving me against the wall with a dull thud. The welts on my back throbbed painfully as I hit the wall, but I kept quiet. I couldn't, however, stop the small sound of pain when he slapped me, his fingers landing on a place that had been bruised by his belt the night before.

He raised his hand to hit me again and I clenched my teeth, determined that he wouldn't get another sound out of me. He didn't get the chance to bring his hand down as the servants' door at the back of the room suddenly swung open.

For one long second Reed stood in the doorway, fury burning on his face like nothing I'd ever seen before.

He hadn't left me. He'd come back. Again. After all I'd put him through, he'd still come for me. I could see the bruising on his face, the exhaustion in every limb.

The relief rushing through my body came with something else. Anger. No, nothing so tame as anger. This was rage. Not only for what Tanek had done to me, but for what he'd done to Halea, what he'd done to Reed.

I was so done with his shit.

Remembering something I'd learned years ago in a self-defense class I'd insisted on taking before going to college, I jabbed my free hand at Tanek's throat, keeping my fingers stiff as they came in contact. Even as I did it, I brought my knee up as well. I heard the seams of my nightgown tear, but I didn't care. Shocked by the sudden blow to the throat – and not helped by the alcohol he'd consumed – Tanek couldn't think fast enough to protect his crotch. I felt a vindictive stab of satisfaction as my knee made direct contact.

Tanek dropped, his hand unable to hold my arm as he fell to his knees. He curled up, hacking and gasping, unable to make any noise loud enough to let the guards outside know that it wasn't me who was in pain.

I didn't even spare him a look as I ran straight into Reed's arms. His mouth came down on mine more gently than I wanted and I pressed myself against him, not caring that the kiss hurt my bruised lips. I buried my hands in his hair, twisting my fingers until Reed made a noise in the back of his throat and his arms finally tightened around me the way I wanted. My injuries throbbed painfully, but they were nothing compared to the joy I felt at being where I belonged. Heat flooded me, pushing aside all of the pain until all I could feel was him.

I wanted to stay there in his arms, forget everything else, but I could hear Tanek wheezing on the floor and I knew we didn't have time. I broke the kiss, allowing myself a moment to close my eyes, to feel safe for the first time since I'd fallen asleep in his arms. Then I stepped back.

"Oh, baby." Reed's voice was soft.

I looked up into those dark eyes and my heart did a little skipping beat at the emotion I saw there. Anger. Desire. Compassion. He brushed his fingers down the side of my face, light enough that it didn't hurt.

"I could say the same." I placed a gentle hand on his injured cheek. "But I'm okay."

He raised an eyebrow as he reached up and took my hand. "This is far from okay."

"You're here," I said.

"I am." He glanced at Tanek. "And that fucking bastard will never touch you again."

"Halea..." My heart constricted.

"Safe," he said. He lowered his voice so that Tanek couldn't hear him. "Kai and Tomas are getting her."

I breathed a sigh of relief.

"This has to be your choice, Nami." He squeezed my hand. "I want you to come with me. You and Halea. Come to the States, where I can protect you."

"Go...back?" I don't know why that came as a surprise. It made sense. Quite a bit, actually. Reed had connections that could keep us safe until we figured out what to do. Then I realized he was still waiting for an answer. "Yes. Of course, yes."

He smiled. "Let's go."

"*Bitch*." Tanek's voice was little more than a croak.

I stopped mid-step. Reed gave me a concerned look. "I can't leave in this." I gestured as I pulled my hand away from his. "Will you get me something to wear?"

364

As he moved to do as I asked, I walked back over to where Tanek was laying. He was trying to get back up, his mouth working as he was trying to get sounds out. I knew the chances of him calling the guards was about fifty-fifty at the moment. He wanted to hurt me, beat me, maybe to death. And he didn't want anyone to know that a woman had put him down. But, I knew if he thought Reed and I were going to get away, he'd risk it, probably lie to the guards and tell them that Reed had done it.

I wasn't going to risk it.

I looked down at Tanek as he started to push himself up against the wall. All of the rage I'd pushed down, the humiliation, the pain, I let it come up. My hand curled into a fist. I was done. Done being beaten.

"Fuck you!" I put all of my weight behind the swing. Pain flared up my knuckles and my arm, jarring and bright, but it was worth it to see Tanek's head spin around, hear his strangled cry.

His eyes were dazed as he looked up at me, but he couldn't keep himself upright. As he slumped down on the floor, I drew back my foot and kicked him in the stomach, ignoring the sharp pain in my toes. He retched and I pulled back again.

"Nami." Reed grabbed my arm and I looked up at him. His eyes were hard. "You shouldn't do that without shoes." He held up a pair of slip-on tennis shoes. "You could hurt yourself."

I pulled on the shoes and then reached for the dress he'd pulled from my closet. I didn't look down at Tanek who was still coughing and whimpering. I pulled the nightgown over my head, stiffening as I heard Reed swear under his breath, but I didn't look at him either. I pulled the sundress over my head, thankful that Reed had picked something that wasn't too rough against my bruises.

"I'm going to kill him." Reed's eyes were as dark as I'd ever seen them. Pitch black and full of something I'd never seen before. Hate. Not just anger, but pure hate.

"No." I grabbed Reed's arm. "We're not going to kill him." I didn't mention the fact that I'd been thinking of doing just that. Now that Reed was here, I didn't need to do that. Besides...I looked down at Tanek. "Death's too good for him."

I let go of Reed's arm and kicked Tanek again, this time without hurting my toes. He retched again, this time vomiting up whatever he'd been drinking. I made a face but reached down anyway and grabbed him by the hair.

"I will make sure you spend every moment of the rest of your life regretting you ever thought you were good enough to marry me." I hesitated for only a moment before I slammed his head against the floor. His eyes rolled up, body going limp. I dug into his pants and pulled out the envelope before I straightened and turned towards Reed. "Let's go."

Reed's eyes were wide as he stared at me. I waited for him to say something, anything, but he didn't. Instead, I watched two different emotions play across his face. Shock at what I'd done. And admiration. He held out his hand.

"We need to get to the garage. The one where your family's cars are."

I nodded. We'd lost time that I was sure we needed. Tanek's guards wouldn't worry if they didn't hear anything or if Tanek didn't come out soon, but when he did wake up, we'd want to be as far away as possible.

We went back out the servants' door, but instead of going back towards the main hallway, I led Reed the other way. It looked like a dead end, but I knew it wasn't. Most of the big rooms had servants' entrances, which were common knowledge. The new guards Tanek had hired didn't know yet, but other members of the security team did. No one but family knew where we were going. And Tanek wasn't family enough for this.

Saja was a peaceful country, but when my great-

great-great-grandfather had built the new palace, World War II had been enough of a reality for him to worry about his family. He'd had hidden passages built throughout the house. Even generations later, we'd kept the secret, and now I was glad we had.

I found the panel easily and pressed my fingers into the release. I heard a small sound of surprise but didn't look back. I felt along the wall and found the flashlight we kept inside. The beam was fairly weak, but it was enough. I listened hard as we walked, waiting for any sound that would indicate Tanek had woken up.

I slowed as we passed another panel that should lead to the hallway just outside the kitchen, which meant that the next one would be the garage. I had an idea of what the plan was. If Kai and Tomas were getting Halea, that meant they were probably planning to take us all out in one of my family's cars. How we were going to manage that without being seen by the outside guards, I didn't know, but I trusted Reed and the guys. They would get us out of here.

I pushed the release and the panel slid aside. Reed stepped in front of me before I could walk out, bending his arm so that he pulled me close to his back, shielding me with his body. A surge of love went through me, so strong that it brought tears to my eyes. Tanek had used and abused my body for his own pleasure, and even though the last time had cost him his freedom, Reed continued to put himself between me and any threat.

"Nami!"

Reed let go of my hand and moved out of the way so that Halea could run into my arms. I clutched her tightly, looking over her head at Reed. "Thank you." I wanted to keep looking at him, but there were two others I needed to thank as well. I slid my eyes over to Kai and Tomas and repeated the same words to them. They nodded.

"What did he do to you?" Halea's words were muffled and I reluctantly released her. Her eyes were wide and concerned, though I could see the anger underneath it.

"Don't worry about it." I started to tuck her hair behind her ear but stopped when she scowled at me. Shit. She was angry at me.

"Why didn't you tell me it was this bad," she demanded. "Nami..." Her bottom lip trembled and tears welled up in her eyes. "Why didn't you..." Her voice trailed off and I watched things click. "Me. You stayed because of me." She looked at the guys and then back at me. "That's why I had to go with you last time. Not because you were just afraid he was violent in general. Tanek threatened me, didn't he?"

"Nami." Reed's voice was soft. "You may have knocked the bastard out, but we still need to go."

"You did what?" Halea was startled into English.

I lifted my chin. "I gave him back a little of what he gave me."

"Good," Halea said. The anger in her voice surprised me.

"Princesses," Tomas spoke, an urgent tone in his voice. "We need to go."

"Right." I turned towards my former bodyguards. "How are we doing this?"

Tomas opened the trunk to one of the town cars. "I am sorry."

If I hadn't seen the look of chagrin on Tomas's face, I wouldn't have believed it.

"We told the other guards we are taking Halea shopping for your father's birthday," Kai said.

"Which means she can sit in the car," I realized. "But I can't." I looked at Reed. "And neither can you."

He shrugged, his expression blank but his eyes dancing. "It'll be a snug fit, but I think we can manage."

I was surprised at the sudden flare of arousal that went through me. Even with all that had happened, the thought of being crammed into a tight space with Reed...I wanted him. It may have been crazy, but I couldn't help it.

My throat tightened when I saw the same desire shining in Reed's eyes.

"It'll make more sense if I get in first."

I wasn't sure if anyone else noticed the rough edge to Reed's voice, but my body certainly recognized it. I watched as Reed climbed into the trunk and then climbed in after him. As Tomas closed the lid, I settled back against him.

"Is it okay if I put my arms around you?" Despite the desire I could feel radiating off him, Reed sounded almost hesitant.

"Please." I leaned my head back so that it was resting on his shoulder. I sighed as his arms went around my waist.

Neither of us spoke again until we knew we'd passed through the front gate and were on our way to the airport. When Reed did break the silence, what he said wasn't what I'd expected.

"What's in the envelope?"

I'd completely forgotten about the envelope until now, and was almost surprised that I still had it. "Oh, that." I couldn't turn to look at him, but I held it over my shoulder so he could take it. "It's your...confession." I put as much derision into the word as I could."

"Really?"

"That piece of shit got this from the police so he could show it to me. It is the only copy."

Reed chuckled, surprising me again. He kissed the top of my head. "You are the most amazing woman, Namisa Carrmoni." His arms tightened briefly around me. "I love you."

Four words didn't seem adequate to express everything I was feeling, but they were all I had at the moment. "I love you too."

369

Chapter 15

Reed

I grimaced as my vertebrate made loud popping sounds. I stretched my arms above my head and twisted my waist. Being crammed into a trunk two times in a short period of time wasn't exactly friendly on the spine or muscles, no matter how pleasant the companionship had been the second time.

I glanced at Nami and then looked away. I was already half-hard from being pressed tight against her. Continuing to look at her was either going to give me an uncomfortable erection for the plane ride or piss me off. The bruises I'd first seen on her when I'd walked into her room had been bad enough, but then she'd taken off the dress and I'd wanted to beat Tanek to death. There wasn't an inch on her that didn't have a new or at least fading bruise. The only thing that had kept the bastard alive was that Nami had stopped me. I promised myself that I would do whatever it took to make sure Tanek spent the rest of his life as another inmate's bitch.

"Mr. Stirling?"

I turned as the pilot approached. He wasn't anyone I knew, but I'd chartered private jets through this particular international company before and I knew them to be professional and, more importantly, discreet. Right now, the most important thing was to keep as many details as possible quiet for as long as we could.

"My name is Antonio Russo." He flashed impossibly white teeth when he smiled. "I will be flying your party to a private airstrip just outside of Padua. Another plane will be waiting to complete your trip to the United States."

I shook his hand. "Thank you. Are we ready to go?"

"Yes, Sir." Antonio nodded. "Whenever you are."

"We'll board in a minute," I said. "I just need to have a few words with the gentlemen who won't be coming with us."

The pilot nodded again and then picked up the luggage Kai had pulled from the backseat. I gave the bodyguard a surprised look. I hadn't even thought about my things. I was glad he had though. It was one less thing I had to bother with.

"Princess Namisa," Tomas spoke, his voice surprisingly emotional. "Before you leave, we must beg your forgiveness."

Nami's eyes widened in surprise, but she didn't say anything.

"Kai and I had been charged with keeping you safe for years and we have failed in our duty."

"No." She shook her head. "The blame for this lies on no one but Tanek Nekane. You protected my sister. You made sure that she was not harmed by my husband. There is nothing to forgive."

Kai opened his mouth as if he'd protest, but a sharp look from Nami stopped him.

"Now we have to finish what we have started," she said. She looked over at me. "I am assuming that running to Philadelphia is not the end of the plan."

"It's not," I said. "I'll give you the details on the plane, but the short version is that Kai and Tomas are staying here to implement the last part of the plan to get Tanek arrested." I glanced at the plane. "We need to go."

"Reed is correct," Tomas said. He gave a bow to Nami and then to Halea before turning to me and holding out a hand. "Thank you."

"Thank you," I repeated. "And you two be careful."

"We will." Kai shook my hand as well. "Take care of our princesses."

"I will," I promised.

The pair got back into the town car and drove off to wherever they intended to hide it. After that, they'd go to Kai's car and head for Ina's apartment. Then it became a waiting game for them until the king and queen returned. For the princesses and myself, our time of waiting was beginning right now.

I held out a hand to Nami and she took it, then put her other arm around Halea. Together, we headed for the plane.

I hadn't bothered to ask for their nicest one since availability was more important, so it was more compact than some of the others I'd used before to entertain business associates, but it was still better than a commercial flight, even in first class. I'd been thinking of needing privacy because of who Halea and Nami were, but after seeing the marks on Nami's body, I was doubly glad I'd gone with private flights. The last thing she needed was people staring at her injuries.

Halea settled in one of the seats and, after a quick look at me, Nami went to sit beside her. I was a bit disappointed that she wasn't sitting with me, but I could see why she needed to be near her sister. I headed up to the cockpit to let the captain know we were ready to go and then went to the bar to find out what sort of drinks they had to offer.

By the time we touched down in Italy, both princesses seemed to be calmer and I'd finally started to relax as well. That, I assumed, had just as much to do with the couple of now-empty bottles of liquor I'd consumed. It wasn't enough for me to be drunk or even

373

tipsy, but they'd definitely taken the edge off. I wouldn't be completely tension-free until we were home, but Italy was definitely safer than Saja. Kai and Tomas had assured me that, while relations with Italy were good, Tanek would still have to go through a process to try to get Nami and Halea back from there. It'd be even harder once we were in the States, and that would be if he could find us at all. Considering I trusted the only two people who knew we were coming, I doubted Tanek would be able to figure out where we were before the king and queen arrived back in Saja.

The plane in Italy was a little bigger than the first and included a long seat that Halea immediately claimed. As soon as we were airborne and allowed to unbuckle, Halea stretched out, falling asleep in seconds. I found a blanket and covered her with it, tucking it in so it wouldn't fall off. She looked even younger and more innocent, and I felt a surge of anger that Tanek could even consider hurting her.

"He's never going to touch you," I promised quietly. I knew she couldn't hear me, but that didn't matter. Even if the king and queen refused to lock up Tanek, I would do whatever it took to protect Halea and Nami.

"Reed." Nami slipped her hand into mine.

I turned around and looked down at her. I used my free hand to tuck an unruly curl behind her ear. "I don't care what it takes. I will make you safe again."

She raised herself on her toes and pressed her lips against mine. It was a fairly quick, chaste kiss, but I saw the bright flare of arousal in her eyes.

"You will do anything to make me feel safe?"

That wasn't exactly how I'd worded it, but it was close enough. "Yes."

One side of her mouth quirked up in a partial smile. "Good. Come with me."

I was confused, but let her pull me after her. As soon as I realized where she was going, I knew what she

374

wanted. At least, I thought I did, even though I had to be wrong. What I was thinking was crazy.

"Do you know when I feel the most safe?" she asked as she opened the door to the bathroom. She backed inside and pulled me towards her. "When you are inside me."

Fuck.

"I don't know, Nami," I protested weakly.

She reached around me and closed the door, locking it. This bathroom was slightly larger than the one on a commercial plane, but it was still a tight fit.

"Do you want me?" she asked, reaching up to trace my bottom lip with her finger.

"I always want you," I said. And it was the truth. My brain said this was a bad idea, but my cock was insisting it was the best idea I'd heard all day.

Nami slid her hand down my neck and down my chest. Her eyes locked with mine as her hand dropped lower and cupped me through my pants. My entire body jerked as she grasped me. Fuck.

"You're hurt." I tried another protest even though my cock was screaming at me to shut up.

Nami nodded. "So are you."

"Not even close to the same."

She let go of my cock and lifted herself onto the sink. As she parted her legs, she pulled up her dress until the hem rested on her thighs. I let out air in a hiss as she moved her hand between her legs. She made a sound and her eyelids fluttered. I swallowed hard, my pants suddenly and impossibly tight. When she pulled her hand out, her fingers were glistening. Without taking her eyes off me, she raised her hand to her mouth and licked her fingers clean.

"Oh, fuck, Nami," I breathed.

She nodded. "Yes, please." She held out her hand. "Fuck Nami. I need you. I need you to make me clean again."

A better man than me wouldn't have been able to refuse her. I was pushing my pants down on my hips even as I took the two steps I needed to end up right between her legs.

"Fast," she said as she grasped my cock and led it to her entrance.

I nodded. I would go fast in a moment, but I needed to ease inside the first time. I rested my forehead against hers as I moved forward inch by inch. I kept one hand on her back and put the other beneath her dress. If this was going to be fast, she'd need a bit of help to get off and I was determined to give her at least one orgasm.

A sharp pain went through my earlobe as she bit down. Her mouth started to move down my neck, lips and teeth setting my skin on fire. I took that as my cue and started to move. Fast but deep strokes that left her empty one moment and filled the next. My thumb played across her clit and she whimpered, a sound of pleasure and not pain, one that made my stomach clench and my balls tighten. I was so close. Her thighs quivered around me and I knew she was nearly there too.

I thrust into her two more times and groaned as I exploded, unable to hold back anymore. I rocked against her, giving her the friction she needed to follow me over the edge. We stayed that way, locked together in an embrace, our bodies still joined, breathing harsh, blood rushing in our ears. The world outside would wait a little longer. Right now, we were safe and she was in my arms. That was all that mattered at the moment. We'd face the rest soon enough, but I would keep her here as long as I could, letting her know without words that she was safe and I wouldn't let anything bad happen to her again.

Chapter 16

Nami

I wasn't sure when I managed to fall asleep, but with Reed's arms around me and my head on his shoulder, it didn't surprise me. With the exception of that one night in the hotel, I'd only been sleeping in fits and starts since I'd met Tanek. An hour here and there, waking suddenly with a pounding heart and the certainty that Tanek was there in the dark. In Reed's arms, with his scent around me, the memory of him throbbing between my legs, I was able to let myself go. Even in sleep, when the darkness tried to frighten me, I knew he was there and the thought was enough to keep the demons at bay.

"Nami." His voice was soft in my ear, but loud enough to pull me from sleep. "We're almost home."

For a moment, I felt panic and my eyes opened. Then I realized what he meant and the fear faded, though the adrenaline had made me suddenly and completely awake. Reed gave me a concerned look as I sat up.

I didn't give him a chance to ask if I was okay. I had a feeling I would be sick of that question very soon. "Did you sleep at all?" I asked him.

He nodded. "A bit, but I don't think I'll really relax until we're in a place I know no one can get to you." He reached out and put his hand on my cheek, his touch light enough that it didn't hurt.

"Where are we going?" I asked suddenly, realizing I didn't know any details.

"Philadelphia," he said. "I have some friends there I can trust."

"Friends, not family?" I put my hand on his arm.

"No," he said. "I can't try to work things out with them and worrying about you at the same time."

"I don't want you worry about me or Halea," I said.

He gave me the kind of smile that said I just didn't understand. "You're my world, Nami. How can I not worry about you?"

Before I could think of something to say, he was on his feet and heading for the cockpit.

"I like him." Halea sat down next to me. Her face was pale and she looked tired even though I knew she'd slept through most of the eight hour flight. She reached over and took my hand. "I know you think you have to protect me, but I am stronger than you think."

I smiled as I squeezed her hand. "It wasn't your strength I doubted. It was mine. I could bear what Tanek did to me, but I couldn't have handled anything happening to you."

Tears spilled over, running down Halea's cheeks and she buried her head against my chest, her arms wrapping around me so tightly that it hurt. I didn't ask her to stop, putting my own arms around her and kissing the top of her head. My own eyes burned with tears.

"It's all right now, little one," I murmured. "Shh. We're safe now."

By the time Reed came back to tell us that we'd be landing at a private airstrip just outside of Philadelphia in a few minutes, Halea and I had both regained our composure enough to excuse ourselves to freshen up. I returned to my seat just as the pilot announced that we needed to put on our seat belts. I sat next to Reed. Now that the immediate concerns were out of the way and we

378

were now simply waiting to hear from Kai and Tomas about my parents, I found myself growing nervous. Not at what was going to happen with Tanek, but rather what would be waiting for us in Philadelphia.

"Your friends," I asked as the plane began to descend. "Are they picking us up at the airport?"

"They are." Reed reached over and laced his fingers between mine. A faint flush stained his cheeks. "Do you remember me telling you about Piper?"

It took me a moment, but then I placed the name. "The woman whose decision to go with another man sent you to Europe?"

The corner of Reed's mouth twitched and his ears began to turn red. "I wouldn't have put it exactly like that, but yes. She and her boyfriend are picking us up. They moved in together earlier this summer, but she has an apartment in Fishtown that still has a lease on it. She hasn't been able to find someone to sublet it to, so we can stay there as long as we need to."

"That's very generous of her." I hoped I didn't sound suspicious, but I found it strange that a woman who'd rejected Reed would go to all this trouble to help him.

"Nami, there's nothing between Piper and me but friendship."

I looked up at Reed and found his expression serious. He raised our hands and kissed the back of mine.

"She's actually the one who told me that if I loved you, I needed to go after you and not let anyone stop me." He squeezed my hand. "What Piper and I had...it wasn't real. She and Julien are meant to be together." His eyes were warm as they met mine. "Just like we are."

Because of the six hour or so time difference, it was a little past one in the morning as we left the airplane and I shivered as a gust of wind whipped across the landing strip. Reed slid his arm around my waist and pulled me against him as we walked towards the couple who were waiting next to a normal-looking car. That was surprising.

I'd assumed that Reed's friends had as much money as he did.

I looked at her first. She was about my age, maybe a year or two older. Bright red hair that she had pulled back in a ponytail. Dark green eyes and a light dusting of freckles across her fair skin. She was quite pretty, but the way she looked at the man standing next to her kept me from being jealous. She was clearly in love. He was tall with black hair and bright blue eyes, a handsome man, I thought, but not my type.

"Thank you guys so much for helping us," Reed said as we reached his friends. He put out his free hand and shook Julien's hand. Piper came forward to give him a half-hug, then gave me one as well, surprising me enough that I couldn't cover it.

She smiled. "Julien and I both know what it's like to have everything working against you." She reached behind her and he took her hand. "Any way we can help, we're more than happy to."

"Thank you," I said. All of the anxiety I'd had at meeting her melted away. She had one of the most sincere faces I'd ever seen. "I'm Nami and this is my sister Halea." I gestured towards Halea who gave Piper a shy smile. I purposefully left off our titles, though I supposed Reed had told his friends who we were. I didn't want them to think of us that way though.

"We brought the car rather than having someone drive us," Julien spoke up. "Figured it would be the best way to keep from drawing attention." He glanced at me and offered an additional explanation. "The apartment's not in a bad neighborhood or anything, but a town car would be noticed, even this early in the morning."

"Thank you," I said again.

He opened the back door and I climbed in while Halea walked around to the other side. Reed got in beside me as his friends put Reed's luggage in the trunk and then got into the front of the car.

As Julien began to drive, Piper half-turned in her seat so she could see us while she talked.

"You asked us to keep an ear out for any international news," she said to Reed. "There hasn't been anything yet." She looked at me, her expression open and compassionate. "I am so sorry for what happened to you."

I didn't know how much Reed had told her, but I knew at least some of the evidence was still clear on my skin. I nodded, swallowing hard. Reed put his arm around my shoulders. My stomach flipped and I closed my eyes for a moment, fighting a sudden wave of nausea. It was jet lag, I told myself. Jet lag and nerves. I'd been sick every day since Reed had been arrested.

"The place is mostly empty," Piper was saying. "We wanted to keep it furnished in case we had a renter who preferred it that way, but it's pretty plain. I went over right after we got off the phone and cleaned, then went shopping."

I opened my eyes and caught Halea looking at me, concerned. I managed a smile and turned my attention to the city I could see through the windshield. We didn't go downtown though, heading off to a neighborhood outside what I would have considered the city. Piper informed us that Fishtown was part of Philadelphia, but not the business or historical district. I was going to ask why they called it Fishtown when one of the streetlights illuminated the image of a fish on the side of one of the buildings. Not like a drawing or anything like that, but rather a metal cast. I couldn't see much detail as we passed, but it was enough to confirm it was a fish.

"Here we are," Julien said as he pulled up to the curb.

We were on a cobblestone street off of the main one, parked in front of what I would have thought of as a row house rather than an apartment. It was a rustically beautiful red brick building. I was sure it would be even nicer looking in the daylight.

Piper went up the steps and unlocked the door while Julien grabbed Reed's bags. He kept his arm around me as we followed Piper and Halea followed us. We stepped into a living room just as Piper flicked a switch, lighting things up. It had been painted fairly recently, I saw. Not enough that we could smell it, but enough for it to be clear that she'd done some work on the place.

"It's lovely," I said.

"Thank you." Piper gave me a warm smile. "I brought over some clothes for you to wear if you needed them. They're upstairs in the main room. Linens are in the hall closet just outside the bathroom. The fridge is stocked with food and drinks."

"You didn't have to do all of that," Reed said.

"Yes, I did." Piper turned her smile on him, but it was clear it was only platonic. "You did so much for me, it was the least I could do."

"It's late," Julien spoke up. "We'll leave you to get settled. Give us a call if you need anything, no matter the time."

"Thank you." Reed put out his hand again and Julien shook it.

The three of us stood in silence for nearly a full minute after Piper and Julien left. The apartment was quiet and any sounds from outside were muffled. Reed released me to walk over to the door and turn the deadbolt. I had a feeling he wasn't doing it because he thought we needed protection from people in the neighborhood.

"Why don't you two head upstairs," he said. "I'll see what Piper has in the kitchen and whip us up something while you're showering. When you're done, I'll bring up some food and take a shower. There are two bedrooms. The bigger one's on the right. I'll be in the one on the left."

"No," Halea spoke up. "You and Nami will share the bigger room."

382

"Halea." I could feel the heat burning in my cheeks.

"I am not a child, Namisa." Halea's eyes narrowed and, for the first time, I saw myself in her face. "You two need to be together. End of discussion."

As she started up the stairs, Reed turned to me with a half-smile on his face. "That is definitely your sister."

I laughed softly. "Yes, she is." I held out my hand. "Shall we find something to eat before going upstairs to our room?" I liked the sound of that.

He took my hand and then sighed.

"What's wrong?" I asked.

"We finally get a room where we won't be interrupted and I'm too tired to do anything but sleep."

I laughed again and stepped into him, wrapping my arms around his waist. His automatically closed around me as well. I rested my cheek on his chest. "That's okay. We have plenty of time. And falling asleep in your arms sounds like the best thing in the world right now."

He kissed the top of my head. "Yes," he agreed. "It does."

Chapter 17

Reed

Waking up in that bed, with Nami in my arms, the bright sunlight streaming in between the curtains, the smell of whatever it was Halea was cooking wafting up the stairs, it was like something out of a dream.

Piper had left some of her clothes for the girls and I still had a clean outfit or two in my bags, but it was pretty clear that one of the first things we needed to do after breakfast that morning was go shopping.

I called a car and the three of us went into the city. There still hadn't been anything on the news about the girls being missing and I was beginning to suspect that there wouldn't be. Tanek still had until tomorrow evening before the king and queen knew something was wrong, I was willing to bet that he would do whatever it took to make sure they didn't find out. That probably meant he'd try to figure out where we'd gone and come after us. I just hoped that by the time he realized we'd left the country, Kai and Tomas would have gotten Ina to the king and queen.

I wasn't going to worry about that though. We were safe for now and it was Nami's first time in Philadelphia, and Halea's first time in the United States. I may have had issues with my family and some of the members of Philadelphia high society, but I did love my city and I intended to show it off. We went to Macy's first, so the girls could get clothes and so that I could see the expressions on their faces when they saw the gigantic pipe organ that covered the upper parts of the walls.

When we left a couple hours later, we had enough clothes to last all three of us several weeks. We took them back to the apartment and then went out to walk. The weather was absolutely gorgeous. A bit hot considering it was the end of June, but there was a nice breeze and I could tell that the freedom of being out and about without having to worry about bodyguards or anything like that made the air smell twice as sweet.

The three of us spent the rest of Tuesday and all of Wednesday in various parts of the city. We walked and ate and talked. Halea quickly became enough at ease with me that she didn't seem self-conscious anymore, and even tried teaching me some of their native language. Nami's face lost its look of pinched worry and she began to get her color back even as her bruises faded. She still looked a bit peaked in the mornings, but I wasn't worried. It would take awhile for her frayed nerves to mend. We didn't know how long our peaceful time together would last, but none of us talked about it. We wanted to enjoy what we had and not think about anything else. When things started to change, we'd deal with it, but for the moment, we were safe and happy.

Thursday morning, we were up early and in the kitchen discussing what we'd be doing after breakfast when someone knocked on the door. Immediately, the mood shifted. Julien and Piper both had keys, and although they might knock just to be polite, something in my gut said that it wasn't either of my friends.

"Stay here." I was technically talking to both of them, but I looked at Nami. Halea would follow her sister's lead, and I didn't want Nami doing something foolish.

Nami raised her eyebrow but didn't argue. I took that as agreement and went out as the person at the door knocked again.

I could've asked who it was, but it'd end up the same either way. If, by some strange fluke, it was Tanek, he wouldn't be getting into the house, no matter who was with him. American police wouldn't come in without a warrant or an invitation. And if Tanek himself tried, I'd yell for Nami to call the police.

As soon as I opened the door, however, everything changed. It wasn't Tanek on the other side, or any of the bodyguards. It wasn't even the American police, called by Tanek, which was something I'd had in the back of my mind.

No, the two people standing on the doorstep were familiar-looking. And the last two people I would've expected to see standing here.

"Your Majesties." I managed to keep my voice polite and even, though I merely inclined my head instead of bowing. They may have been a king and queen, but I wasn't in their country and they had given their daughter to a monster. I wasn't about to give them any more than the slightest courtesy, and only that because of how much I loved Nami.

"Mr. Stirling." King Raj shifted on the step as if he planned to come inside.

Immediately, I folded my arms across my chest, solidifying my presence in the doorway. If he wanted inside, he would have to get by me, and I didn't like his chances. He wasn't a small man, but I was bigger, and younger. And I was pissed.

"Please, let us see our daughter," the queen spoke this time. There was a pleading note in her voice, but I didn't move.

"Reed."

Nami spoke up from behind me and I glanced over

my shoulder.

"It's okay."

I had my doubts, but they were her parents. As long as they didn't try to take her out of the house by force, they couldn't hurt her by coming in. I knew I didn't have to worry about them talking her into coming back to Tanek, not with Halea still in the kitchen.

I stepped to one side and the queen rushed past me and threw her arms around Nami. I wasn't sure who was more surprised, her or me. Then the king stepped inside and turned towards me, his hand out.

Well, shit.

As I shook his outstretched hand, movement outside caught the corner of my eye. When the king moved to embrace his daughter as well, I looked towards the road. Kai and Tomas were standing at the car. They gave me identical nods and I felt a rush of relief. The fact that they were here meant, I hoped, that they'd gotten Ina to the king and queen, and that Tanek was done.

I closed the door behind me and turned to find Halea in her father's arms and Queen Mara wiping her eyes. Nami looked at me, her own eyes wet and shining. She motioned towards the couch and chairs that Piper had left behind.

"Let's sit."

I let them all settle, unsure where I should sit. King Raj took one of the chairs and Halea perched on the arm, grinning from ear to ear. Queen Mara sat on the couch and Nami took the seat in the middle. She looked up at me and smiled, gesturing to the spot next to her. I took it, but didn't touch her. We needed to deal with one issue at a time.

"Kai and Tomas brought a young lady to speak with us," King Raj glanced at Halea, obviously choosing his words carefully. "Ina told us about her own...experiences with Tanek."

Nami's face tightened.

388

"And then they told us about you." King Raj looked at me, his eyes narrowed. "About how you and Nami met, and the time you spent together."

Oh, fuck me.

I didn't know what the expression on my face was, but I did see the stubborn set to Nami's jaw, the rebellious glint in her eyes. She reached over and took my hand.

"Did they?" Her voice was cool.

"They did," Queen Mara said dryly. "Enough that they knew they could be in serious trouble for their dereliction of duty."

My fingers twitched against Nami's, but she remained calm and collected.

"What else did my bodyguards tell you?"

I caught a flash of something in the king's eyes, something that looked like a combination of admiration and annoyance. It was quickly replaced with something else. Regret.

"The truth about what we had done to you." King Raj stood and crossed over to where we were sitting. To my shock, he went down on his knees in front of Nami. "We were wrong, my child. So wrong." His voice caught on the last word and he grabbed Nami's free hand. "I will never forgive myself for what that..." He uttered a word in their native language that, based on the shocked look on Nami's face, I assumed was suitably appropriate for Tanek. "For what he did to you."

Nami's fingers tightened around mine. Kai and Tomas didn't know the worst of it. I hadn't told them all the things I knew Tanek had done, only that he'd been abusing her. That meant the king and queen didn't know.

"He's in jail," Queen Mara said. She smoothed down Nami's hair. "And he will never hurt you again."

King Raj turned to me, still on his knees. "Thank you, Reed, for saving my daughters when I was too blind to see what was happening."

I didn't know if this was the right time, but I

wouldn't go another moment without saying it. If they knew that Nami and I had slept together when we'd first met, and it seemed like they did, they needed to know the whole truth of it. "I love her."

Nami's hand squeezed mine almost to the point of pain. She clearly hadn't expected that, but she didn't look angry at my confession.

"Do you?" Queen Mara's voice was cool, but not cold.

"I do." I made the words firm as I turned to meet the queen's eyes. They were Nami's eyes, almost the exact same shade of blue-green. "And I'll protect her with my life."

"From what we hear, you almost did just that." King Raj stood. "And we won't forget it."

"Neither will I," Nami said softly. Her parents looked at her. "What I want to know is, with all this talk of being sorry coupled with what you owe Reed – have you learned anything?"

The atmosphere immediately changed and I could feel the tension radiating off of all three of them.

"You say you'll never forgive yourself for what happened," she continued. "But that doesn't mean anything to me if you're not willing to change."

"Change?" King Raj's voice was soft.

Nami lifted her chin. "You forced me to marry a man I didn't choose. A man who beat me. Raped me. Repeatedly."

My fingers were nearly numb from how hard she was squeezing my hand.

The queen made a noise, confirming my previous suspicion that they hadn't known about the rapes.

"All because of tradition." Her voice was steady, but I could feel her body shaking against mine. "You never once asked what I wanted. Never asked my opinion on anything." She looked at her mother and then at her father. They both flinched at the look in her eyes. "And

390

this is what happened because of it."

"What do you want?" Queen Mara asked. "What can we do?"

"Annul my marriage."

Okay, that one took me off guard, and judging by the look on her parents' faces, they hadn't been expecting it either though I wasn't sure why I was surprised. Of course she wouldn't want to stay married to Tanek. I just hadn't realized that her parents had any power to control that.

"Annul the marriage," Nami repeated. "And let me choose. Choose my own life."

"And if we do," King Raj said slowly. "If we let you choose, what will your choice be?"

"I will be Queen," Nami said. "I accept that responsibility." She took a deep breath and then added, "And I choose him."

My heart gave an unsteady thump.

King Raj looked at me, a stern expression on his face, and then turned to his wife. She nodded and they both looked at Nami.

"Agreed," King Raj said. "Let us discuss where we go from here."

Chapter 18

Nami

I put my hands on the edge of the sink and bowed my head. The bathroom was full of steam, my skin still glistening. The hot water had done a great job of easing the knots in my back and shoulders, but my whole body was still tense. The past few days, hell, the past few weeks, hadn't been easy, but today had been what Americans would have called a roller coaster of emotions.

Joy at seeing my parents. Horror and humiliation when they said Kai and Tomas had told them about what Tanek had done, about the truth behind mine and Reed's relationship. The surge of love hearing Reed say that he loved me and he'd protect me. A mix of feelings so complex that I couldn't explain them or sort them as my parents asked for my forgiveness, acknowledged that they owed Reed. And then surprise at my own boldness when I challenged them.

They would annul my marriage, had promised to make the necessary calls that very afternoon. By the time we returned to Saja tomorrow, I would be free of my vows. Free to publicly choose Reed.

I swallowed hard. If he still wanted me.

I pulled the towel off of my head and let the wet curls tumble over my bare shoulders. I hung it up on the door hook and turned back to the sink. I had another towel wrapped around me and I took that off now. I looked down at my body. The bruises were nearly gone. I'd never bruised easily and they'd always healed quickly. It wasn't them I was looking at though.

I was looking for other changes.

"Nami?" Reed knocked on the door. "Are you okay?"

"Fine," I said. "I'll be out in a moment."

I pulled the towel back around me again, looked one more time at the little piece of white plastic, then threw it in the trash. After a moment's consideration, I covered it with a bit of toilet paper even though there were only two of us in the apartment at the moment. Halea might have gone back to the hotel with my parents, but I didn't want him finding out that way either.

No, he deserved to hear it from me.

I walked out of the bathroom and across the hall to the bedroom Reed and I had been using. The fact that my parents had left the two of us here, knowing we were sleeping together, was their way of saying I could make my own decisions. That they'd accepted my choice. In a few minutes, I'd know if my choice would accept me. I knew he loved me, that he was willing to go to jail for me, but this was different. For some men, this would break them.

"Are you sure you're okay?" Reed came towards me as I stepped into the room. He took my hand, an expression of concern on his face. "You look like you're feeling sick."

I shook my head even though he was partially right. I did feel like I was going to throw up, but this time I knew it really was from nerves. The other times I'd told myself it was nerves, I knew now I'd been lying to myself. I'd probably known it then, but so much had been going on, I hadn't wanted to think about it. And I certainly hadn't wanted to think about the implications.

"I have something I need to tell you." For the first time today, my voice shook.

"Nami, sweetheart, what's wrong?" He put his hand on the side of my face. "You're scaring me, love."

"I–" Words failed me and I ducked my head.

"You can tell me anything." He cupped my chin, raising my head so that I was looking at him. I could see the fear mingling with concern. "Even if it's that you changed your mind about me."

I shook my head, tears burning in my eyes. "I haven't. I love you and I want you. I wish I would have chosen you from the beginning."

"I wish that too," he said, brushing his thumb across the corner of my eye. "If only to have spared you from the pain of what happened."

"It's not just that." I took a breath and wished I had the courage to take a step back, the strength to say this without needing his touch.

"Please, just tell me."

It was the desperation in his voice that did it.

"I'm pregnant."

I waited, but other than a slightly stunned look on Reed's face, there was no reaction. No cursing. No pushing me away. Neither was there joy or excitement. I hadn't expected that though. Shock had been the best I'd hoped for. After all, I hadn't thought anything of it when Reed and I had made love those few times since he'd come for me, hadn't thought to tell him that we needed to use a condom.

I was able to move away now and his hands fell at his sides.

"There's more," I forced myself to say it. "I haven't taken my birth control since we were in Venice. So when we've...and when Tanek..." Bile rose in my throat and I choked it down. The words that came out next were just

395

as bitter on my tongue. "I don't know who the father is."

Tears streamed down my cheeks and I dropped my head, unable to look at Reed, to see whatever expression was on his face. Rejection. Disgust. Even pity.

Then his arms were around me, pulling me against his bare chest. He held me tight, making soothing noises that had no words. His skin was hot and I welcomed the heat, my own body cold from my confession.

"Do you know what I know?" Reed's voice was soft, but there was no hesitation, no wavering. "I know that it doesn't matter whose DNA that child has, I am its father."

I caught my breath and looked up at him, not daring to hope that I was understanding him correctly.

"I don't care if this is too fast or if people think I'm crazy." His expression was fierce. "I love you, Namisa Carrmoni, and if you'll have me, I want to marry you."

I wanted to say yes so badly, but I couldn't. Not when I knew why he was saying it. Maybe we would get there in some distant future, but I didn't want it to come like this.

"I won't let you do that," I said.

"Won't let me?" he asked.

"I won't have you marrying me just because I'm pregnant."

He shook his head and released me, taking a step back. "If you don't want to marry me, Nami, all you have to do is say it. I would never force the issue." He looked away. "I just thought, that since you said you wanted me, that you chose me..."

"I do," I said. "And I did choose you."

"Then why won't you marry me?"

The question was so sad that my heart broke. "I do want to marry you. I just don't want it to be because..."

I didn't get to finish because Reed's mouth was covering mine, swallowing my protests. The towel fell to the floor and his hands were on me, running down my back to my ass and back up again, leaving burning trails

396

of fire along my skin. His tongue slid between my lips, curling around mine and drawing it into his mouth. I moaned, everything else forgotten but the feel of his chest under my hands, the way his teeth were scraping against my bottom lip.

I made a muffled squeak as he picked me up and felt him smile. He lowered me to the bed, finally releasing my mouth so that he could kiss his way down my neck. His lips danced across my skin, up my breasts, pausing to circle my nipple with his tongue, then moving to the other one. I expected him to either return to my mouth or move lower to the aching place between my legs. Instead, he stopped at my stomach, placing a kiss just above my bellybutton. He ran his fingers across my skin, his expression thoughtful as he looked at my stomach.

"Is that really the only reason?" he asked softly, not looking up at me. "You don't want me to feel obligated?"

"Yes." I reached down and ran my fingers through his hair.

He looked up at me, his eyes deep pools of black. "I love you, Nami. And that has nothing to do with...this." He spread his hand across my stomach. "I want to marry you." He smiled softly, his fingers moving slowly over my still-flat belly. "Not in spite of, or because of." He leaned forward and kissed my stomach again. "I want to have a family with you. It doesn't matter to me that things are moving faster than I'd thought they would. It's what I want because it's you." He looked at me again. "What do you want, Nami?"

I gave him the truth. "You." I cupped his chin, using it to pull him back up my body.

"Then marry me," he whispered against my mouth.

"Yes." I pulled his head down so that our lips crashed together.

His hands moved down my body as we kissed and then I felt his cock between my legs, pushing against me. He pulled his mouth away long enough for our eyes to meet and me to nod my consent. Then he was sliding inside me and the world was reduced to just the two of us. Our bodies moving together, hips rising and falling in perfect sync. The pleasure was building fast inside me, driving me towards the inevitable explosion. And when it happened, Reed was there with me, calling out my name.

This was what I wanted. Not only the sex, but the completeness that came with joining with someone who knew me, understood me on some level that no one else did. Reed wasn't just a great lover, he was my other half. He made me a better woman. He was the one I wanted to spend the rest of my life with, the man I wanted to be the father of my children, no matter what biology said.

I didn't know how the people of Saja would react to any of this, but for the first time in my life, that wasn't what mattered. For the first time, I was going to have something I wanted.

Chapter 19

Reed

We left Philadelphia Friday morning and Nami didn't ask why I hadn't gone to see my parents before we left. I'd been a little worried that she would think I didn't want them to know about the engagement or the baby, but she seemed to understand that I wasn't ashamed of her but rather didn't want to deal with all of the shit that would inevitably follow a visit to my parents.

I did, however, take her with me into the bank where I'd kept a small safe deposit box with a few things I didn't want to take with me as I traveled. One of those things was my grandmother's engagement ring. It hadn't been expensive enough for Britni, but I knew Nami didn't care about that. The moment she saw the ring, her face lit up and she held out her hand.

Judging from the expression on her parents' faces when we met them at the airport, the ring came as no surprise. Halea, however, was thrilled. We took a private plane back to Italy and she spent at least half of it talking to Nami about what the wedding would be like. The queen joined in, assuring Nami that before the plane landed in Saja, the marriage to Tanek would be annulled. The only question was how long we wanted to wait before we held the wedding.

I felt Nami's eyes on me when her mother asked the question again. I looked up from where I'd been on my phone, reading all the emails I'd ignored over the past week. My parents were responsible for at least half of them, some business, some personal. I supposed they figured that at least this way there was a chance they'd get to have their say. I put all that aside though. My parents could wait.

"Whatever you want," I said quietly. I understood what she was asking and I would let it be her decision. If we married quickly, then announced the pregnancy in six weeks or so, we might be able to pass off the child as having been legitimately conceived on our wedding night, just born early.

I didn't know what Saja annulments required, but there was a chance that they were the same as American annulments which, as far as I knew, required a marriage not be consummated. In my mind, consummation meant consent, but I didn't know about the laws in Saja. If an announcement of the marriage being annulled meant that the people of Saja believed Nami and Tanek hadn't slept together, then they would believe that the child was mine.

It was mine, I thought fiercely. Nami was mine. My family.

"We would like to marry as soon as possible," Nami said. "There is no need for something lavish. As we all know, that does not guarantee a happy marriage."

"We will be arriving late and we will need to adjust to the time change," King Raj said. "But if you wish, we could conduct the ceremony tomorrow." He looked at me. "Do you have any specific religious affiliations that you wish us to include?"

I was surprised by the question. While the king and queen were honoring their word about letting Nami choose what she wanted to do with her life, I'd expected them to tolerate me, especially since they knew little about me save that I'd had sex with their daughter before

400

she'd been married to Tanek. Well, that and the whole rescuing thing, which I sincerely hoped made them think better of me than the rest.

"My family attended church back in Philadelphia, but it was a social thing. They go because it's expected of them. I'm happy to follow whatever customs Saja follows." I smiled at Nami. "Nami is my family now."

I saw her hand go to her stomach and wondered at how quickly the gesture became natural.

"And speaking of family," she said.

I was a bit surprised she was going to tell her parents and Halea, but I'd meant what I'd said. I would support what she wanted.

"I'm pregnant."

Queen Mara's mouth tightened for a moment, her eyes going from Nami to me and back again.

"Who is...?" The king was obviously thinking the same thing, but couldn't quite bring himself to ask it.

Nami's eyes met mine and I knew she'd let me decide this one. It wasn't even a consideration. "I am."

"For certain?" King Raj gave me a cynical look.

"Yes." I stood and walked over to Nami. I reached down and took her left hand, raising it to kiss her ring. "They're both mine." Her eyes shown and she tilted her head up so I could kiss her lips. Mindful of the eyes on me, I kept the kiss chaste and brief. Still, it sent electricity through me and I had to remind myself that I only had to wait until tonight, tomorrow night at the latest, and I could indulge in a more thorough kiss. That and more. I ran the back of my hand down the side of her face. I'd never get enough of her.

"Tomorrow, then," Queen Mara said. "We have plenty of time on the journey home to plan a wedding."

"And a nursery." Halea was beaming. "I wonder if it is a boy or a girl."

I left the sisters to talk with their mother and went to get a drink for myself and the king. I had a feeling, with all of the wedding and baby talk, King Raj and I were going to need a drink. Him, because of the events of the past couple days. Me, not because of my impending marriage or fatherhood. I wasn't nervous about either one, at least not about my choices. No, I was going to do something else that was freaking me out.

I was going to send an email to my parents with an invitation to my wedding and an offer to pay for a private plane.

By Saturday afternoon, I still hadn't heard from my parents and I put it all aside as I made my way out of the guest chamber where I'd slept last night. Alone, unfortunately, but understandably. Very little about this wedding would be traditional, but I could at least stay away from Nami until the ceremony. A ceremony where I would have no one at my side. My parents had made their decision and my conscience was clean. I'd leave Philadelphia and my family in the past. Today was about moving forward. New life. New home. New family.

As soon as I walked into the garden – the little one that Nami loved so much, not the big one – I saw two familiar faces.

"Piper! Julien!" I stared at my friends as they hurried over.

"Nami called me when you guys landed in Italy," Piper said, pulling me into a quick hug. "She wanted you to have someone here to stand with you." When she stepped back to Julien's side, her smile faltered. "Unless you think this is too weird."

"No." I shook my head and gave them both smiles. "It's definitely good to see some friendly faces."

"Yeah, those two don't exactly look like the friendly type." Julien gestured over my shoulder.

I glanced back and laughed. Kai and Tomas were standing on either side of the entrance, looking very much like the menacing former linebackers I'd once thought they were. "Actually, they're good guys. Threatened to kick my ass a time or two...and one of them once said he'd castrate me if I got near Nami again, but we've worked out our differences."

Julien glanced down at Piper, a smile playing on his lips. They had one of those moments of silent communication that I understood now.

"It's good to see you happy, Reed," Piper said sincerely. "Ever since...well, it's all I wished for you."

"I know," I smiled at her. "I am happy, and I owe you two quite a bit for that."

"Not at all," Julien said. He held out his hand. "It's what friends do."

"Yes," I agreed as I shook his hand. "It is."

The music changed as the string quartet saw the king and queen ready to enter. Piper and Julien hurried off to stand with a handful of other spectators I didn't know but assumed I'd be meeting later on. I took a step backwards until I was off the path and gave a slight bow as my soon to be in-laws walked past.

Halea followed them, dressed in a simple pale blue dress that made me realize that Kai and Tomas were going to have their hands full soon, keeping guys away from her. Halea and the queen moved until they were across from the other members of the audience and the king stood at the top of the path. He looked at me and I took a deep breath. It was my turn.

I walked up the path and took my place to the right, turning as the music changed again. It wasn't a traditional American wedding march, but that didn't matter. The moment I saw Nami walk between Kai and Tomas, nothing else mattered. The heat, the fact that my parents hadn't even acknowledged my invitation, not knowing how this country would accept me. Right now, I didn't care about anything except the beautiful woman walking towards me.

Her dress matched Halea's, a shimmering blue that contrasted with her darker skin and made her eyes glow even more brightly. She wasn't far enough along to be showing, but I found myself looking anyway. Beneath the soft curves of her body was a child. Our child. My heart constricted painfully and I wondered how my body could handle everything I was feeling. It was strange, I thought, how I'd once thought I'd loved Piper. What I'd felt for her was so small compared to what I felt for Nami, and even though it seemed impossible, I found myself loving Nami more with each passing day.

I barely heard King Raj speaking as Nami took her place at my side. As I'd been instructed, I held out my arm and she placed hers so that our hands were on top of each other. We'd agreed for a less formal ceremony, cutting out a lot of what the king had said at the prior ceremony, so it was only a short time later that I found myself repeating a vow to love and honor Namisa Carrmoni as my wife and my queen. Her voice was steadier than mine when she said her own vow, but I could see the tears glistening in her eyes as I slid her wedding band onto her finger. It was a beautiful piece of workmanship, surprisingly complementary to my grandmother's ring. Simple white gold, it had been handed down through the generations, though Tanek had refused to use it in place of his own mother's rings. I was glad he hadn't. It meant so much to Nami and there were no negative memories associated with it. While I knew both of us would never forget what had happened, neither of us wanted the memories to haunt us, taint what we had. Fittingly, the inscription on the inside of the band, roughly translated, said 'Your past is gone. We are the future'.

And then I was instructed to kiss my bride. I looked down at her and gently took her face between my hands. It didn't matter that her parents and sister were here, that people were watching. This moment was about her and me, a promise that this was it. Neither of us were going to run away. No matter what the future held, we would stand together.

I let her see all of that in my eyes and then I bent my head forward to, for the first time, kiss my wife.

Chapter 20

Reed

I stood over the cradle and looked down at my daughter. Four months and I still couldn't get over the wonder that was Angelique. My little angel. She'd been so small when she was born I'd been afraid to hold her.

I reached down and lightly touched the dark fuzz that covered her head. Her eyes were blue, like almost all infants were, but that could change. I knew the immediate family – the only ones who knew the truth of when Angelique had been conceived – were waiting to see if the eyes would grow dark like mine.

As the due date had gotten closer, I'd wondered if I would have the strength to continue to tell Nami that I didn't want her to do a paternity test. I'd truly believed that I didn't care who the biological father was, but there were times I'd doubted myself, wondering if I would feel the same if the child looked like Tanek. And then Angelique had been born and I'd known it didn't matter. She could have looked exactly like Tanek and she still would have been mine.

She didn't though. She looked like Nami. That was for the best, I knew. Even if people suspected that Angelique could be Tanek's, as long as she looked like her mother, the rumors could be kept to a minimum.

"*Good-night, my angel.*" Saja's native tongue came more easily now than it had a year ago when Nami had first begun teaching me. I'd actually caught myself thinking in it once in a while.

The people of Saja had been reluctant, at first, to accept me, but as Nami and I had toured the island on our honeymoon, they'd begun to thaw. Nami had told me once that it was because everyone could see how much I loved her. If that was truly the case, I didn't have to worry about it because I still loved her and I always would.

"She is sleeping through the night quite well."

I didn't turn as Nami slid her arms around my waist. I felt her kiss my back before resting her cheek there.

"I know you didn't want me to." Her voice was soft. "But I had to know, for me."

I turned and looked down at her. The light in the nursery was dim, but I could make out the expression on her face. She was worried I'd be angry at her.

"I had the paternity test done. I had to know."

I captured her always wayward curl. "I don't need a test to tell me that she's mine. Biology doesn't determine family."

Nami nodded. "I know." She reached up and ran her finger along my bottom lip. "And I think we should start trying to give her a brother soon." Her eyes were the deep blue-green of the ocean. "A full-blooded brother who looks exactly like her father."

"Nami?" I made it a question.

She nodded, a smile breaking across her face as she pushed herself up on her toes so she could press her mouth against mine. It was a hard kiss, a fierce one. "After all," she continued. "Her father is the most handsome man in the world."

I wrapped my arms around her and lifted her so that we were face to face. "Do you mean it?"

"Yes." She rested her forehead against mine. "The

test..."

"Not that," I interrupted. "About wanting to try for another baby already?"

She laughed, a soft sound so as not to wake our daughter. "It probably won't happen right away since I'm still breast-feeding her, but yes."

"We should still probably get started." I shifted my grip on her, moving my hands down to grab her ass. She wrapped her legs around my waist and I walked her back to the wall.

"Here?" She gasped as I kissed her neck.

"Yes," I said. "Here. Now."

I tugged on the belt of her robe, making a sound low in my throat as the silk fell away to reveal her amazing body. She'd worried, I knew, that I wouldn't find her attractive after Angelique was born, that the way her body had changed would repulse me. I'd spent an entire night focused on worshipping every inch of her so that she would never feel that doubt again.

"What if she wakes up?" Nami asked, then moaned as I lowered my head to flick my tongue across her nipple. Her breasts were even more sensitive and responsive than they had been before. I'd actually made her come once just from paying attention to them. Turns out I love the way she tastes.

"I guess you need to be quiet then." I grinned at her as I reached between us and pushed down the shorts I'd been planning on wearing to bed. Now I was thinking that naked might be the way to go.

I was already hard, my body begging me to bury myself inside her, but I waited. I twisted my fingers, ignoring the awkward angle, and slid my hand between her legs. She moaned again, biting her bottom lip to muffle the sound. She was already wet when I slipped a finger inside her. So wet and tight.

"Please, my love." She dug her nails into the back of my neck.

409

I positioned myself and grabbed her hip, holding her as I slid home. We groaned in unison, eyes closing as we came together. With all of the responsibilities that came with being the heir to the crown, as well as refusing to yield to the common practice of allowing a wet nurse and nanny take primary care of our daughter, time alone was precious. And far too infrequent.

She clung to me as I moved in deep, even strokes that filled her completely. Her full breasts pressed against my chest and she wrapped her arms more tightly around my neck, her breath hot against my skin as she whispered endearments and encouragements in two languages.

I could feel the tension coiling in my stomach and fought against it. I needed her to come first. I swore quietly as her teeth scraped over my throat, then bit down. The pull of her mouth as she sucked on my skin made my muscles tremble and I knew I wouldn't last much longer.

"Come, baby. Please," I begged her, surprised that I could even remember the words.

She shuddered and I rolled my hips, pressing harder against her clit. Her teeth clamped down painfully on my neck as she came. The jolt that shot down through me met with the delicious pressure of her pussy contracting around my cock and that was it. I went down to my knees as I came, wrapping my arms around her and holding her to me, on me, as we rode the waves of pleasure. I could feel her heart thudding against her chest, beating a counterpoint to my own rapid pulse.

My legs began to cramp and I shifted us, wrapping Nami's robe back around her as I tugged up my shorts. I settled us on the floor, leaning back against the wall and pulling Nami onto my lap.

"So." I threaded my fingers between hers. "I was thinking that for our one year anniversary, we could go back to Venice and then Paris."

"Really?" Nami smiled. "That would be wonderful. A few days in each city."

410

I nodded. I looked down at our hands, our rings glinting in the dim light. "And maybe we could end the trip in Philadelphia. Have Halea bring Angelique to us."

"Philadelphia?"

"Piper and Julien did invite us to their engagement party."

"They did," she said slowly. "Is that the only reason you want to go? And why you want our daughter with us?"

"No." I shook my head. "You know that my parents and I have been writing for the last few months."

"I do."

I'd ignored them until Thanksgiving, then had taken Nami's advice and told them about the baby. Things had been tense, but slowly easing since then. I'd even spoken to them twice. Once at Christmas and then to tell them that Angelique had been born. Neither time had been as bad as I'd feared. I didn't ask about the business and they didn't volunteer. They were still at the house on Chestnut Hill and Rebecca had run off with some rich married man, but it had been Piper and Julien who'd told me that. I could tell they were trying to be careful, and though they never came out and apologized, I knew they wanted to make up for what had happened between us.

"I think, maybe it's time for my parents to meet my wife and daughter." The words weren't as hard as I'd thought they'd be.

"I'd like that very much," Nami said. She kissed my chin. "Now, I think we should take advantage of the fact that our angel is sleeping and go back to our bedroom."

I grinned at her and kissed the tip of her nose. "You've got to give me a couple more minutes before I'll be any good to you."

She rolled her eyes. "I meant to sleep. We haven't gotten much of that either lately."

I bent my head and covered her mouth with mine. The kiss was deep and thorough, leaving us both gasping

411

for air by the time I raised my head.

"You win," she said. "More of that, then sleep."

"Deal."

As we stood, I glanced over at the cradle one more time. My daughter. My angel. I smiled. Maybe she did look a little like me after all. Nami squeezed my hand and I let her pull me through the adjoining door and into our bedroom. Even as the door closed behind us, I took her into my arms and walked us over to our bed. I planned on taking my time now. If Nami had her way, we'd have half a dozen kids in as many years and who knew how many opportunities we'd have for leisurely love-making.

I wouldn't have it any other way.

THE END

All series from M. S. Parker

Pure Lust Box Set
Casual Encounter Box Set
Sinful Desires Box Set
Twisted Affair Box Set
Serving HIM Box Set
Club Prive Vol. 1 to 5
French Connection (Club Prive) Vol. 1 to 3
Chasing Perfection Vol. 1 to 4
Pleasures Series
Exotic Desires Series
A Wicked Lie
A Wicked Kiss
A Wicked Truth (Release September 15, 2015)
Blindfold (Four part series coming in September, 2015)

Acknowledgement

First, we would like to thank all of our readers. Without you, our books would not exist. We truly appreciate each and every one of you.

A big "thanks" goes out to all the Facebook fans, street team, beta readers, and advanced reviewers. You are a HUGE part of the success of the series.

We have to thank our PA, Shannon Hunt. Without you our lives would be a complete and utter mess. Also a big thank you goes out to our editor Lynette and our wonderful cover designer, Sinisa. You make our ideas and writing look so good.

About The Authors

MS Parker

M. S. Parker is a USA Today Bestselling author and the author of the Erotic Romance series, Club Privè and Chasing Perfection.

Living in Southern California, she enjoys sitting by the pool with her laptop writing on her next spicy romance.

Growing up all she wanted to be was a dancer, actor or author. So far only the latter has come true but M. S. Parker hasn't retired her dancing shoes just yet. She is still waiting for the call for her to appear on Dancing With The Stars.

When M. S. isn't writing, she can usually be found reading– oops, scratch that! She is always writing.

Cassie Wild

Cassie Wild loves romance. Every since she was eight years old she's been reading every romance novel she could get her hands on, always dreaming of writing her own romance novels.

When MS Parker approached her about co-authoring the Serving HIM series, it didn't take Cassie many seconds to say a big yes!!

Serving HIM and Pure Lust are only the beginning to the collaboration between MS Parker and Cassie Wild. Another series is already in the planning stages.

Printed in Great Britain
by Amazon